A Hiss Before Dying

A Hiss Before Dying

A MRS. MURPHY MYSTERY

RITA MAE BROWN & SNEAKY PIE BROWN

Illustrated by Michael Gellatly

BANTAM BOOKS

NEW YORK

Copyright © 2017 by American Artists, Inc.
Illustrations copyright © 2017 by Michael Gellatly

Published in the United States by Bantam Books,
an imprint of Random House,
a division of Penguin Random House LLC, New York.

BANTAM BOOKS and the HOUSE colophon are registered trademarks of Penguin Random House LLC.

Library of Congress Cataloging-in-Publication Data
Names: Brown, Rita Mae, author. | Brown, Sneaky Pie, author.
Title: A hiss before dying : a Mrs. Murphy mystery / Rita Mae Brown.
Description: New York : Bantam Books, 2017. | Series: Mrs. Murphy ; 26
Identifiers: LCCN 2017002158 | ISBN 9780553392494 (hardcover) |
ISBN 9780553392500 (ebook) Subjects: LCSH: Haristeen, Harry
(Fictitious character)—Fiction. | Murphy, Mrs. (Fictitious character)—Fiction. |
Women detectives—Virginia—Fiction. | Women cat owners—Fiction. |
Cats—Fiction. | BISAC: FICTION / Mystery & Detective / Women Sleuths. |
FICTION / Humorous. | FICTION / Suspense. | GSAFD: Mystery fiction.
Classification: LCC PS3552.R698 H57 2017 | DDC 813/.54—dc23 LC record
available at https://lccn.loc.gov/2017002158

Printed in the United States of America on acid-free paper

randomhousebooks.com

246897531

First Edition

Dedicated to Major Sara Bateman, U.S. Army Ret., ex-MFH.
We've been through a lot together and most of it was your fault.

The Cast of Characters

The Present

Mary Minor Haristeen, "Harry"—Hardworking, task-oriented, she runs the old family farm in Crozet, Virginia. A loyal friend to both human and animal, a quality not lost on those who care for her. If she has a weakness—perhaps best explained as a personality trait—it is that psychology has no interest for her. Harry doesn't care why you do anything. She simply deals with the result.

Pharamond Haristeen, DVM, "Fair"—Tall, powerfully built, at forty-three he is one year older than his wife, Harry. His equine patients trust him as do most humans. He is more sensitive, more introspective than his wife.

Susan Tucker—Harry's friend since cradle days, she loves Harry as only an old friend can. The two can disagree but will always come to each other's aid. Susan's deceased grandfather was a former governor of Virginia. Her husband, Ned, is a representative to the House of Delegates.

BoomBoom Craycroft—Another childhood friend who can find herself swept up into one of Harry's messes. BoomBoom often asks the obvious question. Obvious to her.

Deputy Cynthia Cooper—She rents the old Jones homeplace, a farm next to Harry's. As she was not raised in the country, Harry and Fair are a great help to her. She does her best to deflect Harry's curiosity. If Susan and Fair can't contain Harry, it's a sure bet Coop can't, despite her shiny law enforcement badge.

Reverend Herbert Jones—He's known Harry all her life. She is a faithful congregant of St. Luke's Lutheran Church. He learned to lead men as a young combat captain in Vietnam. On his return after the seminary, he did his best to lead women, too, to faith, charity, and peace. He is a good pastor to his flock.

MaryJo Cranston—Smart and successful as a stockbroker, she invests for some of the Virginia tribes. Of course, she cannot reveal financial standings but no one complains. She has a nose for money and also gives to environmental causes as well as to rebuilding a school once used for tribal children, then called "Indians," as well as African American children, then called "colored."

Liz Potter—She works with Harry, MaryJo, Susan, and Boom-Boom on wildlife projects as well as the above-mentioned school. She, herself, is African American, owns a high-end store in Barracks Road Shopping Center. She's easygoing and well liked.

Marvella Rice Lawson—In her sixties, she will never be described as easygoing. She's one of the powers-that-be at the Virginia Museum of Fine Arts. She and her brother, each an art collector of vastly different tastes, have amassed art worth a small fortune. When the highly intelligent Marvella walks into a room, she parts people like the Red Sea.

NOTE: Harry was an Art History major at Smith College, Northampton, Massachusetts. Her father couldn't believe she'd major in something so useless. Her retort was that this was her only chance in life to do so, as once she was out of college she would need to work. Both parents were killed when she was in college, before her father had the chance to appreciate the woman she became. Now, at forty-two, some lights are being turned on upstairs. She and Marvella will wind up working together. Neither knows that in this book.

The Eighteenth Century

Catherine Schuyler—At twenty-two, intelligent, levelheaded, and impossibly beautiful, she is learning from her brilliant father about business. She already has a reputation as a leading horse-woman.

John Schuyler—A former major in the Revolutionary War, only a few years older than his smashing wife, he is powerfully built and works hard. As he is from Massachusetts he can miss some of the undercurrents of Virginia society.

Rachel West—Two years younger than her sister, Catherine, she, too, is beautiful, but her beauty is softer, sweeter. She's easy to please, ready to help, and possessed of deep moral conviction.

Charles West—Captured by John Schuyler at the Battle of Saratoga, the then nineteen-year-old marched all the way to The Barracks prisoner-of-war camp outside Charlottesville. The second son of a baron in England, he had the good sense to stay in America. Like John, he is dazzled by his wife and knows how lucky he is.

Karl Ix—A Hessian also captured. He and Charles became friends in the camp and continue working together after the war.

Maureen Selisse—The daughter of a Caribbean banker, she was a great catch for her ruthless late-husband, Francisco. Keenly aware of her social position, she is also accustomed to getting her way. She hated that he carried on with a beautiful slave, making little attempt to hide it.

Ewing Garth—The father of Catherine and Rachel, a loving man, brilliant in business. He is a creature of his time, but one who can learn. He helped finance the war and hopes the new nation can hold together. A widower, he misses his wife, a true partner. The economic chaos of the Articles of Confederation affect his business as well as everyone else's. He sees doom ahead for the new nation and no way out.

Jeffrey Holloway—Young, not wellborn but divinely handsome, he married the widowed Maureen Selisse, to everyone's shock.

Yancy Grant—Shocked and infuriated more than anyone by the above hasty marriage, he hates Jeffrey. Being challenged to a duel by Jeffrey gives him the chance he's been praying for: to get rid of the past.

The Slaves: Big Rawly

Sheba—Maureen Selisse's lady-in-waiting. Really, she's Maureen's right hand and she enjoys the power. She'll destroy anyone who stands in her way.

DoRe Durkin—He works in the stable and limps from an old fall from a horse. He mourns his son Moses, after Moses's flight up North in the wake of the death of Francisco Selisse, who brutalized Moses's love, the beautiful Ailee.

The Slaves: Cloverfields

Bettina—A cook of fabulous abilities. She's the head woman of the slaves, thanks to her fame, her wisdom, and her wondrous warmth. She also has a beautiful voice. Bettina's view: "I could be a queen in Africa, but I'm not in Africa. I'm here." She made a vow to Isabelle, Ewing's wife, as she died. Bettina vowed to take care of Catherine and Rachel. She has kept her pledge.

Serena—A young woman, learning from Bettina both in the kitchen and out. She has uncommon good sense and will, in the future, wield power among her people.

Jeddie Rice—At eighteen, he is a natural with horses. He loves them. He's been riding, working, and studying bloodlines with Catherine since they were children. Like Serena, Jeddie has all the qualities of someone who will rise, difficult though the world they live in is.

Tulli—A little fellow at the stables who tries hard to learn.

Ralston—Fifteen and thin, he, too, is at the stables. He works hard.

Father Gabe—Old, calm, and watchful, he accepts Christianity but practices the old religion. Many believe he can conjure spirits. No matter if he can or can't, he is a healer.

Roger—Ewing's house butler, the most powerful position a male slave can have. He has a sure touch with people, black or white.

Weymouth—Roger's son, in his teens. The hope is he will inherit his father's position someday, but for now he's fine with being second banana. He's a good barber and in truth not very ambitious.

Barker O.—Powerful, quiet, he drives the majestic coach-in-four. He's known throughout Virginia for his ability.

Bumbee—Fights with her husband. Finally she moves into the weaving cabin to get away from him and to comfort a lost soul.

Ruth—Mother to a two-year-old and a new baby. How she loves any baby, kitten, puppy, and she gets to show this love to save a little life.

Richmond

Georgina—Early middle age, quite attractive but putting on weight, she runs a tavern that also serves ladies. She knows everything about everybody, almost. No one uses last names in this world except for the male customers, men of means, in the small city.

Sam Udall—As a dedicated customer of Georgina's, he appreciates her shrewdness. He realizes the financial world has changed since the colonists have won the war. He also understands that the old Tidewater grandees are slipping. A new man is emerging with new money if the financial chaos can be corrected.

Mignon—A runaway slave from Big Rawly, she serves in the kitchen. A tiny woman with big eyes, she was set up as a thief by Sheba. Now there is a reward out for her capture.

Eudes—As the outstanding chef at Georgina's, he brings the customers in for the food. He is quite an independent thinker; he's a free black man who, like Georgina, doesn't blab everything he knows.

Deborah—The most expensive of the delicious offerings at Georgina's thanks to her beauty and her self-possession. She literally can drive a man crazy. She's a runaway slave, as are many of the girls. The white girls also ran away. Spared slavery, they were not spared brutality, unwanted sexual congress, or poverty. All of which binds the girls to Georgina, who treats them decently—plus they make good money.

Binky—An idiot. It's hard to believe he could work at Georgina's and be so stupid. He is, however, a pretty young man.

The Animals

Mrs. Murphy—Harry's tiger cat who knows she has more brains than her human. She used to try to keep Harry out of trouble. She gave up, knowing all she can do is extricate her human once she's in another mess.

Pewter—A fat gray cat who believes the world began when she entered it. What a diva. But the Queen of All She Surveys does come through in a pinch, although you'll never hear the end of it.

Tee Tucker—Bred by Susan Tucker, this is one tough, resourceful corgi: She knows she has to protect Harry, work with the level-headed Mrs. Murphy, and endure Pewter.

Owen—Tucker's brother. They adore being with each other. For Tucker it's a relief to sometimes be away from the cats.

Shortro—A young Saddlebred ridden as a hunter.

Tomahawk—Harry's old Thoroughbred hunter who hotly resents being thought old.

The Eighteenth-Century Animals

Piglet—A brave, smart corgi who went through the war and imprisonment with Captain Charles West. He loves living in Virginia with the other animals and people.

Serenissima—Francisco Selisse's fabulous blooded mare whom he sent to Catherine to be bred to her stallion, Reynaldo.

Reynaldo—An up-and-comer, with terrific conformation, but hot. Catherine and Jeddie can handle him.

Crown Prince—A younger half brother to Reynaldo. Both are out of Queen Esther, and fortunately Crown Prince has her temperament.

King David—One of the driving horses. He's heavier built than Reynaldo and Crown Prince. Solomon is King David's brother. They are a flashy matched pair.

Castor and Pollux—Two Percherons who do heavy-duty work. They are such good boys.

Sweet Potato—A saucy pony teaching Tulli to ride.

A Hiss Before Dying

1

*A*blood-red sugar maple glowed next to the farm lane as the autumn sun shone through its leaves. Two cats and one dog walked in the pleasant sixty-degree weather toward the barns, the Blue Ridge Mountains at their backs.

The bottom rim of the sun, hovering over the spine of the mountains, would soon dip down, ushering in an explosive sunset followed by a beautiful twilight. The changing seasons specialized in twilights of various blues.

Animals moved about as day gave way to night. Day hunters and feeders headed for home, the night creatures popped their heads out of dens, stuck beaks out of tree hollows, preparing for activity. The deer moved toward their sleeping places, which were usually sheltered from the winds in a thicket. Even the beavers stopped timbering, carrying a few thinner branches toward their lodge. That would be tomorrow's task, trimming the branches.

Mrs. Murphy, the tiger cat; green-eyed Pewter, the overlarge gray cat; and Tee Tucker, the intrepid corgi, relished this time of day. With a few barks from Tucker, the retiring deer bolted as the

3

domesticated animals chased after them. Deer were so much bigger, to see them scatter away just puffed up the three amigos. A few harsh words might be exchanged with the fox whose den extended under the roots of an ancient walnut.

The turtles, the salamanders, the fish and crayfish prepared for night. When they sat by the creek, the cats would stare at the freshwater creatures, but in the main they found the fish boring. Birds, on the other hand, squawked, chattered, spit seeds, dropped earthworms on them, cussed the cats unmercifully.

A blue jay looked down from a poplar tree. *"Empty-handed."*

"We weren't hunting." Pewter detested that bird.

"You couldn't catch a mouse if your life depended on it. Fat, fat, water rat," the handsome bird taunted.

Before Pewter could return the insult, Tucker looked up. She'd heard the sound wind makes through feathers built for speed as opposed to feathers designed for stealth.

Overhead, not too far, a fully grown bald eagle carried bloody flesh in its talons.

The three froze. Even the blue jay shut up.

The eagle tucked its wings close to its body and made a taunting dive toward the three pets, who flattened on the lane. At the last minute, the bird opened its wings, a span seemingly as long as a Cadillac, turned slightly, and with one mighty, taunting flap, off he flew.

"Did you see what he had?" Mrs. Murphy asked. *"All I saw was bloody flesh."*

"A piece of rawhide hung from above his talon." The dog looked at the huge bird fast disappearing, thanks to his uncommon speed.

"An eyeball. He carried an eyeball in his talon, hanging from the flesh," the sharp-eyed blue jay informed them. *"It was swinging. Blue. A blue eyeball. As blue as my feathers."*

"Sometimes a horse will have blue eyes," Tucker mentioned.

"Human, a human eyeball. They're easy to identify, really. Somewhere out there is a person with half a face," the blue jay proclaimed, opened wide his own wings, lifted off toward the house.

The three looked at one another, then resumed walking toward the house and the barn.

Tucker, puzzled, wondered, "Maybe the rawhide held the eagle. You know, he was somebody's pet and he got loose."

"Tucker, a person would have to be crazy to keep a bald eagle. They're ferocious, huge, and wild," Mrs. Murphy replied.

"We were once saber-toothed tigers." Pewter puffed out her chest.

"Yeah, and you sold out for tuna," Tucker teased.

"Better than Milk-Bones. Dogs are really dumb," Pewter shot back.

The dog and gray cat argued past the pastures and paddocks. The horses kept eating. They'd heard it all before, including knock-down, drag-out fights in the barn when the two would chase each other, buckets flying, brushes, even halters, pulled off their hooks.

Mrs. Murphy generally exhibited more decorum.

They pushed through the animal door at the large screened-in porch, then through the door into the kitchen, which also had an animal door.

In the kitchen, every cabinet door above the sink was open, dishes stacked on the counters.

Mary Minor Haristeen, "Harry," stood on a half ladder, wiping down the interior of the cabinets with a wet rag. This was to have been a short task. That was three hours ago.

"Don't step on the dishes," she admonished the cats, already on the counter.

"These are old bowls. Throw them out," Pewter advised. "You don't have to keep everything. Look how chipped this stuff is."

"It was her mother's," Mrs. Murphy said.

"Guess what? Her mother isn't here to see it. I am. I don't want to eat out of old bowls. I'm a modern cat." Pewter sat beside the stacked bowls, tempted to push them off the counter.

Through the window over the sink, in the setting sun Pewter saw her blue jay nemesis settle on an overhanging tree branch. The bird turned his head to the right, then to the left to afford a clear view.

"Fatty!" he shrieked.

Pewter charged the window, nearly knocking the bowls to the floor, spit loudly, and slammed a paw into the window.

The jay giggled, then hopped up a branch, closer to the window.

"I will kill him!" Pewter promised.

"Get off here. You nearly knocked Mom's bowls over," Harry chided.

Harry climbed down the half ladder, put the rag in the sink, wiped her hands. Then she picked up the bowls, climbed back up, and slid them into place. She repeated this until everything she'd put on the counters was back in place.

Just as she finished, the back door opened and her tall neighbor, Cynthia Cooper, a deputy in the sheriff's department, stepped inside.

"Now you come over. I could have used you to put away this stuff." Harry pointed to the cabinets.

"A cleaning fit." Cooper nodded.

"Fall and spring. Best time." Harry stepped down, folding the ladder.

"You say." Cooper leaned over to pet Tucker.

"Sit down. Hey, look at the sunset before you do."

Cooper walked over to look through the sink window. "Like someone tossed a match into the sky."

"I never get tired of sunsets, or sunrises, for that matter. Get off work early?"

"No. It's six-twenty. Tell you what, it's been a long day."

"Accidents?"

"No."

"Dad's home!" Tucker rushed outside through the animal doors to greet Fair Haristeen, all six feet five inches of him.

"She's so obsequious." Pewter pouted.

Fair stepped inside the screened-in porch, stomped his boots to remove the dust, then opened the kitchen door. "Hi, honey." He kissed Harry on the cheek, then kissed Cooper, too. "Never pass up the chance to kiss a pretty woman."

"You're the worst." Cooper laughed at him even as she enjoyed the attention.

Fair was one of those men people liked, men and women.

"You know, honey, I actually understand that," Harry responded and laughed. "And I'll have you know you've walked into a better organized kitchen. Anyone want a drink? Tea?" Harry offered.

"Too late for tea, but if you have a beer, I will indulge, and I owe you a six-pack," Cooper promised.

"You do not." Harry pulled out glasses and three beers.

"We saw an eyeball!" Pewter wanted attention so she jumped on Fair's lap. *"It was bloody. A big, blue eyeball."*

"The bald eagle had it." Tucker filled in detail.

Harry, wisely, put down some treats. Pewter liked Fair, but dried chicken twists trumped affection.

"How cold is it supposed to get tonight?" Cooper asked. "I haven't had time to check the weather on my phone. Like I said, a long day."

"No frost. We usually get the first frost mid-October, but it's warmish right now," Fair replied.

"Which reminds me, time to close in the screened-in porch," Harry noted. "We can do it this weekend and then switch the horses' schedule."

The horses remained out at night in the summers, and inside out of the sun during the day, with the reverse rotating in the cold months when fall truly arrived.

"They look good. I noticed driving in how shiny their coats are," Cooper complimented Harry, who took care of them.

"Curry comb. Hair is starting to grow. They're getting ready for the cold. I just brush out the dirt, then brush with a smoother combination, and bingo, they shine like patent leather. Good food helps, too, like some rice bran. Anyway, you said it was a busy day. If it wasn't accidents, robberies?"

Cooper smiled. "No. But I got a call from our dispatcher, go to Route 250 right at the top of Afton Mountain before it plunges down the east side. Two-fifty has a hell of a grade. Drove up there. Nothing urgent, just a call for an extra pair of eyes. Got there and here is this big transport loaded with brand-new Volvos, motor running, everything fine but no driver. No one in sight. The keys were in the ignition, the emergency brake was on, nothing was damaged. We checked his shipping papers. He was on his way down to Volvo of Charlottesville. Called them. He was due in. No one had heard a thing. We called Louisville, Kentucky, where he'd picked up the freight. Everything was fine. No driver. No cell-phone. Only shipping paperwork."

"That's odd," Harry said.

"His wallet was in the truck. Sunglasses. Not a thing touched that we could tell."

"What did you do?" Fair thought it peculiar, too.

"The Volvo dealer sent up three men, one to drive, one as a passenger, and one to follow. Luckily there was someone in the dealership that could handle that big boat. As there was no crime, no report, we thought it best to get the new cars to the dealer," Cooper added. "We looked around for the driver. No sign of him. As a precaution, we dusted the cab for fingerprints."

Harry, ever imaginative, thought out loud. "He could have been carrying contraband."

"Well, they go through every new vehicle to prepare it. If something is amiss, I reckon we'll know. But, *poof*, just disappeared with that big rig idling by the side of the road."

"Maybe he stopped to go to the bathroom and had a heart attack," Fair offered.

"We'll have bona fide search teams out tomorrow. It's rugged terrain. Really, could be just what you said, but that doesn't mean we'll find him easily."

"Coop, someone might have picked him up," Harry, always excited by a mystery no matter how tiny or removed from her own life, said.

"Don't know." Cooper shrugged.

"Just think, what if that had been a Brink's truck, a truck jammed with bags of money?" Harry grinned. "An unlocked truck."

Fair laughed. "I remember when I was in third grade. Dad and I were down on Main Street, we'd walked back to Water Street, and a truck full of beer turned over. Cans rolling everywhere. I mean in minutes half the male population of Charlottesville was there scooping up them cans."

"See, there are good accidents," Harry said and laughed.

"*Well, I saw an eyeball. That's not a good accident.*" A tidbit of dried chicken fell out of the side of Pewter's mouth, as she loudly made her points.

"*Pewter, they don't care about eyeballs any more than you care about a rig full of new cars.*" Mrs. Murphy shrugged.

She was right. For now.

2

October 18, 2016 Tuesday

*C*rackling logs, the odor of sweet pearwood, gave the Virginians for Sustainable Wildlife meeting a cozy air. Harry hosted this month's gathering, which had started at 6:30 in the evening. The members took turns hosting, which brought them closer together. A few of the people had known one another for years, but others were new to Crozet, to central Virginia. Being invited into someone's home provided an opportunity to learn more about them, a sense of their taste, perhaps even their priorities. Anyone coming into Harry's living room might share a seat with Mrs. Murphy or Pewter, both loath to move. Tucker had the sense to sprawl on the floor.

Jessica Ligon, doctor of veterinary medicine, young, well liked, finished up her report. "So we're still seeing fleas and ticks. Granted, raccoons, possums, other quadrupeds deal with it. Fleas can give animals tapeworms. So when deer season starts and your house dog chews on a carcass left behind by an irresponsible hunter, then your dog gets an infestation. Just keep a lookout for them. But tapeworm is easy to purge, fortunately. Do the mammals have Lyme disease? I'm sure some do."

"Why can't we break the cycle in the wildlife?" MaryJo Cranston, an investment broker and the treasurer of the group, asked.

"The horrendous expense, for one thing. Plus, MaryJo, you can't be sure the animals you want to purge of parasites are the ones ingesting the meds. An animal can carry the tick as well as be bitten by it. As for Lyme, we'd have to trap them, get blood. If infected, it's an antibiotic protocol. Just can't do it with wild animals, as it takes so many consecutive days of pills. We'd need to keep them in cages until the antibiotic cycle is complete; also, Lyme fatigues them. It's just close to impossible."

MaryJo, newer to the group, nodded. "It does sound complicated."

Susan Tucker, president of the group and Harry's childhood friend, checked her notes. "Jessica, thanks, we're always fascinated with new developments in veterinary medicine for all animals."

"The research being done now is amazing, especially with stem cells. That's a whole other topic for another meeting, but it is in the future."

"I read somewhere that veterinarians are better at managing chronic pain than doctors. You all are taught more about it," BoomBoom Craycroft, another childhood friend of Harry and Susan's, responded.

"We've made tremendous advances." Jessica reached for her drink.

"Liz, you have your fowl report. Actually, why don't I amend that to winged report." Susan grinned.

"Good." Liz Potter, a middle-aged African American woman passionate about the environment, checked the Apple tablet on her lap. "To date, a three percent increase in woodcock population in central Virginia. Also, grouse are increasing, especially in the Rockfish Valley. We're getting ready for the raptors' migration, so they'll be in the thermal spirals along the Blue Ridge, especially in our area. That will allow us to count as many as we can and to monitor health. The migration is ten days later than usual this year and we think it is due to the unusual warmth. No frosts yet as you know. They are also late in New England."

"Isn't it wonderful to see those hawks just lazing in circles?" BoomBoom had been watching this fall phenomenon since she was a child, a phenomenon that drew birders from as far away as Japan.

"How are we doing with the bald eagles?" Harry said. "I see them here, usually flying along the creek."

"Big comeback." Liz nodded.

"Is it true that if you find a dead eagle, osprey, or red-shouldered hawk you can't take feathers?" BoomBoom asked.

"Sure is," Liz replied.

"Well, Liz," BoomBoom prodded, "what difference does it make if the bird is dead? You haven't harmed it and the feathers are beautiful."

"State law." Liz leaned forward. "The Apaches have gotten a pass from the government to wear eagle feathers, but if I walk into your house, say you have worked protected feathers into a big fall floral wreath, how do I know where you found them? Since no one can prove how they come by feathers, teeth, claws, fur, the idea is to ban ownership of anything of protected species unless you're a member of a federally recognized tribe, and even that's dicey. Think about the bracelets years ago of elephant hair— you remember, the thick black wristbands? Almost looked like rubber. Two or three would be bound by gold wire. Expensive. You can't wear them today. I'm super-sensitive to this because of the antique clothing I carry in the store. Anything I carry that's

Native American I produce chain of title. You wouldn't believe what I went through to establish that quilled Sioux dress as having been made in 1880. I sold a Flathead vest, beaded, made in 1900, and the paperwork was as heavy as the vest."

Harry, surprised, blurted out, "People think you killed the birds or bears for furs and talons?"

MaryJo replied, "That's why she has chain of title."

"People trap endangered species as well as animals with thick winter pelts. Whenever the pelt prices go up for furs, the trappers work overtime just killing beaver, fox, wolf, even bear," Liz told them, disgusted.

"Good thing cat fur isn't valuable." Tucker giggled. "Pewter, you'd be first on everyone's list. Why, your pelt would be as big as a coyote's."

Pewter, on the back of Liz's chair, narrowed her green eyes. *"Yours would make a good coat. Warm, too."*

Mrs. Murphy, in Harry's lap, added her two cents. *"Corgi fur isn't as soft as ours."*

"Whose side are you on?" Pewter sat up.

"She's right. Your fur is softer. If someone didn't want a coat, they could use you for a big pillow."

Pewter shot off the chair, attacked the dog. The two rolled around on the floor, complete with sound effects, unleashed claws, gnashing teeth. Quite the spectacle.

"Harry, you have an attack cat." MaryJo, never having met Pewter before, was apprehensive.

Susan laughed. "We always feel safer when Pewter's around."

Tucker freed herself from the grip of the large cat and scrambled out of the living room with Pewter right behind. The humans heard the door flap smack in the kitchen door, then the second door flap smack in the screened-in porch.

They also heard a yell. "Watch it!"

Cooper came inside, took off her coat, hung it on the coat peg

in the kitchen, and joined the group. "Harry, they about took me out."

The women laughed and chatted with Cooper until Susan restored a semblance of order. "Cooper, we were just finishing up. Bow season's started for deer. We were talking about poachers."

"Not my department, but bow season's more calm than black powder or regular season, which starts November nineteenth."

"Think we'll ever see open season on humans?" BoomBoom half-jokingly said.

"Boom, we have that now," the sheriff's department officer replied.

"I thought this was a quiet year?" Susan leaned back in her chair, inhaling the fire's fragrance.

"Actually, it has been a quiet year. So far only two murders in the county, both domestic violence."

"Weren't those two murders related?" Liz asked.

"They were," Cooper replied. "A small meth lab behind the high school, of all places, run by a husband and wife and another couple. Argument escalated. The usual. Let's hope that's it for the year."

The door flap smacked again and Pewter sauntered in with a satisfied look. "I terrified that miserable dog. Just scared the poop out of her."

The tiger cat complimented her friend. "Is she hiding in the barn?"

"Cowering in the tack room. Shaking. Pathetic sight. Don't mess with me." Pewter puffed out her considerable chest, strolled to the fireplace, sat down in front of the screen, and licked a paw.

Tucker had outrun the fatty. Granted, the dog did run to the barn and did shoot into the tack room—because Harry always had a dish of food for her there.

Liz, never having been in Harry's old farmhouse, observed the preening cat. "That may be the biggest cat I've ever seen."

"And you could open a beer can with your nose," Pewter sassed.

Liz's nose evidenced a slight hook, but it wasn't that bad.

"We'd love it if you'd join our Virginians for Sustainable Wild-life," MaryJo invited Cooper, handing her a printed sheet with wildlife statistics and issues.

"I'll be supportive, but MaryJo, I can't really commit to meet-ings. I'm never sure about my schedule. I'm studying ballistics online. I really do think that what you all are doing is terrific," Cooper replied.

"What got you interested in ballistics? It seems an unusual area of study," BoomBoom questioned.

She shrugged. "So much of what involves solving crimes is technical. I need to keep learning. Ed Clark suggested I study on-line."

"Ed Clark. Really." MaryJo was impressed.

Ed Clark, one of the founders of the Wildlife Center of Vir-ginia, had a passion for firearm history, even owning old rifles and pistols.

"I was over at the Lyndhurst building. Wanted some wildlife information, recovery rates, that sort of thing, and when I walked by Ed's car, I noticed a beautiful flintlock rifle in the backseat. I asked him about it," MaryJo continued. "He really does know a lot."

"Some of those firearms are works of art. The engraving on the metal, just exquisite. Plus, I like the proportions of the old guns." Susan appreciated anything aesthetically accomplished.

"Harry, you have an old flintlock," BoomBoom remembered. "When we were studying the Revolutionary War in school, your father showed it to the class."

Harry got up, pulled the small library ladder to the bookshelf, climbed up, pulled a wooden box off it, stepped down, and opened it to show the group. The well-preserved firearm rested on satin.

"Harry, take that to a gunsmith. First, it's valuable. Second, it's probably serviceable," MaryJo enthused.

"I never thought of it. Kind of like my great-grandfather's Army saber. It's always been there." She looked closely at the pistol, realizing it was beautiful.

"Who did it belong to?" Liz wondered.

Harry replaced the pistol and returned to the circle. "Mother's family. They fought in the Revolutionary War. One of my great-greats was at Yorktown. Dad's family, Johnny-come-latelies, didn't get here until afterward. I used to tease Mom and tell her we've been here since the earth was cooling."

Susan sighed. "Both of our families go way, way back. My paternal grandmother had a few snotty moments about it. She's gone now, but Harry's mother nor mine ever took the grand and airy road."

BoomBoom laughed. "Oh, there's nothing quite like a Virginia blood snob."

"Charleston, south of Broad, is pretty bad." Susan's mouth, closed, curled upward.

"Charleston is so beautiful. If we lived there we'd all be snobs." Liz Potter laughed.

MaryJo returned to her flintlock subject. "Harry, do take that pistol to a gunsmith." She put her hands on her knees. "Well, let me tell you the best part about Ed's flintlock.

"He took me away from where the animals are kept. He didn't want noise to upset them, and he showed me how to fire the rifle."

Cooper smiled but said nothing. In his enthusiasm he'd had her fire a flintlock pistol. Animal control, wildlife preservation was not her territory, but Cooper met Ed years ago when he was testifying in court about pelt values, illegal trapping. They struck up a friendship, both finding common territory over firearms.

"Cool!" Harry enthused.

"Isn't it complicated?" Jessica inquired.

"Well, you have to ram the bullet, a ball, down; actually, first you have to put the powder in, or if it's a rifle with a pan, you put the powder there," MaryJo babbled on. "Anyway, I guess it is complicated. You have to do the steps in the exact order."

"And?" Cooper used a Glock in her line of work.

"You pull back the trigger, which as you know is fancy and stands upright, and *boom!* Lots of smoke. I loved it."

"Keep your powder dry." BoomBoom grinned.

"It's the truth. Anyway, Ed told me about an old firearms club; they have a firing range and I'm going to join. It's like living history," MaryJo enthused.

"Now you've got me curious," Harry admitted.

"All we need. Her in the back pastures with a flintlock rifle," Pewter grumbled.

"You can be very accurate," MaryJo continued. "But obviously the range isn't terribly far. I mean, that's why at the Battle of Bunker Hill the officer said, 'Don't fire until you see the whites of their eyes!' about the advancing British."

"Those men had courage," Cooper said admiringly.

"Tell you what. I think whether you marched in a cohort or wore chain mail or stood in a square to repulse a cavalry charge, you had guts." Harry paused. "I was reading last night about the Battle of Borodino in Russia, Napoleonic Wars, and it made me cry." She paused for a moment. "I read military history. My husband reads novels. We're a pair."

"A pair of what?" Susan teased her and they all laughed.

BoomBoom rose to stand before the fire, next to Pewter, who was not going to move. "Hey, Cooper, did you ever find the driver of that rig? The one left on Afton Mountain yesterday?"

"Funny you should ask. Rick called," Cooper responded, referring to Sheriff Rick Shaw, her boss. "The search team found him about a half hour ago, wedged under a big boulder."

"Wedged?" BoomBoom voiced the question for everyone.

"Like he crawled there?" Harry pressed.

"I didn't see him, but the boss said it appeared he either fell next to the boulder or tried to protect himself, using it as a shield. Half his face was shredded. One eye is missing."

"Shredded?" Susan exclaimed.

"The sheriff's exact word." Cooper's eyebrows were raised as she said it.

The door flap sounded again. Tucker quietly walked into the room.

Pewter announced, *"Hey, they found a body, a one-eyed body."*

"What are you talking about?" the dog wondered.

"The eagle." Pewter lifted her head up slightly.

"The eagle and the eye," Mrs. Murphy chimed in.

"Just because they found a defaced body doesn't mean the eagle did it." Tucker didn't feel like giving Pewter any credit.

"Doesn't mean he didn't." Mrs. Murphy stayed in Harry's lap. *"With talons like that I figure an eagle could tear off the side of a Volkswagen."*

"You've got a point there." The dog shuddered.

Pewter loudly announced to the humans, *"See! See! This wretch is terrified of me, shaking. I'm the top dog here."*

"Pewter" was all Mrs. Murphy said.

A single lamp allowed "the boys," as their wives called them, to play cards at what had been termed the "colored" schoolhouses, which their wives were now trying to save. Fair Haristeen, Ned Tucker, Bruce Cranston, and Andy Potter avidly studied their respective hands. While each husband esteemed his wife's community involvement, he did not feel called upon to imitate it, at least where wildlife was concerned. The old schoolhouses elicited a bit more of their interest.

Dr. Jessica Ligon and Cooper were not yet married, and Boom-Boom had been married once, one too many times for her. So those "girls," as the men called them, had no fellow at the table. Given one's mood, depending on wins or losses, that may have been a blessing.

Fair's eyebrows lifted slightly. Not a great hand, but not a bad one, either. As they bid, put down cards, picked up others, they chatted. Sometimes escaping into nonessential activities minus the very essential wife proved restorative.

"That damned skin has been hanging in her shop for a year," Andy grumbled about one of Liz's prized pieces of merchandise.

"It's expensive. It only takes the right person to walk through the door," Bruce Cranston counseled.

Bruce, a landscape architect, wed to MaryJo, stated the obvious, to himself anyway. Ned Tucker, Susan's husband, was the district's delegate to the Virginia House of Delegates. Fair was an equine vet, Andy Potter ran an insurance company founded by his grandfather, the first African American insurance company in central Virginia.

"Selling is an art. You sell designs, service, really, just like as you need to prepare the ground, plant stuff. I sell security, peace of mind." Andy folded his hand, not a good one. "Ben Franklin sold insurance. Fair, you sell your know-how, and Ned, it scares me to think what you sell."

The fellows laughed.

Ned could take a ribbing. "Mock me if you must, but I sell good government."

"Ned, do you think anyone gives a damn anymore?" Bruce shook his head.

"If it affects them, yes. But so few people think about the big picture now. That's tearing us apart."

This set off a spirited discussion, which put the card game on hold for a while.

"We sure don't want to work with one another." Fair laid down his cards.

"Everyone needs to be right and who is? Politics is lots of hot air, give and take, now it's just hot air and take." Bruce sighed. "Ned, I don't see how you stand it."

"You can inch a few things forward at the state level. Nationally, it's a disaster. Look, take these two schoolhouses and the identical shed. Three buildings that represent our segregated past and the mess from 1912 of lumping what they called 'colored' and 'Indian' together. If this were a national project there would be layer and layer of supervision, school buildings. By the time we cleared all the hurdles the buildings would no longer be salvageable and we'd be dead."

"Racism, don't you think?" Bruce looked at Andy.

"What am I, the expert?" He half smiled, then did answer. "Our governor is focused on business, on bringing money into the state. Virginia relies on so much federal funding, partly due to all the military bases. That funding has been cut back. Our governor and the delegates haven't the time for historic preservation unless it's the Founding Fathers, and even then." He shrugged. "But their lack of interest has given us a free hand, more or less."

"You're right," Fair replied. "We can do something about these buildings, and thanks to your wife, Andy, and to Tazio Chappers, I think we will save them, in time, in good time."

"I'm on it." Ned tidied his cards.

Tazio was a young mixed-race architect bursting with ability.

"The key was raising the twelve thousand for the three heat pumps, then another five to repair the standing-seam tin roofs, which, considering all, have held up, but they did need help. No pipes froze, so we could turn the water back on—which hadn't been on for about thirty years—and damned if it didn't do just fine. The well is good, we replaced the old pump just to be sure, but these buildings really were built to last." Ned ran down the list of what they had accomplished already. "And Governor Holloway, may he rest in peace, helped us with the kickoff. Tazio and Liz were smart enough to let him speak about segregation." Andy was quite proud of his wife's acumen, it was just the damned Sioux regalia for sale at her store, the stunning deerskin long dress covered in dyed quills, some beads, that he questioned. The late Governor Holloway was Susan Tucker's grandfather, a vital man in Virginia history.

"I'm supposed to meet with the girls November ninth." Ned got up to throw another log into the potbellied stove. "I do what I can, same as I do what I can for the wildlife group."

"Bears and eagles are everywhere," Fair noted, making already successful preservation efforts. "The Center for Conservation Biology at William and Mary have counted one thousand seventy bald eagle nests."

"How about that?" Bruce whistled.

"There are many factors. I think the biggest one is banning certain pesticides." Ned took his seat. "This whole struggle over chemicals like Roundup, the weed killer, is one of the toughest things we're facing down in Richmond. What it comes down to—and this doesn't really impact America's symbolism—is, I think, now everyone understands the danger of DDT, but realistically how much do you want to pay for a tomato? Really." The others looked at him, so he continued. "Without some chemical help, farmers will lose, in some cases, eighty percent of their crop. Some crops are fragile by nature. Think of all the bugs that can ruin apples, or deer eating them? We've got to find some sort of balance to protect our wildlife and our plant life, as well as provide affordable food for our people."

"A balancing act. I guess all business comes down to that. Mine certainly does," Andy said.

"MaryJo has to assure people she's not investing in companies that use cheap labor in foreign countries. She even has a client who won't invest in any company doing business with China. Half of what she does is hold hands."

"Is MaryJo still working with Panto Noyes?"

Panto Noyes, a lawyer from one of Virginia's unrecognized tribes, oversaw investments from people who considered themselves Native Americans. The Federal Bureau of Indian Affairs deemed otherwise. Virginia suffered for more than a century because the federal government refused to recognize any tribes. Given that Virginia began in 1607 and subsequent Caucasians and African Americans married Native peoples, proof was far more difficult than for someone from Montana.

"Ned," Andy asked, "still working on getting Virginia tribes recognized? After a century-plus we did get, what?, eight recognized by the federal government? I know that's a big deal for Panto."

"I am." Ned sighed as he looked at his cards. "I don't know if there's anything we can do for those unrecognized tribes or individuals. It's complicated, and places like this schoolhouse created the complications."

"How?" Fair finally held a good hand.

"Well, when Walter Pletcher got his damnable legislation passed for the state records in 1912 which said any blood not 'white' blood is 'colored' blood. I mean, that's really it in a nutshell. What could anyone do back then? And kids who went to schools like this, who maybe didn't live with their tribe, lived and worked outside those boundaries, they married each other. It can't be untangled, truthfully. Doesn't mean I and others won't keep trying to provide some kind of benefits, to hold the federal government's feet to the fire. The paperwork a person must fill out to prove tribal affiliation is just about impossible for most Virginians. And, of course, DNA proof is inadmissible. Pletcher muddied the waters by calling, legislating, everyone colored."

"And it's an issue way on the back burner," Andy noted.

"Right now, anything that doesn't involve the presidential election is on the back burner. These elections literally paralyze government every time around, and it seems in between now, too. Nothing gets done." Ned hated it.

"That's a good thing." Fair laughed. "Remember what Ben Franklin said: 'No man's life or property is safe when Congress is in session.'"

They all laughed.

$$3$$

A shiny, fit pack of beagles stood, tails wagging, ready to rumble. The Master and huntsman, Dr. Arie M. Rijke, finished thanking Mary and David Kalergis for allowing the beagles to hunt Sugarday, their farm. The Blue Ridge Mountains occasionally peeked out from the ever-lowering clouds. The temperature hovered at fifty-two degrees but would surely drop, as it was already 3:00 P.M.

Sugarday rested on what was the old footpath that ran east and west even before the Europeans arrived in Virginia. At one time, this had been the Wild West. Just a few miles west was the site of the Revolutionary War–era prisoner-of-war barracks, a complex that once encompassed two hundred acres, with more added over time. All that was left of the active, overcrowded camp was a stone marker. A few of the old estates from that time like Big Rawly, or remnants of Cloverfields, Ewing Garth's vast holdings, still stood.

The beagles cared little about the eighteenth century in Albemarle County. What the beagles cared about was flushing and running rabbits. Anyone who called a rabbit a "dumb bunny" had obviously never hunted one.

The little guys, patient as possible, eagerly waited while Dr. Rijke mentioned that the pack, founded in 1885, was the oldest continuously hunting beagle pack in America. Finally, touching his horn to his lips, he blew a few opening notes. Humans then walked over a rolling swell, hounds cast, set to work.

Harry, Fair, Susan, Ned, BoomBoom, and Alicia Palmer, Boom-Boom's partner, walked briskly with the thirty other foot followers. Their dear friend Miranda Hogendobber, in her late seventies and fit, chose to help set up the breakfast in the house. Mary and David generously opened their doors to the beaglers, many of whom, in truth, were muffin hounds. They walked and ran along just to get to the breakfast afterward. Hunters on foot with a pack or those on horseback, for whatever reason, have always called the repast afterward to restore energy and spirits a breakfast. Often the emphasis rested on spirits.

The four whippers-in positioned themselves with two forward and two behind. Wearing formal coats of a hunter-green thorn-repelling twill; white riding breeches and knee socks, also of green; sturdy shoes and baseball caps, black, with a white circle, an embroidered WB in the center, they were extra-alert. Some of the foot followers also wore Waldingfield Beagles caps.

Hounds worked a bit of covert, tails swishing faster, but no one spoke. Nor did the people in the field. Harry's mother and father loved following the beagles. She had tagged along as a child and always felt close to them when hunting, even now. She liked to think, in spirit, her parents followed.

A chirp. Other hounds rushed to the spot. More furious sniffing. Bob Johnson, silver-haired, tall and lean, a whipper-in, deftly took a step back, as it seemed they might reverse. They did, and on full throttle, too. Then just as quickly they cut a corner, shot off to the right, flew over a still green pasture to dip toward the west in the direction of the strong-running Ivy Creek. They paused, lost, cast themselves. Amy Burke, a forward whipper-in, was on the right side. Her brother, Alan Webb, mirrored her on the left. Foot speed, highly desirable, took second place to experience. The wrong move by a young whipper-in might turn your quarry. It takes years to make a good whipper-in. Arie was fortunate to have that experience in most of his people. His youngest, fastest whipper-in, Jacque Franco, was absorbing as much as she could.

The Huntsman stood still, waiting. The field, led by Colonel Shelton, a powerfully built retired Army officer, staff in hand, waited close enough to see everything but not close enough to interfere.

A mature hound, a bit stocky, Empress, let out a bugle call. Cyber, much younger, ran to her. He opened and now the entire pack flew over the meadow. The rabbit could be seen up ahead at a distance using all his speed. The little white tail bobbled, then disappeared in a narrow wood. Hounds bulled through the brush. The cry intensified but changed in its tenor. Nor, strangely, did the beagles emerge from the thicket when the rabbit did. As Amy tallyhoed, the field also saw the rabbit. Hounds continued speaking, but no one quite knew what was going on. Was there a second rabbit? The staff didn't want to spoil the sport, to turn the rabbit or confuse the hounds. After a suitable wait of about four minutes, Arie slowly walked to the edge of the thicket, beating back the bushes with his knob-ended crop. The whippers-in wisely stayed closer to the edge in case the pack should emerge.

"Bob," Arie yelled.

The field patiently watched, wondering what really was going on in there, while Bob used his whip to also push through the brambles.

"There's something wrong," Suzanne Bischoff, Arie's wife, murmured.

Colonel Shelton, now next to her, replied, "I hope no one is injured in there. Hounds caught up in wire or something."

No one was injured, but someone was dead. Being a physician, Arie knew the minute he saw the corpse that the individual had been dead overnight. No point trying to revive him.

The cold night preserved him, but a few wild animals had gnawed on his fingers and nose.

"He's been dead between twelve and fourteen hours, I would say," Arie observed.

"Look here." The man lay partially on his right side, and Bob pointed to his back.

Two bullet holes were visible in the back of his heavy hoodie, right in the area of his heart.

"Bob, I need to pull the hounds away from the body before they do damage. Do you have your cellphone?"

"I do," Bob replied.

"Call the sheriff." Arie took a breath, blew a toodle. He almost sang "Onward Christian Beagles," which he would often do to settle them, get them ready for a new cast, then thought better of it.

The minute he emerged from the woods, his wife knew something big was wrong, although to one who did not know him, Arie appeared calm. Calm he was, but surprised, nevertheless. Who had killed a man, an African American looking to be about fifty, on the Kalergis's property?

The three other whippers-in silently took their positions. Bob emerged from the woods, running to catch up.

Reaching the field, Arie announced, "We have an unusual circumstance and I must put the hounds up. I'm sorry to cancel the hunt—but the breakfast will start that much earlier." As he smiled tightly, a siren could be heard in the distance. Deputy Cooper, working this Saturday, had just left Barracks Road Shopping Center after ejecting a drunken customer in Buchanan and Kiguel framing shop. That loopy soul was now in another cruiser, heading for the county jail.

The field slowly walked back to the house as Cooper drove down the driveway.

Harry reached for Fair's hand. "Boy, it must be really bad."

As the Waldingfield Beagle staff quickly put the hounds in their party wagon, counting each one as they did so, Cooper stopped next to them.

"Who found the body?" she inquired.

This was the first the other whippers-in heard of it.

"We did." Bob shut the wagon door, then pointed to Arie Rijke.

"Hop in," she ordered. The three drove back across the fields as Bob and Arie directed her to the site.

The ground was hard, there was no danger of sinking into mud. She stopped at the tree line.

Arie disembarked at the wood's edge, leading the way through the bushes to the body.

Cooper walked around the corpse. "Shot in the back. No other marks on him. His sweatshirt is torn in spots from these thorns. Has anyone else seen the body?"

"No," Arie answered.

"Gentlemen, we'll need to wait here until the rest of the team arrives, which won't be long." She questioned them for the details as to when and how they found the body, when they pulled the hounds off, and confirmed that neither of them knew the deceased.

She checked her watch. "Forty minutes from your discovery until now."

Seeing a glitter around the dead man's neck, Cooper knelt down, pulled a pencil from her coat pocket, and gingerly hooked it under the chain. A brass rectangular chit hung at the end of the chain. It read in eighteenth-century script *Garth* and the number 5, large, centered above the name.

"Hmm" was all Cooper said.

The two tall men bent over.

Bob ventured a guess. "Some kind of ID."

Arie, from South Africa, replied, "I don't know."

"Harry will know. She's the history buff. This is old." Cooper got on her cellphone. "Darrel, stop at the house, pick up Harry."

Ten minutes later, Harry joined them in the woods.

"What is this? Bob says it's an ID, maybe?"

Harry, not backed off by the sight of a murdered man, knelt down as did Cooper, who again lifted the brass rectangle with her pencil.

"This belongs to the Garth family; they owned at one time over four thousand acres. Sugarday was part of that land. At the time of the Revolutionary War, Cloverfields was about two thousand acres, but Ewing Garth, a brilliant businessman, continued to add to his holdings over the years. He finally persuaded the state to sell him The Barracks, which brought his acreage up to four thousand."

"So this belonged to Ewing Garth?"

"It would have been given to anyone who was a slave leaving the plantation on an errand for Ewing. If he sent ten people out, they would each have one of these."

"What's the point?" Darrel asked, not one to read much history.

"To allow the bearer to do business unmolested. Also, back

then there were gangs of mostly white men, but not always white, who would steal slaves to sell them down in the Delta—hence the expression *Sold downriver*. No one could say slavery was an easy ride, but in the Delta it sure was rougher than in the Mid-Atlantic."

"So the chit would keep a man or woman safe?" Darrel asked, intrigued.

"Most times, especially if the person was owned by a powerful man. Ewing and his daughters were very powerful, both here and in North Carolina, where he also owned a great deal of land. The Holloways were powerful, Susan Tucker's people. *Holloway* is her maiden name. They owned and still own Big Rawly. Her grandmother does."

Cooper rose and her knees cracked as she stood up. "What in the devil was this fellow doing with it around his neck?" As an afterthought, she added, "Shot twice in the back."

"This is the second corpse you've found in a week. Right?"

"The other man was pretty well torn up," Darrel added.

"Do you know how he died?" Everyone there knew how Harry was, her tireless curiosity.

Cooper sighed. "No. That will take the medical examiner. Could very well be natural causes, even with his injury."

"This guy's in good shape except for the bullet holes." Darrel shrugged.

"Exactly. Which is why I want you to go up to the house and ask Mary and David if they heard anything last night, say between three and five in the morning. Did the dogs bark?"

"Right." He turned to leave.

"Was he killed here or moved here?" Harry asked.

Cooper nodded. "Hopefully we'll be able to identify him. Makes the work easier. I can't tell if he was moved, but I bet our forensic team can weigh in on that.

"You two notice anything else?" she asked Arie and Bob.

"No, but we had to get the beagles out of here before they damaged the body. Carrion," Arie succinctly replied.

As Arie had served in the South African Army and Bob in the U.S. Navy, both had been trained to keep cool and decisive in a crisis.

"All right, you all go back up to the house. Pretending nothing has happened isn't going to work, so tell people the truth, the little fellows found a body. You don't need to elaborate. Harry, this means you."

"Yes," Harry simply agreed.

As the others walked away, Cooper methodically searched the ground. Nothing unusual.

Waiting for the team, she lit a cig. She'd sneaked back to smoking again and she needed the nicotine, a calming puff. Two dead men, why? Not that the deaths were related, but the circumstances around each body were unusual, not to mention the relative scarcity of unnatural mysterious deaths in the area.

Hearing more squad cars and the ambulance, she inhaled as much as she could, then ground out the cig on the sole of her shoe before dropping it in her pocket. No point in advertising that her no-smoking plan had fizzled.

Sheriff Shaw soon reached her in the woods. Wordlessly, he studied the body. He, too, noticed the chit, and Cooper filled him in on the background Harry had provided.

"Umm."

"Boss, two dead men in a week. A quiet year and now this. The driver had to be forced under that boulder," she said. "I don't see how he could crawl."

"Maybe not. People find unusual strength if they're scared enough. He had half a face, so he was scared," the sheriff countered.

"Must have been terrified. Who can do that to flesh? He was

killed, yes, but by a human?" She found the means of death puzzling.

"Now this." He looked up at a perfect fall sky. "And really it has been such a quiet year."

"Not anymore." They sighed, almost in unison.

4

December 31, 1785 Saturday

A fragrant cherrywood log crackled and popped in the fireplace of the inviting parlor, John Schuyler, in a chair, opened his eyes.

"Four more minutes." John Schuyler's wife, Catherine, smiled at him.

He smiled back and looked at the large grandfather clock that had cost his father-in-law a fortune to import.

Fortunately, Ewing Garth possessed a fortune, which his two daughters, Catherine and Rachel, and their husbands would someday inherit.

Charles West, Garth's other son-in-law, a former British captain in the late war, stood up, lifting his glass, as they'd been visiting in the library after dinner.

The others stood also.

Bettina, the head woman slave and cook, came in from the kitchen, as did Roger and Weymouth, Roger's teenage son. Roger, as the butler, was the male slave with the most power, which he used judiciously. Bettina, also wise about these things, expressed herself more than Roger, but everyone thought that was because she was a woman.

Charles looked around the room at these people whom he had learned to love. "Happy New Year."

All, Bettina, Roger, and Weymouth, too, lifted their glasses and toasted the New Year and one another.

"Did not the Romans understand this day better than ourselves?" Catherine, at twenty-two, was reaching the apogee of her beauty. "Janus, who can see the past and the future."

Charles, tall, blond, impeccably educated, nodded. "A dubious gift."

Ewing, late middle age, smiled indulgently. "Oh, now, Charles, if a man is speculating, Janus could certainly add to his fortune."

"Well," his son-in-law tilted his head, "yes."

Bettina looked out the hand-blown glass windows. "Snowing heavier."

The others followed her gaze.

"January." Rachel, not a late-night person like her husband, Charles, was struggling to keep awake. "The dead of winter."

"I try to remember that. The leaves are sleeping and will unfold in springtime," Ewing remarked. "Old as I am, every year spring comes as a miracle."

Roger walked over to the window, putting his hand on the glass, which was cold. "Might I suggest that Catherine and John, Charles and Rachel head home before this grows worse? No one wants to get lost in a snowstorm."

Bettina scolded. "Roger, did you leave prints on that glass?"

"No." Roger smiled at her. He knew her ways and she his.

"Didn't one of Paul Axtell's sons die in a blizzard?" Catherine asked.

"Terrible thing," her father replied. "You and Rachel were just little things. No one was prepared for the ferocity of the storm.

We knew it was going to snow. You can feel that in your bones—but this was as though Borealis was extracting his revenge." Ewing cited the Greek god of the north wind. "Started in the late afternoon. Isabelle and I," he recalled his late, much missed wife, "took you two outside to play in the large twirling snowflakes, but within an hour the sky grew dark, the wind picked up. In we came and within minutes the house felt as though someone was pummeling it. The noise of that wind! The snow was so thick I doubt people could see the hand in front of their face. Paul's son, a big, strapping boy, Samuel, went out to bring in more firewood. They found him when the storm passed, almost twenty-four hours later; he lay between the woodshed and the house, not twenty yards from the back door."

"Poor fellow, so close," Rachel, always kindhearted, said.

"Mother Nature can be cruel." Ewing rose from his chair. "Poor Paul never really recovered, and now, these many years later, his mind is completely gone. His daughters must watch him all the time. He wanders off. Forgets where he lives. A sad life, and once he had everything. I suppose there's a lesson there, but I prefer to focus on a happier one for the New Year."

"Mother used to pray for thankful increase, so let us hope that is what 1786 brings to us." Rachel smiled as Charles took her hand and kissed it. "Happy New Year," Charles said.

"Yes." Rachel kissed his cheek.

"I'll fetch your wraps," Bettina offered, while Roger, not waiting for more direction from Bettina, who could be bossy, left for the back of the house.

Weymouth preceded his father down the long hall, heart pine shining, each man now carrying a lantern with a candle in it. They set their lanterns on the long, elegant hall table, which Ewing also had shipped in from England. Most of the furniture in the big house, as it was called, came from there. The Garths weren't much for the French fashion, they found it too ornamental, too frilly.

The men helped the women on with their wraps. Roger opened the door and Ewing's daughters kissed him good night.

The two couples walked together through the snow, then parted ways as Catherine and John headed toward a tidy two-story clapboard house toward the west and Rachel and Charles turned east toward its duplicate.

"Happy New Year," they wished one another, glad to see the candles shining in their own windows.

When Charles opened the door for his wife, they were greeted by his Welsh corgi, Piglet, who had faced the war with him, and the aroma of a good fire. Their two daughters, one two years old, an adopted child, and one a year old, along with Catherine and John's son, a year and a half old, were sound asleep down in Ruth's cabin on the double row of slave quarters, the buildings facing one another.

Ruth loved children and they loved her. All the children, slave and free, played together as toddlers.

Charles, unwrapping his scarf, smiled at his wife. "We're alone."

She teased. "We have Piglet."

Taking her in his arms, he held her, then kissed her. "That we do. Let's make the most of this peace and quiet."

Catherine and John came to the same conclusion.

Down at the weaving lodge with its huge shuttle loom, the peace and quiet was disturbed. Bumbee, a gifted weaver, slept near the enormous fireplace. A knock on the door awakened her. She wrapped a shawl around her shoulders and hurried to the door, but she didn't open it because her worthless husband, whom she had left in high drama, often tried to win back her affections, if only for a night.

"Who is it?"

"Mignon."

"Good God." Bumbee threw open the door to behold a tiny shivering young woman, half dead from the cold.

"Sit by the fire." Bumbee led her to a rocking chair in front of the fire, picking up another heavy log and placing it on the flames. "How did you know to come to the lodge?" Bumbee asked, worried.

"I didn't. I came up from the path by the creek. My lantern died, but I knew by the big rocks I was near Cloverfields, so I climbed the path upward and knocked on the first door I saw through the snow."

"Are you hungry?"

"No, I can't feel my feet. I just want to be warm and I'll slip out in the morning."

"Mignon, the snow will be deep. I can hide you here for a while, up in the loft. No one goes up there and there's a back stairway that leads right into the woods. What happened?"

"That devil Sheba beat me with a cane. She didn't hit me in the face because she didn't want it to show. I ain't never going back down there. She and Mrs. Selisse are the Devil's own."

"That they are." Bumbee knew only too well of the violent temper of Maureen Selisse, now Holloway, the lady of a great estate, Big Rawly. Her lady's maid, Sheba, proved even worse. Maureen's temper would explode, then usually fade, but Sheba seemed to enjoy inflicting pain. Neither mistress nor slave ever forgot and forgave what they considered an affront to their person.

"I took a ribbon from Mrs. Selisse's table. All I wanted to do was hold it up to my face to see if the color suited me, and that bitch Sheba walked in just as I did it. She screamed I was stealing the mistress's pearls, how I was a slut always trying to entice the men, and then she picked up a lady's cane from the big Chinese jar and beat me. The more she beat me the crazier she got. I ran away. She ran after me for a bit, but then grew tired. She's crazy wild."

"Mignon, strip off those clothes. Soaking wet. I'll bring a blanket. You can wrap yourself up in that." Bumbee headed for the stairs, where she kept blankets, a few pillows, odds and ends tucked under them.

The loom sat in the middle of the large downstairs room. Bumbee had the carpenters on the estate build her shelves that were made up of large and small squares. Into these she placed wool, cotton, and even some hemp, organized by color, material, and weight, a carefully variegated embodiment of her organized mind. She returned with blankets, which she wrapped around the still-shivering younger woman. Then she draped Mignon's wet clothing over a bench sitting at a right angle to the fire. She wasn't worried about anyone coming into the lodge; generally only those women she had trained to weave and now worked with her joined her in the lodge. They would shut up. No slave of Cloverfields would ever reveal a person fleeing a harsh master, or even a good master, for that matter.

Slowly Mignon warmed. "I'm heading for a city. Maybe Richmond, maybe Philadelphia. I can get lost there."

"Cities can be rough. Don't really know myself."

"I don't care."

"Mignon, you're tired, you're probably hurt, and I hope you don't have frostbite. Your nose looks all right. What about your fingers and toes?"

"I could keep my fingers warmer than my toes. I'll worry about that in daylight." Exhaustion began to wash over her.

"Come on. Let me get you upstairs. No one will know you're here. You need sleep. The bed's a pallet bed, but it's warm. We can talk in the morning and I'll make breakfast. I reckon not much is going to happen until some of this snow melts down."

Nodding yes, Mignon allowed Bumbee to lead her upstairs. She climbed onto the pallet, Bumbee taking the blanket wrapped around her, placing it on top of the other blankets. Mignon fell asleep instantly.

Bumbee stared down at the fragile-looking woman. How was this tortured girl going to get out of the county? She'd leave tracks in the snow. Once people could move about, Maureen Selisse would quickly report a runaway slave. God forbid she lost any money. Whoever returned Mignon was sure of a reward and Mignon would be sure of tenfold more misery.

Bumbee toted another heavy log for the fire, blew out her candle, and crawled into bed. The wind whistled outside. Worried as she was about Mignon, she was glad the intruder hadn't been her worthless husband.

"Sweet Jesus, give me strength," she prayed, then she, too, fell asleep.

5

January 1, 1786 Sunday

*B*lue, the world shone soft blue. Snow continued to fall, tiny little flakes. Even though the walkways among all the buildings had been cleared, two inches already rested on those paths. Another hour and the men would be back at it.

Catherine, like most well-born women of her generation, rarely used the word *slave*. One tried to circumvent what may be unpleasant. A cheating husband was rarely called that. Behind their fans, women might murmur that the husband suffered from the usual malady. Catherine avoided talking with the ladies if she could. Bored her to tears. Like her father, she adored business, growth, new ideas, and, of course, profit.

It would never do to be direct; being direct in Virginia betrayed a common mind, hence vulgarity. This rule did not apply sometimes—with one's own family.

The back door opened. "Sister."

Catherine hurried to the door and took her sister's hand to help her over the threshold. Footing was slippery.

"Rachel, what are you doing out in this weather?"

Throwing off her heavy coat and unwrapping her scarf, Rachel shook her feet. "Charles and the two girls are making more noise than a cannonade. I thought two girls would be easy. I must have been out of my mind. Add in my beloved and handsome husband and I have three children. He was so lonesome for them when we woke up this morning he pushed through the snow to fetch them home. I would have been happy without them for a bit longer." She looked around as she followed Catherine into the kitchen, the huge walk-in fireplace warming the room wonderfully well. "Where is John?"

"Out clearing paths."

Both sisters had children close in age. Rachel's true daughter, Isabelle, was named for her mother. Marcia, an orphan under cover of belonging to a distant relative, was also raised as her own. Marcia would never know her true parentage, although the sisters and their husbands, plus Bettina, knew, but then Bettina knew everything, as did most of the slaves.

"Sit down. I was just boiling a pot of tea so I could go over Father's logging plan for his land along the James River. But I'm sleepy."

"Snow. Rain. Makes me fight to keep my eyes open unless I'm in the house with those hellions. Catherine, I don't think we were that bad."

Catherine laughed as she picked up the boiling tea kettle. "No one ever does. I'm sure we gave Mother fits."

"Mmm." Rachel remained unconvinced.

"Cream?"

"Sit down. I'll get it." Rachel rose to retrieve the pitcher sitting in a small sink, cold water keeping the cream at a good temperature.

"I'll go half blind from all this reading of maps, number, harvest years. We've three hundred acres about Scottsville. The demand for lumber is rising sharply. Father wants to cut it all, then replant. I want partial cutting. Let the rest stand and get even fatter. I don't think the demand is going to falter."

"Why not?"

"People are pouring in." Catherine sipped her tea, grateful for the small jolt.

"That they are. Charles has already had to enlarge his plans for St. Luke's. The cornerstone, as you know, was laid in the fall, but the weather, so strange, halted most of the work. Now he's doubled the size of the church itself. Spring can't arrive soon enough." She looked out the window. "No time soon."

Charles was designing a Lutheran church sited at Wayland's Corner.

"I think not. It will arrive. It always does. Remember how Mother and Bettina would have a robin party when they saw the first robin?"

Rachel leaned back. "I find myself looking back more now, especially since the children came. I wish Mother were here to see them."

"I wish Mother were here to help!" Catherine laughed.

"Which reminds me, where is JohnJohn?"

"With his father. My husband is like your husband. He rose, dressed, ate breakfast, then hurried to pick up JohnJohn, his little shadow. That boy wants to do everything that John does. Poor little fellow gets in the way, but eventually he falls asleep and John carries him back down to Ruth. If it breathes, Ruth loves it. I think she'd mother frogs if she could. If it's warm, she puts him under a tree or in a wagon."

The two smiled for Ruth, in her early thirties, who loved young things and showed a real gift for children. They took to her and she knew when and what they were ready to learn, whether it was how to build a box or their ABCs. If a woman, slave or free, couldn't handle or understand a child, usually that woman found her way to Ruth, including powerful mistresses from other estates.

"He's going to be the spitting image of John." Rachel again looked out the window, and it was snowing harder. "I've discovered I like working with Charles, like the drawings, like the walking over building sites. I could never understand how you could sit and go over business plans with Father. Now I do. When something fills your mind, best to learn and do."

"We'd both die fiddling with needlepoint. Which reminds me. Father told me that Maureen Selisse is having great success with the foundry, but here's the odd part, she is allowing Sheba to advertise and sell fabrics and needlepoint."

"What? Since when did that holy horror ever evidence any flair for texture, color, much less needlepoint design? All Sheba can do is make other people's lives miserable," Rachel remarked with feeling.

Catherine shrugged. "The real story is Maureen is keeping her lady-in-waiting happy."

"Curious." Rachel tapped her fingers on the smooth wooden tabletop.

"Indeed. Sheba knows what really happened when Francisco was stabbed to death. I don't believe their story about Moses killing him. Never did."

Francisco was Maureen's husband, who bedeviled and violated regularly a gorgeous slave woman, Ailee. The story told by mistress and lady-in-waiting was that Moses, Ailee's true love, killed Francisco. The two slaves fled, never to be found by the authorities.

Rachel, usually quiet in groups, easily chatted with her sister and all the people on Cloverfields. "But why fabrics?"

"Maureen imports all those expensive silks and brocades. Maybe there's money in it?" Catherine wondered.

"I think Sheba and Maureen will use this to gather information. Who is losing money? Who is making money? Who is having an illicit affair with whom? Women will come and a bit of sherry here and there, tongues will loosen."

"Rachel, I would never have thought of that," Catherine honestly replied.

"No good will come of this."

"Not to us, but probably to them." Catherine sighed.

6

*S*oft October light bathed St. Luke's Lutheran Church in spun gold. The gray fieldstone seemed warmer, the slate roof glistened deep gray. The midday sun glowed on the hand-blown window-panes. St. Luke's boasted many windows, quite an expense back in the late eighteenth century when it was built. The parishioners exhibited pride and success—but not too much. This was and remains Virginia, after all.

The Very Reverend Herbert Jones, service over, having bid the congregants goodbye, stood with Harry and Fair, a slight breeze touching his robes and hand-embroidered vestments. As they walked to the back quad, the three Lutheran cats, Cazenovia, Lucy Fur, and Elocution, followed them.

Reds, golds, orange, yellow, deep scarlet leaves still clung to the trees, but their days were numbered.

The human and feline group stopped at the first quad and turned to inspect the back of the beautiful church with its two matching arcades, the arches graceful and sturdy, having held up for centuries.

The sun shone to their left, just slightly west, as it was about one o'clock. The service had run a bit over, with the choir director indulging a fit of too many choruses of "A Mighty Fortress Is Our God," written by Luther himself.

Harry, elected to the vestry board, in charge of buildings and grounds, pointed to the back roofline. "See."

The Reverend shaded his eyes. "No."

"It is a little difficult, but the weather stripping is cracking at the back second-story window, where you put the old desk and file cabinets. Who uses that room?"

"I do. I move files up there every two years. When I was young there wasn't so much paperwork. Now it's an avalanche, and not just from local and state and federal authorities. The diocese feels compelled to inundate us. My job is to serve my parishioners, not fill out forms."

"Amen," Fair uttered with solemnity.

The Reverend turned to him, smiling. "You probably have as much, if not more, than I do."

"Veterinary medicine is on an arc to catch up with human medicine. Just give it a little time. We will soon be operating with a lawyer at our elbow."

"What's the most expensive horse upon which you've operated?" Herb had never thought of the money involved.

"One and a half million dollars," Fair promptly replied.

"I am grateful our Lord has not put a price on me." The genial pastor laughed.

"Incalculable." Harry reached for his hand.

She and everyone dearly loved this man, who had been a captain in Vietnam, survived, and dedicated his life to God, to being the best pastor he could be. He thought sometimes that the seminary took as much thought and preparation as battle, although it was far more pleasant.

Fair looked up. "See what you mean."

"Well, let me jump on it this week." Harry addressed the Reverend. "It's that time of year. You never know when the weather is going to turn and I don't want water to leak into the window frame or, worse, the roof, then freeze and thaw."

"Fine with me, but you aren't getting on that roof." The Very Reverend, average size but still bigger than Harry, looked down at her.

"Oh, don't start that again." She fussed because years back she had part of the slate replaced and Herb pitched a fit when he found her on the roof. "I don't need to get on the roof. I just need a tall ladder to reach the window."

Elocution rubbed against Herb's leg. *"Poppy, you'll set her off."*

"I'll hire a glazier or a roofer and he can climb up there."

"Actually, I'm the one who hires anyone for buildings and grounds with your permission, and you can't keep treating me like a hothouse flower. I can fix that in a skinny minute. I have the tools, just need to dig out the old flashing and lay in new. It's easy unless I find more damage, but I sure hope I won't. Anything involving a roof, plumbing, or electricity is expensive."

"Now, listen here. I have known you since you were tiny. I'm not having you on a two-story ladder. We went through this before." He looked to Harry's husband. "You talk to her."

"Why did you let me get elected to buildings and grounds if you won't let me do my job?"

"Harry, you do a great job, you do the mowing, the trimming, repairing stone walls if need be. You do just about everything, but I don't want you up there." He held up his hand. "I am an old man, so chalk this up to a generational difference, but I don't think women should do some things. That's what men are for."

She had heard this argument before and really didn't feel like fighting it. He was truthful. This was more of a generational thing.

These days many a young man didn't even bother to stand up when a woman entered the room. That just shocked her, and she attributed it to them being raised by Yankees who had moved south. Not always true, of course, but it gave her some comfort. It did not occur to Harry that a woman might not be able to have it both ways. And being a Virginian, she felt men should certainly perform all the proper courtesies.

Fair put his arm around his wife's shoulders. "Honey, he is the Very Reverend, you know," he said in his light baritone. "Time may come when you need Herb to put in a good word for you upstairs."

They laughed, walking back to the church building. He was her pastor, her friend. He buried her mother and father when they were killed in a car accident while she studied at Smith. He comforted her and guided her. He married her to Fair and he never shrank from helping when Harry or another parishioner, indeed anyone, was in need. She decided to shut up.

"Let's have a cup of tea or something more exciting. My throat went dry during the sermon." Herb opened the doors to the small gathering room just off his office.

"Sounds wonderful." Fair smiled.

The three cats shot ahead of their human, skidded to a stop in front of the cabinet at the small kitchen.

"*Treats,*" they sang in chorus.

"Whatever got into Edgar today?" Fair smiled as he asked about the choir director.

"We can't clap for encores in church, but he was going for encores." Harry laughed. "Every now and then Edgar and Dot," she named the new organist, as the older lady had finally retired, "collude, I swear they do. She must have hit every note on that organ."

Herb chuckled. "They don't lack for enthusiasm." He took a

long, much-needed sip. "Feels better. I must have preached an overlong sermon. I'm too dry."

"Twenty minutes," Harry informed him. "I keep count."

"So I see." His eyes brightened. "I'll remember that when I'm up there, looking down at you. To change the subject, what really happened yesterday at Sugarday? I've heard a few reports."

"Susan, Ned, BoomBoom, and Alicia were there from St. Luke's. Miranda was up at the house. Lots of people. The meet was well attended. Everyone wants to be out in this fabulous weather. I expect they told you the hounds found a body in that line of woods to the west of the house?" Harry remarked.

"Yes, and they also told me that Officer Cooper had you sent down to view the body," he replied.

She nodded. "Sheriff Shaw and Coop wanted me to look at a brass rectangle on a chain around his neck. He'd been shot, fairly recently. He hadn't been lying there for days. I was grateful for that."

"What about the brass rectangle?" Herb was curious.

"Engraved on its center was *Number Five* and under that, *Garth*. About two inches long by an inch and a half wide. I took it to be a slave pass."

"How odd." The Reverend rattled the ice in his glass. "Did it look original? Not a copy or reproduction?"

"Looked original to me. I don't think anyone makes reproductions." Harry considered this. "Could make some people angry."

"Would," Fair agreed. "Assuming that pass was authentic, what might it possibly mean? Why wear it?"

"Why get killed in the first place?" Harry added.

"Well, it is peculiar," Herb said. "St. Luke's was built with slave labor as well as parishioner labor. I wonder if they needed those chits?" He thought for a moment. "Probably not since they came from the Garth estate and Mr. Garth's son-in-law was the architect. We forget how highly skilled both slaves and freemen were. Well, we forget until we look at the evidence. St. Luke's has stood for over two hundred years, and you, being head of buildings and grounds, know how sturdy those structures are."

"I do. Downstairs in the vault where you keep the old papers, well, those on parchment, right?" Herb nodded, so she continued. "Did you ever find objects? Not passes but china pieces, stuff like that?"

"Whatever has been found over the two hundred years is in the vault. Mostly bits of glass, pipe bowls, and the reason for that is, I would guess, that most objects are underneath us. As they built, dropped, or discarded things, they built over them."

"Probably," Harry agreed.

"Still, they had to have had a garbage pit." Fair finished his drink. "If that's ever found and, say, architecture students or archeology ones create a dig, who knows what they'd find?"

"As long as it isn't bodies." Harry half smiled.

7

October 24, 2016 Monday

"*I'm not talking to you.*" Pewter sashayed in front of Tucker.

"*Good. I need the break,*" the corgi fired back.

"*You think you're so smart.*" The gray cat fluffed her tail slightly so as to enlarge her person.

Truthfully, her person did not need enlargement.

Mrs. Murphy, trailing behind, veered clear of the two arguing animals.

Never took much to set off Pewter, but Tucker had sworn she saw a red-tailed hawk—of which there were many—and one should seek cover.

The cat naturally disagreed, said it was an osprey, a water bird, and the two barely resembled each other. Both started the day peevish over their breakfast bowls. How any creature, four-legged or two, could be peevish on such a spectacular October day was a mystery.

The sky sparkled a deep robin's-egg blue with a few wispy, pure clouds high above. Last night was the first light frost. A slight wind caused the remaining leaves to rustle. There was enough color to lift one's spirits, to celebrate fall in central Virginia.

The animals, domestic and wild, showed their lush winter fur, a dense undercoat adding more fluff and more protection.

"Think we'll see more eagles?" Mrs. Murphy finally spoke.

"Making a big comeback," Tucker replied. *"That's what Liz Potter said at Mom's wildlife meeting, remember?"*

"Nasty birds. Hate 'em," Pewter declared.

"I still wonder why the one we did see was flying from the mountains. Eagles nest by water, big, high nests. Mom says there are lots down on the James River and even some on the Rockfish," Mrs. Murphy mused.

"You're right, but I'm sure he had a reason. Maybe fishing was better that day in the Shenandoah Valley," Tucker said.

"Doesn't explain the eyeball." Pewter sniffed. *"I really do hate big birds."*

"Birds like eyeballs," Tucker announced, as though they didn't know.

"Crows and vultures. Eagles are fish eaters," Mrs. Murphy replied. *"I suppose any animal, including a human, will eat carrion if nothing else is available. Some protein there."*

"Remember the time we came upon the corpse dressed as a scarecrow and the crows mobbed it? Sang a song about eyes, too, which was really horrible."

Pewter puffed her tail out more. *"Birds have no respect."*

"Neither do humans. It was a human who hoisted the body up on the pole," Tucker wisely noted.

They chattered on. Being creatures of the moment with no need for ideologies, they accepted the habits of other animals. Humans attached theories and ideologies to habits, some correct, some not correct. The two cats and dog never did that. They looked life square in the eye, which doesn't mean they always liked what they saw.

"It's getting close to Halloween. Might have something to do with it. I hate Halloween, too." Pewter spoke as though she was on Mt. Olympus.

"I'm not overly fond of it either," Mrs. Murphy confessed.

"What I don't understand is why do they want to look like skeletons, dead things? Zombies? Monsters? They'll all be dead soon enough, why push it?" Pewter sensibly said.

"If I knew the answer to that, I'd think like a human, God forbid." The sturdy dog raised her nose in the air. "Girls, up a tree. Someone's coming. A coyote."

The two cats needed no further prodding, for coyotes would kill and eat anything.

Within a minute, Odin, a young fellow, approached Tucker, legs farther apart, braced, in case. On seeing a friend, the corgi relaxed.

"Scared me there for a minute."

"I didn't think anything scared you." The handsome fellow smiled at the dog.

The cats and dog had helped Odin survive a bitter winter when he was scrawny and half grown. They'd debated about it but then moved by his plight, pulled food and garbage out to him behind the barn. Odin never forgot and would bring the threesome tidbits of gossip from the wild animals, things he'd observed at other farms.

"Heard about the body at Sugarday?" Tucker asked.

"No, that's pretty far away. Might hear about it in a day or two, but there aren't many of us that far east of here. Coyote, I mean," Odin replied. "The only thing I heard was a human was found under a boulder up by 250."

The cats in the tree and Tucker related the details of the beagles finding a body, shot twice in the back. As Harry had seen the body, their information was good. Pewter also, in glowing detail, described the eagle carrying an eye, which she was sure belonged to the corpse under the big rock.

The coyote sat on his haunches. "Guess he didn't stand a chance. Either one."

"Maybe they didn't deserve one," Pewter called down.

"If we ever get to see the Waldingfield beagles, we'll ask them. The humans usually miss something." Tucker didn't mean that as a slam, but it was what she'd observed in her lifetime.

As it was, Deputy Cooper, in her tidy office, was going over the known facts of the two corpses.

Sheriff Shaw popped in. "Anything strike you?"

"If we can get an ID on the second body, that might help. For the first guy, good record, truck driver for a Louisville company for eight years. No accidents. Everything we found out has checked out since the day we called the trucking company. No record of any sort. Clean. The trucking company, mid-South, obviously, ships east as far as Boston and as far west as Denver. No problems there that have shown up, anyway. All trucks state inspected. All drivers vetted for criminal records. Random blood tests to determine if anyone is on drugs or drink. Noland Charmin was clean. Married. Father of two. No one can think of what happened to him. Waiting for the medical reports. I'll track down habits, you know, did he like basketball? Sometimes interests tell you more than records."

"Mmm," Rick said.

"Second victim still unidentified, obviously."

The sheriff stared at Cooper for a moment. "Patience. It always takes patience."

And so it would. But like so many things in a criminal investigation, by the time they found out what they needed, they would be a day late and a dollar short.

8

January 2, 1786 Monday

The storm seemed tethered over the mountain. Flurries would fade, then an hour later more heavy snow would fall accompanied by fierce gusts.

Catherine joined the boys in the barn, to check on the horses. Jeddie, eighteen, almost nineteen, wiry, a good rider getting better, delighted her no matter what.

Serenissima, a quality mare she bought from Maureen Selisse, dozed in her stall, a warm blanket over her. All the horses, whether the blooded horses or the draft horses, contently ate or dozed, happy to be inside. With fresh hay, constant water changes if the water froze in the buckets, and their stalls picked clean, life was good.

Chores done, Catherine sat down in the tack room, warmed by a small woodburning stove placed on thick slate that sat on packed earth. The rest of the floor, unplaned oak, had been worn smooth over the years. Tired, she removed her gloves, blew on her hands, then held them toward the stove.

"Miss Catherine, I can make tea on the stove," Jeddie offered.

"No, thank you." She looked up at his open, honest face. "Aren't we getting close to your birthday?"

He smiled. "Not too close."

"Nineteen?" Her eyebrows raised.

"Yes." He grinned. "I'm old enough to get married."

She tilted back her head, laughing. "Jeddie, I had no idea you wanted to get married."

He laughed with her. "I don't. Momma's lecturing me about it."

"And your father?" she asked.

The young man shook his head. "Saying nothing. He doesn't want to get on the wrong side of Momma."

"Wise man. No one wants to get on the wrong side of your momma."

"She's saying if I marry the right girl, I can be happy. A wife will take care of me."

"She's right."

"And I'll get my own cabin. Ours is crowded. I think Momma wants me out."

She grinned. "Oh, I don't know about that." She paused. "Springtime. I'll talk to Father about building more cabins. We have enough, he'll say, and we do, but I'll remind him that it's best to be prepared and some of our younger people will be married soon, new babies. You know Father loves babies." Her eyes twinkled. "Wants to pick them up. I remember the first time Marcia wrapped her tiny fingers around his finger. His eyes misted, he fell in love. Tell me, Jeddie, what would we have done if he hadn't fallen in love with her?"

"She's a pretty little thing," Jeddie remarked.

"We can't hide the fact that she's an outside child, but we can hide whose outside child. It's been fun watching ladies talk behind their hands about how our cousin fell from grace, the one in South Carolina. Then someone else whispers, 'No, it was the cousin in Charlottesville.' People love to talk and they don't much care if it's the truth or not. What they care about is looking as though they have the real story."

He nodded. "I listen, especially when we're at another barn or a horse race. Lot of puffed-up people."

"Speaking of races, haven't heard of anything planned, but I don't think we will until April. It's going to be a long, hard winter. Do you think Serenissima has caught?" She used the expression for a mare who has gotten pregnant.

"I sure hope so."

"We should know right around the time of your birthday."

This made him laugh.

Catherine knew bloodlines, especially the new blood coming in from England. She had a gift with horses and could find the right training for one just by watching the animal. As Jeddie loved horses, she passed on to him what he could memorize. Each year he learned more.

Jeddie heard through the pipeline that more northern states planned to abolish slavery. Vermont already had done so. Connecticut, Rhode Island, Pennsylvania, and New Hampshire said they would adopt policies to gradually abolish slavery, but nothing much had happened. Some young slaves talked about heading out if they could just make it. He listened but didn't say anything. Jeddie thought it stupid to talk about freedom within earshot of anyone. And he had never heard of those states being good horse states. He was born to work with horses. So he listened, watched, and kept learning.

He loved Catherine. They'd worked together in the stables for as long as he could remember. She took so much time with him, rode with him, showed the damage a stifle injury could do, showed him how to read age from teeth. The odd thing was, if he had ever expressed curiosity about freedom, she would be the person he would discuss it with, even though his father told him over and over again to never trust a white person. He did trust her and she trusted him. They never spoke about it, they felt it.

When Moses and Ailee fled Maureen Selisse's plantation, Big Rawly, they hid in the small cave down by the creek. Eventually Moses escaped to Pennsylvania hidden in a wagon driven by John and Charles, both of whom feared for Moses as well as for themselves. As if the young man was accused of murder, he would be killed without much of an argument. He didn't kill Francisco Selisse. His wife did—but there was no proof, and almost everyone believed Moses did it in a rage over Ailee, whom Moses loved and Francisco violated. Maureen and Sheba beat Ailee, smashing in her one eye, but Moses and the once beautiful woman escaped. However, Ailee, in no condition to travel, was hidden in the loom room once she was strong enough to walk up there. The slaves knew. Catherine, Rachel, John, and Charles knew. Ewing did not. No one would ever speak of the fact that Marcia was Ailee's baby by Francisco. She looked white; hence the fabricated story about a cousin, which Ewing knew perfectly well was a story, but he didn't know how much of a story. Marcia would never know her true parentage. People liked to talk, but in this case no slave on Cloverfields would ever utter a word. Maureen and Sheba were hated and feared. Maureen would get even, as would Sheba, with any slave anywhere as well as any white person.

Marcia's secret, the second secret of the illegal hiding and transporting of a slave, was buried with Ailee when she killed herself. That didn't mean it wouldn't have repercussions over the years.

Jeddie, young though he was, knew what was at risk. He sat next to Catherine.

"Does this mean you have a girl in mind?"

He looked at her. "No."

She smiled.

"I don't. Really."

She poked him in the arm. "That's what you say now, but someday you might change your tune. Things just sort of happen."

"Like when you fell in love with Mr. John?"

That tinkling laugh again. "If anyone had told me I'd fall in love with a poor soldier from Massachusetts I would have told them they were out of their minds. And here I am. And I am lucky, for he's a good man and a brave one."

"He's a war hero."

"That he is, but Jeddie, he's brave in other ways. He acts on what he believes is right. He's not much of a talker. He's a doer. I love him, but more, I respect him. And Rachel respects Charles, son of an English lord, no less. A second son, I add."

"All those titles. Too confusing."

"Is." She looked out the window. "Well, Father will be fretting. I told him I'd go over the timber tract maps with him. Still dark. You'd never know it was midmorning."

"I'll walk back with you."

"I'd enjoy your company. Always do."

He walked next to her in case she slipped. The paths kept getting shoveled out, but the snow and now a bit of ice kept ahead of the shovels. They talked about Reynaldo and his brother, Crown Prince, two exceptional horses.

"Jeddie, Bettina's in the back. Slip in and grab a biscuit. She made a pile this morning."

"Yes, Miss Catherine." He trotted around the back to the kitchen for one of the best biscuits in Virginia.

Ewing, in his office, was poring over last year's figures for tobacco hogsheads when his daughter came in, took off her scarf, coat, and gloves to sit across from him. Wordlessly he shoved papers her way. Two peas in a pod, really.

Bumbee, down in the weaving cabin, kept at her loom. Two other women also worked the shuttles, the click and clack, warp and weft, filling the room with rhythm. The large fireplace kept it pleasant. Every now and then the wind would rattle the windows, real blown windows, no oiled skin for Cloverfields.

Bumbee turned to stare outside. "Is this ever going to end?"

Grace, sixteen, attractive, leaned toward her smaller loom. "Good you got that wool and carded, too."

Liddy, maybe eighteen, sat on a low bench, twisting some strands of wool together, pulling, testing. "Bet no one is going to Sheba's fabric shop now."

"We will never need to do that," Bumbee forcefully said, then paused, "but Miss Catherine and Miss Rachel will have to go, I expect, to keep up good relations."

"And to buy silks." Liddy shrugged.

"True." Grace nodded. "But that's not our job anyway. Goes to Regina."

Regina was the seamstress, prized for her ability to see a drawing of a dress and reproduce it.

In the corner, near the fireplace but close to the stairway so she could hide if necessary, Mignon folded odd cloth bits, leftovers from larger projects.

Bumbee used these to make hooked rugs, odds and ends. *Waste nothing* was the motto.

Grace spoke to her. "You're quiet as a mouse."

"Am I? My mind wanders," Mignon replied.

"Your feet hurt. It's not as bad as I feared, but keeping them wrapped helps," Bumbee said.

"Mignon, I know you want to go, but your feet do have to heal and the snow needs to melt some. Anyway, you don't want to leave tracks," Liddy sensibly said.

Mignon looked up from her task. "I'm praying for a thaw."

Bumbee smiled. "While we're sitting here, tell us about those French and English fabrics."

Mignon rolled her eyes. "Lord, girls, you could buy a good horse for what those fabrics cost, and they are beautiful, colors, so many colors. And Sheba wants feathers, dyed feathers and furs. She even got some sable. But those colors, oh, my."

"Like what?" Grace loved clothing.

"Mint green, sky blue, deepest red, and a pale yellow nearly white but so thin. Some of the silks are heavy, others are like air. You put the fabric over your hands and can barely feel it. And there is one bolt that is deeper than a robin's egg, a blue beyond compare, a blue like a big expensive jewel next to a bolt of pale melon, which shimmers. As much as I hate Sheba and that harridan Maureen, they know fabrics."

"Let's hope it keeps them busy," Grace said. "We want them all to stay at Big Rawly. I can't look at either one, can you?"

"No," Liddy offered.

"Me, neither." Bumbee pulled the shuttle down with a practiced hand. "I see Ailee's smashed face, the cheekbones, her eye."

"Vicious." Liddy again looked to the window.

"Well," Bumbee changed the subject, spoke to Grace, "your mother is telling me she hopes you will marry Jeddie Rice."

Caught off guard, Grace mumbled, "Oh, well, Mother, you know how she is."

"I do. I do." Bumbee and the others laughed. "What I want to know is how you feel. You are of age, should you so choose to marry."

"Bumbee, he hardly speaks to me. Mother has this in her head. She says, 'That Jeddie Rice is going places, plus the Missus loves him.' She goes on about how I will live well with a respected young man who will become an even more respected man."

"He does have a gift. No one can ride like Jeddie," Liddy pitched in.

"Maybe so, but he still doesn't say three words to me. Mother's dreaming."

"Better to marry someone at Cloverfields, because if your husband's master won't sell him to Mr. Garth, you'll hardly see him. Too much traveling," Bumbee wisely counseled.

Liddy popped up. "There's always Rollie."

Grace shot her a hard look. "That is the dumbest man ever born."

"I didn't say he was smart, but he's here and he's young. He's a good carpenter," Liddy defended him.

"You marry him, then," Grace shot back.

True, Rollie was not overly bright, nor was he handsome. The girls wanted handsome husbands. Most girls do.

"What I can't understand is why some woman hasn't married DoRe," Mignon said.

DoRe, head of the stables at Big Rawly, lost his wife a year back. He was Moses's father. So many sorrows for such a good man.

"Don't you even mention it. Don't breathe it." Bumbee sat up straighter. "Bettina has her eye on him."

Liddy giggled a little. "They're both old."

They were in their early forties.

"He has a good position. Old means nothing. Position counts. I know, I know, when I was your age my head could be turned by a handsome man. Look who I married and look what I got," Bumbee snapped.

A silence followed this.

A knock on the door shut them up, although Bumbee did whisper, "If that's Mr. Percy, I will knock him upside the head."

She called him by his surname.

"Come in," Liddy sweetly called as Mignon hurried up the stairs.

"Ladies." Zebediah, thirties, stuck his head in the door. "We're finishing up shoveling for now. Need anything? More wood? More water?"

Bumbee smiled. "You brought in so much this morning I think we'll be fine until this time tomorrow. Zeb, how does the weather look to you? Slowing down?"

He shook his head, then closed the door.

"All the good men are taken," Liddy lamented.

"Oh, someone will come along. Just don't make the mistake I did," Bumbee counseled, voice softer.

"But there must have been good times?" Liddy inquired.

"Well—yes." Bumbee laughed and the others laughed with her.

9

January 3, 1786 Tuesday

Although noon, the dark sky gave no hope of relief from the snow, which started New Year's Eve, light enough, then turned into a thumping snowstorm that wouldn't end. Six men ate corn bread, freshly churned butter, fried chicken, diced potatoes in cream with parsley, and green peas preserved from the summer in a tavern blessed with a gifted cook. Preserving fruit proved far easier than vegetables, but some vegetables were put up. Always tasted flat. Some of the luncheon customers drank French wine. Yancy Grant, a horseman from Albemarle County, and his impromptu tablemate downed coffee, the best coffee in Richmond.

"What brings you to Richmond, Sir?" Yancy asked Milton Sevier.

The man, close to Yancy's age, middle-aged, a full head of hair, no powdered wig, reached for corn bread. "Had I known this storm would prove so severe I would have waited to come to Richmond. Land contingent to my own has become available and I hope to work out terms with the seller's attorney, based here instead of Williamsburg. The seller has become befuddled with age and his daughter does not feel she is adept at such a large business decision."

"Might I ask what county, Sir?"

"Appomattox. And you?"

"Albemarle."

Milton nodded. "Well, we will both need prayers to Hermes to arrive home safely."

Just then the door opened and a young, handsome African man, bundled up, snow on his shoulders and cap, called out to the proprietress, "Miss Georgina. River's freezing."

Georgina, well padded, still attractive, nodded to Binky, who removed his cap, disappearing back to the kitchen. Wearing a lacy mobcap on her suspiciously red hair, Georgina stopped at each table. Usually the room was jammed for a midday meal, but now it was so quiet the men could hear one another at the separate tables.

Arriving at Yancy and Milton's table, she beamed. "Two of my favorite gentlemen have met at last. Should travel become difficult, I will halve the rate for rooms. No one can control the weather and if you stay at Yorktown Victory Inn or down to Grace Street at Charlton's Ordinary, the cost may be prohibitive if rooms are available. I have a feeling many a man is stranded today. I had hoped we'd endure some snow, that the worst of this would stay west of us, but no, snow, snow, snow."

"You are most kind." Yancy smiled up at a lady he'd known over the years. "I will avail myself of your generosity."

Yancy had stayed at a small rooming house, but left this morning, thinking the storm would finally pass.

"And I thank you, Madam, but I am staying with my sister and her husband. I do think I would enjoy myself here, though." He smiled broadly.

Georgina operated a fashionable house of pleasure. The tavern part of the house allowed businessmen to make appointments with other businessmen, thereby covering their tracks, should their wives wonder. Of course, wives were not to know such places even existed, but they did, pretending they did not.

The less gorgeous girls acted as waitresses for midday meals. Certainly attractive, but often not as truly stunning as the ladies reserved for the evening guests, they helped Georgina turn a profit.

"We both have distance to travel. Two days if all goes well. I came down by the river. What of you, Sir?" Yancy asked the round-faced fellow.

"Yes. Always easier to travel downriver than up, but the roads are impassable. Now I find the older I get the less I like being jostled in a coach."

"Quite." Yancy finished a delicious chicken breast. "May I inquire as to your business?"

"Tobacco. The land now available is good tobacco land. There are fingers of soil reaching almost up the James, which support the crop. Yes, the best land is in our southern counties, but I have been most fortunate in my Burley tobacco."

"Let us pray," Yancy said with a chuckle, "that our former adversaries never lose their taste for Virginia tobacco."

"Or the French, the German principalities, the Swedes, and you will be surprised to learn I do a brisk business with Poland."

"I am, Sir, indeed."

"Coffeehouses now fill every European city and those gentlemen love to sip their coffee, smoke our tobacco, and discuss politics."

"Our world is changing. I think perhaps we Virginians no longer discuss politics with the fervor we did before the war. We should, you know."

"Yes. Banking is chaos. And I feel strongly that monies must be able to move freely between the states, between banks, between countries, really. As to goods, the same. It seems to me that everyone is so uncertain that no one can move forward."

"I quite agree."

"Mr. Grant, may I ask of your business?"

"Horses, Sir. Also barley, corn, oats. All is well until Mother Nature refuses to cooperate. These last years have proven good for crops. I am as dazed as every man concerning our political difficulties. Prices for grains fluctuate sometimes wildly, as do shipping costs. I try to sell close to home, and even there people are pulling back. Fortunately, I can store any excess, but for how long?"

"We are all in the same boat, are we not?"

"Yes, yes. I had hoped to create more stability through marriage. I was drawing close to Francisco Selisse's widow. I knew them both well and after the murder I did what I could to be of service to her. She simply cannot run that large an estate and I fear her slaves have taken advantage of her."

"All of Virginia, no, all of the original thirteen know of that murder. And the killers were never found. Of course, the estate— Old Rawly, is it not?" When Yancy nodded, Milton continued, "Is a large responsibility but I thought it had been well run."

"It had. Francisco brooked no interference nor laziness. He babied his wife, just babied her, so when he was killed, she was helpless except for her lady-in-waiting, a slave called Sheba. It is my thought that this woman truly controls the estate."

Milton's brow wrinkled. "It would not be the first time. People can exert strange power over one another, regardless of station. But did the lady not remarry with somewhat indecent haste?"

Yancy breathed deeply. "To a man almost half her age. Handsome. A carpenter's son. Between Jeffrey Holloway and Sheba I think Mrs. Selisse, I can't call her Holloway, will come to ruin.

The man knows nothing. Perhaps he could build you a cabinet but run a large estate, no. She will be bankrupt in a few years' time, mark my words."

"I do hope not, Mr. Grant, but I fear this may apply to many of us if we can't straighten out the political morass in which we find ourselves."

"Indeed," agreed Yancy, who himself suffered financial reverses, not that he wished anyone to know. "How do you find your beef, Sir? This chicken is excellent."

"Wonderful. Georgina excels at pleasures." Milton allowed himself a double-edged statement.

They finished their meal with pound cake nestled in a little pouf of raspberry sauce for dessert. As Milton took his leave, Yancy wished him success with his land transaction and hoped to see him in the future. As for himself, this storm would delay his meeting with a gentleman, Sam Udall, he hoped would extend him funds against his land holdings. He also hoped he could find a way to discredit Jeffrey Holloway and make Maureen his own.

Not only had the mistress of Big Rawly shocked him by marrying a pretty boy far beneath her station, she had sold her young mare, Serenissima, to Catherine Schuyler. Francisco bred the mare, she was not quite one year of age when sold. He had a good eye, the late Francisco. Yancy had offered Maureen a good sum. He wanted to train and race Serenissima. Instead, the lady sold the horse to Catherine for the unbelievable sum of seven thousand dollars. Seven thousand dollars. Yancy suspected Sheba was behind keeping the mare from him. She, no doubt, received some money, as well. Seven thousand dollars. Did Sheba use Jeffrey as a cat's paw? He knew Jeffrey had called upon Catherine to discuss horses, which sounded Yancy's alarm. Jeffrey Holloway barely knew one end of a horse from another. Jeffrey was not yet married to Maureen. What he knew was that Maureen did not sell him the mare. As for Catherine, he bore her no ill will. She was a consummate horsewoman.

Once in the room, clean, one wooden chair, one high bed, one sturdy desk, a decent woven rug on the floor, he dropped in the chair. The fireplace, though small, kept the room warm enough, a pile of cut logs near it.

The flickering lantern was needed as the sky darkened. More snow as he looked out from the second story down below to the large yard, stables. The weather vane even held inches of snow, frozen.

He would try to secure a loan when all this snow, wind, cold diminished. He had to hang on until springtime, when he knew his horses could win some races. And he had to hang on for his revenge against Jeffrey Holloway.

10

*H*arry stared at the case filled with original jewelry, beaded belts, handmade items, some heirlooms, gorgeous Plains Indian clothing, saddlebags, other treasures. "Liz, where do you find these things, especially the beadwork items? These bracelets and belts are incredible. The colors of the beads seem saturated."

"South Africa and our own west. Each tribe has its own way of doing things. The Crow, the Sioux, the Flatheads, the Crees, the Cherokees. Everyone has their style just as the tribes do in South Africa. Such painstaking, beautiful work."

Harry moved to another glass case, then stopped abruptly. "Where did you get this?"

"You know what it is?"

"I do." Harry pointed to a brass rectangle with a large 9 in the middle and *Garth* in script, ornate, underneath.

"Hootie Henderson brought that in. Actually, he brought a handful. Look." She pulled out a drawer and took out a small leather bag, emptying the passes on top of the counter. "Fabulous, aren't they?" Hootie, an older farmer, had cleaned out his attic in a worker's house once on Cloverfields in its prime.

"Did Hootie say how he came by these slave passes?"

"Found them in the attic wall upstairs. He put up new insulation, found this, found some old accounting books. He figured no one would pay for the accounting books but they might buy these, as they really are pretty and the history means so much."

Harry allowed Liz to pour some of the passes into her cupped hands. "I wonder who wore them or kept them safe in a deep pocket."

"Garth's people. You know, I hate to see things like this stored away at a museum, only brought out for special shows. It is our history. I think more of us should be part of it. We may have different viewpoints but we share it," Liz declared with feeling.

"Even white people? You wouldn't be offended if I wore one?" Harry was fascinated.

"No. I have one." Liz pulled up her necklace with the pass, Number Seven. "Lucky seven." She paused, then continued. "It's history—something we should never forget," she repeated, emphasized. "I know you'd never think of it as mere ornamentation."

"Has anyone bought one?" Harry felt her heart beating faster.

"Last week a well-dressed fellow bought one. He knew what it was."

"And was he African American?"

"As African American as I am. We had a good talk about it all. Obviously well educated, and I got the feeling rich, rich and important."

"Liz, I must call Coop. You read in the paper about the unidentified man found at Sugarday?"

"Yes. Strange, really, that anyone would be out there."

"Liz, do you remember the number you sold your rich customer?"

"Number Five," Liz answered instantly.

Harry pulled out her phone, reached Cooper, and Liz listened, mouth agape.

"I can't believe it."

"I can't either, and it took a minute for it to register. She's coming over . . . well, you heard, to see if you can identify him."

"I don't have to go to the morgue, do I?" Liz looked ashen.

"No. But try to remember everything that you can."

The two sat quietly behind the counter. Within fifteen minutes Cooper sailed through the door, as Liz's shop was in Barracks Road Shopping Center and the detective had been just on the county line.

Cities and counties operate separate governances as well as separate law enforcement agencies. Liz's shop was in the city and therefore under the protection of the Charlottesville police. Cooper, a deputy in the sheriff's department, Albemarle County, had every right to question Liz, as the body was discovered in the county. As it was, the two departments cooperated as opposed to engaging in useless competition. One would be surprised at how much needed to be covered in both jurisdictions, most of it having to do with traffic and domestic violence.

Liz stood up. "Cooper, what can I do?"

Gently, the tall blonde woman put her cellphone on the counter. "Now, Liz, this isn't too bad. Don't worry. He hadn't been dead long. Do you recognize this man?"

Liz gasped. "He's the one who bought the chit, the pass."

"Can you tell me anything? Even the smallest detail may prove useful."

Liz repeated what she had told Harry, who remained quiet.

"Do you remember what he wore?"

"Not that sweatshirt. He was in a good suit, expensive. He wore a gorgeous silk rust-colored tie that was exquisite. I asked him where he bought it and he said Ben Silver in Charleston, South Carolina. He knew which beaded bracelets and belts were from South Africa and which were North American. He also knew, and this surprised me, that the deerskin fringe dress behind me on the wall, dyed quills on the top and the sleeves, as from the last quarter of the nineteenth century. He recognized the design, knew it was Sioux. He pegged the price at $25,000 without asking me. I thought at first he was a collector. He did mention, not to make a point, that he worked in fine art. He was somewhat acquainted with American tribal work but declared he was no expert. He was based in D.C., traveled everywhere, and loved seeing Native art as well as Rubens. Knew the high-class galleries in the west, especially Santa Fe. A nice fellow. I thought, anyway."

"Liz, you've been helpful."

"You don't know who he is? No missing persons or stuff like that coming through the department?"

"No, and given how you described him and his appearance, that is doubly strange." Coop turned off her phone.

"Rich people don't disappear unnoticed," Liz flatly stated.

Cooper said, "Maybe he wasn't rich."

"I can tell," Liz declared. "I need to read a customer the minute they walk through that door."

"Never thought of that," Harry replied. "And you're still friends with me. My purchases are modest."

Liz smiled, a relief from her surprise at having talked with a man subsequently murdered. "Your friendship is priceless."

Harry put her arm around Liz's waist and squeezed. "Coop, what now?"

"Thanks to Liz, I'll call the Ben Silver shop. They may remember him if he visited in person. But if he shopped online, I can track down rust ties."

"Thousands of transactions. Lots of rust ties." Harry sighed. "You'd think someone would know who this man was. Did he say why he was here?"

Liz shook her head. "No. I got the impression he was simply killing time. He did say he had family from here, but they dispersed after 1865. He bought the Number Five and left."

After Cooper left, Harry stayed back for a few minutes. "You okay?"

"I am. I'm a bit shocked that he was or is the victim, but who knows, Harry? We're here one minute and gone the next."

"That's the truth."

"It is highly irregular that a man like that would not be reported missing unless his business was, shall we say, irregular?"

"Like drugs?" Harry replied.

"Yes, but I didn't feel that. I can't say that I have drug radar, but sometimes one does get a feeling. I almost always know if someone is gay. I don't know why. I'm not. I felt he was gay. Subtle. But it wasn't that. I just had the sense that maybe his business wasn't entirely straightforward, I don't know."

"Your husband would be surprised."

Liz laughed. "Oh, I don't know. Andy has gotten used to me being a maverick. Actually, stay here while I call him."

Andy picked up the phone, listened intently to his wife.

"Honey, you like good clothes. Tell me about Ben Silver."

"English goods, Scottish cashmere sweaters, everything is top drawer. Low-key. Quiet money, that sort of thing."

"Your kind of style." She smiled.

"I have a Ben Silver cashmere sweater that is eleven years old and isn't worn thin. Looks great."

"How is it I didn't know you shopped there?"

"Liz, you did. I get the catalogues."

"Oh. I'd better pay more attention to men's catalogues." She thought for a minute. "But I have a husband who can dress himself, unlike so many women."

"And I have a wife who can undress her husband."

"Andy."

He laughed. "See you later, sweetheart."

She clicked off her phone. "That man. Get Fair to go online and see if he likes the merchandise."

"Will."

"Harry, consider it gathering information. If the man spends money you aren't going to wind up in the poorhouse."

All Harry's friends knew money gathered mold in her purse.

Later that night, Harry and Fair sat before his enormous computer screen. Given his profession, he needed it and he spent thousands on that computer. At Ben Silver's website, the goods or furnishings if properly described in nineteenth-century terms, were outstanding, very male, very understated.

Fair lingered over a silk-and-wool jacket with a pale aqua windowpane pattern over the basic color.

"No."

"Honey, I'm not going to buy it, but I like it."

"You can't buy anything unless you try it on. Six-foot-five-inch men can't buy online." She stood her ground.

"You have a point there, but I could go to Charleston. You could go with me. A getaway weekend." He leaned toward her and kissed her cheek. "Romance. Church bells. Palmettos. Great restaurants."

"Yeah, yeah. You just want to go shopping."

"If the victim shopped here he really did have money, taste, and possibly power. Powerful men don't wear flash. Entertainers do, but real power, never. Not in the English-speaking world, and have you ever noticed a powerful man never carries a briefcase?"

This made her think. "You're right."

"To call attention to yourself by dress means you're insecure. A man should be smartly turned out, but not so people gawk. Think Cary Grant."

"Name someone alive."

"The Prince of Wales."

"Can you imagine his budget?" Harry laughed.

"Another one. David Beckham. He's sometimes a little out there, but when it matters, subtle."

"They are all three Englishmen."

"I guess it means we Americans still aren't quite sure of ourselves." He laughed.

"I guess." Harry evidenced no interest in fashion, a quality that drove her girlfriends crazy, and sometimes her husband as well.

"You mentioned that the victim recognized the beadwork in the cases and even knew the tribes who had made the items. He could tell from the work, the patterns."

"Liz said he could."

"A man with aesthetic training."

"Then how does he wind up shot twice in the back on Mary and David Kalergis's farm? It's nuts. Furthermore, I think it upset the beagles."

"If they could talk they might know more than we do. Scent."

"*Right,*" Tucker called up from the floor.

"*I am sick of dogs getting all the credit for their noses. Cats have good noses,*" Pewter fussed.

"In good time, I'm sure the sheriff's department will figure out what the murder is about. Cooper is highly intelligent, you know."

"The strangest thing, Fair. I mean, apart from Liz having done business with the man killed. I had an overpowering urge to buy one of those brass chits. Number Eleven. Overpowering."

He put his arm around her. "Past life?"

11

Mrs. Murphy and Pewter sat in the hayloft, the second-story doors thrown open, always good for hay to be aired. The front of the barn also had such doors. The farm produced outstanding clover and orchard grass hay but Harry twice a year paid good money for pure square alfalfa bales. The hay dealer could back up to either end of the barn, position the ladder with the rollers, and literally roll the bales up. Harry would be in the second story, pick up the bale, place it where she wished. As she had filled up the hayloft two weeks ago in preparation for winter, the aroma added to the pleasing stable smells. Pleasing to the cats, Harry, and horsemen, anyway.

They sat there looking out at the back pastures at the horses as each one that was turned out would make a run, a little buck, and snort.

"Doesn't take much to make them happy," Pewter noted.

"All horses, cattle, and sheep need to do is put their heads down to eat, walk a bit, eat some more. They don't have to catch anything," the tiger cat wisely replied.

"Until there's a drought or a flood." The gray cat watched as Shortro, a young horse, performed a pirouette to the snorting of the others.

"Then we're all in trouble."

Below, the morning frost, light, coated the world in silver. A ground fog lifted from the back meadows while pockets of mist, also silver, began to rise from the crevices and bowls on this east side of the Blue Ridge Mountains.

Tucker trotted out the back of the barn, unaware of the cats above. The corgi, watching the horses, sat down. For some strange reason, many humans don't think animals can appreciate a beautiful day. Tucker, senses superior, could appreciate this perfect fall morning better than the humans. She breathed in the odor of the fall leaves, could smell the bark on the trees, the earth beginning to release the frost. She also knew a small herd of deer had walked behind the barn before daybreak with the pungent, heavy odor of scent mingled in with powder coming up from the fallen leaves. Foxes and deer ate very different food, but foxes, curious and sometimes sociable, might amble along with other species for a time, their sweetish scent trailing the deer scent. Tucker liked foxes, but then they possessed the canine mind. The feline mind was a different matter.

Above her, Pewter pushed out a flake of hay. The rich-smelling hay fell right on target, which made the dog jump sideways.

"Ha." Pewter laughed.

Tucker turned around, looked upward. "Come down here."

"Not a chance," the gray cat fired back.

"A good choice. You're too fat to run fast for long and I'd catch you."

"Dream on, Bubblebutt."

Mrs. Murphy, in no mind to play referee, left the two of them to argue while she walked to Simon, in his possum's nest. Simon, curled asleep, as he was nocturnal, snored a little. He made a lovely nest in a hay bale, which kept him warm in the winter.

Harry's closing up the barn on the very cold nights helped, but the hay proved a good insulator. He stole rags and towels to create a toasty bed. His treasures, neatly organized, filled his nest, a tube of shiny lipstick, half of an old but colorful crop, bright quarters and pennies, pencils, a purple ball cap in good shape which read Brookhill, a rawhide strip, and his biggest prize, a compact of Harry's that he filched when she forgot to close the desk drawer in the tack room. When awake he would open and close it, fascinated by the mirror. If Harry missed it she kept the loss to herself.

One eye opened, then the other. "*I ate so much.*"

"*Simon, you smell like sweet feed.*" Mrs. Murphy inhaled.

"*Half a scoop was spilled in the feed room. Oh, what a treat.*" He grinned, half sat up.

"*You've added some items to your collection.*" She patted the golden-hued lipstick tube, rolling it a little.

"*Fell out of Susan Tucker's car. She parks in the same place. I watched from the hayloft. Sunset. The tube glowed. I snatched it the minute she walked into the house.*" He grinned.

"*Did I tell you she won the club golf championship after being runner-up these last few years? Pewter, Tucker, and I ride in the golf cart sometimes but we weren't allowed on the course during the tournament. I love to ride in the golf cart.*" The cat smiled then changed the subject. "*Why do you have a rawhide strip, well, it's a long one. Harry has plenty.*"

"*She does, but I found this by the creek. Smelled like bird. And it's longer than the strips Harry uses to tie stuff together.*"

Mrs. Murphy leaned down to sniff the strip. "*Nothing left now, just smells like leather.*" She hastened to add, "*A really good smell.*"

"*It's one of the reasons I like being in the barn. I don't know if I could ever build and live in a nest outside. This is heaven.*" He yawned.

Loud voices diverted Mrs. Murphy's attention. Pewter thundered toward her, then turned around, backing down the hayloft ladder a few moments later, more arguing, barking, hissing.

"*I'd better get down there.*"

"*Murphy, they're impossible.*" The possum curled back up.

"What's going on? You two settle down or you're not riding around with me." Harry emerged from a stall, walked up to the battling pets as Mrs. Murphy climbed down the hayloft ladder.

"*She started it!*" Tucker pouted.

"*Bubblebutt, Bubblebutt, Bubblebutt.*" Pewter relished every syllable.

Tucker growled but Harry cut her off. "I'm not taking either one of you and I'm going to The Barracks."

Tucker's ears fell, her mouth dropped, distress registered in her gaze. "*No, no. Take me. I protect you.*"

"*Bubblebutt, Bubblebutt.*" Pewter rubbed against the corgi's chest to add to the dog's torment.

Poor Tucker couldn't even curl her lip.

"Are you going to behave?" Harry pointed a finger at the dog.

"*I'll do anything, anything to go with you.*"

As the dog begged, Pewter, tail vertical, sashayed away from the dog, toward the barn doors. Burlesque music should have accompanied this parade.

Harry turned to watch the cat. "I know you're behind this."

Pewter didn't even turn her head. Kept walking.

"*I hate her. I really hate her.*" Tucker followed Harry into the tack room, where the human wiped her hands, checked the mirror, full-length on the wall, to brush off hay bits and dust.

She walked out of the tack room, closing the door, and the minute she did so, the mice came out from behind the tack trunk.

Mrs. Murphy walked alongside Harry, keeping in step.

"Murphy, you are the only animal with sense."

"*Thank you,*" the lovely, sleek tiger cat replied.

Jumping on the running board, the two cats leapt into the 1978 Ford F-150 when Harry opened the door. She then picked up Tucker, grunted a little at the dog's weight, placed her on the seat. Tucker refused to look at Pewter so, of course, the cat leaned on her.

Slipping her cellphone under the visor, Harry turned the key, and was rewarded with the rumble of a real, old-fashioned V-8.

Gas mileage had improved, all manner of electronic devices festooned vehicles now, trucks boasted luxury interiors, some of them just over the top, but nothing sounded like a true old V-8 and Harry loved that deep purr.

She popped the truck in gear, down the farm road they drove, deer still in the front meadows, lifting their heads, then returned to feeding.

Once on Garth Road, the thin sunlight streaming from the east lighting some trees still in color, Harry turned left to The Barracks stables, passing Ivy Farms on her right. New, huge homes appeared over the last few decades at the edges of what was once all Garth land. And a high-end development, big wide tree-lined lanes; big homes, all colonial; Continental Estates, filled up the back side, out of sight of the stables. Harry continued on the curving road, turned right by the stables and slowly drove to a two-story clapboard house a mile from the stables, due east.

She'd called ahead of time, filled a basket with Pippin apples as she had a few old-fashioned types. She and Fair filled baskets last weekend for their friends, themselves, and always for their horses as well as those of friends. The Pippin apple, harder to grow than the supermarket varieties, was once highly prized in central Virginia, being a favorite of Queen Victoria.

Martha Henderson, hearing her truck, came out the door of the clapboard two-story house built in 1790.

"Just what I wanted. Hootie's been pestering me for apple pie."

"I expect he'll be happy."

"Come on in. Come on, Tucker, Mrs. Murphy, and Pewter. I know you want to ask us about the slave chits."

"How do you know that?" Harry stepped over the swept threshold.

"Because Deputy Cooper called on us yesterday and you can't resist a mystery. There are so many here on this land, all those prisoners-of-war, then Ewing buying up the camp and, well, there's no end to history, is there? It's always around us."

"Sometimes I feel ghosts close to me. Silly, I know."

"Sit down, honey." Martha, in her middle sixties, had always been motherly, even when young. "What can I fetch you?"

"Not a thing."

"*I'll take a treat*," Pewter piped.

Harry ignored her as Martha put out a plate of scones that she'd made that morning. Who could resist?

Then she made a pot of tea, set down fresh butter on a little plate, a few jams, and sat down herself.

"Where's Hootie?"

"Upstairs. He wants to show you the old account books."

Just as she said this, a heavy footfall was heard on the wooden stairway. Carrying large, leather-bound books, Hootie, large himself, came in, placing them on the table. "Good to see you, girl. I don't get to see enough of you."

"Nor I you. Farming, especially during the changing seasons, is no respecter of socializing."

He laughed as Harry spoke. "I couldn't live any other way, could you?"

"No." She reached for a scone while Pewter emitted a piteous meow.

"Poor kitty." Then Martha roared. "Poor starving kitty. Oh, well, even if she's fat she has to eat." Martha, pleasantly plump, rose, opened a cupboard, and retrieved a box of cat treats and one of dog treats. Her pets, outside, hadn't come in but they, too, evidenced too many good meals.

"You won't believe how many of these account books there are. I brought down the earliest ones. Starting in 1786. Goes right up to World War Two." He flipped open Book I, revealing black cursive handwriting, beautiful, and the numbers, too, showed artistic flair.

Harry followed his finger. "Shipped three hundred bushels of apples to Richmond. Fifty cents a bushel. Six wagon wheels over to Maureen Selisse Holloway and one full oaken wagon to Father Donatello." She looked up. "There was an early Catholic church?"

"The Italians. Remember there were Hessians and Italians imprisoned at The Barracks." Hootie was a history buff. "Most stayed behind. They started St. Mary's. Just like the Lutherans started St. Luke's."

"What a find." Harry whistled. "And in such good condition."

"Covered with dust. Martha cleaned them all up." He smiled at his wife.

"These have historical value." Harry touched the page.

"That's why I'm not giving them away. You give them away and they wind up in storage at the university library or a historical group. No. If someone pays for these account books I bet they will actually read them. I called Jerry Showalter," he named a local antique book dealer who traveled the country. "He'll find the right home for them and Martha and I will enjoy a bit of profit. We reinsulated the attic, not cheap, which is how I found all this."

"And the slave chits?" Harry wondered.

He carefully closed the book. "A leather bag of them."

"I don't think this was a slave house." Harry looked around.

"Who knows? The Garths took good care of their people but as the business expanded Catherine added as much as her father once she took over. I expect they had to hire a true bookkeeper and some secretaries. No way one person or even the two sisters could handle all the paperwork." Then he leaned back in his chair. "Imagine how many people you'd need today? I'd reckon that the average American loses four to five days a month on paperwork for the federal, state, and county governments. A hindrance to productivity."

"Hindrance, hell, a nightmare." Harry pressed her lips together.

"I figure all these questionnaires, tax papers, it's all designed to create government employee jobs. Eventually half the population will be government employed. Jobs that don't create profit," Martha, once a schoolteacher, said. "Government can't make money, can't be for profit. I understand that but as more and more people no longer understand the necessity of private profit I think we'll all go down the tube. As so many work for the government or take money from the government, contracts and such, they keep voting themselves more money."

"You all think much more deeply about this than I do. I'd better catch up." Harry smiled.

"Oh, we get riled up. Now, the chits? What are they? What were they doing here? That was the officer's question. She's a nice girl. And not married?" Hootie's eyebrows shot upward.

"Well, you are." Martha poked at him.

"She's dating one of the baseball coaches at UVA. Back to the chits. Any ideas why they were here? Any idea at all?" Harry inquired.

"No. Whoever lived here was good with detail. Maybe that was another detail." Hootie reached for a scone himself.

"Pretty important." Martha knew her history. "You can't have chits out in the open. Were as valuable as money back then. 'Course, after 1865, I reckon they were worthless."

"I never thought of that." Harry finished her delicious scone.

"How very strange that that fellow, the one killed, was wearing Number Five and he'd just bought it. Deputy Cooper talked a long time with us and I don't think we were much help. I have no idea why that fellow was killed or why he was wearing a chit. As I recall the five was quite elegant, just as the Garth name, in script, was elegant."

"I told Fair last night after I'd been to Liz's shop and seen the chits that I had an irresistible urge to buy Number Eleven."

"That's a pretty one, too." Martha smiled. "Think you might? Buy it, I mean?"

"I don't know. I know I don't want our past hidden, or anyone's past, for that matter. We have to acknowledge it regularly. How else can we learn? I remind myself that most people did the best they could with what they had. They weren't thinking about big issues. They were thinking about food, clothing, and shelter. Not much has changed there."

Hootie added, "Deputy Cooper told us Liz was selling the chits for one hundred dollars a pop."

"We sold them to her for fifty apiece after a lot of back and forth." Martha pushed another scone toward Harry, who took it.

"That's retail. Called keystone. You double the price. You figure out rent on a good location store, utilities, advertising, the cost of decorating and display. The retail business is hard. How can someone anticipate what people will want to buy? At least with farming we know everyone's got to eat," Harry opined.

Hootie laughed, a deep, throaty sound. "Got that right."

"Well, let me get back to work. I've thatched the pastures and want to put down fertilizer. I like a light dressing before winter. I think the freezing and thawing helps get the good stuff into the soil," Harry said.

"Does." Hootie agreed, then added, "Glad you came by. If your mother were alive she'd read every one of those account books before I sold them."

"I bet she would." Harry smiled.

Martha, voice soothing, said, "I don't see how the chit or the Number Five can be important. Just a coincidence. Why would anyone kill someone over an old slave pass?"

"I'm sure you're right." Harry rose. "Then again, people do crazy things."

12

A profound silence enveloped Cloverfields when everyone awoke. The sunrise first touched the top of the Blue Ridge Mountains, a thin outline of pink. This widened as the sun rose, pink turning to gold. The mountains themselves, baby blue because of the snow set against a startling blue sky, glowed.

Catherine, wrapped up, as was John, walked toward the stables. Little John remained at home, cared for by his nurse. Both sisters could work as they pleased since nurses took care of the small children. If the children weren't home they were with Ruth, whom they called Auntie Ruth. Rachel loved playing with her two girls. Catherine loved her son, but it was apparent her interest would increase once he could ride, once she could really talk to the boy. John proved a better mother, happily listening to the two-year-old's babble, picking him up, taking him on his chores. Today, the cold won out. No little children, black or white, would be outside, plus the drifts, deep, could easily swallow a small child.

The drifts also could easily swallow Piglet, who prudently padded along the shoveled walkway. Charles waved at his sister-in-law and John, approaching them from his own house, east of theirs.

By the time the three reached the stables, Jeddie, Ralston, and Tulli, all of nine, had broken the ice on the buckets, fed everyone; each young man, and even Tulli, shoveled a path to the paddocks behind the stable in which he was working. Two large stables, aligned on the same axis, housed the prized carriage horses and the blooded horses for riding and racing if Catherine would chose to do that. She hadn't yet made up her mind. The third stable, the oldest of the structures, solid, at a right angle to the other two, was home to the draft horses, playful gentle giants.

The two larger stables each had a small raised roof along the spine of the main roof. This was high enough for an interior walkway. On either side of the raised wooden walkway, rows of windows ran fore to aft. The stables, flooded with light, filled with fresh air when the windows were opened, proved models for other horsemen. Ewing Garth spent a great deal of money on these stables. Catherine convinced her father that light and constantly flowing air, if any breeze was available, made for happy, healthy horses.

Today, no windows were open. The glass was covered with snow, there had to have been at least two and a half feet, but some light filtered through those high roof windows. Given the slipperiness, that snow would not be shoved off the roof. At the base of the roofline, a row of wrought-iron clamshells would catch snow as it melted. This did not ensure that no one would get dumped on if and when the temperature rose, but it wouldn't be as bad as it might without the little wrought-iron impediments.

Every structure at Cloverfields, whether a slave cabin, a stable, the weaving room, the icehouse, the blacksmith's forge, all had been built to stand for generations. All had rain barrels to collect water just as every single structure, even an equipment shed, the carriage house, every single one, boasted glass windows. That cost half a fortune alone. But Ewing reasoned, as a young man and then again with his eldest daughter's prompting, that lots of natural light meant fewer lanterns or candles. Fire was ever a fear everywhere not just at Cloverfields. Once the sun set, people did light lanterns, chandeliers. But by that time, most everyone was home, the stables empty of people.

Catherine, John, and Charles laughed as the draft horses were turned out. The matched pair, Castor and Pollux, charged through the heavy snow, kicking it up, running through the sparkling snow fountains they'd created. The other horses, also being turned out, watched the big boys, deciding it looked like fun. Soon squeals filled the air, the snow muffled their trotting.

"You know, I think snow helps tighten their legs," Catherine mused to her husband, not a horseman, but he could ride.

Jeddie, seeing the three, walked down the newly shoveled path, through the stable, and popped out on the other side to speak to them. Had he tried to reach them by walking off the path to where they stood he'd still be struggling with snow.

"Miss Catherine, Mr. John, Mr. Charles, good morning."

"Jeddie, you must have come out here before sunup?" Catherine smiled at this young man she loved.

"Did."

"How'd you find your way in that darkness? Pitch black as the Devil's eyebrows," Charles wondered.

"Oh, I slept in the tack room. Ralston slept in the driving stables and Tulli started to sleep in the other stable but he got afraid and crawled in with Ralston. We wanted to stay close to the horses because it seemed like the snow would never stop."

Appreciating his dedication and foresight, John put his hand on Jeddie's shoulder. Broad but on a thin, wiry frame, the young man was built for riding. "Jeddie, you think of everything."

"Thank you, Sir."

"Well, let's go tease Tulli." Catherine was already headed to the older stable, where the little fellow could be seen standing at the paddock gate clapping to the horses.

On reaching him, Catherine called out, "I hear you were afraid of ghosts."

"Uh-uh." He shook his head, cap pulled down around his ears.

Ralston joined them from the middle barn.

Charles added, "We heard you slept with Ralston. Didn't want to be in the dark alone."

"Well . . ." Tulli frowned.

"I made him sleep on the floor." Ralston, sixteen, poked Tulli. "And he snores."

"Uh-uh." Tulli's vocabulary was not serving him this morning.

Piglet sat down, observing the boys. He could smell their happiness with one another. The stable team, so young, was a good team.

"I have an idea." Catherine looked from one to the other. "Sweep out the aisles. Should take, oh, fifteen or twenty minutes. Carry some water out to the paddocks. Hang the buckets on the inside of the fence. You won't be able to reach the water troughs. You can't even see them. When you're finished we'll meet you in the kitchen at the big house. You know Bettina will be working her magic."

Tulli beamed, as did Ralston.

Charles piped up. "You tell Jeddie when you're done so he can come, too."

Jeddie was already hauling water buckets to Crown Prince and Reynaldo, an unpleasant job, as some of the water sloshed out.

Hand pumps, inside the barns and outside, could usually be coaxed to bring up water. When the ground froze hard, the inside pumps served everyone.

Pulling her shawl tighter around her shoulders, Catherine looked toward the mountains, a clear sky, the mountains bathed in light. Gorgeous but really cold.

"Let me check the sleigh. Make sure the runners are waxed and the tack clean." Charles headed toward the large carriage house.

"Why? We aren't going anywhere," John wondered.

"We don't think we're going anywhere, but you never know." Charles smiled, his teeth still good, not stained.

"True." John thought for a moment. "I don't think anyone is going anywhere until much of this melts. I bet the James is frozen. Nothing is moving."

"Probably." Charles watched as Catherine headed toward the cabin rows.

She turned, calling back, "I'm going down to the weaving lodge. Won't be long. Will one or both of you go tell Bettina, the boys plus ourselves will be in the kitchen? And I'm hungry." She grinned.

John smiled and waved and she hurried down the long, wide row between the cabins, smoke curling out of chimneys. Each cabin now had a stone or brick chimney, an advancement for safety. In the old days, chimneys in inexpensive dwellings and workshops often were made from charred logs. Usually it worked. When it didn't, everything burned to a crisp. Ewing, over time, made certain every single structure at Cloverfields had a safe chimney as well as the glass windows, no oilskins or heavy hides. He had no motto, but if he did it would be "Do it right the first time."

High fur boots kept Catherine's feet warm, but the air chilled her cheeks. As she hurried down the row, tears formed in her eyes. Most of the front porches had not been shoveled out. One or two had, including Father Gabe's, the healer. A thoughtful, quiet man, if anyone needed him the way would be cleared.

Each cabin rested on a quarter to a half acre, the back being a large garden. People sat on their front stoops in warm weather, called out to one another, or gathered at Bettina's stoop to sing. Winter drove everyone inward, reinforcing family ties or tensions, depending.

The last cabin, the large lodge, on the right sat a quarter mile from the first cabin, for the double row was long. The lodge had more distance from the living cabins. It faced the woods, which slanted a bit until finally dropping precipitously to the hard running creek below. Rock outcroppings attended this creek, a narrow footpath leading in both directions. Rarely used, when it was, it allowed slaves to visit one another at the plantations along the creek. Summers, long twilights propelled people to sociability, but most especially a young man courting a young lady. Sometimes if this resulted in marriage the couple might live together. If not, then the partners traveled on off days determined to see each other. Ovid wrote, *"Amora vincit ominia."* Love conquers all, and it did.

Catherine was not thinking of love, but warmth. The hearth in the weaving lodge, big enough to stand in, threw off wondrous heat. Smoke spiraled straight upward from the large chimney. Bumbee was working. Bumbee didn't think of what she did as work. She loved it, creating designs, using colors in novel ways, experimenting with wools and fabrics. The woman possessed an artistic gift.

Catherine threw open the door, too cold to knock. As she did, Mignon, shocked, stood up, overturning her stool.

Bumbee, startled, looked up from her loom. "Miss Catherine,

Mignon was stirring up some warm milk. Would you like some or might you use some in coffee? We've made strong coffee." Bumbee chattered as though this was the most natural thing in the world.

"I . . . I'd love some coffee." Catherine sat on the curved maple chair that Bumbee's husband, ever in disgrace, had made for her.

Mignon softly asked, "Milk or coffee with milk, Miss Catherine?"

"Coffee with milk, thank you."

Once the coffee was delivered, Catherine held the cup in her hands, then began this discussion sideways. "Bumbee, I am freezing. I need a heavier shawl. Actually, I need to wear two shawls. This one and a heavy one overtop."

"It's going to be a long winter." Bumbee pulled the shuttle down, the rhythm of her weaving consoling.

Glancing around, Catherine's eye fell on a rich green wool in one of the squares holding materials. "What about that color?"

"Mmm, too thin. You need a heavier wool like the navy. Feel it."

Catherine rose, put the coffee cup on a table made out of the same maplewood as the chair. Reaching the fabric, she felt it between her thumb and forefinger. "See what you mean." Then she touched the wool in the next square, a deep maroon. "That would look wonderful on Rachel."

"Everything looks wonderful on you and your sister." Bumbee smiled as Catherine sat down again.

"Mignon."

"Yes, Miss Catherine."

"Does Mrs. Selisse, I mean Holloway, know you are here? After all, you may have been trapped by the storm."

"No, Ma'am, she doesn't, but she and Sheba want to get their hands on your wool." Mignon stopped stirring, moved the pot away from the fire by lifting it off the wrought-iron rod, hanging it on another inside but at the edge of the huge fireplace.

"May I ask what you are doing here?"

Bumbee kept pulling down the shuttle, lifting it back up, humming to herself.

Mignon's voice was clear. "I ran away."

"Dear God," Catherine whispered.

Bumbee spoke up. "She fell through the door the first day of the big storm. She hadn't planned to come here but found the path from the creek up here, which is good or she would have froze to death."

"Yes." Catherine's mind raced.

"I won't bring harm to you. I promise I will be out of here once I can move through the snow."

"Mignon, that's a hopeful thought. If the authorities should visit here before that, we better come up with a good story, and I can't think of one." Catherine drank some coffee.

"I'm sorry, Miss Catherine. I never meant to bring danger. I was exhausted, my feet throbbed, they were so painful, so I followed the path upward. I didn't know where I was. When I saw the lodge, I did."

"Done is done." Catherine sighed.

Maureen Selisse's brutality, known throughout the county, infuriated people, but no one could do anything about it. As for Sheba, there were those who would happily kill her if they thought they could get away with it.

Catherine and Bumbee knew they had to protect Mignon until she could move. The fewer people that knew, the better, but any slave that would report a runaway would eventually be killed by others. Silence. Ever and always: silence.

"Miss Catherine, she can hide here. For now." Bumbee stopped weaving.

Catherine nodded. "Let me talk to Bettina."

None of them could have known or dreamed that Mignon's fate would haunt the twenty-first century.

13

October 26, 2016 Wednesday

*H*arry stopped for a moment, rake in hand, at the base of the large marble statue, the grave marker for Francisco Selisse, murdered on September 11, 1784. Well-carved marble, tremendously expensive even in the eighteenth century, the Avenging Angel, flaming sword in hand, guarded the East of Eden. Francisco's death was never avenged. Life went on as it always does.

A big pile of leaves giving off the distinct sneezy odor of fallen leaves awaited transfer to the canvas laid on the ground.

Harry leaned against the base of the huge statue, then straightened herself. "Susan."

"What?" her best friend, also raking, replied.

"Come here a minute."

Susan dutifully put down her rake, her pile quite large, joining Harry at the base of the impressive statue.

Putting her finger on the base, the slender Harry asked, "Do you know what these little scratched squares mean? I kind of remember them from the few times we played in the graveyard, but mostly we avoided this nasty angel."

"He's frightening even now." Susan smiled, then studied the scratched squares. "I have no idea. Seven of them, some look more recent than others. Not like our time, but you know."

"It's an old family graveyard. Someone must know or have known." Harry changed the subject. "Your grandmother looks well."

Penny Holloway lost her husband, in his nineties, on August 15, 2016. A few years younger than her husband, a former Virginia governor, a dynamic man, a World War Two hero, she missed him terribly. However, Penny was not a woman to dwell on sorrows, much as she felt them. She continued her work for nonprofits, attended to her gardening and her two daughters, one being Susan's mother. Her "girls" were in their early sixties. Time moves along at blinding speed, except when you are waiting for a check.

"She does. Thanks again for helping me plant those spring bulbs. She loves to see them pop up. Well, she loves fall, too." Susan returned to her leaves, raking them onto her canvas.

Mrs. Murphy, Pewter, and Tucker, intending to be of assistance, followed them to the graveyard when they began working. All three fell asleep under a towering oak easily three centuries old. Little moats of dust spiraled into the air as they breathed out.

A half hour later, Harry and Susan finished up. The leaves now added to the big mulch pile that Sam Holloway, Susan's deceased grandfather, had built for his wife. It was a long rectangle dug into the earth, three sides held firm by stakes and wooden boards. Each spring, Sam would back the wagon to the edge, then shovel the "cooked" mulch onto it, spreading the mulch on his adored wife's gardens.

As they walked away from the mulch pile, the wind picked up, a twenty-mile-an-hour gust, subsiding to a steady thirteen-mile-an-hour wind.

"Boy, we got that job done in the nick of time." Harry pulled her baseball cap lower on her head lest the wind carry it off. "My weather app didn't say anything about a stiff wind."

"Just comes up. You can't really predict the weather by the mountains, maybe big storms but not the little things like this. The other day driving back from Harris Teeter," she named a high-end supermarket, "a wind devil shot right across the intersection to Crozet. Wind devil? It really was a tiny tornado."

"Susan, a tornado has to be one of the scariest things on earth. Just the noise alone, and I read somewhere that the average mouth of the funnel is about one hundred fifty yards, but some monsters are much bigger than that."

"Look at Pewter. My God, she looks like a beached whale." Susan laughed.

Harry, observing her cat under the oak, laughed, too. "Let's go say goodbye to your grandmother and I'll pick up these three amigos when we leave."

"You pick up Pewter. I'm not strong enough." Susan laughed again.

Trotting to the back door of Big Rawly, Susan crossed through the spacious enclosed porch. Her grandmother and mother busied themselves in the kitchen, easily visible from the closed-in porch.

Opening the door to the main house, Susan called out, "We're done."

Penny, drying her hands on a dish towel, beamed. "Thank you. Step inside. I've got brownies for you and Harry. If you don't want to eat them now, don't fret. I put them in containers."

"Thanks." Susan loved brownies.

Harry, on her heels, also thanked Mrs. Holloway, then asked, "Mrs. Holloway, have you ever noticed the tiny squares scratched into the base of Francisco Selisse's big tombstone?"

Millicent Grimstead, Susan's mother, replied, "Actually, I know what they mean."

"You do?" Her mother was surprised.

"Mother, do you remember Cash Green, older than dirt, when I was little?"

"Cash Green." Penny's face broke into a big smile. "That man could talk a tin ear on you. What a good soul he was. He used to tell Sam and me he was born in 1872 right here on Big Rawly and he never left. Lord, that was back in the midforties just after the war. Sam said as long as he could remember, Cash was here."

"He knew about the squares?" Harry asked.

"He did. He said little squares on the tomb of someone hated called down a curse. Little crosses on the tomb of someone loved called down blessings. He used to add that this came from remembered spirits from Africa. He'd lean toward me and whisper, 'It's the old power of my people.' What stories he could tell!" Millicent grinned and wished she'd had the wit to write them all down, but she had been only a child then.

No one mentioned that Big Rawly had witnessed its share of hard luck over the many decades.

Millicent picked up the conversation after that brief pause. "I bet Cash told the same stories to Father when he was little. Mother, did you ever hear the one about buried treasure?"

"No, I missed that one." She folded the blue-striped hand towel. "I seem to have missed a lot."

"According to Cash, and this was relayed with long pauses, drama." Millicent grinned. "There is buried treasure on Big Rawly. Jewelry and cash. There's buried treasure at St. Luke's and at Ebenezer Baptist Church. Tons of treasure. That's all he ever said."

"I expect every old estate in Virginia has its buried-treasure story." Susan took the containers. "Wouldn't it be wonderful if they were all true and people found them?"

"Sure, then there could be lawsuits about who does the treasure really belong to and why." Harry shrugged.

"No. If you own property, you own its history as well," Penny firmly stated. "So if you girls find the jewelry, it's mine. I could use a new pair of earrings."

Laughing, the two friends left to pick up the three animals, still sound asleep.

Harry placed her hand on Susan's forearm. "Wait. Let's get in the car and start the motor. That will get them moving."

Turning toward the front of the house, they slipped into Susan's Audi A7, cut on the motor. Tucker lifted her head, blinked, then ran like the Devil for the station wagon.

"Wait. Wait for me!"

Mrs. Murphy, hearing her friend, quickly followed suit.

Pewter opened one eye. Then two popped open. *"Don't you dare leave without me! I'll get even!"*

As the large gray cat hurried toward the car, her belly flab swung from side to side, which made the humans laugh. Mrs. Murphy and Tucker shot into the car when Harry got out to open the back door.

"Hurry, Pewts," Mrs. Murphy encouraged.

Pewter reached the opened door. *"If you left me, you'd fall apart. Humans can't think for themselves. You need me."*

Susan, hand on the shifter knob, remarked, "She's saying a mouthful."

"Better we don't know what she's saying." Harry got back in, closing the door. "I doubt it's praise. Hey, before you drop me back home, let's go down to Barracks Road."

"I am not taking you to Keller and George." Susan named a high-end jewelry store. "You've mooned over that pearl necklace for years. You are never going to buy it. It costs thousands and thousands of dollars. And we all know how tight you are." She paused. "But it really is beautiful, and given that it's Mikimoto, every time they sell the one you want they order a new one."

Exhaling loudly, Harry confessed, "It's so beautiful. But no, I want to go to Liz Potter's."

"Don't you dare get involved in a murder case. That's another thing you can't resist." Susan had been at the beagling plus she knew about the brass chit since it was reported in the paper.

"I am not getting involved."

"*Liar, liar, your pants are on fire,*" Pewter helpfully called out from the back.

The parking lot, enormous, made it easy to find a spot, except for Christmastime. The two walked to Liz Potter's attractive store, inviting display window, near Barnes & Noble, which always enjoyed a lot of foot traffic.

When they pushed the door open, Liz looked up. "How are you two?"

Susan offered, "Good. We just cleaned up the family graveyard at Big Rawly."

"Your ancestors thank you." Liz came out from behind the counter to give each woman a hug. "I've been in contact with the Wildlife Center of Virginia. Got more brochures and stuff for our next meeting. You know the real problem is the state's restriction on veterinary treatment of wildlife. Oh, and MaryJo wants to finally report on her research about contraband animals."

"We know about the vet issues," the two said in tandem.

"That has *got* to be changed. We can help so many more animals and relieve suffering. It's just bloody stupid." Liz grimaced. "Besides, why shouldn't a young veterinarian like Jessica Ligon be able to branch out?"

She was referring to the Virginia state regulations that prohibited a veterinarian from treating injured wildlife. If one finds a harmed raccoon, say, it was necessary to drive all the way to a veterinarian certified to treat same. By the time you drive the fifty miles or whatever it is, the poor animal has died in pain more often than not.

"This is an issue that will take people in every county leaning on their delegates." Harry knew the drill. "We've got to educate the public, then mobilize them. Usually an elected official is smart enough to know what side his bread is buttered on. And, of course, there are always those jerks who try to make a splash by arguing against anything no matter what it is. Has it ever occurred to anyone that democracy is an expensive, inconclusive system that just drags out suffering on every level?"

"Harry." Liz's bejeweled hand flew to her breast. "I've never heard you speak like that."

"Oh, Liz, I didn't mean to upset you. Sometimes our foolishness, the corruption, just gets to me," Harry said quietly.

"Who was it that said democracy is a terrible system but better than anything else?" Susan wondered.

"Good thought." Liz walked behind the counter. "Anything tempting?"

"Everything." Susan admired a gorgeous beaded bracelet from South Africa.

"I want to buy Number Eleven." Harry pulled her checkbook from her rear jeans pocket.

Rarely using credit cards, Harry paid by cash or check. She figured given how often credit card information was stolen, and the time it took to rectify matters, it was best not to use them except in those cases where it is much easier, like buying an airline ticket.

Susan, now herself surprised at her best friend, asked, "And what are you going to do with Number Eleven?"

The bag of chits, on the counter now, had the contents emptied out as Liz sifted through the beautifully engraved pieces with the Garth name for Number Eleven.

Susan quickly added for Liz's comfort, "I'm not trying to kill a sale, but we all know Harry probably has tucked away the first dollar she ever earned."

Liz laughed. "Harry, you're no doubt smarter than the rest of us, but I operate on the principle that you can't take it with you."

"Hear. Hear," Susan chimed in.

"Ah." Liz held up Number Eleven.

Susan examined it closely. "The script is gorgeous." Then she checked out many of the other brass rectangles. "They're really lovely, and when you think that they conferred temporary freedom of movement, I wonder about the important errands a slave must have carried out to be given one of these. Delivering goods, news, reporting emergencies, reaching people who needed things."

Harry held Number Eleven in her palm, turned it over. "Looks like a little mark." She flipped over other chits, also marked. "Hmm, maybe the engraver was testing his tools before actually engraving *Garth* and the number."

The door opened.

"Ladies," Panto Noyes greeted them. "Susan, I just came from a meeting with your husband about the old schoolhouses. He's behind us and I've contacted all the tribes, recognized and not, to write their state legislators."

"Great," Susan exclaimed. "You have more contacts than anyone."

"Helps that I've been dancing in powwows since I was a kid. I do know everybody."

"Big plus for a lawyer, too." Liz smiled. "What can I do for you?"

"As always, I came in to admire that Sioux deerskin. The red-and-white quills, the design, well, it inspires me."

"Me, too," Liz agreed.

"And I came in to see if you would donate an item to our tribal fund-raiser. It's for scholarships." He saw the chits but didn't comment.

"Of course."

"The best year we ever had for the fund-raiser was 2007. Fifty-two thousand dollars." He beamed. "Then came the crash. We were lucky to clear ten thousand, but bless MaryJo. She invests for the tribe, nonprofit, and she does a hell of a job. Before she came on board I did the investments. No one else would do it. But she's a star."

"She must read tea leaves," Harry joked.

He smiled. "I wonder about that myself, but, you know, some people just have a knack."

"Like Warren Buffett." Liz nodded.

"That's the top of the top. But around here think of guys like Mark Catron, Derwood Chase. There's a small club of shrewd investors."

"Men?" Harry lifted her eyebrows.

"Mostly. Marge Connolly, although she retired. No, there are women," Panto quickly replied. "And younger women are moving into finance."

Harry paid for Number Eleven, chatted a bit more, and the two returned to the station wagon where three crabby animals awaited, the windows cracked for the cool, fresh air.

"You should have taken us," Pewter complained.

None of the three thought about the wisdom of running about a busy parking lot.

"Home," Harry cheerily said to the three in the back.

"Tuna better be there," Pewter grumbled.

"*Steak.*" Mrs. Murphy felt like red meat.

Tucker, uninterested in the food discussion, leapt into the front seat by scrambling over the divider between the two front seats.

"Tucker. You're bigger than you look." Harry grasped her small sun-yellow shopping bag from Liz, the interior tissue an azure blue.

"Now that it's the two of us, why did you buy Number Eleven?" Susan inquired.

"I don't know. It's . . . it's almost a compulsion. I'm putting it on a gold box chain I have and will wear it under my sweaters and shirts. I don't know why and I paid one hundred dollars, so you know it's a compulsion."

Someone else shared that compulsion, more or less. They sat in the parking lot, computer at hand in their lap in the dead of night and disabled Liz Potter's shop alarm system. Whoever it was went in, took all the beaded bracelets, short jackets with beaded shoulder stripes, as well as the $25,000 western Sioux dress, and other things.

14

Sitting side by side in front of Cynthia Cooper's desk computer, Sheriff Rick Shaw and his deputy stared intently at the screen.

He breathed out his nostrils. "It's a match."

Also exhaling, Cooper nodded. "Is."

"Go back to the building," he told her.

Within seconds a pale beige brownstone with dark green shutters appeared on the screen. Next to the lighter green wooden door, a handsome brass plaque appeared. *Pierre Rice Inc.* was engraved in lovely script with flourishes. Underneath the name, also in script, was *Private Investigator*, and underneath that, also beautifully done in old script, was the number 5.

"That number again." Rick pushed his chair closer to the screen.

The county had upgraded all their computers, hardware, everything electronic. The image on the large screen was crystal clear, not a hint of fuzziness.

"Well, it is the house number on a very expensive Georgetown Street in D.C.," Cooper reminded the sheriff.

"I know," he grumbled. "Still, he wore the chit around his neck. Number Five."

"Well, Boss, maybe he liked that he found a slave chit with his street address."

"Maybe, Coop, but how did he find Liz and her store? And why? According to Liz, she put pictures of the brass rectangles on the store website a month ago. Says the website is invaluable to her business."

Fingering the keyboard, she quietly replied, "I don't know, but it probably isn't insignificant. What I want to find out is how much money he made. He owned that house. A brownstone in Georgetown is hideously expensive."

"Anything in Washington is hideously expensive." Rick snorted.

"That's my point. He probably had contracts for government work or corporate investigations. As he was not employed by the government he could use methods frowned upon by Congress, the judiciary, et cetera."

"You forgot executive."

She smiled. "No, I didn't. The executive branch will break or bend the laws first."

He laughed. "Amazing what you learn as time goes by, isn't it? But whatever he was working on, it frightened someone else. No files, no computer, no cellphone. No records found anywhere. And the FBI went through his place with a fine-tooth comb. Nothing there. Did Pierre destroy records or did someone get there before the FBI? Whatever Pierre Rice was investigating, someone or some agency had something to fear if the FBI was there."

"The lack of any records is unnerving. Our running down this crime might put us in the political crosshairs." She paused. "And I don't give a damn."

"Coop, the government can ruin any of us in a heartbeat. Can and would."

A long silence followed this. "I hate to think of my country as that criminal and corrupt."

"Some individuals and some agencies are. But I still believe there are honest public servants and I especially want to believe that many of them are in law enforcement."

Without replying, she, again, scrolled through pictures of the interior of Number Five.

"Just in case we missed anything."

Rick, nose nearly on the screen, sat back when she handed him his glasses, which he snatched from her hand. "All right."

"I didn't say anything. Everyone needs glasses as they get older, right?"

He ignored the statement. The elegant living room, walls a pale peach, furniture very Sister Parrish, which is to say traditional, opulent but subtle, filled the screen. A large painting hung over the Sheraton sofa. Cooper zoomed in.

"Jesus Christ," Rick blurted out. "That's a Frederic Church. My God, Coop, if that's original—and it looks like it is—it's worth millions." He stopped a moment, caught his breath. "Have Darrel track the provenance. If Sotheby's doesn't have it, Christie's will," he said, citing the two top-of-the-line auction houses in the country.

Darrel, a young officer, proved a whizz at finding anything via computer. He could also fix just about anything.

Cooper blinked. Occasionally she would traipse with the girls to the fabulous Virginia Museum of Fine Arts, but mostly she was ignorant of the field. "Millions?"

Nodding, Rick added, "And he had to know what he was doing. I think this is what's called the Hudson River School of painting, but don't hold me to it. At any rate, Church, immensely talented, painted the mountains, the rivers, he struck out on a new path when others still imitated Europe or painted wealthy Wall Street bankers, senators, and society ladies. He was a true original."

"The painting is beautiful and it looks like the Hudson River." Cooper enlarged it.

"Is. Pierre Rice clearly had taste, money, and some form of art training or passion."

They then looked at other artwork, all of it American from the eighteenth century up to the twenty-first. Many of the hangings on the wall were pencil sketches for paintings. Pierre Rice started small, not quite so expensive. When he made money he began to spend very big.

After going from room to room, Cooper returned to the front of the brownstone. "Boss, we caught a break that his maid came in, found the place immaculate but no Mr. Rice, no computer, no file cabinets, and no car. We're lucky she called the police. They looked for unclaimed victims, missing persons and the like. Our photo of Mr. Rice, not horrific but certainly sad, proved the key. The maid knew him when the officer showed her the photo. My next question, where's the car?"

He grunted. "It's bound to show up somewhere." He glanced at a list. "You track down other private investigators in D.C. Find out who knew him. If they did, did they like him, and did they know what projects he investigated or people he investigated?"

"Right. He has a sister in Richmond."

"The Richmond police will need to inform her about her brother. Has to be done in person. Then we'll call on her. We're lucky there is a next of kin close by. I hate to push people after they've heard painful news but the sooner a witness or family member talks to us, the better off we are. Time blurs memories."

Cooper glanced at the address. "She's not poor, either. I think she's an important person in the arts. I know I've heard that name. On Monument Avenue near the Virginia Museum of Fine Arts. Finding out about the Rices is going to be very interesting."

"A wealthy man is shot twice in the back and left on Sugarday estate. He's wearing a hoodie and jeans. The Number Five slave chit is hanging around his neck on a chain. The Kalergis's heard no shots, no sign of any disturbance. And this is what bothers me, no tire tracks. Either he was chased and dropped nearby, then carried to Sugarday or killed farther away, brought to the estate, then carried into the copse. It's hard work to do that, hard work and unusual. The ground, dry as a bone, had no tracks. Why not shoot him and leave him in his car?"

Cooper rattled off the details on the missing vehicle, which Rick knew by now. "A black 2014 Tahoe four-by-four. Nice car. Terrible on gas, but it will go through anything. Also, a Tahoe would not elicit suspicion or interest. If he drove a BMW SUV or a Porsche he would stand out. So apart from his wealth and good taste, we know he was smart about blending in."

Rick slapped his thighs, stood up. "Let's get cracking. And let's hope this doesn't leak into the media."

"They'll broadcast that we've ID'ed the body."

He moaned a bit. "Which means your neighbor will be hot on the trail. Do what you can to keep Harry out of it."

"Yes, Sir."

He stopped at the door and smiled. "Sometimes I think finding the killer or killers is easier than keeping Harry Haristeen out of the picture. She has more curiosity than her cats."

"They're more sensible," Cooper replied.

They both laughed as Rick left her office.

15

*S*weat trickled down Charles's brow. As St. Luke's continued to raise money for a proper church, the congregants worshipped in a sturdy, large log cabin, a potbellied stove smack in the middle of the center aisle so as to distribute heat as evenly as possible. Except it wasn't possible, and Charles and Rachel's pew stood too near the stove. Those in the back of the cabin shivered.

The pastor had given a rousing sermon on the need for unity, for all Christians to work together. The men especially knew this was about the failing Articles of Confederation, which prompted one argument after another.

The women, while not uninterested, had no vote in the matter. Given their husbands' businesses, they certainly heard about the failures.

The choir sang a last hymn, the congregants filed out as the lovely song ended. The cabin had a large vestibule, a necessity given all the pews in the worship space.

Charles, raised Church of England, and his wife, Rachel, raised an Episcopalian which was, more or less, an American version of the Church of England, wound up at this Lutheran church thanks to Charles's commission to design it. The more the young couple learned about Martin Luther, about the tenets of this faith, the more they were attracted to it, until both joined St. Luke's as communicants.

Crowding into the vestibule, everyone spoke of their trials during the everlasting storm.

Karl Ix, who had been a Hessian prisoner-of-war with Charles and now lived and worked at Cloverfields, enthusiastically spoke with a group of other Hessian former prisoners. These men escaped, but the colonials, as they were then called, rarely hunted them down. Manpower was scarce during the Revolution, and if a farmer found a strapping fellow he didn't inquire too closely about his broad German accent. The same was true of the Italians, and once the war ended, they, too, remained to form St. Mary's Catholic Church. Virginia benefitted from these Europeans who grasped freedom when they could. Given that many were highly skilled, they found ready employment when times were good. They also learned to work side by side with slaves who excelled at a trade. It made for an interesting combination.

"We have got to petition the state to build roads, good roads." Karl clapped his hand on Gunther Swartzman's back.

"Ya. Ya, but where's the money?" Gunther agreed totally with Karl.

"That's the problem. We have engineers, we have men who want to work but all we hear from our delegates is how poor we are. Is New York this poor or Pennsylvania with rich Philadelphia?"

"Ah, Philadelphia." Charles smiled. "They managed to make money while occupied and make money after the British withdrew. We'd better pay attention to those Quakers."

The others laughed, but most Quakers did succeed at any form of business. The Quakers in Virginia, not as numerous as those in

Pennsylvania, suffered during the war since they did not believe in war or violence. They persevered and slowly were making their way back into society.

"If a man fails at business and is a Quaker, do they not reject him?" Michael Taylor, looking a bit too thin, asked.

"They do. They do. Perhaps that's what spurs a man to succeed against all odds." Gunther smiled as Big Billy Bosum joined them.

Nearing thirty, the tall fellow had served in the American Navy but was sent to a French ship as an exchange sailor, a kind of noncommissioned officer liaison. He learned a great deal, as did the Frenchman, on the U.S. ships. As the ships were built in different state ports those states petitioned the new government for some repayment, some help to bolster faltering state budgets. No monies were forthcoming and states fought one another in the national legislature. The congressmen barely worked with one another, each state trying to get what it could for itself alone. Things were going from bad to worse.

Charles filled him in. "We were talking about building roads."

"Roads. Ships!" Billy raised his voice. "Every year the firepower increases, the accuracy increases. The French are building more ships. The English intend to encircle the globe. We do nothing. We have nothing!"

This provoked a full discussion concerning the lack of central leadership. Each state could commission an Army and a Navy, but not the national Congress, which was, however, the only body that could declare war.

As the men deliberated this mess, the women spoke of Maureen Selisse's continuing problems with her people, as they referred to the slaves.

"Well, I heard another woman ran off. Sheba caught her stealing pearls," Jutta Rogan declared. "Not that I believe it."

"How can you?" Billy's wife, Lillian, replied. "First of all, no woman over there at Big Rawly would be stupid enough to steal anything."

The others nodded.

Rachel innocently asked, "Who was it that ran off?"

"Mignon," Jutta answered. "The little woman, tiny like a house wren, youngish, I'd say. Certainly younger than Maureen, who wants us all to believe she's still twenty-eight."

The others laughed.

"Maybe a woman is only as old as the man she marries." Rebecca Smythers unwound her scarf for the small stove made the vestibule comfortable unlike the big potbellied stove inside.

The room, filled with cherrywood's sweet burning odor, proved more pleasant than the big interior room. Chairs lined the walls and many took advantage of them, the elderly women being seated first.

"He is a handsome young man," Jutta wistfully remarked.

Gunther Swartzman's wife smiled, looking at Rachel. "What is it you horsemen say? Your sister says it, pretty . . ." She paused.

Rachel filled in the expression. "Pretty is as pretty does."

As the ladies enjoyed one another's company, Catherine, John, and Ewing Garth were engaged in similar discussions at the small clapboard Episcopal church east of Ivy Creek, on the high hill that looked down on the creek.

As it had taken this long for the rutted roads to be somewhat passable, business proved a lively discussion just as it was at St. Luke's. The ladies did not refer to a missing slave from Big Rawly, as all were too excited that Elizabeth Hart had become engaged to Roger Davis, a young man on the way up politically. Everyone declared it a brilliant match.

As the churches throughout Albemarle County were filled with people glad to get out finally, Mignon slipped away from Cloverfields.

Bumbee, Bettina, Ruth, Grace, Liddy, and the other women provided her with layers of clothing, plus a sturdy pair of shoes, as hers had been ruined in the blizzard. Bettina wrapped biscuits and cold ham in a dish towel along with a small cup so the runaway could drink water. Father Gabe gave her a good knife.

They watched her as she made her way down the steep wooded path to the creek.

"I hope she makes it to Richmond. There's enough people there that she can disappear. Maybe she can get on a boat bound for Philadelphia," Bumbee murmured.

"No point heading north. They'll be looking for that. Charleston, that would be good, or Savannah. Work at a shop down by the ships," Bettina wisely said.

"That's a long way," Father Gabe quietly replied.

"I wish I could have given her a chit," Serena, who also helped make extra food, said.

Bettina quickly replied, "And if she's caught, we would all be in trouble. Mr. Garth would be questioned. We would be questioned and the constable, in particular, would blame us. Serena, think."

"Yes, Bettina."

The powerful cook softened for a moment. "Chile, much as we want to help someone, we have to stick together first. Always think of Cloverfields."

"I pray she makes it. I fear she won't," Ruth whispered.

"And if she doesn't?" Serena's eyebrows raised.

"You know as well as I do. She will be returned to Maureen and she will be dead within a year. An accident, of course." Bumbee's voice was sharp. "I pray that someday, some way, I will be able to kill Sheba and Maureen for what they did to Ailee." Her bosom heaved. "I pray for vengeance."

"Ah, Bumbee, vengeance is mine, saith the Lord." Father Gabe touched her arm.

"The Lord is mighty slow," Bumbee grumbled.

16

Marvella Rice Lawson, informed of her brother's murder Friday by the Richmond chief of police, sat on her divan, hands folded. The fact that the chief of police personally delivered the news bore testimony to how important the Lawsons were. Marvella's husband, Tinsdale, was partner in one of the most powerful law firms in the Mid-Atlantic. The Lawsons entertained on a lavish scale and were entertained in turn by Virginia's governor, her two senators, the mayor of Richmond, and other people of note.

Rick sat across from the elegant woman, late fifties, as did Cooper, notebook in hand.

"Thank you for seeing us, Mrs. Lawson," Rick opened.

"Of course. Anything I can do to assist in finding my brother's murderer, I want to do it." She spoke with the precision of a well-educated woman who moves in the highest circles.

"Did he ever discuss his business with you?" Rick asked.

"Sometimes after a job had ended, but usually, no. He would tease me and say what I didn't know wouldn't hurt me. Now I think perhaps he wasn't teasing." She leaned back slightly as her maid entered with a tray of tea and shortbread cookies. As Rick and Cooper were on duty, they couldn't drink liquor, but tea sounded good on a cold Halloween day.

"Did he ever seem fearful to you?"

"Pierre?" Her eyebrows raised. "Fearful, no. Foolhardy, well, yes."

"In what way?" Rick pressed.

"He knew how to spend money." She inhaled. "In his defense, he bought beautiful things and the paintings have accrued in value. We often argued about art, especially art." The salmon cashmere sweater she wore offset her skin tone, as did her lipstick. Elegant enameled Tiffany barrel earrings, royal blue, added to her subdued glamour.

"Any special reason?" Rick paused. "We have seen the interior of his Georgetown house, and yes, there is impressive art on the walls. The department up there, D.C., videoed a walking tour of his home for us."

She smiled. "He had an eye. Not something you expect to find in a private investigator. I was the art history major. He majored in business. We were both at Howard. I wanted to go to William and Mary, but Daddy said, 'Why deal with white people? Put all your energy into your studies. Howard.' And Daddy was right for the time Pierre and I were at university. I digress. I'm not quite myself. I loved my brother very much and I can't understand—" She stopped before the tears came.

Rick said, "I'm sorry to bother you, but we don't want to waste a minute. The more we find out, the closer we may come to apprehending whoever did this. Is it possible someone was furious over a painting? The artwork in his apartment is astonishing."

She smiled a bit. "Millions. He built such an impressive collection and he started small. Do I think someone killed him over a

Thomas Hart Benton? No. You can see by what art interests me that we differed somewhat. Hence the not really arguments but lively discussions."

"He must have met many rich people," Rick simply stated.

"Pierre could get along with most anyone. Even as a child. He was two years older, he had an entertaining way of observing events and people. As for his art collection, we took classes together. He had an interest but declared that men don't go into art history. Hence the business major."

"How did he wind up as a private investigator?"

She laughed. "He liked business, he liked politics, and in his senior year he worked on a local campaign. That's when he discovered that politicians and businessmen are two hands washing each other. The corruption intrigued him, especially how congressmen and businessmen were not above blackmailing one another, not that the word would be used. A private investigator always had business. Given Pierre's discretion, he was a natural, and, well, he was smart. He originally found a job at Minton Agency in Washington, where he learned his trade, and oddly enough, he loved it."

"When was the last time you talked to your brother?"

"Last weekend. He came down for a gathering of old classmates at Quirk Hotel. He also wanted to see the artwork displayed there."

"Do you remember the friends?" Rick inquired.

"I thought you might ask that. I wrote down the names and his relation to each one, not just those at the gathering but in his circle generally. I marked with a star those that are closer to Tinsdale and myself, but Pierre did know everyone."

"Did he have a girlfriend? Or an ex-girlfriend? Someone who might be angry at him."

Marvella paused for a long time, then looked into Rick's eyes.

"My brother was a homosexual. It is—or was, anyway—more difficult for a black man to be gay than a white man. Pierre, when young, engaged in furtive affairs. We would talk. My biggest regret for my brother is that he never found a partner or thought that he could. When I would bring it up, citing that times have changed, he'd say, 'Marvella, no one wants a fifty-eight-year-old man.' As far as I know, he never spoke of this in his work or his social life. And I hasten to add, Pierre did not indulge in rough trade. He didn't have a hidden sex life or a bar kind of life. I guess you would say he had evolved to the point where he lived in a closet with an open door, but unfortunately he lived there alone."

Cooper lifted her eyes from her reporter's notebook to gaze on a beautiful Parisian street scene, a young woman fashionably dressed in baby blue, stepping into a carriage, the hackney horse as elegant as the woman. Her left ankle is clearly visible covered by a sheer white stocking. Risqué for the time.

Marvella noticed. "Jean Béraud. When I first started collecting you could purchase his work for a song. All people wanted were the Impressionists, Picasso, paintings like that. Béraud was a sly social commentator and the draftsmanship is secure, the paintings themselves lovely. I snapped up as many as I could, all the while Pierre kept telling me, 'Focus on Americana.'" Tears suddenly spilled down her cheeks. "How I will miss him. I don't think it's hit me yet."

"Mrs. Lawson, you've been generous with your time." Rick rose, reaching inside his front uniform pocket, retrieving a card. "If you think of anything, no matter how trivial you believe it is, call me or call my deputy."

Cooper also gave Mrs. Lawson her card.

"Two lists." Marvella handed him neatly handwritten lists on expensive paper. "These are his dearest friends, and then others in his acquaintance that I can think of farther down. And this one is, to the best of my memory, when and where he acquired each of his paintings and the pencil sketches. Those sketches brought him into contact with so many people. When he was ready to buy oils, he had made many friends." She took a long breath.

Cooper walked closer to the Jean Béraud. "You almost feel as though you're in the painting. That it will come to life."

"Yes, you do."

Now at the front door, the maid, standing in as a butler, opened the door. She was watchful of Marvella suffering from this shocking loss.

Rick did not step through it but turned. "Mrs. Lawson, have you any idea why this might have happened?"

"In a sense, I do. Pierre was handsomely paid by his clients. Whatever this is about, there is a great deal of money at stake and possibly reputation. My brother was a careful man. Someone killed him before a public investigation could come to light."

17

"*D*ammit to hell!" Ewing Garth slammed down a letter he'd been reading.

Weymouth, Roger's son, jumped.

Roger, hearing his master's voice raised in anger, hurried down the hall, looked at his handsome son, eighteen, a contemporary of Jeddie Rice, standing behind Ewing. Weymouth raised his eyebrows and shrugged. He'd brought Ewing a huge pile of mail fifteen minutes ago after paying Jarvis Hoffman, who had dropped it off now that the travel proved a bit easier.

Ewing's mail bills alone totaled more than a thousand dollars per year. One paid the postage when a letter arrived and the postal service, disorganized and miserable, left no one happy. Given that Ewing's business interests spanned the thirteen original colonies, England, and France, the mail, critical, infuriated him as well as everyone else.

England and Europe enjoyed royal post, announced with a hunting horn when the mail arrived. The United States, lacking royal authority or any central authority, tried to anoint a postmaster general, but the chore of setting up and maintaining a national service without good roads, without enough money, proved overwhelming. Ewing paid for each letter sent to him. He need not pay when he sent out mail, but what he did do was become terse in his communications. Anyone receiving a letter from Cloverfields knew it would not be expensive and eagerly accepted it.

"Master?" Roger quietly said.

Ewing looked up from the offending document. "Roger." Exasperation filled his voice. "Do you know where Catherine is?"

A voice called from the hall at the back of the house. "Father, what's wrong? Bettina and I can hear you all the way to the kitchen."

Taking a deep breath as he listened for her footfall, Ewing waved away both Roger and Weymouth.

Weymouth, who shaved Ewing daily, noticed a small spot he'd missed at the older man's jawline. He hoped his father didn't notice or he'd hear about it.

Catherine swept into the well-proportioned office, a fire crackling in the fireplace keeping the room warm on a cold January day, too cold, really.

He smacked the letter on his desk. "Connecticut has raised its tariff on tobacco. Our agent up there has written to inform me that this will decrease our profit by two percent."

"Father, it's a long time before we cure tobacco and send it to Connecticut. By that time perhaps they will repeal the tariff."

He settled in his seat a bit. "Never. Once an agency raises a tax they never reduce it. This is designed to weaken Virginia. They have always been jealous of us. Is it my fault their soil is poor? Well," he thought for a moment, "most of it."

"You were wise, Father, to sell early at a fixed price so they know your prices won't jump. You won't lose business, you'll lose a bit of profit. Actually, I'm surprised they aren't charging more. Connecticut is still moaning about its war debt."

Ewing waved his left hand, a large signet ring on his third finger. "One hundred fourteen million dollars. The total for all thirteen states. I know the debt amount but I am weary of Connecticut citing the sum as though this is all their own problem." He inhaled deeply. "Actually, my dear, I don't know how any state can recover from this. We don't recover by trying to slap extra taxes on out-of-state goods. It's madness."

Catherine pulled up a light wooden chair with back slats to sit next to her father. He handed her the Connecticut letter.

Reading it, she shook her head. "You're right but you usually are. The only thing I can see that will help each state climb out of this terrible hole is increased trade with England and France or any European nation. We aren't going to clear this hurdle by stealing from one another."

How like her mother she was, Ewing thought to himself. Clear, a good head for business, and logical. Catherine was not given to excessive emotion.

"Add to this, now the states are printing too much money just as the Continental Congress did. Worthless paper. Worthless." His voice fell.

"Perhaps someone could use the old bills for wallpaper." She laughed.

That made him smile. "You'll enjoy this." He handed her North Carolina currency. "They have a printer at last. No more North Carolina script. However, what is a North Carolina dollar worth compared to a Virginia dollar or a Connecticut dollar, since that state seems determined to get all our money?"

"Father, do you fear the war was for nothing?"

He sat bolt upright. "No, I do not. We had to get rid of the king. But this, this is chaos. You know, dear, this is one of the few times

I would like to talk to Francisco Selisse." He mentioned the wealthy, disliked, late Francisco. A man accused of sharp business practices.

"I can't say that I share your feeling." Catherine had hated him.

"He came from the Caribbean, he understood their banking procedures, was familiar with her ports, both free and encumbered. I tell you there is no such thing as a poor Caribbean banker." He smiled slightly. "Helps that they do business with pirates. I think, my dear, the solution to this crisis must come from someone who has prospered in business elsewhere. As it now stands, I don't know if I would trust any plan arriving from the resident of another state. I think each man will favor his own home, so to speak."

"Possibly." She rose to throw another log on the fire.

"Roger or Weymouth can do that. No need for you to trouble yourself."

"I wanted to stand up." She picked up another log, a light one, examining it. "Sleeping bugs. I can't throw them in the fire. I'll tuck them lower on the pile here."

"My dear." He smiled. "I'm not sure the bugs will thank you. Sooner or later they'll be in the fire."

"I'll watch that log. I want to see them when they awaken."

"April," he simply stated.

"John hears from men with whom he served. He mentioned last night that Light Horse Harry Lee is speculating on hundreds, maybe thousands of acres of land. Everyone is giving him credit. They're running over themselves to give him money."

"A man can be a great general but a poor businessman. Now is not the time to buy land." Ewing picked up the North Carolina ten-dollar bill. "I don't know what it is time to do."

"Our holdings are secure."

"Yes, but holdings are not gold or silver. One must make money, must create profit." He threw up his hands. "I apologize. Some days are darker than others. Before I forget, when Jarvis Hoffman brought the mail he told me that another of Maureen Selisse's slaves had run away."

Catherine sat down. "I would not be surprised if one day she wakes up and there is not a soul at Big Rawly other than her new husband and Sheba."

Ewing laughed out loud. "Quite so. But this time it was a woman who Sheba says was stealing jewelry. Jarvis says the report is she was stealing enough to buy her way to Vermont, where she would be free."

"That makes a good story, but Vermont is a long, long way off."

"And cold."

"That, too."

"They never did find the two slaves who were accused of killing Francisco," Ewing said. "They simply disappeared. Unusual."

"Yes, it is, but the world is full of mysteries. Did Louis the Fourteenth have a twin? People love to imagine things." She picked up more papers from her father's desk, reaching across him. "Did Jarvis give the slave's name?"

"Mignon. I don't recall her, do you?"

"Bitty woman."

He shook his head as he couldn't picture her. "I do recall Ailee, the beautiful woman who fled, the one accused of helping to kill Francisco. I often wonder why more women, regardless of station, don't kill men who abuse them. I'd kill."

"Father, women are taught to endure." She let out a peal of silvery laughter. "After all, Mother endured you."

"My angel. There were times when I tried her patience."

Catherine gently touched her father's hand. "Now that I am

married and a mother, I have ample occasion to think of what you and Mother endured from Rachel and me. And I confess there are days when I look at John and I could just throttle him."

"Marriage forces one, if one truly loves his or her mate, to try and see the world through another's eyes. I learned more from your mother than from any other person in my life, including my own parents. Perhaps if we can remember those lessons we can, the states, I mean, find a way through this morass. I hope so." Then he handed her the ten-dollar bill. "For your wallpaper."

18

November 1, 2016 Tuesday

"Every time I came into the shop I was mesmerized by the color, the shape. Fabulous. To think it's stolen."

Mrs. Murphy, Pewter, and Tee Tucker sat on a bench against the wall while Harry listened to MaryJo.

"It was extraordinary," Liz quietly replied, wondering if MaryJo would be nosy, ask insurance questions.

Liz changed the subject. "MaryJo, given your investment business, with the market all over the map, I don't know how you have the time to do all the research for our wildlife group. You've done so much just on the Chesapeake Bay alone."

Nodding, the soft light in the store enhancing her youthful look, MaryJo drummed her fingers on the counter. "Well, the biggest problem is the death of bald eagles. Yes, it is better than it once was, especially during the Reagan years. All that pesticide being used by farmers along the bay, along the James River, well, all the pastures and croplands by our rivers because that is the best soil. Anyway, furidan, now illegal, isn't used anymore. The problem is, it can be stored, just not used. So we must remain vigilant."

"Didn't Virginia use stuff like that in our schools?" Harry inquired.

MaryJo, happy to be the repository for facts, quickly replied, "Schools and public buildings used chlordane. You needed a license to buy the stuff but not a license to use it, and it does kill germs. So janitors, who couldn't read the labels, used chlordane in our schools. The stuff seeped through walls. Kids suffered from chronic ear and sinus infections."

"And this stuff kills wildlife?" Liz's eyebrows lifted upward.

"If it gets into the soil, but nothing is as bad as derivatives of nerve gas, which so much of the old stuff was. Makes a box turtle's head swell. If humans are exposed, it throws off judgment, makes some people appear drunk. And even though we now have safeguards thanks to Governor Baliles when he was in office, there is a ton of stuff out there, stored."

"Well, MaryJo, that is not comforting." Harry smiled slightly.

"Can't the State Pharmacy Board do anything?"

"First, they have to find it. Second, they must find who is using this awful stuff." MaryJo's voice grew louder.

"Better living through chemistry," Liz sarcastically added. "People worry about oxycodone, heroin, it seems to me we are awash in rivers of bad stuff."

"Well." MaryJo drew herself up to her full height, about five-eight. "That's why, Liz, you don't want anything in this shop that could be mistaken for contraband or part of an animal killed, whenever, by something like furidan."

"MaryJo." Liz swept her arm toward the items in the case. "Why would anyone even think that? I'm a lot more concerned about whoever disarmed my security system and made off with the most expensive things. How they disarmed the security, bizarre."

MaryJo paused dramatically. "Bizarre?"

"Is bizarre," Liz corrected her. "So bizarre, so clean and neat, that I wonder how long before he comes back or some other electronic wizard, to disarm my security system and clean out the cash register before I take the cash to the bank. I take my proceeds to the bank every day now but it's time consuming." She slapped her hand on the counter. "I don't want to live like this."

"Smart. Who can sit around in a shop all day?" Tucker observed.

"Depends on what's in it," Pewter remarked. *"What about PetSmart? Or another pet store full of treats and toys. Not so bad."*

"Still, you're inside." The dog was ready to go home and chase some squirrels.

"Panto is happy to help you if you need him to give you a figure for insurance, value, rarity," MaryJo offered, forgetting Liz's husband owned an insurance agency. "He knows so much. He travels all over the country for meetings, powwows. As he himself is Native, people trust him."

"You've gone out west with him?" Liz asked.

"Bruce and I traveled with him last year to Arizona. We met with southwestern tribes. We did go off eventually by ourselves to see the Grand Canyon. Spectacular," MaryJo enthused. "The Apaches are spectacular, too. They know and transmit their traditions."

"Are you thinking about closing the shop?" Harry registered Liz's frustration.

"I am. It will make Andy happy. He complains he never sees me. I always thought I'd like retail and I do. Trying to figure out what people will buy, staying just ahead of the curve. It's a challenge," Liz honestly told her. "I need to think about all this a bit more, more calmly. I don't know why that robbery shocked me so much but it did. And I think what really got to me was what was taken. And what wasn't. There's something about it that makes me wonder. The Sioux dress, the beadwork bracelets, short deerskin shirts, museum quality. You see stuff like that at the powwows, the dancers. Everything modern was untouched. The chits stolen . . . I had them next to the bracelets. I expect the thieves will toss them, as they aren't that valuable compared to the other stuff." She inhaled. "And Christmas shopping is starting. I'd like to clean out my merchandise. Oh, I should shut up, I'm dispirited."

"Liz, that makes perfect sense." Harry consoled her. "Maybe you should bring Sugar to work with you. She's big, if anyone has a funny idea, I think Sugar will dissuade them."

Sugar was Liz's majestic German shepherd.

"That's why I have always left her at home. I didn't want her to frighten anyone. People are afraid of shepherds and Dobermans."

MaryJo stepped in. "Harry is right. Bring Sugar."

"Well—"

"Liz, until you know what you're going to do, make it easy on yourself," MaryJo advised.

"*I can smell old feathers,*" Tucker idly mentioned.

"*On the stolen deerskin, shoulders.*" Mrs. Murphy, half asleep, woke up, as she noticed anything connected to birds.

MaryJo and Harry left together, the three animals on leashes with Harry. As the day proved cool, she wasn't worried about the hot asphalt of the parking lot, so she brought them along. Finally, it was feeling a bit like fall.

"You know, contraband animal parts or animals themselves are a business of billions of dollars. People will kill for money, animals, even other people," MaryJo forcefully said.

"I don't think it has anything to do with Liz. She would never willingly support anything like that." Harry stuck up for Liz, whom she much liked.

"No, I didn't mean to imply that. I just wanted her to be aware of how people think today. Maybe whoever took the old dress felt it belonged back with the tribe that created it. When you think of some of the clothing created between 1870 and 1900 you realize how well made it is, how unique. Those jackets, tight, made out of skins with the fur left on, extraordinary. I can picture a brave wearing one."

Harry smiled. "Me, too. Fur is warmer than cloth or the so-called new fabrics. Fur is perfect. Why do animals grow it and we don't? You know, I can't bring myself to wear a man-made fabric knowing it's made from an old soda bottle."

MaryJo responded, "That stuff always rustles." She then added, "Still better than killing and skinning animals."

"I read somewhere that chow chow owners save the fur they comb out of those thick coats, wash it, card it, and spin it into sweaters," Harry said.

"*Pewter, you've got enough fur for a sweater.*" Tucker's tongue hung out a little bit.

"*Very funny. People don't save cat fur.*" She reached Harry's Volvo, stood on her hind legs to paw the door with her front legs, claws un-leashed.

"*Because you lick it off, then throw up hairballs.*" The dog let Harry pick her up when she opened the door.

Pewter shot in behind the corgi to attack her.

Screams followed as Mrs. Murphy crawled into the front seat to avoid them. More screams, bits of fur floating through the air.

"Harry, that really is a dangerous cat," MaryJo said.

"She's my guard cat." Harry laughed.

19

January 31, 1786 Tuesday

*B*eing tiny allowed Mignon to hide, squeezing herself behind barrels and hay bales in barns. She followed deer trails when she could, fearing exposure on roads. She knew if she boarded a boat anywhere, that would be it. A description of her was posted in stores in Virginia emphasizing that she was tiny, early thirties, upturned nose, attractive, skilled as a cook's assistant.

The cold nights, especially cruel, tested her. She'd curl up inside a shed, a barn, anything to escape the wind, but the cold seeped through cracks. Sometimes she'd find an old unused horse blanket in a barn. She'd tell herself to awaken at dawn and she would, and move on.

She'd hitched a ride with a free black man who told her to wrap a bandana around a hat he had, tie it under her chin. She posed as his wife, finally making it into Richmond. She wanted to get out of Virginia, but she needed money for that. That man took her home to his wife, who allowed her to wash up. Mignon gratefully took an old skirt and a sweater from the wife. They suggested she see if she could find work at Georgina's.

They didn't mention that Georgina's was a house of ill repute with a tavern of excellent food serving as a cover, but everyone knew. Mignon figured it out quickly enough when she was interviewed. Georgina, a white lady of some girth, needed help, and anyone who could cook was welcome. The lady, perhaps forties, did not inquire about Mignon's background.

The reward for a runaway slave would be a pittance against one Saturday's profits, and part of those profits included seeing that men had good food and good drink. Georgina prided herself on running an elegant establishment, which she did. If she had seen a sheet advertising a runaway slave, Georgina paid no attention. There were too many of them anyway.

Mignon kept to her duties, not showing her face in the main parlor.

Georgina's girls were white and colored, as she called them. However these women came to her, the madam kept to herself. All were young, beautiful, eager for profits.

The head cook, Eudes, a free black, bossed Mignon around, but once he determined she knew what she was doing—which only took one night—he shut up and they worked side by side.

Tuesdays were slow but a steady trickle of well-dressed men did arrive, sitting in the parlor, talking to the girls. The parlor, with English furniture, allowed the men to watch the ladies as they offered them wine or stronger spirits.

Georgina bustled back in the kitchen. "Mr. Billiart would like mulled wine. He said he took a chill walking here."

"He's rich enough to have a carriage," Eudes grumbled.

"Indeed he is, Eudes. And half of Richmond would know exactly where he is. Most especially his wife. This is her sewing circle night." Georgina turned on her heel to leave, calling over her shoulder, "Not too much spice. He likes his mulled wine mild."

"I know what he likes." Eudes turned to Mignon. "You haven't worked here Friday and Saturday nights, but most of Richmond's finest are here. And they're all in church on Sundays with their wives."

Mignon said nothing.

Abby, young, gorgeous, sailed in, picked up a tray, placing it in front of Eudes, who put an entire decanter of mulled wine on it along with some crystal glasses.

Winking at Mignon, Abby bragged, "Gonna make me seventy dollars tonight. Seventy dollars."

Mignon whispered to Eudes as the beauty left the room, "Can she make that much?"

"Can. Some of the girls have specialties and make more. Deborah specializes in teasing, driving them wild. She brags she can make two hundred a night on the weekends." He looked Mignon up and down, figuring she knew little of the trade. "If there's a position a fellow prefers, some like special clothes, the smart girl figures out how to give it to him. This way she gets a tip and Boss doesn't interfere. Georgina knows how to keep everyone happy. For the most part." He laughed at her. "Country girl?"

"Yes, Sir."

Shrewd, Eudes, voice low, said, "You're safe in the kitchen. And if the constables come around, we can hide you."

Her eyes wide, she nodded.

"Honeychild, you're not the first runaway to wind up at Georgina's."

She bent her head low, for she wouldn't admit to being a runaway. She did say, "It's good work."

"'Tis. Some of those girls out front, they decided why give it to the master for free? This way they can make money. They find their way here, Georgina changes their looks a little. Gives them etiquette lessons. No one's the wiser. Can you read?"

"No, Sir."

He flipped a steak into chicken grease. "Reading is power."

"Yes, Sir. I don't know as I'm smart enough to read."

He laughed a genuine laugh. "Girl, you look at those dumb clabberfaces in the front room. If they can learn to read and write, anyone can."

With that he grabbed a bag of clabber off the shelf, sprinkling a little into the grease to thicken it. "I'll help you."

She smiled a little. "Yes, Sir."

"You can call me Eudes."

"Yes, Sir." Then she laughed at herself and he laughed, too.

20

*T*he fieldstone living quarters, built at the same time as St. Luke's, were set on an east-west axis to catch the beautiful sunsets. Sun set earlier now as the winter solstice loomed ahead. Over the decades the well-proportioned structure first had lanterns and candles, then gas lighting, then electrical lighting. A coal furnace gave way to oil which just last year was supplanted by a brand-new heat pump costing $7,200 with installation. The water bubbled up from a deep well, good underground mountain runoff water.

Inside the fireplaces, chimneys cleaned each year, augmented the modern heat. As power often failed, the fireplaces proved essential. Maybe the house temperature hovered in the midfifties on those powerless days, but at least the pipes didn't freeze. By the fireplace it would be warm.

The floors, old random-width heart pine, glowed with the centuries of use. The walls, repainted regularly, kept to the original colors, pale yellow, pale mint, pale blue. Anyone from the later eighteenth century would have called upon the pastor and felt right at home with the exception of electrical lighting, harsh to an eighteenth-century eye, and the soft purring of air from the vents. But the home was as it had always been. The attached stable became a garage, a toolshed was hidden behind the house, and a well-stocked woodshed attached to the kitchen side door by a covered walkway. Granted, one had to carry in all the cured wood, but it remained dry thanks to the sturdy shed with one old light fixture overhead.

Elocution, Lucy Fur, and Cazenovia commanded the pillows on the bed on the second story, facing east to wake up with sunrise. Facing east afforded a bit more warmth, as the winds usually socked the house from the northwest. Also facing east meant one need not overlook the graveyard, tranquil though it was, on the western side of the property. The graveyard sat below the two descending gorgeous church quads, the one surrounded by the arcades of the church. The huge, lower-level one was set off with a low stone wall, as was the graveyard. A hand-forged iron gate rested in the center of the graveyard wall, which stood at two and a half feet. Inside, various stones stood, some dating from the founding year of the church, 1781. The large log cabin built then had provided protection from the elements. The old cabin had been broken up in 1810 to make way for landscaping, Capability Brown's ideas being all the rage. The few parishioners who died during that time rested in a tiny enclosure closer to the stone church itself, having been enlarged twice during construction, again on the west side. The later graveyard, established when the church and house were finished in 1786–87, bore testimony to the excellence of design and execution. All had stood the test of time. Over the years tombstones began to appear, as well as a few statues. Then, too, small square, low stones nestled by large tombstones. Usually a date and a faded name had been carved on the tiny stones that covered deceased infants and young children. No man or woman could ever assume that all their children would survive to adulthood. Fevers, whooping cough, sometimes measles, accidents carried off the young.

The cats complained as Reverend Herb slid under the comforter, the one blanket, and the sheet. He plumped up two pillows behind him, which didn't disturb the cats, but they complained nonetheless.

A fire threw off dancing light. One lamp on a nightstand provided reading light. Wearing an old T-shirt, long sleeves, Herb opened Elizabeth Longford's Vol. I on the life of Wellington. He'd read both volumes years ago but wanted to refresh his memory. He liked Mrs. Longford's work and he loved the Iron Duke.

A light wind slightly rattled the windows on the west side of the house. The wind brushed the east side of the house. The denuded tree branches swayed a bit. A perfect night for reading oneself to sleep, Herb thought.

"*He always reads about war stuff,*" Cazenovia remarked. "*He could read us 'Puss and Boots.'*"

"*He was a soldier before becoming a minister.*" Elocution wrapped her tail over her nose.

"*You'd think if a person went to war, they wouldn't want to be reminded of it,*" Lucy Fur suggested.

"*True, but this is about old war, not Poppy's war, which I guess is turning into an old war,*" the calico, Cazenovia, said.

The Reverend Jones's war was Vietnam, where as a young captain he learned he had the gift of leadership. He determined if he survived the war, he would study at the seminary and hope to lead men and women to God.

The cats thought all this fine but knew that the human version of the Almighty was usually represented as a man with a long beard. Naturally, the Almighty was a splendid cat but the humans would never get that, so the cats worshipped their way and left their beloved Reverend to his way.

Sharp ears, the cats heard a truck motor up by the church, which was just about one hundred yards away by the paved roadside. Five minutes passed and they heard something out in the graveyard. Reverend Jones's human ears couldn't hear it.

Elocution, nosy, hopped off the bed, hurried to the west bedroom, hopped onto the window ledge. *"Hey, come see."*

The other two shot off the bed to join Elocution. The night dark didn't stop them from clearly observing a figure, couldn't see his or her face, pushing over two tombstones. He knelt down, peered at the earth under the headstones with a flashlight, then turned it off and left.

"Could you see his face?" Cazenovia asked.

"No, but whoever it was didn't move like an old person. No hitch in his giddy-up." Lucy Fur watched a regular walk.

"Should we rouse Poppy?" Elocution asked.

"No. It's dark, he's in his nightshirt. Whatever it is it will keep until morning," the calico prudently advised.

Not only did it keep until morning, it kept until the early afternoon. Instead of walking to his office Thursday morning, he elected to drive, kitties in the backseat. Once in his office, he worked at his desk.

Harry came at one o'clock, said hello, then climbed upstairs. She opened the window to check and see if she could fix the flashing from inside, hanging out the window. Realizing it was, in fact, precarious, she knew she would need to hire a workman to do the job outside on a ladder. Herb wouldn't have it any other way.

As she closed the window, she stood for a moment and looked down over the grounds and noticed two tombstones knocked over.

Back down the stairs, she stuck her head in the pastor's office. "Reverend, two tombstones are down in the graveyard. I'm going to have a look."

"What?" He glanced up from his papers.

"Don't worry about it. I'll check." She left and all the cats followed her, for she'd brought Mrs. Murphy and Pewter. Tucker, the lone dog, also stayed at Harry's heels.

The graceful, simple markers, four feet high, in the old section of the graveyard, lay flat down.

The animals inspected the damage.

"Whoever did it had to push hard." Mrs. Murphy noticed the dug-in heel prints in front of the tombstones.

Harry knelt down. The slightly larger stone belonged to Michael Taylor, born February 2, 1729, died October 15, 1786. The second tombstone belonged to his wife, Margaret Taylor, born June 11, 1740, died October 15, 1786.

"Hmm." Harry figured there would be records somewhere in St. Luke's, but when a husband and wife died on the same day or close together in time often it was illness or accident. The same with children.

Then she bent down closer to the earth and noticed marks like someone had plunged a blade into the soft earth. The earth underneath each marker had this feature.

Standing up, hands on hips, she thought for a moment, then bent down, trying to lift up a tombstone. As it was very heavy, she couldn't do it.

"Dammit," she swore.

Tucker sniffed the earth. *"Old."*

"Of course, it's old," Pewter sassed.

"Old bones," the dog continued.

"How can it be old bones?" Mrs. Murphy wondered. *"People were buried in caskets, pine boxes at the least."*

"*Being an undertaker was a good business,*" Lucy Fur said. "*Still is.*"

"*No. There are old, old bones down there. Maybe three feet from the ground surface. I'm a dog, remember.*" Tucker held her ground.

"*Well, who cares? Dead is dead.*" Pewter lifted her nose.

Harry, already walking toward the church, hands in pockets, wanted to know about Michael and Margaret Taylor.

Once inside, she trotted back to Herb's office. He looked up and from her expression knew something held her attention.

"Do you have the records of everyone in the graveyard? I mean, easily accessible."

"Yes. Remember we put all that on a computer disc four years ago. That was a job. The original docs are in the safe downstairs and temperature controlled, I might add." He smiled, pleased that the congregation had been so supportive, interested even in that project.

"Would you pull up Michael and Margaret Taylor. Died, both of them, October 15, 1786."

"Give me a minute." He tapped onto his keyboard.

"*Where are the crunchies?*" Pewter asked. "*There are always crunchies in this room.*"

"*Where they always are. On the counter by the sink.*" Elocution no sooner said that than Pewter was on her way.

"*Fatty,*" Lucy Fur whispered and the others giggled.

"Michael and Margaret Taylor. Married twenty-eight years in Christian harmony. Both taken by the wasting disease on the same day. October 15, 1786."

"Usually that means tuberculosis, doesn't it?" Harry inquired.

He glanced back at the large screen. "Did. Actually, many of the causes of death were very accurate. They knew heart attacks and strokes. They may have used different language, but it's clear. Tumors were mentioned and, of course, the sweating sickness. Malaria. Those were almost always summer deaths, and fortunately not many of them. St. Luke's kept very good birth and death records. The interesting thing about malaria is if we have some facts about someone's life, we often know they had been to the Caribbean or down to our Low Country. And, as you know, some people can live years with malaria. Now, might I ask why you wanted to know about the Taylors?"

"Their tombstones are knocked over. Pushed."

"Why didn't you say that in the first place?" He stood up to leave the room.

Harry, all the animals save Pewter, face in bowl, followed him.

Once at the graveyard, Harry pointed down to the dirt. "Can you see those straight marks, like knife plunges?"

"Yes." He knelt down. "I think I can push these up with the front-end loader."

"Don't. You might chip the tombstone. I'll call Fair. He's so strong. If Fair and Ned come on over, they can right these in no time."

"You're right. I didn't think about chipping anything."

Hours later, Fair and Ned righted the tombstones. Harry had returned to the church to watch and Herb also watched. The two men, Fair at six-five, Ned at six feet, put the stones exactly in place, but Harry first pointed out the odd marks.

Fair, job finished, said, "There, the Taylors can rest in peace. They weren't disturbed."

No, but someone else was.

21

"We'd dance all night." Dr. Beverly Ely smiled. "I knew Pierre would be in my life the first time I danced with him, which was at a Save the Bay fund-raiser in, I think, 1994. I was turning thirty, finished my residency, felt I could finally make some real decisions about life. Pierre was maybe thirty-six. Handsome. So smooth and handsome. I said that, didn't I?"

Cooper sat across from the attractive cardiologist, her trusty notebook in hand. Both she and Rick worked their way through the people list that Pierre's sister, Marvella, had written out for them. Sometimes they questioned a friend or business associate together. Other times, like today, Cooper worked alone.

Dr. Ely, at fifty-two, remained slim, attractive, well spoken. She had a practice with four other physicians associated with Martha Jefferson Hospital, which had become gargantuan. Needless to say, Dr. Ely made a very good living, close to a half million annually.

"Did he ever talk about his work?"

Dr. Ely removed a pencil lodged behind her right ear, rolled it between her hands. "In his way. He never spoke of a case while he was in the middle of it and he once told me this was for my own protection. Most all of his work involved corruption, whether it be political misdoings or financial or both. He warned me that some people would kill. Once a case was resolved he might mention it, but not in detail."

"When was the last time you saw him?"

"The day before he was killed. He was here in town, in Charlottesville, and we met for lunch at the Keswick Club, where I'm a member. Golf." She smiled. "I'm not really the country club or private membership type, but I am crazy about the new Pete Dye golf course." She paused. "Had Pierre wanted to be a member, I think he could have. I mean the old days of refusing African Americans are gone, at least with the Keswick Club. No one looked twice at a white woman with a black man. Times have changed, thank God."

Cooper smiled. "For some of us, Dr. Ely. For those who are poor, uneducated, struggling, not so much, and of course, I see too much of it."

Putting the yellow pencil on the side table next to her chair, Dr. Ely nodded slightly. "Yes. Yes, and thank you for reminding me. My work is, well, as you see—" She indicated her office, expensively decorated. "And my colleagues are all well educated, as was Pierre."

"I was stunned at his art collection. Actually, our sheriff, Rick Shaw, knew how valuable it was. He told me. I'm culturally limited."

"Perhaps your interest rests elsewhere. Yes, Pierre's collection is stunning and so is his sister's, which is radically different. Marvella cowed me when we first met back in the nineties but over the years I've learned her reserve is just that. She's really a warm person and she loved Pierre."

"Did you know that Pierre was gay?"

A silence followed this, then Dr. Ely quietly answered, "Yes. It was one of the things that brought us together." She paused. "This may sound strange to you, Deputy, but his homosexuality and my own allowed us to love each other without unrealistic expectation. I don't hide my orientation, but I don't lead with it. Yes, things are better, but I am fifty-two years old, a physician, and when I started out, being truthful would have severely impacted my career. So the two of us would go to events where a date was expected and Pierre would laugh. He could be sly. He'd say, 'What would be worse?' indicating the people in the room all dressed to the nines for the fund-raiser. 'Would it be worse that they know we're gay or are they choking on the fact that a white woman, a good-looking white woman,' he was always charming that way, 'is dancing in the arms of a black man?'" She threw up her right hand. "Then I'd laugh, but, Deputy, not to harp on this, there are still elements right here in Charlottesville where the racism is gilded, not exactly hidden, just gilded, and as for being anti-gay, that's more ignored than explored, if you know what I mean."

"Actually, Dr. Ely, I don't. I do recognize the racism and I hear, from time to time, a smartass comment about faggots from another cop. Not a lot, but enough, and it's always from a male. I ignore it. I'm not going to report it. Putting someone on the hot seat, by my observation, deepens the prejudice."

"Would Sheriff Shaw do anything about it?" Dr. Ely was interested.

"Actually, he would. He accepts, he doesn't understand, but rather than drag someone on the carpet he prefers to work with them, find the way into the prejudice. Not that it's my department's priority." She closed her notebook for a moment. "My first priority is finding Pierre Rice's killer."

Dr. Ely's brown eyes clouded over for a moment. "I will do anything to help, anything. Here I've nattered on. I don't think I've told you one thing that's useful."

Cooper smiled. "You have. I'm learning to know him a little. Is there anything that crosses your mind? An offhand comment by Pierre? Maybe something he said during lunch?"

Dr. Ely reflected, then spoke again, "He told me over the years that if he had evidence, he would turn it over to whatever agency he was working for. Often, well, for instance, years ago he found a large company was polluting the river down at West Point. When the Environmental Protection Agency had the goods, they didn't immediately prosecute. They made a deal. They kept it out of the courts, out of the papers, and the company paid an enormous fine plus enacted cleanup. Pierre said that a company would never admit they had violated the law, they would fight and he would wind up in court testifying for whoever hired him. But if they had violated the law, and a deal was offered they almost always made the deal. He said he thought keeping out of court was in everyone's self-interest. The company doesn't get dragged through the mud. The taxpayer's money isn't spent on exhaustive legal proceedings and endless appeals plus something actually gets done. He made me think about so many things. He made me question my assumptions."

"I'm sure you made him question his."

She laughed, a laugh of relief and remembrance. "Oh, he declared I ended whatever sexism he might harbor. He'd tease me that I can't cook, I'm not so socially adept, and he could read people better than I can. He was right, too." She leaned forward. "Deputy, he was my best friend. I hope you have a friend like

Pierre, someone who will tell you the truth, someone who will help you out of a jam even when they told you not to do the stupid thing you did to get there."

Cooper smiled again. "I do. One last question. Did you know of a routine or process Pierre had to prepare for a case?"

"Yes," came the instant reply. "I could guess what he was working on by what he was reading. And he was careful about checking out books from the library. One can get records now, although it's only supposed to be the authorities, but let's face it, a computer whiz can get everything. Often he would ask me to buy books. They would be on my credit card, not his. Again, he often said he was up against people with a lot to protect. He needed to fly under the radar."

"Any recent purchases?"

"*The Genius of Birds* by Jennifer Ackerman," came her reply. "And books on Native American customs. He was showing an interest in tribal regalia, accurate clothing that a person must wear if they wish to perform in festivals. He knew about the Indian children being recorded as colored back in the early twentieth century. *Colored* was the legally acceptable word and it obviated recognition of tribal blood, affiliation. He was making quite a study of the Virginia tribes, their legal disappearance, but I can't imagine where it would have led."

"That's something. Certainly out of the ordinary," Cooper mumbled, then looked at an ornate wall clock. "I have taken up so much of your time. Thank you."

"As I said, Deputy, I nattered on but you made me feel so comfortable."

Cooper stood up, and Dr. Ely did also. She was nearly as tall as Cooper. The officer handed her card to the doctor, who read it, tucking it into her front pocket.

"Call me, Dr. Ely. If anything should occur to you, even if it seems not important, anything at all about Pierre, call me. We want to find his killer. No matter how odd something seems, no matter how unbelievable someone's murder, I promise you it makes sense to whoever committed the crime. Once we know why, we can almost always find who."

22

"Wore the Mistress's sapphire necklace." DoRe relayed this compelling information to Bettina, whom he had come to visit.

Getting off Big Rawly, never easy, was made a bit easier when DoRe asked Maureen Selisse if he could go over and pick up a small enclosed carriage. Ewing Garth, knowing Mrs. Holloway wished one for herself, was happy to lend it to the wealthy woman to use. If she really liked it, then her young, handsome husband would find one for her or arrange to have one built in Philadelphia. Everyone knew the order would go to Philadelphia, after a show of considering alternatives, for Maureen needed to appear extremely fashionable, and that meant the best, most expensive small conveyance possible, one that would certainly outshine the Garths'.

DoRe ran the stables, knew what he was doing, and was finally coming back to life after the death of his beloved wife and the disappearance of his son, Moses. These punishing events both happened within a year and a half.

Bettina sat across from the big, middle-aged man in the im-

156

pressive carriage harness room, the potbellied stove keeping it just right as the beginning of a light snow started outside.

And the stable help was working at the three stables but did not pop their heads into the wood-paneled room. Everyone at Cloverfields knew Bettina set her cap for DoRe. Not only had she set her cap, she commanded Serena and a few of the other girls to cart down a feast. Bettina believed the way to a man's heart was through his stomach.

"Mrs. Selisse's sapphire necklace? Lord, Lord." Bettina exhaled.

"Can't get used to calling her Mrs. Holloway. I slip, too. Bettina, I didn't know where to look when Sheba came down to the stables wearing that fur, the beaver skin, and a sapphire necklace. She's the only slave got a fur, I can tell you that but then we all know Sheba's not exactly a slave, according to her."

"But where was Mrs. Selisse? That witch wouldn't let Sheba wear her sapphire. Anyway, Sheba has some jewelry of her own. She gets something every Christmas and I know it's hush money. I know it."

He bit into a biscuit, so light it melted in his mouth. "No one can cook like you." He beamed, then cut into a piece of pork braised on one side, with tiny slivers of lemon rind also on it.

Bettina had dried fruits, canned vegetables, all manner of flours. She wasn't considered one of the best cooks in the state of Virginia for nothing, and that alone set Maureen Selisse off. She wanted the best cook, the reputation for the best table and entertainments and, of course, now the best small carriage.

"The Missus was down on the James at the foundry. She is running the business. She's running it as well as Francisco. She pretends that Jeffrey," he named the young, handsome husband, "is the boss but we all know that story."

"Yes, we do." Bettina slid more biscuits his way.

"I feel a little sorry for him. Yes, he married himself a rich,

rich widow, but he's at her beck and call and that's no life for a man. It's a funny thing, Bettina, he goes on down to the cabinet-maker's shop, builds some things. Works right along with the men there. He makes her pretty things and she *oohs* and *aahs* over them but tells him not to get too close to *those people*, as she calls us. He's always good to all of us."

"Just so he isn't good to the women. We know what happened last time."

"Poor, poor Ailee. The last in a long line of pretty girls that Francisco played with. And my poor, poor boy."

Bettina, voice lowered even though no one was around, said, "Moses is doing well. The man and wife up there, the man Charles was in camp with, Captain Graves, I think is his name, they write back and forth. Moses works hard. Has made friends with the freemen there, and there are a lot of them."

Moses, thanks to John and Charles, now lived and worked in York, Pennsylvania.

A soft smile creased DoRe's face, his silver mustache curved upward. "He's a good boy. He was a good son. I often wonder if his mother had lived, could she have talked sense to him? I couldn't. That boy lost his mind over Ailee. Lost his mind."

"She was extremely beautiful and he was young." Bettina smiled kindly. "And I don't know if your angel wife could have stopped him. Things happen, DoRe."

He cleared his throat. "You help me find peace, Bettina." He put down his fork, his plate was clean. "I am thinking I can live again. I know my boy's alive and that lifted a heavy weight. And I thank you, Bettina, I thank you with all my heart for getting me little messages, for calming my spirit about Moses, and right under Mrs. Selisse's nose." He laughed, as did she.

"Time heals us," Bettina simply said. "When my Norbert died,

I never thought I would smile again, but a year passed, then two and three. You heal."

"Norbert was so much older than you, Bettina. You are a woman in the prime of life."

"Thank you."

"You know what I think?" He leaned toward her. "I think your Norbert and my Claudia, I think they want us to live. We, I don't know, we kind of insult them if we don't."

"I'm mighty glad to hear that, DoRe. You have suffered enough."

He smiled a big, broad smile at her. Yes. He was going to court her but he would be slow. A man can't be too careful and they were owned by different people. It was complicated but not impossible.

Catherine burst into the stable, her son running after her. She opened the carriage room door.

"DoRe, how good to see you."

"Miss Catherine, you spoil me. Yes, you do." He stood up as she took his hand.

"JohnJohn, this is DoRe. He is head man at Big Rawly. All the horses, all the carriages and sleds, DoRe is in charge of it all."

"Like Barker O.?" The little boy named the slave in charge of driving, the driving horses, and plow horses at Cloverfields.

Bettina laughed. "JohnJohn, Barker O. and DoRe have been competing against each other for years. When the weather is good and each man is up, oh, my, what a show."

DoRe blushed a bit. "Now, now."

Seeing that Catherine was in the room, Barker O. burst in, slapped his rival and friend on the back. Jeddie, Ralston, and Tulli squeezed in. Everybody wanted to say a word to DoRe. Everyone had known Moses. DoRe didn't know that Ailee had hidden on Cloverfields with Moses. He only knew that somehow, he didn't know how, the white folks got his boy to York, Pennsylvania, to a safe place, a job, good people. Nor did he know Ailee killed herself. No one would tell, and even if they could, they wouldn't. Why spread sorrows? But DoRe was a respected man and no one could figure out how he could stand Maureen, but what could he do? She owned every hair on his head.

Everyone was talking at once. Talking about the weather. Talking about Yancy Grant babbling about running his horse, Dark Knight, when spring came. Talking even more about how Yancy Grant hated Jeffrey Holloway because he, Grant, wanted that rich widow for himself. He had debts to pay plus her fortune would raise him up, he believed he belonged on top. Catherine listened intently because slaves knew more than the white people. And the slaves at Big Rawly watched Maureen with the searching eye, as the old phrase goes. Soon as they were at another plantation the gossip would fly.

Then John, Charles, and Karl Ix piled in. The room, small, was jammed. The only person missing was Ewing himself, buried under paperwork in his office. The good fellow didn't know there was an impromptu party.

Rachel walked in, squeezed next to her sister.

DoRe, properly, said, "You two beautiful girls take my seat. You're both small enough to sit side by side."

"Rachel, sit here." Bettina stood.

Catherine, knowing Bettina was sweet on DoRe, she'd known it since Francisco was murdered, ribbed her sister. "Actually, we just wanted to say hello. We'd better get back to our tasks before the snow decides to come down."

"Well, I'd better be going, too." DoRe smiled.

"Jeddie, hitch up the Charleston green carriage for DoRe." Catherine looked at the man. "I noticed you rode one horse and brought the other. Good thing. Carriage needs two horses." She smiled. "But then you remember everything."

"I do try, Miss Catherine. I do try."

Catherine inclined her head to her husband, who got the message, and one by one the folks filed out.

As the carriage was being hitched up, the brass on the trappings shining like gold, Bettina wrapped food in dish towels, her tried-and-true method, put all in a large basket, and covered that with another towel.

"You are trying to fatten me up." He smiled at her, then said low, "I thank you and I will do what I can to warn you about Sheba. She's up to no good. Blaming little birdy-boned Mignon for stealing jewelry and ribbons. Says she took the pearl necklace, too. I wonder where that witch has hidden that necklace?"

"No one has seen Mignon, so maybe she made it."

"I hope so. If that little lady spotted a penny in the dust she'd try to find the owner. We all know how honest Mignon was. Sheba has Mrs. Selisse, somehow she has her."

"I think we have a good idea what she's holding over Maureen's head," Bettina remarked.

"Sheba knows what really happened with Francisco, but there's not one thing we can do about it. Not one thing." DoRe shrugged.

"Well, you can keep clear of her."

Jeddie knocked on the door. "Ready, DoRe."

"Be right there, boy." He took the offered basket, cleared his throat again. "Bettina, if it's fine with you, I would like to call upon you when I can."

"Oh, my, yes." Impulsively she kissed him.

She couldn't believe she did it.

DoRe was glad she did and felt that kiss on his cheek the whole way home.

23

November 5, 2016 Saturday

*H*arry cut the motor on her lightest tractor, the John Deere forty-horsepower, already twenty-three years old. She turned around in the seat, satisfied with how straight the rows were. Then she cut the motor on, lifted the disc attachment, drove out of the large garden, and cut the motor again. She swung down.

"Straight as an arrow." Cooper admired Harry's work.

Like most farmers and gardeners in the Mid-Atlantic, Harry prepared the ground for spring in the late fall. Usually mid-October proved ideal, but the unusual warmth pushed the discing, harrowing, dragging chains to the first week of November. Get the timing wrong and shoots will pop up only to be killed by frost. Do the prep work too late and the fertilizer and winter seed, if planted, don't properly work into the soil.

Harry loved trying to figure it out. Cooper, bravely attempting to garden, loved it less. Harry, knowing this and that Cooper wasn't a country girl, took over.

Harry brought over equipment plus saved horse manure to

make a rich mixture of commercial fertilizer, manure, and old straw.

Cooper observed all this, making a mental note to do her part in the spring and get the jump on weeding.

"Let's unhook this and hook up the manure spreader. Oh, pour some bagged fertilizer into the manure, will you?"

"How many bags?" Cooper asked as they unhooked the disc and hooked up the manure spreader, a sturdy cart.

"Mmm." Harry eyed the twenty-five-pound bags leaned up against the big tree. "Let's start with five and see how it goes. You were smart to buy the lighter bags, by the way. We have nothing to prove by toting fifty-pound bags of fertilizer. That's what my husband is for." Harry laughed.

"That man could toss one hundred pounds like a basketball." Cooper knew how strong Fair Haristeen was.

"Could." Harry smiled.

Like many women, she appreciated a super-strong man.

The two cats and dog watched the humans work from the well-kept Jones family graveyard not far from Cooper's large garden.

"Her garden is twice as big as Mom's," Pewter noted. "She must be feeding half the sheriff's department."

"Ha." Mrs. Murphy flicked her tail. "When she paced out this garden in the spring, she had no idea what she was getting into. The good thing is, Mom didn't have to do her garden. There was enough in Cooper's."

The three laughed. Cooper did overdo and Harry knew the tall deputy would never be able to keep up with even the tomatoes, much less the rest of her sprawling, ambitious garden. So Harry would help her weed, attack the beetles, pull up the okra, really good okra. The two women liked working together and having a friend to pull weeds with and chatter about this and that. And Cooper learned, yes, she did.

"Okay." Harry turned around. "Two more bags and we've got it. Stuff is mixing in just great."

Cooper opened two bags, pouring them in, Harry started the PTO again and the manure spreader churned out the cooked straw, old manure and the fertilizer producing an odor, not offensive yet most distinctive. Harry, smart, used what she had on the farm. Every three years she'd call up Rachel at Southern States and do an extensive fertilizer spread on her acreage, depending on the crops. Fertilizer prices could fluctuate with gasoline prices. Last year, Rachel convinced her to try carbon packing which added $58 per acre. Best thing Harry ever did. Her pastures, good, became spectacular. So she paid the money for another packing, this would be two years in a row. Then she thought she'd wait and see how many years the process held before doing it again.

Like all farmers, Harry knew Mother Nature was a harsh business partner. Sometimes she held a cornucopia. Other times, you lost everything. But sun, soil, and water were the key, and fortunately for Harry, she had all three in a potent combination.

Cooper, on the other hand, just west of the dividing creek, had poorer soils. So instead of working on all her pastures, Harry focused on the garden. If she could help her wonderful neighbor, a former suburban girl, learn from that, then in the future she might be able to convince Cooper to grow hay. You can always make a bit of money on high-quality hay.

"Done." Harry triumphantly finished the garden fertilizer run.

Cooper, wiping her hands on her red kerchief, looked at the now-covered quarter acre. "Thanks to you, I really did have a terrific yield."

"Wait until next year. Your asparagus will be up. Harvest it every two years. You can't believe how good it tastes from your own garden. The next thing you need is chickens."

"You don't have any."

"I used to, but the cats chased them. You can turn your chickens out in the morning and drive them into a pen at night. You will be amazed at how effective they are, so you don't need to use chemicals. I hate all that pesticide stuff. I don't care what anybody says, it gets into the water supply."

"Yeah, I think so, too. Well, the chickens will have to wait until spring."

"Good, then we can come over here and chase chickens." Pewter puffed up.

"Waddle is more like it." Tucker guffawed.

The gray cat shot straight up in the air, turned to land on the dog's back. She dug her claws into Tucker's shoulders, which forced a yelp.

"You two stop it!" Harry hollered.

"Kind of like Israel and Palestine." Cooper put up her tools.

"Actually, they behave better than those two." Harry drove her tractor into Cooper's shed. She intended to drive it back to her place tomorrow. The sun was low, it set fast this time of year: Boom, it would just drop below the horizon. There might be a smashing sunset but no long, lingering twilights as in summer.

The mercury was dropping, that early chill touched your bones. The two women walked back to Cooper's house, the old Jones place, the Reverend Herbert Jones's family. He rented the house and farm to Cooper. Both were happy with the arrangement.

"Open the door!" Pewter insisted.

Harry stepped back onto the porch and did just that. The three animals joined them.

"Hot tea, cold beer, hot chocolate, um." She looked around. "Port. I forgot I had a bottle of port."

"Coop, save the port. I'd love a hot chocolate."

"Tuna!" Pewter demanded.

"*A greenie.*" Tucker wasn't shy, either.

As Cooper kept treats for Harry's animals, Harry walked to the cupboard and pulled out the goodies. Soon the humans and the animals were all happy.

"Good hot chocolate."

"Milk. Always use milk." Cooper smiled. "Thanks again for all your work and the use of your equipment."

"That's what friends are for." Harry stopped. "Funny how you change, learn things. When I was at Smith, I'd stay up for bull sessions. I thought that was friendship, you know, all this talk. Then one day I realized I wasn't as smart as I thought I was. I felt closer to people by working with them instead of showing off how smart I thought I was. I like accomplishing something. Talk doesn't do that."

"Yeah. 'Course I was at Christopher Newport." Cooper named a school down in Newport News, Virginia. "I never was the intellectual type. And then when I studied law enforcement, everyone thought I was really weird. Not many women in law enforcement then. Now I think in Virginia we're around twenty percent of law enforcement officers. Loved it. Still do, but Harry, no matter what you do, someone is ready to jump on you."

"The times." Harry sighed. "Even Fair. How can you jump on a vet, but just the other day a client, new and rich, I might add, chewed him out because he didn't tell her about navicular. And here's the thing. Her horse didn't have navicular. Just had a stone bruise, but she was sure Fair was keeping something from her. Called in other vets."

"Crazy." Cooper finished her hot chocolate, rose, and poured more for them both from the saucepan on the stove.

"Any luck on the fellow who was found at Sugarday? The paper gave his name. You know, Rice is an old Virginia name."

"I knew we couldn't get through the day without you poking

around a case." Cooper shook her head. "As it happens, yes, there's information piling up, but nothing that points to murder. We've spoken to his sister in Richmond, Marvella Rice Lawson."

"Marvella Lawson! She practically runs the Virginia Museum of Fine Arts. She's a big deal and her husband is, too. Full partner at that powerful law firm, the one full of ex-governors and ex-senators," Harry said.

"I liked her. She held it together. Helped us as much as she could, but the whole thing is odd."

"You always say that until facts begin to make sense. Murder isn't odd, it appears to be very human."

"True." Cooper agreed with her friend. "Pierre Rice, the victim, whose name you read in the papers, often worked for large corporations or government agencies. But we have no records, no phone, no computer. He was so circumspect he didn't even buy books with a credit card, you know, if he was researching something. He would have his best friend do it, a cardiologist here. Beverly Ely."

"I know Beverly. Not well but she rides, so I see her at meets. Seems solid."

"She does. Whatever he worked on, he kept a low profile but this time, somehow he got caught. Or he frightened someone badly.

"Rick contacted the Environmental Protection Agency. Years back, Pierre uncovered a huge pollution problem down at West Point, thousands of pounds and gallons, more probably, of debris pumped into the river. But the EPA, who admitted knowing him, said he was not on a case for them."

"Any thoughts about the Number Five chit?"

"After talking to Dr. Ely, I called her back because she had had lunch with him the day before we found him. He wore the chit."

"And?"

"According to Dr. Ely, Pierre said he was descended from the Rices at Cloverfields. Then he teased her and said this would lead to buried treasure."

Harry laughed. "If we dug at all the places where there's supposed to be buried treasure there wouldn't be an undamaged lawn in Albemarle County."

"We still haven't found Pierre's Tahoe. If we had that it would help."

"Black Tahoes are ultracool. All someone would have to do is put on new plates. Lots of Tahoes with tinted windows, too."

"I know. We just need a break."

She was about to get one out of left field.

24

November 7, 2016 Monday

"Better here than at a firing range." MaryJo lifted the flintlock rifle to her shoulder, fired.

The metallic sound when the shot hit the empty soda can sounded great.

"Good shot." Harry was impressed.

"You shoot. Glad you got the pistol revamped."

"The firing pin is so graceful. The trigger fits my finger curve perfectly. These things are works of art."

"Couldn't help myself. I bought this rifle last week. Ed Clark fired my imagination, forgive the pun." MaryJo continued, "I'm learning to make my own cartridges. Bruce stopped in his tracks when he came home from a small job out at Continental Estates. I had powder, paper, string lined up on the oilcloth tablecloth I bought just for this. Fortunately, he's an understanding husband."

The cats sitting on the top rail of the three-board fence way in the back pasture observed all this. Tucker sat below.

"Let's hope she doesn't get obsessed with this," Mrs. Murphy remarked.

"Just wait. Old firearms, history." Pewter's tail hung straight down.

"She'll start reading about battles where those things were used. She'll have to practice and be a good shot. She's using a pistol her ancestor used in the Revolutionary War. Who cares?"

"The horses are watching like we are. Two humans shooting at a target. Just seems boring."

After a half hour of this the two women walked back to the barn. MaryJo, rifle over her shoulder, stopped to place it in her Range Rover.

"MaryJo. If you have time let's drive over to the school. I'll call Cooper and Tazio. Maybe they can meet us there," Harry suggested.

MaryJo checked her Baume and Mercier watch. "We'll need to take separate vehicles. I have to go home to dress for dinner with a client."

"Business must be good," Harry said.

"Good enough for me to buy that rifle." MaryJo smiled. "You and Fair should consider more aggressive investing. Just a thought."

Within twenty minutes the two women met Cooper and Tazio at the formerly named Crozet Colored School. In respect of history, however painful, changing the name seemed a bad idea.

Tazio opened the thick door to the ninth- to twelfth-grade building. As she did so, her dog Brinkley, a yellow Lab; Tucker; and the cats decided to stay outside and play as the sun was low on the horizon.

"Looks pretty good, doesn't it?" Tazio beamed, her smile warm.

"Does," Harry agreed.

"Bruce told me they cleaned it up after he and the boys had their poker game here while we had our wildlife meeting," MaryJo added.

"Thought if we were here, we could come up with an idea for

a fund-raiser. There's still work to be done," Harry told them. "Ned is approaching the county commissioners about using this to teach history. Having students from the county spend some days or a week studying as did the children from the past. Given all the schools we now have that would cover months."

"Susan called me about that. Great idea. But a fund-raiser?" Tazio questioned.

Harry jumped in. "The more people that see this, the better. We can print up a card or small booklet about the history. We've got three buildings. Let's use them for a blowout party. Cocktails in the elementary school. Dinner here. Dancing in the storage shed, which is this size. That will take some work but we can do it."

"When?" Cooper was intrigued.

"What about an early spring party or St. Patrick's day?" Harry tossed out those two times.

As the humans deliberated, mulling over how to decorate the buildings, work out food, the animals chased a deer who easily dumped them.

"*Fast,*" Tucker acknowledged.

"*And she knows the territory better than we do.*" Mrs. Murphy sat down.

Brinkley turned back toward the school. Nearing the buildings, a squirrel scrambled over the storage facility.

"*Go away!*" the squirrel shouted.

"*Oh, shut up.*" Pewter bared her fangs.

"*I'll throw acorns.*"

"*You have to find them first.*" Brinkley laughed.

"*Drop dead.*" The gray fellow with the flicking tail ducked into an opening he'd made where the roof and sidewall met.

"*Let's get him.*" Pewter was working at the door.

With joint effort they only managed to pound on the locked door, but the noise was considerable.

"That doesn't sound good. Let me check this out." Harry opened the door to the high school, the racket loud now.

"My dog's in on it." Tazio joined her.

Didn't take them a minute to reach the storage building, four frantic animals at the door.

Tazio fished the keys out of her pocket, opened the door, and was nearly knocked over as they rushed in.

Harry stepped inside, cut on the light. "What the—?"

Cooper, now behind her, also stopped.

As the squirrel disappeared, the animals shut up, then Tucker said, *"Old cologne."* The others agreed.

MaryJo walked through the door.

A black Tahoe sat on the low wooden floor. Two large barnlike doors at the rear of the building would allow a vehicle to be driven in, unloaded.

They could see a mesh cage, a few large feathers inside, in the back of the Tahoe. Cooper opened the front door of the vehicle, opened the glove compartment

She read the registration.

Pierre Rice.

25

"*B*. See. Butter." Eudes pointed to a small crock of freshly churned butter.

Mignon, standing next to him at the long, clean preparation table, stared down at the ABCs she had written and rewritten over the last two weeks.

Eudes thought the best way to teach Mignon how to read was through cooking. So for *a*, he had her write out *a* for apple, *b*, butter. Each time he would place food on the table, he would tell her how to write it down. She'd search through her letters, then put them together.

Eudes also taught her the sounds for each letter. She pleased him being a quick study.

"It's magic." She grinned.

"What?"

"That scratching on paper means something. Magic."

"Mignon, that magic goes back thousands of years. I can hear a man's voice from ancient Athens."

"You can?" She was dazzled.

173

"I could if I read Greek, which I don't, but I have some translations."

"Eudes, you are a learned man."

"And why am I a cook in a whorehouse, pardon me, a place of relief and renewal?" He laughed. "Money. If I taught Latin to that handful of boys, free black boys, who wanted to read I would starve. Not a penny in teaching, plus I would be curt with a child who didn't want to learn."

"How did you learn?"

"First off, I'm a free black man, as is my family. I asked my father, a joiner and a good one, would he send me to school. Instead he hired a tutor. No distractions. No other boys. Just old Mr. Disston and me. I learned. When I began to shave, my father declared it was time to learn a profession. I liked his work but he said it relied on whether men were making money or not. Pick a trade that people always need. Well, they need to eat."

She looked at him admiringly. "I wish I knew how to think like that."

"Honeychild." He patted her forearm. "Where you were, what good would it have done? You did what the master told you to do."

She nodded. "But people learned things. Mr. Selisse had coopers, and barrel makers, he had men who could plane timber so you could see your reflection in it. And the boys and men in the stables, they knew a lot."

"Guess you're right. What did you learn? You don't talk much, Mignon. I'm a deep well. You can tell me anything."

She felt she could. "As a little one, I was in the kitchen, where I learned to make and cut out cookie dough. When I was bigger, I could knead it. The cook, she knew a lot, but she was jealous. I had to watch her and there were older girls above me. But I learned a bit."

Georgina blew through the double swinging doors. "Friday. We'll have our afternoon crowd and it's bitter cold out there. What do you have planned?"

Eudes smiled. "Black bean soup with a little pork fat. I'm roasting capons and I'm experimenting with a hot spiced wine. Mignon gave me the idea." He indicated Mignon.

Georgina eyed Mignon, barely five feet and thin. "Did you, now?"

Mignon nodded, her hands covering her papers.

Eudes, wishing to promote this woman who touched him, boasted. "Georgina, since she came to us, I have gotten more done, more ideas. But I need a serving boy who isn't asleep at noon." He pointed to the big clock on the wall. "Twenty to noon. Where is Binky?"

As if on cue, a young handsome fellow pushed open the doors with one hand, buttoning his shirt with the other.

Seeing the boss, he fashioned his best grin. "Miss Georgina, and in blue. Matches your eyes."

"You worthless thing." She glared at him but did like the compliment. "You were up there with Deborah. Well, set the table and right now. Eudes," she looked at her cook, "has the full complement for a nasty day. Hot soup. And put out small glass cups for spiced wine and do it now. My God, can't you keep that thing in your pants! I ought to charge you for fooling with that girl."

"I love Deborah. She loves me." He protested as only a young man can.

"Love you she might, but she has customers to serve. Now get out there." As he left, Georgina turned to Eudes and Mignon. "My girls need to keep their strength." She glanced at the clock, one of the weights shaped like a pinecone dangling a touch longer than the other. "Half the girls are still asleep. Well, our afternoon crowd will have choices but don't forget, Friday. Tonight we will be packed unless a storm comes up." She smiled. "Cold weather encourages a man to get warm."

With that wisdom she left the kitchen. Eudes just shook his head.

Mignon breathed relief. "I was afraid she'd see my papers."

"Georgina doesn't care if you learn to read, but she will care if she sees you do anything but work. I'm the one that needs to be more careful." He walked to the open fire, bread openings on the side of the laid brick. This way he could make biscuits, bread, anything needing dough while he cooked soups. The capons crackled in an oven, wood fired. The wonderful hickory often infused the meats.

Many men stopped by Georgina's for a hot midday meal but did not hire a girl afterward. Apart from the girls, the place had a reputation for conviviality and excellent food. Eudes's creations were so good they brought the people in.

Most of the sex customers crowded the place at night after the cares of the day vanished. Or perhaps they hadn't vanished—but an hour or more with a good-looking woman banished them temporarily.

Eudes and Mignon worked side by side. She knew exactly what to do. He ladled the soup in a big silver tureen. She dressed this up by putting small pine boughs around the tureen. She kept a supply of greens and dried flowers to set alongside dishes. To keep the biscuits warm she folded over the heaviest, prettiest dish towels, carefully covering the biscuits with a ridge in the middle so the towel could be easily lifted.

Eudes enjoyed this. He had help in the kitchen before, but Mignon anticipated his needs as no one else had done, plus she enhanced the look of the dishes. He didn't need to manage her.

An hour later, Binky came back in, his shirt still neatly tucked inside his pants. "More spiced wine. They are drinking like fish."

Eudes turned to the long stove on the wall as Mignon quickly washed out the large jug. This was the sixth refill and the noise outside the door testified to the good spirits the wine provided.

Binky, finger through the top piece, dashed back outside.

Mignon couldn't help it. She peeked out the doors, then quickly ducked back in.

"Eudes, my master is out there."

"What?" His face darkened.

"My master. Jeffrey Holloway. The true master is the Missus, but Mr. Holloway married her soon after her husband was killed."

"Does he know who you are?"

"I don't know. He didn't come into the kitchen but he could have seen me. I'm hard to miss." She knew her small size distinguished her.

"How big is your reward?"

"One hundred dollars. I mean, that's what the good people who took me in told me."

"Is he a brutal man?"

"No. He's at least twenty years younger than Mrs. Selisse. He spends his time in the carpentry shed."

"Don't leave the kitchen. When he goes, you'll be fine. Describe him."

"He's in his twenties, English-looking, handsome. Lean. Thick, wavy hair, a touch of chestnut. He's a quiet one."

Eudes stepped outside the kitchen, instantly recognized Jeffrey, who was listening carefully to Samuel Udall, a banker on the make, a different generation than the moneymen of ten years ago. "Mr. Holloway, I know your estimable wife has a good head for numbers. Expansion needs to be prudent, security is all important. If I can be of any service in the protection of your funds, I am happy to do so."

"I appreciate your advice, Sir, which I will share with Mrs. Holloway. As the daughter of a banker, her knowledge is considerable. She was saying to me a few days ago that she wished her father were here to help make sense of our financial contradictions."

"Contradictions." Sam's heavy eyebrows lifted.

"The entire nation. Europe, too. She says the world is changing so rapidly. Also, a skilled slave woman has run off, a person of value. My lady is quite upset." He paused, his light hazel eyes flickered. "You may find this heretical, Mr. Udall, but I feel the effort, energy, and watchfulness over a person, free or slave, who doesn't want to be in your service undercuts their value."

Sam, fork in hand, paused. "It is a conundrum. I prefer indentured servants from England, Ireland, Scotland, or Wales myself. I have four such individuals working in the bank. They came highly skilled."

"You are wise." Jeffrey smiled. "Unfortunately, with a large estate like Big Rawly, we need those who are skilled and those whose primary value is a strong back."

Eudes knew Sam, watched the two men in rapt conversation, and then went back into the kitchen. "Your old missus. Rich?"

"Very. Rich as the Garths." She paused, realizing Eudes did not know central Virginia. "Rich as the Randolphs. The old Tidewater families. Rich and cruel."

"Vain?"

She smiled. "Don't men think all women are vain?"

"Not at all." Eudes peered through the crack between the two doors again. "I'd say Sam Udall has a fish on the line."

Finally, the tables cleared as most of the men left to complete their day of business. A few stayed behind, having selected their human dessert. Jeffrey departed with Udall after leaving a nice tip for the serving girls on top of a printed description of Mignon and the reward amount.

"Mignon, he's gone."

"I will be extra-careful," she whispered.

"I'll find out if he returns. The good thing is he doesn't live here. But he knows about Georgina's, so I expect he will be back sometime. Funny, he doesn't want a girl, I mean if his wife is old."

"Middle-aged. Good-looking. A bit plump, but riches make anyone beautiful."

Eudes laughed.

Binky brought the last of the china to the sink. He rolled up his sleeves. "Not a crumb left."

Eudes, happy, nodded. "Cold weather raises an appetite."

"So does a good cook." Mignon raked the coals in the fireplace.

"Well, we've got about four hours before they come back, and Georgina is right, it will be a big night. A night for roast lamb with mint jelly." He watched Binky. "Boy, you got a good job here with prospects. A man can rise, run things, make good money. Don't throw this away on Deborah."

"I'm not. She loves me. I love her."

"It's her job to tell men she loves them, to tell them no one is as good as they are."

Binky turned to face Eudes. "She tells me everything she does. Says she can't even feel them inside. They're no good at it, you know. Says I make her feel wonderful and I want to marry her."

"And support her on your salary or will you let her keep working here?" Eudes asked sharply, as Mignon, her eyes wide, observed.

"I don't know."

"Well, you'd better figure it out. And don't upset Georgina. Then we'll all pay. Stick to business."

"What do you know, Eudes? I don't think you ever had a woman. It's the best feeling in the world."

Eudes's face darkened but he kept control. "The best feeling in the world is respecting a woman worth your time. I don't want some silly fool fopping around about bonnets and bows. I don't want some whore, either. A woman can take you down in a hurry. Think. And how can you support children? Think, Binky."

"Oh, shut up."

Mignon found her voice, surprised herself. "Binky, he's telling you the truth because he likes you. He wants you to succeed."

Binky had sense enough not to sass Mignon. "I know it looks bad, but we'll find a way. And I will do my job. I won't disappoint Georgina. Deborah and I will need the money."

Eudes slapped his hands on the sides of his thighs. Mignon returned to her papers, which she'd slipped onto the shelf under the long table when they became really busy.

Putting them on the cleaned table she read, "B is for bonnet and bows."

Eudes looked at her and couldn't help it; he laughed.

26

"The cerise tie." Ed Clark, animated as always, motioned to his own tie. "I'm far more conservative. Just popped right out at me."

Cooper sat across from Ed, a man of middle age in excellent condition, in the spartan lounge at the sheriff's office. Ed lived in Waynesboro but had driven over for an afternoon meeting with Susan Tucker, MaryJo Cranston, Liz Potter, and Harry for the Virginians for Sustainable Wildlife. As this was election day, they didn't know if the direction of the American public's desires would be clear by the afternoon, but today was the one time most of the group could meet with him. While the president could upgrade or downgrade focus on issues, the rank and file of the various agencies such as the Forestry Department, the amorphous and confusing Environmental Protection Agency, and others would remain the same, for a time, anyway.

Ed Clark, the founder and director of the Wildlife Center, traveled all over the world at various governments' expense. He had traveled to Russia, South Africa, Brazil, European countries. His expertise, transmitted with energy and fair-mindedness, ensured his welcome. He was also called upon to testify in court cases as to the financial damage caused by poaching, killing, defiling animal habitats. He was friendly but formidable.

"Pierre Rice called upon you?"

"He did and he drove over to Lyndhurst where we have our headquarters, where many of the animals rescued are rehabilitating. He asked for a tour, which I gave him. Clearly intelligent and well informed. I liked him immediately. Of course, the tie made me like him even more. A man's got to have ..." he hesitated, then added, "... guts to wear cerise."

Cooper smiled. "Maybe women do, too. You obviously observed him carefully."

"Carefully. His shoes had to have cost at least eight hundred dollars. They were butter-thin Italian calfskin. He wore gray slacks and a well-cut, bespoke, probably, navy blazer. He was not at all what I expected."

"Which was?" Her pencil was poised over her reporter's notebook.

"A policy geek."

Cooper studied the handsome man before her. If his hair had not been silver, she would have assumed he was perhaps in his early forties, but she couldn't discern his age. High energy, a man who loved what he did, one of the lucky ones with a grand passion in his life, which also included his wife, a beauty. Ed was a celebrity of sorts, and many who knew him or thought they did all mentioned Kim, his wife.

"Narrow, rectangular black glasses, shirt hanging out of his pants, sweater with a rolled-neck collar." She described her version of a geek.

"Don't forget the fact that the latest high-tech cellphone would be attached to him like an enema bag," Ed noted acerbically.

Cooper roared, she couldn't help it. "I hadn't thought of that."

Collecting herself, she returned to Pierre. "So Pierre Rice seemed to be in a class by himself?"

"Yes. Easy to talk to, no throwing his weight around, and as I mentioned, it was obvious he was well educated, well connected, and rich, rich with taste. I would have killed for those shoes." He stopped himself. "Sorry, wrong thing to say under the circumstances."

"Actually, maybe not. Let me show you the photograph forensics took when we found the body. It's not too bad." She scrolled up the hooded figure on her portable computer, gratis the county.

Ed shook his head. "I'm sorry and I hardly knew him. I can imagine his friends and family are inconsolable."

"Up to a point. Everyone knew his work would take a dangerous turn. His sister, Marvella Lawson—"

He interrupted, "*The* Marvella Lawson?"

She nodded. "She's hit hard but in her way understands. He did not discuss his cases during or after with his sister or his friends. Finding your card wedged between the Tahoe seat and center console was our first real break. That and a cage in the back."

Ed peered at the picture of the supine figure again. "Like Sherlock Holmes."

"Beg pardon?"

"Disguises. Holmes would go out in disguise. No one would pay much attention to a black fellow in a hoodie."

She thought. "Yes. But someone was and someone was on to him or at least whatever it was that he was investigating—which is why I must ask you the nature of his questions."

"Certainly. One of my functions when called into court on a black market case—"

She held up her hand. "Black market?"

"For feathers, animal parts. You would not believe how lucrative it is. Billions. And this black market is worldwide, but it has flashpoints, if you will. He wanted to know about eagle feathers, not just the sale of them but who might be stockpiling them. He knew that thousands of cardinals, the state bird of Virginia, are being captured and sent overseas. Goldfinches, too. Huge market for them as well as bear claws, black bear gallbladders, antler."

Cooper held up her hand again. "What for? Forgive me, Mr. Clark, gallbladders?"

"Ed. Please call me Ed." He took a deep breath. "Our nation has many constituencies with different, um, spiritual ideas than our own. The eagle feathers, for instance, are vital to the Apaches for their ceremonies. They aren't the only tribe cherishing eagle feathers for their regalia, but you get my idea. Asian men believe body parts of rare animals will restore their fading potency. Many cultures, not just African, believe rhino horn cures impotency. They even have special bowls for the ground powder. That's just the people living in our own country. Look out at the world and you get an idea of how vast this killing, poaching, et cetera, is. If a species is thought to be near extinction—say, elephants—these criminals stockpile the parts and then raise the cost. Really raise the cost and as you probably understand, a man who can't get an erection is ready to buy anything, pay any price."

"Haven't they heard of Viagra?"

"They come from different cultures. All some of them have to do, the really smart and rich ones, is declare the use of such animals is part of their right as Americans."

"The First Amendment?"

"Deputy Cooper, I have heard this amendment used to sanitize outrageous acts against other living creatures." He paused. "Including humans. I would hazard a guess that more people have been maimed and killed in the name of our amendment or God than anything else."

"I fear you're right. So Pierre seemed to be investigating this black market?"

"Here. Yes. I could tell from his line of questioning that he had studied the issue, and he had to have been working for either a government agency or someone running a national nonprofit."

"And whoever hired him probably had to be protected. At least until Pierre had enough evidence for a possible conviction."

Ed took a deep breath. "Yes, but as all such government agencies are mandated to be transparent, that presents tremendous problems for a director, especially a director trying to slow down or halt this trade."

"No slush funds?"

He held his hands palms upward. "I would expect every agency has some, but I would also expect that there are reporters, media people, whose entire purpose for living is to expose wrongdoing in government and this could be perceived as wrongdoing even though they were trying to halt an illegal activity."

"Ah, yes, the principle is always more important than life itself." A note of bitterness crept into her voice.

He stared at her. "You've seen it, too. People who are enraged concerning so-called abuse of power or language which offends them but they do nothing to stop child abuse, violence against women or animals. Obviously, I'm focused on the animals, but I swear to you—and I mean swear, I will swear on a Bible—that the abuse of children and women begins with animals."

She remained silent for a long time. "Yes. As a law enforcement officer, I know that, but I have to keep my mouth shut."

"Fortunately, I don't. Let me tell you what I think Pierre Rice was doing. He may have been investigating for an agency, but my hunch is he was working for a congressman or -woman who needed facts, and even better a huge bust so he or she could introduce legislation to ban these activities. It's also probable that the profits from these activities could be going into the pockets of those who had contributed greatly to some elected official's company, or worse, been directed toward a dark account which couldn't be traced to, say, a senator. It's easy to do."

This jibed with everything Cooper had learned about Pierre's activities, but she didn't have his political experience. "Ed, why can't a clean congressman just introduce the legislation?"

"There isn't enough interest right now. Other congressmen have to see that working for this makes them look good, enlivens their constituency, so to speak. Gets their face in front of the camera. If the lid can be blown off even just one black-market activity like eagle feathers, they have their chance."

"So this congressman would be one of the good guys?"

Ed nodded in agreement as Cooper went on. "And smart enough to bide his time. Good intentions mean nothing in D.C. And let us not forget those who had profited would make life uncomfortable for our good guy or woman. The proverbial hornet's nest."

Ed shrugged. "Add to that, there are so many layers to government right now, it's all 'cover your ass.' It's all about the paycheck and for the really disgusting, their egos. There, I've been indiscreet and said it."

"I'd like to think you're wrong, Ed, but I see it even in law enforcement. I hasten to add that our department is good, good people and woefully underfunded, but I look at some of these megacity police departments and I have to wonder. I always thought I wanted to work, say, in Atlanta or even Washington but now I don't. Too much pressure from without and also from within."

"I understand."

"Did Pierre appear troubled or worried?"

"No. Very cool."

"What about a company whose product, say animal food, is under review?"

"Same thing. Graft. Cover-ups. Done every day whether it's corn meal or dog food. The corporation doesn't give the congressman money but perhaps a second home will come his way dirt cheap. Then again, one can always dump millions in his aunt's bank account. The permutations are endless."

"I see. One last question. Do you think whoever Pierre was working for or with could be in danger?"

Without a moment's hesitation, he answered, "Without a doubt and as we speak, if the ring is big enough, profitable enough, the bad guys are trying to find out who initiated the investigation."

"Like I said, finding your card was our first true break in this case. I know I'll have more questions over time. I'll call and if you think of anything you call me. Now, just one more thing . . ." She reached in her black carry bag.

"Could you tell me what bird these feathers are from?" She put three brownish feathers in his hand.

"Bald eagle," Ed instantly said. "I'm not a man to spread fear, but, Deputy, you are up against what I think is a powerful ring, given the protection status of bald eagles. Only the big guys will have a secure network to get away with killing them, selling live ones, selling feathers, claws. Any protected species is important, but the bald eagle is the most important, to Americans anyway. They won't hesitate to kill."

27

March 15, 1786 Wednesday

Walking toward her father's house, Catherine noticed the plume of smoke from the chimney hanging low, spreading out. That meant more weather on the way.

She passed her mother's garden on which Isabelle had lavished so much attention. Each season was represented by colors selected to demonstrate what Isabelle thought of that season. A few brave snowdrops pushed up through the snow on the ground. Her mother's spring color scheme always started with white, then moved into the yellows, pinks, and purples of croci, from there to jonquils and daffodils. As she passed the rows of snowdrops, Catherine thought how organized her mother's mind was in terms of space, color, harmony, and height. Her father, on the other hand, could remember columns of figures from years back. His mind, very good, was organized in a different fashion. The two complemented each other.

Catherine looked up to her parents' marriage. She and John proved a strong team, radiantly in love. Rachel and Charles surprised each other by their newfound passion for architecture.

Rachel had inherited her mother's sense of proportion, color, aesthetics; Catherine truly was her father's daughter, a fact recognized by men. Women may have been seen as helpmates to their fathers and husbands, but it was a slow-witted man who did not realize Catherine possessed her father's business brilliance. She could see far beyond the nose on her face.

The aroma of maple syrup greeted her as she stepped into the kitchen through the back door. Serena, putting away the cleaned dishes, smiled at Catherine.

"Missus, there's plenty batter left over. Would you like some pancakes?"

"No, thank you, Serena. I made a big breakfast today as John will be at the back bridges shoring up a damaged foot. Well, I call it a foot. And do you know my husband can cook? He made his special eggs while I brewed coffee, wonderful coffee from those beans Father bought from that Jamaican trader. I'm nattering on. Where's Father?"

"Usual."

"Where's Bettina?"

"Down in the root cellar, looking for those peaches we put up this summer. She's determined to make peach cobbler. She says if she does, winter will finally release his icy grip."

"Serena, if you look outside, I think we're due for another handshake."

Serena walked to the paned-glass windows. "Oh, dear. March is cruel."

"Is," Catherine agreed. "Mother's snowdrops are peeking up and it looks like more snow coming. It has to end sooner or later."

"Later." Serena shrugged.

Catherine smiled, hung up her coat, walked down the polished hall to her father's office.

"My dear." He pushed his spectacles up on his nose. "The day will come when I will be buried under papers, an avalanche of papers. People will ask you, 'How did Ewing die?' and you will tell them, 'He suffocated under papers, poor soul.'"

"Oh, throw them on the floor."

"Tempting." He held up one offending document. "Massachusetts has printed more money, devaluing what they owe me and everyone else. You know, I ask myself why do business in my country? It's becoming impossible to make a profit. Indeed, it is the reverse. There is no order."

"Well, we will just have to do business with England and France."

"Yes." He paused, took his spectacles off. "But how can a nation survive if commerce, trade is not promoted? I want to do business with my countrymen. For one thing, sending tobacco, hemp, anything across the Atlantic is expensive and risky. You never know."

"There's a reason people say, 'When my ship comes in.'"

"There is." He rummaged around and handed her a letter executed in a strong hand. "From Baron de Stael."

Years ago when Ewing visited that Continent, a journey expected of educated young men, he met the baron, a few years younger than himself. The two got along and corresponded over the years. Ewing thought the fellow possessed some sense.

Catherine read, paraphrasing, "Calonnet can't control the treasury deficit." She named the French minister of finance, a man of self-importance. "Payments to the Army are delayed, our highways are falling to bits. We must have reform. I give the comptroller general credit, he knows it but I fear for our future. Finance is the base of all stability."

She looked at her father. "The French appear not to be better off than we are."

"One can have the greatest army and navy in the world. One can conquer other countries, but if you can't administer them, if you can't promote trade among nations, encourage your own people, you will fail. I leave the French to themselves. They excel at crisis, then escaping from same, but I don't know as we can do that. We are too new. I wonder will we be strangled in our cradle by our own stubbornness? And you are right. We must concentrate our efforts on England. If there's one thing an Englishman understands it's money." He put the paper back in the pile.

"You'd think we'd all figure that out."

"Catherine, never underestimate human greed or the need to control. Yes, you would think that every state would realize we can't compete against one another. We don't. Is it possible violence will erupt? Have we defeated the British to war against one another?" He flopped back in his chair. "I'm being gloomy. Sorry."

"It's a gloomy day." She leaned over his desk to tidy his papers. "Father, if we stick to tobacco, timber, and apples we should sail through these troubled waters."

"If we trade across the ocean. I don't see how I can do business with other states now and expect fair recompense."

"Maureen Selisse seems to be doing all right."

A silence followed this, he stacked his papers together. "She does, doesn't she?"

"The foundry helps."

"Yes, but the foundry can't be making enough money to cover her lavish expenditures. A copy of our carriage is just one of them."

"Her jewelry is fabulous, she has bedecked Jeffrey in the finest clothing possible, she has sold some horses, then turned around and brought all that furniture from France. I quite like it. Usually I don't."

"Hmm, the black with the ormolu. It is beautiful but one desk would buy a three-hundred-acre farm in the shadow of the mountains. I wonder how much Francisco really left her and even more, how long can it hold out?"

"Sheba, according to Bettina and our girls, has been bragging about how Maureen will send her down to Martinique and from there to Paris. She declares she's on a business mission for Maureen."

"That's absurd. No one would send a slave, a woman no less, to conduct business."

"Perhaps not, Father, but think of the ships that sail into those ports. Filled with wine, furniture, fabrics, expensive everything, and some of these places are duty free. The jewelry alone would produce punishing fees if brought into, say, Charleston."

"Yes, it would. Francisco must have taught her how to outrun the taxman."

"Her father was rich and she married rich," Catherine mentioned. "She's shrewd."

"Shrewd or not, no one can spend money like that without sooner or later facing the bills."

"Maybe she trades. I don't know, but I would like to know and I would like to know the source of Sheba's power."

"Ah, yes." He exhaled, then changed the subject. "They never found the slave who ran away, Mignon. Poor little thing. I expect she froze to death."

"I don't know, but Maureen and Sheba are certainly vengeful when it comes to their people. Broadsheets put up throughout the state, advertisement for reward in Philadelphia's paper. For someone who accused a woman of stealing jewelry I haven't noticed the vacancy of one bauble with the exception of her pearl necklace. I can't imagine that little bird stealing pearls."

He smiled. "What is it about other people's money that's fascinating? For instance, I have heard that our former governor, Mr.

Jefferson, spends money like water. Patrick Henry appears to have more sense, but the man is littering the state with his illegitimate offspring."

Catherine laughed. "Let us give him credit for energy."

"No discretion. Ah, well, foolish men." He threw up his hands. "One should try to conform to one's wedding vows. It was never a problem for me but then no woman could compare to your mother."

"I think some men are just restless. I don't know."

"I expect sooner or later Jeffrey Holloway will become restless." He said this without censure. "Then again, he'd better be careful. He is as owned as one of her slaves."

"Do you think love is a form of slavery, Father?"

"Of course not." He answered swiftly. "Untrammeled passions are, but true love is freedom."

"I think so, too."

"Back to business. You have a good hand, help me write letters to our agent in each state. Perhaps they have a sense of what is going to happen regarding currencies, tariffs. Forewarned is forearmed."

"Indeed it is, Father. But Caesar didn't listen."

He paused a moment. "The Ides of March. A damned unlucky day."

28

"You can tell the difference." Harry pointed to the large paned-glass windows.

"There's nothing we can do about it really." Tazio Chappars, the architect heading the Save the Old Schools committee, sighed. "Who can blow a paned-glass window today? And if they can, he or she will charge us a fortune."

"Got that right." Liz Potter, tired from a long day, slumped into a desk, the chair, wooden, not too horribly comfortable.

Tazio, half African American, half Italian, and all beautiful, headed this group to save the one-hundred-and-forty-six-year-old buildings.

Hester shrewdly realized a woman of color needed to run the show. Liz Potter, African American, came on board after Hester's death. Harry and Ned rounded out the steering committee. Panto Noyes offered his legal services gratis. Ned, with tremendous effort years back, managed to browbeat the county into preserving the schools, designating them for preservation. He could not, however, woo the county officials nor anyone in the House of

Delegates to release funds to further shore up the structures. Ned could and did work both sides of the aisle, but preserving school buildings used by the children of slaves and then their children and on down the line lacked the high-voltage appeal of something that could get a delegate's face in front of the cameras. Politics had become theater, bad theater. With the presidential election yesterday everyone was sick to death of campaigning, mudslinging, et cetera. Ned knew he couldn't try for state funding for at least another year.

The four started a campaign to raise money when Hester died. They raised enough to repair any leaks in the roofs, to install heat pumps, not cheap. The nascent budget was wiped out, but they could again use the wells, the waterlines wouldn't freeze, they'd replaced the old pump.

In the center of the two actual schoolroom buildings reposed a potbellied stove, big and shorn of any aesthetic delights. Despite the Spartan design those potbellied stoves worked as well as the day they were put smack in the middle of each room, the pipes straight up and out the roof.

Ned, first into the high school building, filled the stove up with seasoned oak, kindling underneath. By the time the three ladies showed up, the room was warm and fragrant. The thermostat for the heat pump stayed at fifty degrees to save money.

The four met in the high school building. The primary school was exactly the same, but for whatever reason they met in this one, the floorboards worn shiny from thousands of feet over the decades.

The teacher's desk, a large wooden rectangle, commanded the room from a raised dais. Mrs. Murphy, Pewter, Tucker, and Brinkley sat and listened.

"Ned, any hope that a new president will energize causes such as ours?" Liz asked her delegate.

"If only." He smiled ruefully.

"How many more fund-raisers can Albemarle County endure?" Liz threw up her hands. "There isn't a week that goes by that I don't receive a ball invitation or someone coming through my door asking for an item for a silent auction. We can't compete and we are out of cash."

Tazio, pencil and pad in front of her, scribbled some figures. "Our monthly electric bill, in winter, should hover at about four hundred dollars."

"Four hundred dollars!" Harry's jaw dropped. "That's too much. We just put in three new heat pumps, supposedly state-of-the-art."

"They are, Harry, but these buildings aren't insulated and the windows aren't double paned. We lose a lot of heat," Tazio explained.

"We could insulate," Liz tentatively suggested.

"We could and we should. It wouldn't change the appearance." Tazio had thought this through. "But we have to buy the rolls, not terribly expensive. It's the labor that will kill us."

"We could try to take a page from the Savannah School of Art and Design." Liz brightened. "Students with professional supervision have rebuilt about sixteen hundred homes in old Savannah with the city's cooperation. Why can't we do that here? Use shop classes from the high school."

Ned sat up straight. "Worth a try. Let me approach the city council first and then the county commissioners. One of our confusing difficulties is the city and the county are different political entities. But I'll see."

"Ned, that's wonderful." Tazio loved the idea. "And we get young people preserving their history."

"Then what?" Harry's eyebrows raised.

"What do you mean?" Liz asked.

"She's got her problem look," Pewter remarked.

"What do we do with the buildings? I know Hester thought of a museum, but museums aren't always a big draw. When you think about it, who will come out here to Crozet to walk through an African American and Indian school?"

"You know, she has a point," Tazio agreed.

"Why can't we use the primary school building for those grades and this one for high school?" Liz held up her hand. "Of course, the county will never agree to these being used as an actual school, but what if they were used for history classes? We've talked about this, but really, what if each school in the county and the city had a schedule where they would use these buildings for a day or even a week? They would have to carry in wood for the stove, no computers so they would have to do their lessons the old way. Maybe they would even have to memorize things like, you know, like Lady Macbeth's speech or Lincoln's Gettysburg Address or maybe Martin Luther King's 'I have a dream.' They go back in time and they would have to bring their lunches just like the children did then."

The other three thought about this, then Harry said, "They'd sure learn. It's a wonderful idea."

"We will have a lot of work to do before presenting this, but it's worth a try." Ned smiled. "I like the idea of living history. Maybe we could think of something useful for the storage building, too. It's just as lovely as the two classrooms and now it's got heat. Water's there. Well, we don't have to come up with anything right now."

"A stable or a barn. The kids can take care of some cattle, chickens, I mean if we're going to do this let them live as our ancestors lived." Harry was firm about this.

"Come on, pull on your coats, let's look at the storage building." Harry walked over to her jacket and scarf hanging on a peg by the door.

The four trekked outside, past the primary school building. Tazio unlocked the storage building. The temperature hung inside right at about fifty degrees. The wind came up outside so they stepped in gratefully. Tazio switched on the old overhead lights.

Tucker, who had dashed in with Brinkley, stopped to sniff as did the Lab. "I smell old cologne."

Brinkley inhaled deeply. "Me, too."

The two cats prowled around but, except for some stored desks, nothing else was there. Well, three rolled-up garden hoses.

"Tidy." Harry smiled.

"I check it maybe once a month. You remember all the junk that was in here."

"Broken light fixtures, old wash basins which we rehabbed. Leaves, lots of leaves. Clean now but kind of forlorn. However, it could be useful." She paused. "I think we were too shocked to think because of the Tahoe."

Ned's eyebrows raised. "You aren't considering a garage."

"No, no, but it just hit me. Whoever parked that Tahoe in here knew it was empty, knew our meeting schedule." Harry's voice rose.

"A lot of people know about these buildings. We've had a few fund-raisers in the past," Ned countered.

"How are you coming along with rolling back the Pletcher law?"

"Many of our citizens still can't meet the requirements, so they don't receive benefits. No scholarship money, no anything really. I don't know if the Pletcher law can ever be untangled. We may have gone as far as we can, but that doesn't mean I can't keep trying. A living history experiment here might be a small help.

You never know. Right now, my biggest fight is against Dominion Power and the pipeline. That's been my primary focus, as you know, but anytime something comes up in the House, I try to attend to it."

Harry complimented him. "Big job."

As the humans talked politics, the animals investigated every inch of the storage building.

"This could be a nice kennel," Tucker suggested. "The children could bring their dogs to school."

"What about cats?" Mrs. Murphy asked.

"Cats aren't obedient. You'd disrupt classes," Tucker said.

"Well, you'd beg for food. They'd pull out their lunch pails and you and Brinkley would be awful." Pewter sniffed.

"So would you," Tucker fired back.

"Only for tuna fish sandwiches," the gray cat disingenuously replied.

"What about roast beef?" Brinkley smiled.

"Well—" Pewter's eyes brightened.

"I'd like peanut butter," Mrs. Murphy added.

"Murphy, peanut butter isn't as good as roast beef." Pewter sat near a vent blowing out heat, set at fifty degrees.

The tiger cat held firm. "Is to me."

"I bet if all else failed they could rent these buildings. The two classrooms would make really nice small houses. Not exactly bungalows but nice, the windows make these buildings pretty, light," Tucker remarked.

Brinkley, who had worked closely with Tazio, wagged her tail slightly. "Would, and my mother could turn all this into something special. She's the best, but it's politics. The county would have a fit. I hear the conversations, plus sometimes she reads me her emails. People don't make things easy. There's always someone who protests. She's so patient."

"Well, someone has been in here," Tucker said, "who wasn't patient."

"Tazio keeps the door locked," Brinkley informed her.

"Easy to pick a lock if you know how. Or maybe someone has a key." Tucker shrugged. "Well, it can't be that important and the place is clean. No one has been destructive."

"Think whoever parked the Tahoe wore that faded cologne?" Brinkley wondered.

"Probably," Tucker answered. "It's fainter now than when we first detected it."

Mrs. Murphy mentioned what they all knew. "It's a pity they can't catch a whiff and it's a pity they can't know what we tell them."

29

"A pepper pot." Ewing laughed. "Why our government sent both Jefferson and Adams to France together, well . . ." He shrugged.

Yancy Grant laughed with him. "Perhaps they will balance out each other, but Franklin overshadows everyone so I hear. Then again, our neighbor is most junior to Franklin and Adams. I doubt that is congenial."

"No." Ewing thought a moment. "You, Sir, have lived in France. Should you not put yourself forward?"

Smiling broadly at the compliment, Yancy grimaced slightly. "Ah, Ewing, you know I am no politician. Even Jeffrey Holloway outmaneuvered me."

"That was not being outmaneuvered, that was being subject to a woman's whim and vanity. Allow me to emphasize the vanity."

Yancy shifted in his seat, leaned across the table. "When Francisco was killed, I offered my protection. In time I thought she would look kindly on my efforts to manage her estate. A woman alone will not be able to control those people. For one thing,

Sheba. I believe Sheba is behind the killing and I believe it is that wench's devious ambition that will bring down Maureen. She doesn't see it, of course, but Sheba is turning her people against their mistress, and Holloway, lowborn, lacks any ability to rein in such unnatural, such dangerous thoughts."

Having no desire to be drawn deeper into anything to do with Maureen Selisse Holloway, Ewing simply nodded, then looked up for the waiter. "Shall we start with bread, Sir? Henry," he called the waiter's name, "what has been fresh ground and baked today?"

The two men met by accident near Pestalozzi's Mill, where Mrs. Pestalozzi opened an adjacent tavern so people could eat and drink while their grain was being ground. The huge waterwheel turning, spray shooting off the paddles, added to its allure.

Buying grain, hauling grain down after harvest time was a job for one of his skilled servants, but today Ewing really just wanted to get off his estate so he thought he would pick up a few bags of whatever needed to be ground. Bettina begged for fresh white corn if any had been saved. If not, then yellow and might he find some crimped oats? He listened to her, he usually did for she had a way of framing her desires that made you want to meet them. Also, his late wife prized her cook's abilities and was happy to consider any purchase.

By luck, Yancy was there although not on an errand. Yancy did not offer why he was there and Ewing didn't ask. Everyone showed up at Pestalozzi's Mill sooner or later.

A fireplace at each end of the large room, beams exposed, kept the place quite warm in winter. Today the temperature hovered in the midforties, which felt welcome after the deep cold and snows of January and February.

"Mr. Garth, allow me to bring you a loaf of bread so light, so white, so exquisite it will melt in your mouth," Henry offered.

"And then Mrs. P.," as she was called by those who liked her, "has made her special chowder, parsley, tiny potatoes, and peas, you know what a good canner she is, and fresh clams straight from the Bay." Henry half closed his eyes in gustatory ecstasy.

Ewing, laughing, held up his hand. "Henry, do bring it all and put it on my bill."

"Now, Ewing." Yancy protested but was grateful, for he had come to Pestalozzi's to ask for an extension of credit—not that he wanted anyone to know.

He had secured a small loan when in Richmond from Sam Udall but the loan was far from enough should business falter.

"We will not argue. Your company alone is worth a month of dinners, suppers, and drafts of late-night port."

"You never will tell where you buy your port, will you?" Yancy eyed him.

With a twirl of his hand, Ewing said, "You know, it comes from Portugal and it is dark, deep and dark. Now I do like a tawny port midday, but at night, the end of the day, oh, a rich ruby port or," he paused mischievously, "a wee sip from something distilled by our Scottish brethren."

A glow shone on Yancy's face as he, too, imagined such beneficent liquids. "Ah, heaven shows itself in many forms."

The two chuckled, then Ewing said, "I loved France, but you were there ten years after myself. We've never had occasion to talk much about that fascinating country."

"You know, Ewing, I thought we Virginians possessed good manners but I felt a rube there. The smallest exchange delighted me. The women, of course, were spectacular." He beamed.

"Yes. Yes." Ewing considered this. "I was fascinated by a glass-works outside of Paris. Then when traveling the countryside I saw how rich the soil, how well organized the estates. I had finished my courses at William and Mary and my father declared I needed seasoning, his exact words. And I did learn, indeed I did, but you did not feel constrained? I felt wherever you were born and in whatever station, there you would stay for your life. And everything, so groomed over the centuries, I missed our rugged forests, our untamed land. Had I not been sent on my Continental tour, I don't think I would have realized how new we are."

"Yes, yes, I quite agree. But unlike you, I envied their stability. Here everyone is striving, trying to rise. Perhaps it is the price of freedom. I don't know but some days I am tired." He smiled a bit.

"Yes, I understand."

The bread with fresh churned butter was brought so they began, Henry slicing the bread.

"Your sons-in-law impress me as hardworking young fellows."

"Indeed. As different as chalk and cheese and yet those two men work together in remarkable harmony. Naturally, Charles with his education, well, let me start again. Charles enjoys teaching John a bit of history, higher mathematics. But I think of Catherine, who has a head for figures. And my Englishman," Ewing grinned, "promises he's going to teach the children, even the girls. He's an Oxford man, you know. Naturally, they should learn to read and write but I am not certain my granddaughters need higher mathematics. Then again, the world is changing so quickly, perhaps it will move my granddaughter's education."

Yancy laughed. "That would be a changed world." He savored the bread. "Ewing, do you have any idea of the size or disposition of Francisco's estate?"

"Large certainly. I believe most of the money is in the Caribbean, in her father's bank. I do think Maureen knows. She is shrewd about those funds. Like you, I question not so much Jeffrey Holloway but the tone of operations on the estate. Such unhappiness."

"Never found Moses and Ailee nor the tiny cook's assistant. Waste of money to print the escaped slave notices."

"She was a sweet little thing as I was told."

"Ewing, given our problem with currencies, our difficulties with trade, is it possible that Maureen will be financially embarrassed?"

"We could all be so." Ewing's face froze for a moment. "The French, as you know, are falling behind in their payments to their military. I do not know if businesses are failing but I know ours will if we don't create some form of financial authority. Must you or I create a different set of figures and payment values for each state? How can we do that? And if we are not consistent as a nation, why would other nations want to do business with us? For profitable business, funds should be fluid, Sir."

"Yes, yes, I quite agree. Anything not owned outright is vulnerable, and how can one buy? Land values are uncertain. I predict speculators will be destroyed. If the values fall because no one can determine what is what if the value or currency falls, if the states squabble over tariffs, we are lost."

"Ah, the chowder. Thank you, Henry." Ewing smiled at the agreeable fellow who evidently enjoyed all of Mrs. P's cooking. "Yancy, have you a bank you trust?"

"No. Given the shakiness in Williamsburg, I moved my funds to Philadelphia, and now I am not sure that was wise. Boston, New York? So very far if one needs one's funds immediately. On the other end, Charleston and Savannah, also, too far. Richmond is improving but lacks the depth of men engaged in finance that the other cities enjoy."

"We're in a vise." Ewing thought the chowder remarkable. "I wonder if those among us with resources should not attempt our own bank."

This surprised Yancy, his spoon midway to his mouth. "I, well, our money would be close."

"Money should make money. The question is who could shepherd the funds, guard our treasure, so to speak. She may not be able to manage her estate, but remember, Maureen's father was one of the most successful bankers in the Caribbean. Shipowners, merchants from Europe and America trusted him. And he made them money, pots of it. I have always wondered how much she knows."

"Yes, Yes . . ." Yancy's voice trailed off.

"And would she use her husband to further her own interests? Could she hide, so to speak, and in hiding take everyone else's measure? She is uncommonly shrewd. As to her current situation, that has nothing to do with financial acumen."

"Whatever she told him, I doubt he could understand it. Jeffrey Holloway is a cabinetmaker's son and he himself remains a cabinetmaker."

"Let us both consider the dispositions of our monies. I have become uncertain. Perhaps if we observe Mrs. Selisse," he used her old married name, "she will lead us to the right man or men."

"Or lead us to hell." Yancy exhaled.

30

"Low to the ground." Pewter sniffed as she looked down from the hay storage, windows open.

"*True. Every dog is bred for something useful to humans. Beagles are bred to find small game,*" Mrs. Murphy replied.

"*Well, Tucker is low to the ground and I can't see that Bubblebutt performs useful duties.*" Pewter watched that very same bubblebutt trailing the Waldingfield Beagle pack.

"*Herder. She nips heels,*" Mrs. Murphy sagely commented.

"*Nah. She does that to irritate.*" Pewter noted the goldfinches flying in and out of bushes. "*All that color. You'd think birds would want to blend in.*"

"*I don't know. I guess wings make one superior,*" the tiger mused.

"*Certainly not. Cats are the crown of creation.*" Pewter lifted her chin.

Below, Amy Burke whipped-in on the right front of the pack while her brother, Alan Webb, took the left front. At the left rear came Bob Johnson, who like Arie, the master, had such a long stride others struggled to keep up with him, apart from Arie.

Up front the radiologist walked, his horn hung around his

209

neck with rawhide. On the right rear, Joe Giglia walked, whip with thong in hand.

Harry, Cooper, and Susan followed the beagles. The pack walked some Thursdays at Harry's farm. She and her two friends greatly enjoyed the activity done near sunset. Chores finished for all three in their separate duties, walking the beagles provided a punctuation point for the day and daylight.

In the front of the pack of twenty-one beagles, Empress, a sturdy female with drive, per usual led her friends. The crisp air put a lift to their step. Each human wore a jacket. The harsh cold lurked about a month away but a jacket now was welcome. However, being right by the mountains one never did know. Often storms came up so quickly the weather radar didn't report them until the fury was right on top of you.

Overhead, a whitetail hawk circled. Of course, the beagles, too big, couldn't be snatched up but one could dream.

Harry glanced up to see the impressive bird. "I can never figure out why some raptors head south in October and others, like her, stay."

"Pickings are good here and it's her territory," Susan said.

"You've been reading the materials MaryJo has given us for the wildlife group." Cooper smiled.

"I have. I've always liked watching birds but now I'm trying to become knowledgeable," Susan replied.

"Don't you wonder what she thinks looking down at us?" Harry laughed.

"Bet any creature without wings looks funny." Cooper noted Verdi, a beagle, nudging to the edge of the pack.

"Verdi," Bob reprimanded her, for she could take a notion and scoot.

"I was just looking," the adorable little hound fibbed.

Tucker stuck close to the three women, for if she'd dashed up front she would have upset the pack. They could tolerate other animals when hunting, ignoring house dogs, horses, cattle as they concentrated on finding and trailing rabbit scent. A walk was a different matter. Minds could and did wander occasionally and another dog might upset the applecart. A cat, especially Pewter with her smart mouth, would definitely break their concentration of staying together.

"*Lot of game here,*" Verdi whispered to Cyber, next to her.

"*We can't do anything about it if he doesn't tell us to 'Find a rabbit!'*" Cyber groaned. "*I even smell grouse. Don't smell much of that anymore.*"

They walked a mile out, along the creek, then a mile back cutting through the harvested fields readied for the winter.

Once back at the farm, all stopped as the hounds drank water, waited to be picked up and put in their small wooden trailer.

Cooper parked the black Tahoe next to the barn where the trailer was also parked. She'd picked it up from the dealer, late. Darrel dropped her off and she just ran out of time. She'd take it back to the sheriff's department in the morning.

"*I can smell the dead man's scent.*" Empress lifted her nose, for the Tahoe's windows were open. "*It's faint, but it's there.*"

Curious, the whole pack sidled over to the Tahoe as Amy and Alan quickly walked to each side of them.

"Hold," Amy commanded.

Empress lifted her nose. "*Faint but him.*"

Virgil, on his hind legs, put his front paws on the driver's door. "*Perfume.*"

Empress copied him as Amy carefully pulled the beagles down so they wouldn't scratch the black SUV. "*Perfume or cologne. There was a woman in this car.*"

As sister and brother quietly shepherded the beagles to the trailer, Tucker walked over, lifted her nose. She thought it was cologne but it could have been perfume.

Once the beagles nestled in their trailer, the eight humans re-paired to the now glassed-in porch. Fair readied it for winter over the weekend.

"We can go inside," Harry offered.

"It's so lovely. There won't be many days when we can even sit out here." Amy pulled out a chair by the small round table. "It's not cold here, a little chilly maybe but not bad."

"Well, let me just start these warmers. Once the sun sets that mercury will plunge." Harry positioned two tall warmers, the kind used on restaurant patios.

Immediately, the air warmed. Arie brought out his tin of cook-ies and a drink called The Ridge Lee Special. Harry ducked inside the kitchen, returned with a Pabst Blue Ribbon for Bob, a Corona Extra for Cooper, sweet tea for those who wished it.

"Anyone want hot tea or coffee?" Harry offered. "Food?"

"No, sit down." Alan encouraged her by pulling out a chair.

They ate their cookies, chatted as the rays of the sun grew ever longer. The cats had moved to the opposite end of the barn. They could be seen sitting in the open second-level doors.

"Looks like you put up good hay. The cats are guarding it." Amy laughed.

"You know, our hay crop was spectacular this year." Harry grinned.

Arie asked Cooper, "Any progress on the murdered man?"

"Nothing dramatic, but we know he was a high-priced private detective on a case."

"Anyone know the case?" Alan inquired.

"Not yet, but we know it involved Charlottesville. It could be something as simple, as common, as Charlottesville being a drop for drugs. The town is central to the state. The train runs through it twice a day, the passenger train. Freight more often, but the schedules are erratic. Thanks to 64," she named the east-west interstate, "anything can be easily moved east to west, Route 29, north or south. If this isn't an illegal something, Charlottesville a hub of distribution, it's some kind of stopoff. But we don't know what yet. The drug-sniffing dogs crawled over that Tahoe. Nothing. Very sad."

"That there weren't drugs? But he was a PI," Susan, being logical, pointed out.

"No, not that he was carrying anything, but black Tahoes, with black-tinted windows, are a big fav with criminals, rock stars. We're trying to put this together. Why the Tahoe?"

"Black Tahoes with black-tinted windows are also favored by our government, federal," Bob noted. "The other vehicles are all marked. But if an important person is on the move, there are decoys, unmarked cars. This fits the bill."

"Does." Harry thought about it then turned to her neighbor. "What are you doing with the Tahoe?"

"Picked it up from the dealer. They know their cars better than anyone so our forensic team worked with Price Chevrolet. They took this car apart. Everything. Nothing."

"*Dogs should do their work. Humans miss too much,*" Tucker announced.

Harry gave the corgi part of her cookie. "But, Cooper, what are you doing with it?"

"I was late picking it up, so I called Rick and he said drive it home, bring it in tomorrow. It's terrific to drive. Has everything, I mean this thing is loaded."

"Loaded and expensive," added Harry, who kept up with such things. "That doesn't mean I wouldn't like one."

"What's wrong with your Volvo station wagon?" Alan liked the Volvo.

"Has just over two hundred thousand miles, that's what." Harry slumped in her chair.

"The engine's just getting broken in." Arie smiled.

Harry fiddled with the Number Eleven chit around her neck.

Noticing, Bob remarked, "Isn't that what the man we found wore?"

"He wore Number Five. I bought this from Liz. She had a whole bag full that she bought from Hootie and Martha Henderson. They found them in their attic when they did some work on the house. Found old accounting books, too, all the way back to 1786."

"Wow. They might be valuable," Amy said.

"Hootie will allow me to read them and I asked Tazio to help. What I'm thinking is what if slave prices are in the book? We know Ewing Garth didn't sell anyone on his holdings here but he surely would have noticed costs. And if not that, I'm sure he would at least have noted the price of flour, fabric, medicines, stuff like that. Anyway, maybe we can get them, if they do contain that information, for the schoolhouses." She then told them the idea about actually using the old buildings, about thinking of a fund-raiser for Save the Old Schools.

"Wonderful idea. Put the kids right back in time." Bob smiled.

31

"You'd think after sitting in church this morning, they would curtail their activities." Mignon mentioned the nearly full house.

Eudes replied, "They will do their business and go home. Maybe the hope of spring has the sap rising, I don't know but I do know as long as men are fools for women we have a job."

Outside the kitchen, the candlelight played on the young faces. Men drank a bit, then rose, holding out their hands to the lady they wished. Up the stairs they climbed, some men so eager, they began to unbutton their breeches before reaching the top stairs.

Georgina played whist with three customers, who, having been satisfied, wished a bracing game before returning to their ever-so-Christian homes and hearths.

Despite her love of cards, Georgina kept a sharp eye on her girls. Given that most all of her customers returned home at a reasonable hour, she knew a girl could service two or three clients if necessary. Ladies' maids would hasten upstairs to tie up a corset once a man left, quickly reset hair, and change the sheets if needed. The maids worked as hard as the girls and usually without extra tips. The girls, the smart ones, learned to tip the maids and therefore trotted downstairs at a faster pace than the cheap ones. They served more customers, which equaled more money. The tightwads never did figure that out.

Binky, carrying decanters to each vacated room, stuck his head into Deborah's room while Sarah, a young maid, powdered Deborah's perfect bosoms. Sarah didn't look up at Binky, although Deborah turned to speak to him.

"Binky, you'd better get downstairs. Georgina doesn't want men up here who aren't customers."

As if to second her, a mighty moan could be heard in the next room along with an appeal to Jesus.

"I'm bringing a decanter of wine now that you're free. What did he do?" His lower lip quivered.

"What they all do, Binky. And I pretend I am overcome by their manliness. Some have more manliness than others." She laughed as Sarah now brushed her hair.

"I have a way for us to leave." He retrieved the wrinkled paper from his vest pocket describing Mignon, having picked it from Georgina's wastebasket. "I've kept this for two weeks. Thinking about it."

Deborah snatched it from him but couldn't read, handing it to Sarah.

"Runaway slave. Aged thirty-one. Highly skilled in culinary arts. Distinguishing features, light eyes, short of stature. Name: Mignon. A one hundred dollar reward if found. Notify Jeffrey Holloway at Big Rawly, Albemarle County." Sarah glared at Binky. "You can't turn her in."

"It will give us our start." He nearly spat at Sarah.

"Binky, I can make one hundred dollars on a slow night." Deborah laughed.

"We can make a life. You will never have to open your legs for one of these men again." His voice rose.

"Binky, shut up." Deborah's heavily made-up eyes fluttered. "What kind of work can you do?"

"Anything. I love you. I want to marry you." Tears filled his eyes. "I can't stand other men touching you, shoving themselves inside you."

"You've stood it this long. What's the matter with you?" She put her hands on her small waist, a smallness enhanced by a whalebone corset, which Sarah cinched to perfection.

"I can't stand it anymore." He stepped toward her as Sarah stepped between them.

"Binky, if you don't go downstairs now, Georgina will wonder where you are and where Deborah is, since Mr. Udall has left. Save this for another day, or better yet, forget it," Sarah said.

"Go on, Binky, we can talk about this later." Deborah paused. "You can't turn in one of our people. Mignon isn't the only runaway here."

"But she's the one I can prove and she's the one with the big reward." He walked to the door. "I'm a free black. What do I care?"

Sarah, herself a woman of color, snapped. "You'd better care if you want to live, boy." She folded the paper sheet, tucking it into her more modestly clad bosom.

Breathing deeply, Deborah held Sarah's hand for a moment. "I'd better get down."

"Kevin Murray is waiting. I overheard him ask Georgina where you are. He had a bulge in his breeches."

"Let's hope it's money." Deborah laughed in relief. "God, that man smells like a goat. I should be paid double for tending to him."

With that, she quietly closed the door to her room, walked past the others, some quiet, some not, to descend the stairs like a queen. Georgina glanced up from her cards and smiled as Kevin nearly tripped over his own feet to reach Deborah. Grabbing her hand, he pulled her up the stairs, a big grin on his face.

Georgina smiled as she studied her cards.

Horace Greene also looked up. "A beauty that one but cold, Georgina, cold."

"Well, you will have to warm her up." Georgina snapped her cards together in front of her lips.

Lionel Thomas, another player, raised an eyebrow. "Horace, you do know how to warm up a woman, do you not?"

"Shut up, Lionel."

The players laughed, including Horace, whose wife never indicated she enjoyed his attentions. At least Georgina's girls acted as though they did, except for Deborah. Good at what she did, he never felt she was truly there. He might as well have been on top of Mrs. Greene, except that Deborah was much younger and prettier.

The last customer left at midnight, an early night for the girls. They retired to their rooms along with the ladies' maids who needed to untie their corsets, bring them fresh pitchers of water to wash up, gossip.

In the kitchen, Mignon and Eudes tidied dishes, glasses, scrubbed the work tables.

"Do you have a view from your room, Mignon?" Eudes asked.

"Yes. I can see the backyard."

"Good. One should always have a bit of something to look at." He checked the large wall clock just as the wind rattled the large window over the deep sink. "That one will bite."

"How far must you walk to get home?" she inquired.

"Only two blocks. Brick and tight, my little house. Granted, the wind finds a way in even with the windows shut, but it's pleasing with a front porch." He smiled at her. "When spring truly arrives, I will escort you to my porch and we can watch the world go by like two civilized people."

"That would be . . . wonderful." She smiled, then curtseyed to him, laughed leaving the kitchen.

As Mignon made her way down the long front hall to the back of the building, which was not as tight as she or anyone else would have wished, she passed Georgina's office door, closed, although she faintly heard her boss's voice. She continued on, hurrying to escape the chilly hallway. Her small room would have a fire in the grate. Georgina took care of her people.

Sarah had handed the canny woman the sheet announcing Mignon's escape.

Georgina studied the reward paper. "Where did you get this? I'd throw it away. Sarah, I don't want to know how many of my girls are runaways."

"Yes, Ma'am, but Binky wants to turn her in for the reward."

"He what!"

Sarah leaned toward her boss, who had been fair to her and all the girls. "He wants the money so he can marry Deborah."

"She can't be serious." Her light eyebrows rose almost to her coiffed hair.

"No, Ma'am. She told him that she can make that on a slow night but he's crazy, crazy about her."

Georgina sat down, pointed to a chair for Sarah. "I see. So he doesn't know that Deborah, too, is a runaway?"

"No, Ma'am. She doesn't tell any man the truth and she may not tell us either, but we know more than they do."

"Yes," Georgina drawled, "not having a turgid member is a

great advantage in life. Women can think. Sarah, say nothing. There is no need for anyone here to know who is slave and who is free. All are free here."

"Yes, Ma'am, I know that." Sarah, herself, was a runaway.

"He would turn in one of his own people? My God."

"He doesn't see it that way. He's a freeman and better than we are, not meaning you, Miss Georgina."

Georgina was white.

"Sarah, I am grateful to you for this. Tell no one, no one." Georgina rose, as did Sarah.

The proprietor pulled open a desk drawer, drawing out twenty dollars, handing it to Sarah.

"Oh, thank you." Sarah folded the bills, a good sum, slipping them down her bosom.

As she left, Georgina also left, closing and locking the door. She walked up the stairs with a brisk step, knocked on Deborah's door.

Once there she relayed the problem, as one of her best girls faced her wearing only a thin nightgown, a shawl wrapped around her shoulders.

"He's crazy. This has nothing to do with me."

"Deborah, it has everything to do with you, although I do not hold you responsible." She took a deep breath. "We must act in concert. You keep him occupied, don't give him the chance to report Mignon. I know you can't do it forever but try to keep him occupied for a few days while I consider how to handle this. He will jeopardize other girls, hurt the business."

"Yes, Ma'am."

"Deborah, marry him if you have to. Not that I hope it comes to that but divert his mind. I will take care of you."

"Yes, Ma'am."

"Breathe a word to no one."

"Yes, Ma'am."

With that Georgina left, closing the door behind her. Deborah considered what could be worse, marrying Binky, if it did come to that, or crossing Georgina. The thought of marriage made her ill. The thought of crossing Georgina scared the Devil out of her. She would do as asked. Also, she liked the little woman, Mignon. She liked most all the girls at the house and she knew she was not the only one who had fled for something better.

And no matter what, it was better and she had the bank account to prove it.

32

November 11, 2016 Friday

*H*er black coat shone as she slowly walked toward Mrs. Murphy, Pewter, Tucker.

"Can't you three keep people off this mountain?" the large mature black bear asked.

"No." Tucker looked up at the long snout. "Our mother and her best friend, Susan Tucker, own the eastern side of this. No one should be here unless it's one of them or someone with them. It's trespassing."

"They've set traps. I dropped rocks in them, so the traps are sprung."

"Are they traps big enough for you?" Pewter wondered.

"No. Big enough for coyote, for fox, raccoon." The bear sat down on her haunches. "But how do I know they won't come back for me? Shoot me."

"Odin didn't get trapped, did he?" Mrs. Murphy liked the young coyote even if she didn't completely trust him.

"No, most of the coyote traps are on Royal Orchard, northwest of here." She named a spectacular estate on the mountain's ridge.

"Have you seen who's doing this?" Tucker lifted her head. Opened her nostrils, inhaling the light fragrance of rabbit on the air.

"Usually I see a clean-cut guy wearing a plaid jacket. Sometimes a woman is with him. She looks rich enough."

"Odd," the tough little dog replied. "Usually women don't go in for that sort of thing."

"Maybe the price of pelts went up?" the tiger suggested.

"Sweetpea," Tucker addressed the bear by name, as she would usually be on Harry's land in fall and early winter, then repair to one of the small caves on the mountainside to sleep for the hard winter, "be careful."

"I am. We're all careful ever since that man was stuck under the big rock. Too many people crawling around these mountains. Any time a human dies, never good. Never good at all."

"You all heard about the man found shot at Sugarday? The Waldingfield beagles found him," Pewter remarked.

"We did. Sugarday's some miles from the mountains. It's one thing when people kill one another on city streets. When they're out here, I don't know. I figure it has to do with us, with pelts, or with minerals—something in the ground they've found out about or," she paused, "I don't know. I just know it's not the regular way people kill one another."

"True," Mrs. Murphy agreed.

As the three walked back down the side of the mountain, the temperature rising slightly as they reached the old rutted road or what was left of it, Tucker said, "Sweetpea's right. Has something to do with pelts or something in the ground, like gold."

"That will be the day when gold is found around here." Pewter laughed.

"Maybe the men and women are scouting for black walnut. Cut a few, steal them. Big money." Pewter glared at her. "Mother would shoot them."

"Not if they shot her first." Mrs. Murphy had a bad feeling about all this.

Having the two cats' attention, Tucker changed the subject. "First, Sweetpea telling us about strange people, poachers maybe. Then when Cooper found the Tahoe, that scent."

Tucker lurched a bit to her left. Going up was always easier than going down.

The two cats descended without saying anything. As they reached the lower pastures, following the creek up to the beaver lodge, Mrs. Murphy said, *"Well, you can sure smell the beavers."*

"Mmm." Pewter feigned disinterest.

"And I smelled old bones where the tombstones had been disturbed. You remember, where someone had thrust a knife into the earth a couple of times?" Tucker watched as a beaver dove into the water from the opposite bank.

"Of course you did," Pewter sarcastically replied.

"I did and I said so at the time." Tucker was angry. *"Old bones not in the casket. Whatever it was, it was closer to the surface. Old bones. People don't put bodies in a grave without proper burial."*

"Oh, poof. An old murder." The gray cat tossed her head. *"If it is one, who cares? I don't even care about the new murders. If people want to kill one another, go ahead."*

"I don't know." Mrs. Murphy picked up the pace toward the barn.

"Poof and piffle. When Harry and Fair ate breakfast today, they said it was Armistice Day." Pewter stuck to her guns. *"The end of World War One. They killed millions."*

"They killed even more in World War Two," the dog replied.

"Then why worry about old bones in St. Luke's graveyard and two dead men now? Who cares? People will keep on killing one another. It's what they do."

"But they kill us, too. Sweetpea's sprung the traps. Who knows how many animals they kill each year?" Tucker sadly thought about it.

"Exactly. If they kill us, that's terrible. If they kill one another, why should we care? They're not right, you know. Something's scrambled upstairs."

Neither Mrs. Murphy nor Tucker could answer that.

33

March 21, 1786 Tuesday

*T*he spring equinox brought fair winds, sunshine. Croci pushed fully aboveground. Daffodils peeked up through the soil. The snowdrops were about finished. Winter, long, hard, cruel, seemed to be loosening its grasp, but then Richmond felt spring earlier than the lands west of the fall line.

Georgina walked toward her establishment, passing gardens in front of houses, under windows, behind iron fences, radiant blooms, she adored the blooms and the color. When she passed another woman, she looked neither right nor left. The lady would never acknowledge her but Georgina knew those high-tone bitches, as she thought of them, envied her attire, her sure sense of line as well as adornment. And Georgina paid the milliner extra to be certain that her hats outshone everyone else's, whether it be the wife of a banker, a lawyer, a preacher, or yet another politician on the make. Apart from the poundage, she was attractive, in her middle age, her mind most of all. She missed nothing. Given her business she heard a great deal. Men enlivened by good drink and the ministrations of a beautiful woman often become indiscreet.

She knew Sam Udall's bank was growing. She also knew some of the more senior bankers, especially those tied to the old Tidewater families, were not growing yet seemed self-satisfied. The old money favored the status quo and the status quo suffered greatly during the war for independence. Udall, on the other hand, favored the new man, the businessman. If a bit of graft or payback greased the wheels of commerce, so be it. While he lacked social cachet, she felt he would eventually become the premier moneyman in Richmond. She liked knowing that. She especially liked knowing if she needed funds for expansion, they would be forthcoming at an attractive interest rate.

The new men did not have sons who would dissipate their fortunes. Often their sons worked with them. Dissipation would come with later generations—but they did have daughters, whom they needed to marry off at considerable expense.

Smiling as she opened the gate to the impressive but unadorned three-story home, she paused to consider her portico. Needed something.

Opening the door, she heard an argument upstairs. Removing her hat, she climbed the stairs, stopping outside Deborah's room.

"If you're my wife, you do as I say," Binky hollered.

"But I'm not your wife!"

"But you will be. I will make money. There's more than one way to skin a cat," he shouted.

"Binky, don't be a fool. We have it good here. I don't want to leave. I don't want to work my fingers to the bone, even if it's for my own business. This is good work. In time, I will consider what comes next."

"I come next."

"You have no trade. Your idea of money is to turn in a runaway slave, and let me tell you, Binky Watson, if you do that you will not live to see another dawn."

This had never occurred to the besotted youth. "Kill me? Who would kill me?"

"Any slave in Richmond. Don't be a damned fool."

"I'm free."

"So you may be, but you ought to have the sense to know who your people are. I've heard enough of this. It's time for midday meal."

"You don't work midday." He pouted.

"I will today. It feels like spring. The men will be in here like rutting rams. And this weekend, the money will roll in."

Georgina stepped back, a slight smile on her face. Deborah was no silly whore. The woman had brains as well as compelling allure. She could use Deborah in better fashion than she had. Quietly she descended the stairs.

A door opened as she reached the halfway mark. Lolo Thompson, fully dressed but barefoot, opened her door, peeked out, saw it was the boss, hurried down the steps.

"Miss Georgina."

"You look good in lavender, dear."

"Thank you," she whispered. "I have a rash."

"For how long?"

"A week. I thought it would go away." Her blue eyes implored forgiveness.

Forgiveness did not enter the equation. Profit did.

"I'll send a message to Dr. Foster. It may just be fabric is irritating you or something you're eating, but let's be sure."

"Shall I work the midday meal?"

"Of course. If someone wishes for you," she paused, "after dessert, surely you can find ways to please him without a full-scale assault." She smiled broadly.

As Georgina repaired to her office, Lolo dashed back upstairs to finish her hair, a simpler coiffure for daylight. For nighttime she'd have her lady's maid weave in gold thread or tiny stars. The candlelight reflected especially on the tiny stars.

While officially spring, the temperature nudged into the low fifties but would drop tonight, turning to a light frost. Her fireplace kept the room warm. Georgina prided herself on the rug in her office, a purchase from a faltering French count six months ago. She felt it would not have been out of place at Versailles although she would be, then again perhaps not.

A knock on her door brought forth a sigh. She had hoped to read a bit before customers arrived for their twelve-o'clock meal.

"Come in."

Deborah, ravishing in a rose dress perfect for the day, too simple for the night. "I'm sorry to disturb you."

"Come in. Sit down." She reached for her enamel snuffbox, a small pretty thing that could be slipped into a pocket or bodice.

Deborah shook her head as Georgina offered her a pinch. "Binky shouldn't cause us trouble."

"I'm glad to hear that, but I doubt he has lost his passion for you."

Deborah waved her hand. "That. No. But I told him he wouldn't live if he turned in runaways. You know, he never thought of that. He's a dear boy but dim-witted."

"Why did you ever take up with him?"

"He's a pretty thing." She shrugged. "And he can make me laugh, or he used to be able to make me laugh before he started babbling about love."

"Ah." Georgina closed her eyes for a moment as the delight of the nicotine hit her.

"You said I should marry him if I have to keep him quiet. If I do, I'll be the one that kills him." She laughed.

Eyes wide open now, Georgina responded. "Tell me, do you believe in love?"

"No" came the instant forthright reply.

"Neither do I. What do you believe in?"

"Freedom" came even faster than the "No."

"Mmm, one always wishes to do as one pleases but," Georgina shrugged, "it is rare, is it not?"

"Still better than answering master."

"No doubt." Georgina studied the beauty before her.

"I'll do my best with Binky for now."

"And I appreciate it. Deborah, you drive the men wild, which I'm sure you know. These are uncertain times, and the best way to deal with uncertainty is to be well funded."

A broad smile crossed Deborah's perfect face. "Yes."

"Listen. Listen," she said in a softer voice. "They may speak to you or perhaps you can ask a question, innocent enough. For instance, should you be in Sam Udall's company, perhaps he will reveal where he invests the money. How much business does he do in England? What are they buying over there? Just a thought. He is uncommonly shrewd."

"As are you," Deborah complimented her.

"I will, of course, reward you, especially if the information proves profitable."

"Thank you." Deborah rose, leaned toward Georgina slightly. "Money rules the world. I look at some of the girls and I think they are fools who will wind up in the gutter or in some shanty with four kids hanging on their apron strings. Most of them think they will eventually be kept by one of the rich white men." She dropped her voice. "Never. Never. They don't realize that much of this business is novelty, the new girl."

This surprised the boss. "Well, there is some truth to that. But you need never fear, not with your presence and manners."

"The years will catch me out. Not one of us escapes Father Time, but Miss Georgina, I make you a promise, I will never be poor. Never."

Georgina looked at her girl steadily, then replied, "I have made myself that same promise."

As Deborah left the office, Mignon finished reading the first page of a book Eudes had brought for her. On the right-hand side of the book a drawing of a lion, a thorn being pulled from its paw by a human, complemented the text, which she read haltingly.

"Good." He smiled as the wall clock struck eleven. "Time to work."

"Do you think he really pulled a thorn from a lion's paw?"

"I don't know. I never met any lions." He laughed.

They wiped down the table one more time, brought out a large number of lamb chops, which Eudes rubbed with a bit of pepper.

"Mint jelly?" she asked.

"Right."

They labored in harmony, chattering away. He paused to look at her for a moment, realizing he would do anything to protect her, for he, too, had seen the sheet describing her. Then it hit him. He was in love with her.

34

November 12, 2016 Saturday

"Do you really think this is art?" Harry whispered to Susan and BoomBoom.

"Lovely workmanship," Susan replied.

"But that's not art." Harry folded her arms across her chest.

BoomBoom chimed in. "These shirts and dresses have a religious significance. So to the Plains Indians it's more than art."

Susan studied the beautiful warrior shirt, dyed a turquoise that had stayed bright since the 1870s, and beadwork of exquisite quality. "Maybe the question is would a Lakota think Titian's paintings are art? Isn't it all related to one's background?"

"Well, it is but no one is going to convince me that blown-up comic strips are art." BoomBoom laughed as they left the front exhibition room, walked down the corridor, and she opened the door to the sculpture garden, a favorite with Richmonders.

The Virginia Museum of Fine Arts on 200 N. Boulevard in Richmond had changed dramatically in the last twenty years. One's membership card reflected one's interests. European, African, Asian art, et cetera, would be cited on the card, and the mailings, often colorful and informative, arrived in the mailbox at regular intervals.

Children's programs, senior discounts, changing displays for the various categories kept the place full even in the middle of the week. There were even painting and drawing classes.

The gardens provided one with the fleeting embrace of living plants and flowers as well as more permanent sculptures. Benches allowed one to sit and look and learn.

The day, low sixties, was probably the last of the warmer days, a sweater or a thin coat sufficed. Soon enough the winds would blow steady, the mercury hang in the forties. When winter truly arrived the forties seemed benevolent. This would be a goodbye to sitting outside.

"Hey, there's Bill Hall and Willoughby." Harry noticed a now-retired fellow who worked harder than when employed.

"And Beverly Ely." BoomBoom knew the Charlottesville doctor. "Whoever they're talking to must have spent a fortune on that outfit."

"Maybe she's one of those people who can pull something off the rack and look terrific." Susan mused. "An enviable trait."

"That's Marvella Lawson," Harry informed them as they walked over.

"Bill, allow us to intrude," Susan opened the conversation as BoomBoom and Beverly hugged.

The handsome fellow stood up, kissed the ladies, one of the joys of being a gentleman, and introduced Susan and BoomBoom to Marvella Rice Lawson.

Harry said it was good to see Marvella, who said the same regarding Harry.

The silver-haired patrician lady smiled, clearly happy to meet new people.

"We were just discussing the seventeenth-century floral paintings. So vivid you felt you could touch them." Marvella smiled.

"And so many of them painted by women. Put on a lower rung of art because of it. Whenever there's an exhibition about people kept from their passion but who manage anyway, it always gets me." Bill offered his seat to Marvella, who sat down with a begging Willoughby at her feet.

"You are not sitting in Marvella's lap," Bill intoned.

Willoughby did not sit in the lady's lap, but he focused on the other women just to ignore his human.

They chattered on about what they'd seen, why they traveled down to Richmond today, when Marvella looked at the group.

"There's room if anyone else is a bit weary." She patted the bench.

"Thank you, Mrs. Lawson. I actually am." BoomBoom sank next to the tall woman, two beauties sitting side by side. "We started a discussion but never finished. In a sense it's what is art? Is the gorgeous skin shirt of a Plains brave the same as a painting by Rubens?"

"Boom, Mrs. Lawson and Beverly may not want to dive into such a loaded discussion." Harry smiled, then looked at Bill. "He, of course, will talk about anything."

They all laughed, for Bill was fearless. They knew not to ask him a question if they didn't want to know what he really thought.

"In some ways that's the same question as what is beauty," Marvella calmly began. "Some would say it's structure, harmony, line, color, and subject matter. It's the last that raises the hackles. Subject matter. Think of Mamma Sugar in the warehouse. You all remember the uproar. The black mammy sphinx with a head rag in the old sugar factory."

"Yes. I thought it was spectacular," Susan replied. "And political."

"That's where the problem lies. Is a shirt art? Doesn't that depend on who makes it?" Bill put his hand on Willoughby's head.

"And who buys it," Harry shrewdly added.

They all talked at once, invigorated, interested in one another's thoughts.

"My brother and I loved art but we had vastly opposite tastes. He would purchase a Frederick Church whereas I stayed with European art, especially the nineteenth century. Pierre reached the point where he could appreciate my views and I could appreciate his. I admit that took us until our late thirties." She laughed. "Did you know him?"

Harry, who had known Marvella from fund-raisers, which is to say, not well, knew Pierre but was not going to say "I saw your brother's body in a small covert of trees," so she replied, "I didn't but I have seen his art collection. My neighbor made a copy of a video that she showed me. I was an art history major at Smith. It truly is impressive." She paused. "And I'm sorry for your loss."

Marvella's distinguished face softened. "Thank you."

Beverly spoke up. "Marvella, Bill, and I knew one another through Pierre. He nudged me to collecting on a small scale. Actually, Marvella, Pierre, and I often wound up talking about what is art, how the market distorts not just value but cultural integrity.

"About six months ago we somehow stumbled onto the subject of prices and Pierre told us that something like the turquoise warrior's shirt in the museum would sell for over a hundred thousand dollars." Beverly's eyes widened.

"Wouldn't something like that be easier to fake than, say, Stubbs?" Harry loved sporting art.

"We all didn't get that far," Marvella answered, "but I think it would be. With a painting you'd have to copy the painter's style and use paints from the period. You might have to mix powders and egg white and God knows what else. With a deerskin or beaded shoes one would need to age the leather, use beads from the period, but it might be easier."

Bill stepped in. "Still, where would you find someone who could do the work?"

"Well, I suppose forgers in their own way are almost as talented as the people they are imitating." Susan wedged on the edge of the bench.

"Wouldn't it be easier to use your talents in your own time?" BoomBoom wondered. "Not imitating another epoch?"

"How do you make a name for yourself?" Marvella said. "If you fake something that artist's name is already valued."

Bill then added, "Inside that building some of those works are worth millions. I guess that's plenty of motive."

"Even for tribal clothing and jewelry?" BoomBoom asked.

"Well, if something sells for a hundred thousand dollars and it's expected that the creator is unknown, maybe that's the easiest to fake or forge. Who really was the creator?" Susan replied.

"I don't know." BoomBoom watched a pigeon waddle closer as did Willoughby. "If you're caught, game over, jail. If you cross the wrong parties, zip, they slit your throat."

Everyone looked at her, the same disquieting thought running through their heads except for Willoughby's. That thought being, might this have something to do with Pierre's murder? It was either that, art, a subject about that Pierre knew a great deal, or he had stumbled onto some other form of wrongdoing that generated enormous sums.

Marvella finally gave voice to the thought. "I wonder if my brother was trailing a forger? Looking back, it's possible. Sometimes one can't see what's under one's nose."

"Not me," Willoughby bragged.

35

A week passed since the spring equinox. Daffodils swayed in the light breeze, buds swelled a dark red on trees, a few opened revealing fresh spring green color. Ewing decided a celebration was in order. He'd sent out handwritten invitations on creamy paper one week ago. Each invitation had been hand delivered by a well-dressed slave. Naturally, these tasks proved competitive as everyone wanted to travel, gossip with the other people on the various estates. Then again, being entrusted with such a mission, being well dressed, carried status, a lot of it.

Weymouth, Jeddie, Barker O., Serena, and Bettina performed this task. Bettina and Barker O. traveled together in the simple elegant low coach, which he drove. As Barker O. would also be inquiring about how long Maureen Selisse needed their borrowed elegant coach, Bettina could deliver the invitation to the big house along with some biscuits just to remind Maureen's cook that she didn't know squat. Tulli, for the very first time, wearing a smart cropped navy jacket, rode Sweet Potato while Jeddie rode Crown Prince. On a rawhide string around his neck

Tulli wore his brass chit, Number Fifteen. It was the first time he was so entrusted.

Roger double-checked everyone before their journey. As the butler he would not be asked to deliver messages. A butler was not a messenger, no matter how pleasant the task may prove. Weymouth tucked Number Four in his pocket; Jeddie had Number Five; Barker O., Number Seven; Serena, Number Eleven; and Bettina, Number Twelve.

They spent all of the day and early evening delivering the messages, a drop of wax sealing the invitation envelope eagerly opened as the messenger stood there. An instant reply spared the recipient taking the time to send one of their people. Every single person accepted.

This meant today, March 28, a long line of carriages, phaetons, simple carts, riders on horses came down the tree-lined drive to Cloverfields. The boys in the barns took the carriages and horses after the guests disembarked at the main house. They'd wisely emptied out stalls, moving Cloverfields horses to the back pastures. They also moved some turned-out horses to the back pastures. Jeddie, Ralston, Tulli, and Barker O. didn't have a minute to sit, dealing with each guest's servant if one came along. Even Mr. Percy, Bumbee's errant husband, was pressed into service. The good thing about the number of guests was that these men would enjoy tips, lots of tips.

Given the crush of people, the doors at the house remained open in the back, windows up. Everyone walked outside to see the sunset, a fan of flames edged in gold. The light shone on Isabelle's tomb, the recumbent lamb with a cross across its forelegs.

Inside, the servants lit the chandeliers, the candles on the table, the sconces. As the temperature dropped, the fires flickered in the fireplaces; the guests, each lady on the arm of a gentleman, promenaded into the huge dining room. Bumbee organized the

floral arrangements. The woman had a gift with color, shape, didn't matter the element.

The governor sat on Ewing's right, a wealthy visiting rice planter from Charleston, South Carolina, sat on the host's left. At the opposite end of the table, Catherine acted as hostess. Rachel was two guests down from her sister. Their husbands sat where they could do the most good. Charles found himself next to Maureen Selisse, near Ewing, with Jeffrey across the table from her. When Catherine and Rachel planned the seating, ever a difficult chore, they made certain to keep Yancy Grant as far away from Jeffrey Holloway as possible.

Conversation flowed as freely as the wine, perhaps because of the wine.

"And did you see Beaumarchis's latest play when you were in France?" Maureen inquired of Christopher Shippenworth, a guest from Philadelphia.

"I had the pleasure, Madam, but the news now is that he has gone too far," the silk-clad fellow remarked.

All down the table, discussion of opera, poetry, horses, trade, new piers being built in New York City, the miserable condition of roads throughout the former colonies, expansion into the western territories, the chatter was punctuated with laughter, toasts. By the time dessert was served, an exquisite crème brûlée with a drizzle of raspberry sauce, everyone felt this was a spring party to be remembered.

Although the robins had arrived weeks before, Catherine, Rachel, and Bettina thought of this as their robin party.

Maureen tortured herself because she wanted to top this social event, but what cook could compare to Bettina? Well, she had to do it so she determined to hire a culinary wizard from France. Expensive but she just had to. The drizzle of raspberry and perhaps the last glass of wine inflamed her in this ambition. Where did Ewing get this wine?

The other guests, not fueling social ambitions, paid court to the governor and his wife as well as the people from Charleston and Philadelphia. One must ever expand one's list of acquaintances.

In the main kitchen, the outside kitchen also in use, slaves bussed back and forth. Bettina, a general in the midst of battle, gave orders, walked between the kitchens, declared this needed a pinch of basil, that a dusting of powdered sugar, and the raspberry sauce, when dessert was served, she drizzled herself from a crystal pitcher, the sauce having been made on the estate, stored in the pantry like the canned foods.

Serena, hurrying as another round of dessert toasts were given, gushed, "Bettina, a triumph!"

Bettina, holding a special woven basket covered in a cloth, glowed. "Serena, where's Grace?"

Just then, the young lithe girl, the one whose mother felt she should marry Jeddie, burst into the kitchen, "Oh, Bettina. Everyone sings your praises."

"That's always good to hear. Now, you take this basket to DoRe, he's in the stable. And, Serena, they've all been fed?"

"Were and we even made sure the house folks had a set table. Even Sheba, who says she just has to talk to you about the stuffed capons. I told her you'd been in the kitchen since dawn." Serena smiled.

"Ha!" Bettina laughed.

As the women in the kitchen began to damp down the stoves, put up what little food remained, the men servants waited for the guests to repair to the smoking room while the ladies would go to the east parlor. Once there, they'd enjoy one another, then join together for perhaps a half hour before their carriages rolled up to the front door. People would recall everything they could to one another on the journeys home.

Ewing picked a long broom straw out of a narrow brass can near the fireplace, leaned over to set it alight then touched it to his pipe, one long draw and the tobacco caught, a tendril of smoke floating upward. He threw the straw into the fire. Other men followed suit as Weymouth brought in extra decanters, placing them on the long hunt table.

Christopher Shippenworth talked to the governor across the room.

Basil Sasilieri, the Charleston planter, pipe also in his mouth, walked up to Ewing.

"Mr. Garth, beautiful ladies, excellent food, bracing companionship, thank you for your hospitality."

"Basil, I'm just trying to catch up to you gentlemen from Charleston." He chuckled. "Tell me, Sir, are these currency irregularities affecting business?"

Basil sucked one long puff, removed his pipe. "Affecting, I'd say depressing. Rice, as you know, is not an easy crop. One starts the season with one set of numbers and ends it with another, lower. I don't see how we can continue. A man can't expand, but I'm sure this affects each of us in the room."

Ewing nodded, then observed Jeffrey Holloway pull out a heavy gold pocket watch, lift open the cover to check the time against the large grandfather clock.

Lowering his voice, Ewing remarked, "Why would any sensible man wish to be hagridden by minutes and hours? This incessant looking at new timepieces baffles me. It's enough to have a clock in the house, but to carry one around." He smiled slightly. "The times are changing but time is not."

Basil nodded. "These things come and go. As for time, well, I feel it in the morning when I get out of bed."

They laughed, treading the common ground of middle age.

Jeffrey Holloway, in rapt talk with Charles concerning design, architecture, halted a moment as Yancy Grant joined them. He nodded as custom dictated to Jeffrey, then spoke to Charles.

"Charles, your St. Luke's covers much ground. The stonework will take a great deal of time."

"That it will, but the foundation is dug, as you may have seen, and the two buildings at the end of what will be connected by arcades, that also is dug out. Now comes the real work." He grinned. "Perhaps it's because this is a church, but we work together, sing as we work, very different than what would occur in England."

"Do you ever miss it?" Jeffrey asked.

"Sometimes, perhaps Christmas, I miss hearing the bells peal in the village, but gentlemen," he looked from one to another, "my wife was worth crossing an ocean, fighting a war to find. Sometimes I wonder at my good fortune."

Jeffrey smiled. "You are indeed fortunate."

Yancy snorted. "You, too, Sir. You fell into the honeypot."

Such rudeness startled both of the younger men.

"Charles, excuse me while I take my leave." Jeffrey half bowed to Charles as Yancy grabbed his elbow.

"I know you've seen Sam Udall, the banker, and I know where you've seen him. How would your rich wife like that?"

"Yancy, that is enough." Charles firmly stepped between the two men.

John, noticing the tension, walked over to his brother-in-law's side. Yancy was either too drunk or too angry or both to care.

"Holloway, you've taken advantage of Maureen. You're spending her money without a single idea of how to replenish it and you consort with whores in Richmond and—"

He didn't finish because Jeffrey hit him with a right cross to the jaw. Yancy crumpled like a linen napkin.

Charles knelt over the unconscious man as others gathered around.

"I'll kill him." Jeffrey lunged for the supine man.

John, tall and enormously strong, put his hands on Jeffrey's upper arms, clamped them to his sides. "You will not."

Jeffrey, lifted up like a small boy, was carried out of the room. He had sense to be quiet. John carried him outside and in doing so, two of Cloverfields' larger men swiftly hurried to John's side.

"Let's walk him down to the stables. DoRe can handle him," John advised.

"I don't need handling. That son of a bitch. He's been after my wife's money even while Francisco lived. Furthermore, I am not lying with whores in Richmond!" He was about to sputter more when John silenced him.

Tulli, lantern in hand, scurried out of the stable upon hearing John approach.

"Tulli, fetch some ice." He then released his grip on Jeffrey's left arm. "Steady. Steady. That's what I used to tell my men as we marched toward fire. Your wife may have heard three or four versions of what happened before she arrives down here. Allow as how you lost your temper, how you can't stand Grant's overzealous desire toward her. If she asks questions, try to answer them. If not, especially if she asks about Richmond, say nothing. Forgive me for giving orders."

"You are a major." Jeffrey had regained his composure.

John smiled. "And I have been married longer than you. I expect Mrs. Holloway will be down shortly or DoRe will bring the coach up to the house if you so deem."

"Sir." Tulli led Jeffrey on.

"Put his hand in ice, Tulli," John ordered.

———

Back in the house, Charles called Rachel from the ladies' gathering, briefly told her of what had transpired, and suggested she wait with Maureen while DoRe brought up the coach.

Maureen, center of the drama although she wasn't sure about it, did gather that her husband had belted Yancy Grant unconscious. This display of violence did not displease her.

Back at the carriage, the boys brought up the Selisse carriage from the carriage house, DoRe donned his livery. He tucked Bettina's basket into a wooden box affixed to the side of the carriage, stepped up, felt the smooth reins in his hand, clucked, and they moved forward toward the house, Jeffrey in the carriage, his hand in a small bucket of ice.

Once at the front door, Rachel, now assisted by Sheba, brought up from the women's servants quarters, stood with Maureen. Sheba already soaked up as much as she could. Finally she had a wedge she could drive between husband and wife. No one was going to control the Missus but Sheba.

Rachel walked down the steps, stood at the carriage door while one of the Cloverfields men, in Cloverfields' livery, Prussian blue and gold, opened the door for Mrs. Selisse as he dropped the brass steps from the carriage for her.

"Thank you. What a wonderful feast." Maureen squeezed Rachel's hand.

She then held the footman's gloved hand as he steadied her up the steps.

"Jeffrey, what have you done?"

"Something, my dear, I wish I had done months ago."

Sheba sulked outside the carriage, then Maureen indicated she could climb in and the footman assisted her.

John, walking briskly up from the stables, reached Rachel just as Catherine walked outside for a moment wondering what was afoot.

"Shall I assume the gathering is aflame?" John laughed.

Catherine answered. "Great excitement. We couldn't have asked for more."

Rachel laughed along with her sister. "No one will forget this spring celebration."

"Where is Yancy?" John felt the plunging temperature.

"Carried out to the brood mare barn and placed on a pallet in the tack room. He's still out cold. A blessing," Rachel answered.

A few snowflakes twirled down. They looked upward, seeing low clouds in the night sky. The snow in a minute began to fall faster.

"Good Lord," Rachel exclaimed. "Snow on the daffodils."

"We'd best inform our guests." Catherine felt John's strong arm around her waist, glad for his warmth, as they climbed the stairs. "What a surprise."

There were more to come.

36

"We've kept track of the bald eagle nest in Sugar Hollow," MaryJo Cranston reported. "All eaglets survived and I wouldn't be surprised if more eagles come in this far."

"Why?" BoomBoom asked.

"They've made a big comeback on the James River and the Chesapeake. More population usually means looking for more suitable places to nest. Anyway, all good news," MaryJo responded.

The Virginians for Sustainable Wildlife met this Tuesday at Susan Tucker's. Each month they marveled at how quickly the time had flown by. The reports made, accepted, they finally broke for drinks, food.

Mrs. Murphy, Pewter, Tucker, and Susan's wonderful corgi, Owen, full brother to Tucker, shot into the dining room.

"Sounds like a stampede," Liz Potter noted.

Tucker ever so helpfully spoke up from under the table. *"That's all Pewter. Two-Ton Tessie."*

"Die, dog!" Pewter whapped the dog right across her tender nose.

"Ow. *I'm mortally wounded by a psychotic cat,*" Tucker wailed.

"*Oh, Tucker, when will you learn to leave her alone?*" the corgi's brother reprimanded her.

Mrs. Murphy, never one for these dramatics, sat beside Harry's chair just in case a moment of sharing would wash over the humans engaged in chatter.

"*I smell ham.*" Pewter, happy to have smacked Tucker, sidled up to Dr. Jessica Ligon.

Being a veterinarian might have inoculated the young woman from falling victim to Pewter's charms but, no, she slipped the cat a morsel of ham.

The back door opened, Ned's baritone rang out. "I'm home."

"We're in the dining room," Susan called out as Ned walked in, said his hellos, and joined them.

"I am starved. That damned city council meeting droned on and on and on. I should be paid by the hour. I try to attend one a quarter, give reports from the House of Delegates, but I might just change my mind."

"You are a good public servant," Susan informed him.

As he took a seat next to BoomBoom, the tall beauty remarked, "Isn't the budget in trouble? I mean, didn't they cut the municipal band? Cutting one of the activities that brought us all together."

"The budget is always in trouble." MaryJo shrugged. "Show me a political meeting where there isn't hand-wringing and finger-pointing."

"What we need is a good sex scandal. That will wake us up." BoomBoom laughed.

"Don't look at me." Ned held up his hands in innocence. "I married the best girl in the county."

The ladies applauded and Susan laughed even as she filled a plate for him. He could fill his own plate but she was watching his sugar intake. While he was in good shape, diabetes ran in Ned's family.

"Anything good happen at the meeting?" Jessica inquired.

"Yes, well, the beginning of good things. I first gave a report of how things are going at the House of Delegates, my usual report. Then I presented your ideas, those of you on Save Our Old Schools, concerning rotating studies there so young people could learn about the past."

Harry perked right up. "And?"

"Here's how any new idea is greeted. First, silence. Then someone says we should study that. Someone else remarks money would need to be spent so bathrooms would be in order, the woodburning stoves checked for leakage and healthy inhalation."

Susan said, "Do we need birth certificates? Is the city going to fret over gender?"

"God, we haven't reached that point. This is only the beginning but I'm sure a lively discussion of young people's gender will ensue. However, no one instantly opposed the idea. I didn't even feel that slight resentment from a council member that this wasn't his idea first."

Cooper knocked on the back door, letting herself in. "The law."

"We've got our hands up," Ned teased as everyone raised their hands when the deputy came into the room.

"Sorry I'm late." She gratefully sank into a chair.

"Big day?" Harry asked her neighbor.

"No more than usual, but I finished up over at St. Luke's. Two tombstones were knocked over. Reverend Jones said this is the second time."

Ned put down the pickled egg he was about to eat. "Not Michael and Margaret Taylor's?"

"How did you know?" the deputy asked him.

"Fair and I put it back up. If we'd used the front-end loader, we might have harmed the stone."

"I saw it when I was in the second story of the western part of the main church." Harry thought a moment. "October 15, 1786. There were odd marks in the dirt over the grave, like knife thrusts. Or that's what it looked like to me."

"You don't think the stone could have gouged the soil?" MaryJo stated an obvious thought.

"No. These were thin marks just like a knife. No one thought too much about it but it would seem that grave exerts a fascination," Harry offered.

"*Oh, no.*" Mrs. Murphy groaned.

"*Maybe she'll forget it.*" Tucker gulped a bit of cheese.

"*Ha. Fat chance.*" Pewter tossed her head, looking lovingly up at Jessica.

"Maybe there's something in that grave." Harry's mind started spinning.

"Two old dead people." MaryJo laughed.

"Well, yes." Harry smiled. "But all those stories about buried treasure at the various estates, at The Barracks, well, maybe there's treasure at St. Luke's."

Ned remarked with quiet authority, "You'd need to come up with a compelling reason to exhume the Taylors. I say let them rest in peace."

"I don't know. I mean, yes, we shouldn't disturb the dead but there have been odd, disconnected things. The driver with his face torn off—"

Cooper jumped in. "Harry, that was ruled a . . . shall we say death by misadventure. Something wild killed him. It doesn't appear to be murder."

"Okay. But Pierre Rice *was* murder and then his Tahoe was

found at the old school with a wire cage in the back, eagle feathers inside. And the gravestones got knocked over twice."

"If someone thought something was in there, don't you think they'd be digging?" BoomBoom interjected.

"Maybe they were interrupted or maybe there wasn't time. I don't know. I'm just thinking out loud," Harry said just as the house shook slightly, the windowpanes rattled ominously.

Ned leapt up, hurried to the window while Susan punched into The Weather Channel on her phone.

MaryJo felt the wind hit the house. "Crazy weather. You know, I'd ask a meteorologist if there were severe crosswinds where that Volvo transport was found. Driver could have pulled over to get out of the wind, stepped outside from curiosity." She paused. "Just a thought."

Another blast pounded the house.

"Ladies, get home while the getting is good. The Weather Chanel reports high winds followed by lashing rains and flooding. Came up out of nowhere."

Ned turned back from the window. "Looks ugly."

"Wasn't on my app before," BoomBoom complained.

Susan advised, "Girls, go on while you have a chance. I'll clean up." She held up her hands before anyone could protest.

MaryJo took her coat from Susan, as did Jessica, who also had a hike to get home to Nelson County.

Harry carried dishes back to the kitchen, helped by Cooper. They left last, but within fifteen minutes of the others, as they worked fast.

Heads down they ran for their cars, winds ferocious.

Cooper, driving a squad SUV, hollered to Harry, "I'll go first. If I stop just wait behind me."

Mrs. Murphy, Pewter, and Tucker flew into the car as the door was opened and Harry slid behind the driver's seat.

"Black as the Devil's eyebrows," Harry commented to her animals, who hunched down in the seat.

As she drove out she felt a hard thump behind her but kept going. She wasn't dragging anything and a heavy tree branch hadn't landed on the back of the Volvo.

It wasn't until the next morning, fields soaked, some trees down, as she walked out to the barn that she noticed a hole at the rear of the Volvo.

"That looks like a bullet hole," she said to Tucker.

It was.

37

November 16, 2016 Wednesday

Sitting at the kitchen table, overcast skies adding to the gloom, Fair faced Cooper. Susan was also there. Harry put her hand over her husband's.

"Honey, don't get so upset. Your blood pressure will shoot up."

"Upset. A bullet's dug out from the seat of your station wagon. Yes, I'm upset. Someone shot at you. They didn't take a shot at Cooper, driving ahead of you. They waited for you. If it hadn't been raining so hard, who knows?" He squeezed her hand.

Susan, who had come to take Harry for her six-month cancer checkup, arrived early because her best friend called her, informing her of last night's event, accident, attempted what? Murder?

"Fair, I can't snap my fingers to give you an answer. The bullet will be traced, if possible. We sent the team out first thing this morning and we're fortunate it entered the side of the seat, the entry clearly visible." Cooper wanted to soothe her beloved neighbor, a wonderful man.

"*Dad's really upset.*" Tucker, under the table, cast her eyes upward.

"Just think. I could have been in the backseat." Pewter's green eyes widened.

"Pewter!" Mrs. Murphy bared her fangs for a moment.

"Well, I could have died," the gray cat whined.

"And so could Harry." Tucker was as worried as Fair.

"Why would someone shoot at the Volvo when Mom leaves her Virginia Wildlife meeting?" Mrs. Murphy, always thoughtful, moved closer to Harry's leg as the human sat in the chair.

"Let's review this again," Cooper calmly ordered. "The meeting broke up due to the weather. Who left first? MaryJo, then I think it was Jessica Ligon."

Susan nodded. "Jessica had the most distance to travel. Pretty much Jessica and MaryJo left together, followed closely by Liz. That's what I remember."

"Me, too," Harry confirmed.

Cooper, writing this down in her reporter's notebook, exhaled through her nose. "All right. I will call them to see if each recalls who drove out first. Did they see another car at the end of the driveway, on the dirt road leading out to the paved road? It's possible their headlights caught sight of another car."

"How anyone could see anything, I don't know." Harry remembered the wind and terrible, instant downpour.

"Still, it's possible a glint of headlight off chrome. Now, look, I don't want you two," Cooper pointed at Harry and Susan with her mechanical pencil, "calling them. That's my job. And since no one was hurt, let's keep this away from the papers."

"What do I tell my insurance agent?" Harry's agent, Marsha Moran at Hanckle Citizens, would need information, plus once Harry started talking to Marsha, she couldn't stop. The woman always made her laugh.

"Can you wait a day? I should know my insurance rules better.

But if not, I will also call Hanckle Citizens. It won't take us long to trace the bullet if it can be traced, thanks to the computer. Even ten years ago this would have dragged on. One good thing is arms manufacturers respond almost instantly to law enforcement requests. Obviously, the real problem is secondhand gun dealers."

"Then what?" Fair frowned.

"We take it a step at a time. If the bullet can't be traced to a registered gun, we contact dealers. Many are helpful. The ones that aren't are almost always selling stolen merchandise. We have to prove it. Don't get me going on this. It's a problem across the nation, but as I said, many dealers and also manufacturers are responsible and easy to work with." She looked into his eyes. "Fair, of course you're worried but you know Sheriff Shaw and I will be on it."

Susan reached down to pet Tucker, who came out from under the table. "Coop, there's no way this can be an accident."

A long pause followed, then the deputy spoke. "It does seem unlikely."

Harry raised her voice. "I haven't meddled in anything. I haven't asked a bunch of questions about the private eye, really. I've not interfered. I've been good."

Cooper smiled. "For you, yes."

"Honey," Harry said to her husband, "go on to work. Susan's driving me to the doctor for my checkup. Cooper will be tracing the bullet. I'll be fine."

Later, Harry and Susan stopped at the club for lunch. Susan had waited while Harry endured the boob squisher, had her blood drawn, the usual. The oncologist's office was in the same building as Dr. Beverly Ely, Pierre Rice's dear friend.

The mammogram came out clear, nothing to worry about. The blood test results would take a day. For whatever reason, the day proved busy at the doctor's office.

Harry, attacking a Cobb salad, felt relief. So did Susan.

"Good?" Susan pointed to the salad as she lifted her enormous Reuben.

"It's worth driving across town to Keswick Club for the Cobb salad. I keep forgetting to ask you, how do you like the new Pete Dye course?"

"It makes you think, which I like. I've only played it once and that was with Cindy Chandler so we buzzed around in the golf cart, but next time I'll use you for my caddy. You can see for yourself."

"Mmm." Harry bit into the egg on her salad. "People say Pete Dye courses are unforgiving."

Susan put down her sandwich, wiped her fingers on her linen napkin. "This isn't an easy course, but I don't think it's punishing."

"You're the champion at Farmington. Of course, you wouldn't think it's punishing." Harry smiled at her friend.

"That's good of you to say, especially since you bitch and moan at me when you caddy for me."

"Someone has to do it." Harry laughed, as did Susan.

"Like I said, you have to think. If you're a strong player and you take the more difficult shot and you make it, great. If you're fool-hardy and overestimate what you can do, this course can cost you but any course can. I often think one of the keys to playing golf is not just your strokes but the ability to read terrain. Funny, but that's where our foxhunting pays off. You pay attention to swales, reverse ridges, soil. And that reminds me, we haven't gone out much this season. Hope the weather improves so we can."

"Me, too."

Both hunted. Of course, no foxes were killed. Americans don't hunt to kill, which isn't to say sometimes a fox zigs when he should have zagged. Every now and then one does run a dumb fox, but in the main, they are frighteningly intelligent.

Neither women discussed Harry's results. They were happy when the mammogram was good. Harry was almost at the five-year mark since her breast cancer surgery. Relief was palpable. When Harry awoke from her surgery back then, her husband and her best friend waited in the room. She opened her eyes to the two faces she loved most in life except for those on four feet.

Harry always accompanied Susan for her mammograms, as well. One could go alone but it was one of those procedures where a friend lightened the load. Should the nurse return and say you needed a second mammogram, your friend was there with you. A second was rarely good news.

They listened to the fire in the fireplace, nodded to the other people in the grille, looked out on the course, wrapped in November gray.

"Susan." Harry's voice carried a tone of seriousness.

"What?"

"What could we be doing at Virginians for Sustainable Wildlife that would threaten someone?"

"I don't know. Ned's efforts for Save the Old Schools, seems to me, would provoke some negative response. But since Tazio, all of us have been working on that, there hasn't been much pushback. I mean there's always the possible nutcase."

"Well, Pierre Rice's Tahoe was found in the shed."

Susan shook her head. "That whole thing, the murder, the car showing up later, the chit around his neck, the cage, it's like a dense fog. I can't see anything."

"So, you believe that shot was meant for me."

Susan replied, "Well—yes."

"Here's the thing. If it was meant to warn me, warn me of what?"

"That's just it, isn't it?"

"And here's the other thing. If someone wasn't waiting for the meeting to break up, waiting in the dark which turned into a nasty storm, then whoever fired that shot was at the meeting."

A very long pause followed this. "That has occurred to me."

38

March 29, 1786 Wednesday

*P*iglet felt a tiny hexagonal snowflake on his nose. The snow had fallen off and on since last night, sometimes heavy other times almost a fine mist. The dog trotted along a cleared path to the mares' stable, the accumulation reaching six inches.

He gratefully ducked into the stables, and hearing voices in the tack room, headed there. Charles, Jeddie, and Ralston sat around the small fireplace. The boys cleaned tack while Charles sat across from them, his drawings rolled up, placed on a low wooden table.

"Piglet." Charles smiled.

"You left me. I was fast asleep under the kitchen table." The dog sat next to his human.

"Do you think he'll do it? A duel?" Charles returned to Jeddie.

The young man nodded. "Hot temper."

"Why die for a drunken insult?" Charles took off his gloves, unrolled his drawings, changed the subject. "Here. If we build a carriage house at a right angle to the carriage barn, we'll create a windbreak. Back home stables and kennels are often built around a square area, so three buildings open onto this area, the new building at a right angle." He scribbled at the edge of one of the papers. "Everything is closer, less time going between buildings and the buildings offer some protection from the weather. We've created a short courtyard. Two buildings at a right angle would be more proportionate but the cost will be a problem. Obviously, you can always use more stables."

Jeddie excitedly looked over the plans. "Cobblestone?"

"In the yard. Or brick. Easier to clean, stops the mud, the end-less mess of mud. With good workers, we can cut them, not so round. And see here," he pointed to the rear of the addition, "manure, straw can be taken out this way. Haul it to the midden pile and when my wife wants some for her garden, well, easy to do."

"Has Miss Catherine seen this?" Jeddie asked.

"She has. She wanted me to extend the roof a bit to provide more shade in the summer, keep the snow from sliding off the roof in front of the back stall doors."

"You've got those little clams." Ralston pointed to the fanciful snow holders on the roof.

"Do, but they can't hold back the heavy snows like we've been having." Charles looked out the window. "This one's not heavy but fine. It's almost April."

"Momma says we've had snowstorms in April." Jeddie offered the maternal observation.

"Jeddie's momma wants him to get married." Ralston smirked.

"Does she, now?" Charles smiled.

Jeddie, embarrassed, nodded. "Says a good wife will help me."

"True enough. Prospects?"

Jeddie blushed now. "Momma has some."

Both Charles and Ralston laughed, then Charles said, "Estima-ble girls, I'm sure, but I'd trust to lightning if I were you."

"Sir?" The slender fellow raised his eyebrows.

"Love can be like a lightning strike. You never know when it will hit you." Charles rolled up the papers. "No need to worry about it now. If it happens, you'll know."

"Sir, what if Yancy Grant really does challenge Jeffrey Holloway to a duel?" Ralston inquired.

"Hard to tell. I have no idea if Jeffrey knows how to use fire-arms. Given the circumstances, I would think it would be Jeffrey Holloway that challenges Yancy. Yancy accused him of some ne-farious things."

"What's nefarious?" Jeddie wondered.

"Bad, dark deeds. Man was a damned fool. Drunk." Charles shrugged.

"I never saw a duel," Ralston said.

"And you won't see this one either if it comes to pass. Duels are fought between the two men, weapons chosen by the man who is challenged so it could be a pistol or a sword. Each man is accompanied by a second, a friend who takes his coat, speaks to the other second, sets out the rules. Also a physician is in atten-dance, but spectators, no." Charles emphasized no.

"Do people ever get scared and run away?" Jeddie couldn't imagine standing there waiting to be shot or fighting by sword.

"No. Your honor is at stake, which is why duels are fought in the first place, or so the offended party believes."

Jeffrey Holloway considered his honor. His wife sat in the morn-ing room with him, breakfast on the table. Sheba hovered in the room, pretending to serve Maureen.

"Henry!" Maureen called.

"Yes, Ma'am." An elderly men appeared, wearing house clothes.

"I am freezing. Do something!"

"Yes, Ma'am." He bowed to his mistress, stepped outside the room.

Within minutes two young slaves carried hardwoods and more kindling to the fireplace. The surround was white marble. Her late husband, Francisco, declared a wooden surround not up to his standards. Once he visited upstate New York, beheld the tile that the Dutch used, he had to have that. His personal fireplace in his office was deep blue and white tile.

"I must challenge Yancy Grant. His conduct shocked me. Clearly he is given to both drink and fantasy."

"Do you know how to shoot?" Maureen sensibly asked.

"Not well. I can shoot, though. Father made me take fencing lessons—why, I don't know."

"But you won't be the one to select the weapons," Maureen clearly replied.

Sheba made sure she had heard the accusations Yancy leveled at her mistress's husband. Sheba also pressed that Maureen would be a laughingstock, she didn't say it that way, but that her mistress couldn't afford two philandering husbands. Her honor was at stake, too.

Sheba felt she was sitting in the catbird seat. Of course, Yancy would pick pistols and dispatch Jeffrey, who was holding too much sway over Maureen. Sooner or later, Sheba and Jeffrey would collide, so best to be rid of him now. Powerful though she was she remained a slave. The key to all this was Maureen.

"I thought I might ask John Schuyler to assist me in sharpening my skill," Jeffrey softly answered. "I can't let this go unanswered."

"What shall you do?" Maureen, disturbed by the low talk of Yancy Grant, nonetheless did not wish to lose her handsome younger husband.

"I will write a letter asking for satisfaction," he firmly spoke.

"And who shall be your second?"

"John Schuyler." He looked at his wife.

"He's certainly seen enough bloodshed," she remarked.

"Yes."

"I do hope what's shed is not yours. I can't understand why Yancy would accuse you of keeping low company." Her voice carried an edge.

"Maureen, I told you, yes, I was at Georgina's. I met with the banker, Udall, at his suggestion. I found out more about the tavern once I was there. Had I known, I would have asked for another place to meet."

Sheba, now standing behind Jeffrey, so she faced her mistress, raised her eyebrows just enough to indicate doubt, men are dogs, that sort of thing.

"I should like to see this place." Maureen startled them both.

"My dear. You can't possibly mean that." Jeffrey put his cup down so hard he nearly broke the good breakfast china.

"Yes, I would like to see it, perhaps even go inside." Her face hardened. "I can buy them all and consign them to hell if I choose. I can buy the house and burn it with them in it!"

"Sweetheart."

"If you have betrayed me, Jeffrey, there will be another duel if you survive the first one."

Sheba was in heaven.

"I have not betrayed you. I love you. You wound me, you wound me to think me so crude." He was truly hurt.

"My experience, well, yes, my experience has taught me men will do what they wish."

"I am not Francisco." He nearly shouted, as he slammed down his hand, rose from the table, and strode out.

Maureen sat there, surprised, a hint of realizing she shouldn't have said that bubbling up.

"They're all alike." Sheba's voice carried menace as well as false sympathy.

"You shut up." Maureen stood up, stepped closer to her, and slapped her hard, so hard it could be heard in the hall, then turned and blew out of the room.

Henry, outside the door, wished the plague on both their houses.

39

November 18, 2016 Friday

"She's scanned the walls, even inspecting the cracks in the wood." Tucker sat on her haunches as Harry with a high intensity flashlight slowly went over the storage building at the old school.

"These buildings have held up. I think they should turn this one into a cafeteria." Pewter focused on food.

Mrs. Murphy watched Harry. "Guess they will have to, because what if students bring lunches full of sugar. Parents can't feed their children now because the government figures they're too stupid to do it."

"Feed them mouse tartar." Pewter laughed. "Think of the protein. When we were little it made us healthy."

"Maybe in your case a little too healthy," Tucker teased the gray cat.

"At least I have a tail and, I remind you, claws." Pewter huffed up, dancing sideways toward the dog.

Harry, dropping to her hands and knees on the wooden floor, warned, "If you two get in a fight you'll be grounded for the weekend."

Pewter unpuffed, said, "Where are we going this weekend?"

"It will be spur-of-the-moment," Tucker replied. "Those are the most fun, but probably she'll check the barn, the outbuildings, all that stuff before winter really socks us."

"Then why listen to her?" Pewter smacked the dog just enough to hear a little growl.

Peering at the few gaps between the worn floorboards, Harry grumbled, "Behave."

"Yeah, yeah." The gray cat sauntered over to give the human the benefit of her sharp eyes.

Tucker glanced up in the rafters. "You'd think birds would have gotten in here. A good place for a nest."

As if on cue, Pewter unleashed one claw to slide it in a slight gap between two boards. "Hey, come here."

Mrs. Murphy walked over, Tucker came closer but not too close. The tiger cat also used one claw. The two cats found nothing.

The rumble of a truck caught Harry's attention. She zipped up her worn Carhart Detroit jacket. Once the weather turned colder, she did her chores in this jacket, wearing layers underneath depending on the day. Wet days she wore her Barbour. Farming fashion centers on what holds up, what keeps one dry, warm, and allows the wearer to still move efficiently.

Parking in front of the high school building, Tazio, Boom-Boom, MaryJo, and Liz began to unload old school desks. The Reverend Jones had backed the truck up close to the door, cut the motor, and now he was lifting desks out of the truck bed.

Harry walked out. "Hey, let me help."

"What are you doing here?" MaryJo asked, noticing Harry's old Ford F-150 was parked behind the storage building.

"Nosing around." Harry, now at the truck bed, helped lift down one of the wooden desks with wrought iron on the side to hold up the desktop.

Tazio unlocked the building, came back down the stairs. Within twenty minutes the six desks sat in two rows in the building. Everyone kept their coats on as the temperature hung at about fifty-two degrees. Wouldn't have made sense to fire up the wood-burning stove as they wouldn't be there that long.

BoomBoom, hands on hips, said, "Makes me want to get out my notebook and pencil."

"Where'd you find these?" Harry asked.

The teacher's desk sat on a raised platform at the front of the room. Three student desks remained but with six added, the room began to look like a real classroom.

"Easton's," Liz replied.

"I thought they went out of business." Harry had read that in the paper.

"Did, but the family's still around and on the outside chance that a few odd pieces were left in storage I called." Tazio filled her in. "Sure enough, six old desks from about 1918. These things really are indestructible."

"They'd have to be." Herb smiled. "Farm kids were strong."

"There is that." BoomBoom nodded.

Mrs. Murphy sat in the seat on the left front-row desk, while Pewter reposed on the desktop. Tucker, on the floor, thought the desks breathed life into the place.

"The more we can make this building look like it did back around the time of World War One, maybe the easier it will be to get cooperation from the county and the city regarding renewed classes."

"I hope you're right," MaryJo added.

"Reverend, how'd you get roped into this?" Harry smiled.

"Just happened to be at Tazio's shop when BoomBoom walked in," he replied.

"The good reverend needs more modern insulation for his attic. Will save on the heating bill," Tazio mentioned. "I know you're in charge of buildings and grounds so don't worry, I'm not taking over your job. There are such good products on the market now. They can reduce running costs. If the church decides to do this I think it can be done inexpensively. First, we need to remove the old stuff. Anyway, that's another subject."

"I've got one for here. We've got heat pumps as a backup. If we run them it won't be an authentic experience." Liz sat down at an old desk.

"Let the kids keep the stove going. That way they'll learn what it was like," Harry said with conviction.

"I agree but we have the heat pumps for nights. If kids go home during their one- or two-week living history classes and complain that they're cold, you know how that will turn out." Tazio put her hands in her coat pocket, a warm fleece-lined leather short coat.

"Electric is safer and warm." MaryJo also sat down.

"An old oil furnace from the period, well, we won't be able to find that, but a true oil furnace, not propane, might work and be easier to install. We'd need vents but we can run stuff through the attic, keep the oil down in the basement." BoomBoom wanted to save money. "The point is, you know the electrical service is not always reliable out here."

"Pretty much I think we'll have to go to a gas generator backup for when the electricity goes out, which it will. Those heat pumps we installed can't work without electricity. You can depend on that with winter in central Virginia as you said. Maybe we can get some of the materials and labor donated. And given that we have the woodburning stove we should still be able to keep the electrical costs down." Harry, like BoomBoom, wanted to keep maintenance costs low.

Buying cars, furnaces, air conditioners, was one thing. Maintaining them was another.

"We can't do anything until Ned maneuvers this through the city and the county. Who knows, maybe he can get some money from the House of Delegates." Liz thought out loud.

"If it's not in a delegate's district, a delegate isn't going to vote for a penny."

They all sat down or leaned on the desks, batting around ideas.

Another car pulled up. Panto Noyes bounded into the building. "Inkwells. Got old inkwells."

"I called him. Told him about the desks." MaryJo smiled as Panto placed a shopping bag on her desk, and pulled out some simple, old brass inkwells with a lid. "You all are brave. Kids aren't taught penmanship anymore. Do you know what a mess real ink will be?"

"Think of it as primitive art." Harry laughed.

"Speaking of primitive," Panto spoke. "When I go to pow-wows, visit reservations, especially out west, one of the first things I hear is how tribal children were not allowed to speak their native languages."

MaryJo chimed in, "They are now, but so few elders are left who can speak or teach the language. This wiping out of language, religion, even clothing went on for decades."

Reverend Jones said, "Of course, it was worse for defeated peoples, but immigrants were encouraged to shed the old ways. Their children, born here, didn't want to speak, say, Italian."

"The terrible thing is, people thought this was the right thing to do to fit in," MaryJo responded.

"Give the tribal people credit. They didn't want to fit in. They were forced," Panto declared.

Later, Cooper drove down Harry's driveway with another piece of evidence. The bullet from Harry's Volvo station wagon was from the same gun that killed Pierre Rice.

40

March 31, 1786 Friday

*T*he last day of March ended with high winds, brilliant sunshine. The fine snow of days before melted, puddles and mud everywhere.

People were glad to be back at their tasks, freed from winter's last clutches. They hoped it was the last clutches.

"Did you remember a birthday present?" Bumbee asked Grace as both set before their looms.

"I'm not giving him a birthday present," Grace immediately replied.

Liddy, stoking the fire, turned. "Why not?"

"He doesn't call on me. Besides, what would I give him?"

"A scarf," Bumbee advised.

"I'm not doing it."

"I see." Bumbee focused intently on the garment, expertly weaving a brilliant aqua thread through the navy blue.

Liddy took her place. "Grace, you're sixteen. You'll soon be an old maid."

"Tosh." Grace threw her head back.

Serena knocked on the door, entered when Bumbee called out, "Come in."

"It's so bright in here today." Serena put down a large basket. "Bettina sent down some extra deviled eggs, cold ham, bread."

"That was good of her." Bumbee smiled.

Lifting up the towel, Serena enticed them. "Churned butter thanks to the muscle power of Tulli, who Bettina commandeered from the barn. Honey and strawberry jam, too. Brought knives, if you need them." She sat on the bench by the stairs. "I'm so glad to see sunshine."

"Gray, gray, gray. That has to be the last snow," Liddy hoped.

"Mmm." Serena launched into the news. "Mr. Holloway is up at the big house."

"Are that witch and her handmaiden with him?" Bumbee minced no words.

"No." Serena leaned forward. "The sun really is shining on us. One of these days Sheba will forget herself and give one of us orders. Ha. I'll knock her down, I swear I will. You know what I think? She's so hateful cause she's got all that white blood. Always parading the light color of her skin. Hateful."

The others laughed.

Liddy responded, "The question is, whose white blood?"

This sent them into more peals of laughter.

"I dare you to call her a clabberface," Grace baited Serena.

"Oh, we can come up with something worse than that, but listen, Mr. Holloway sent a letter to Yancy Grant asking for satisfaction."

Silence followed this.

Everyone stopped what they were doing. Bumbee rose from her bench, and sat next to Serena.

"Because of what he said at the party?"

Serena nodded. "But it gets better. Bettina and Roger brought in coffee, morning refreshments, and then Roger waited outside the door. He can be a real quiet sneak that Roger."

"Well, between Roger and Bettina they know everything," Liddy volunteered but without rancor.

"But why did Mr. Holloway come here?" Bumbee inquired.

"Because he doesn't know about pistols. Yancy will get choice of weapons. So he came to ask Mr. Garth if he might come here and have John instruct him."

"I see." Bumbee brought her hand to her chin.

"He also wishes for John to be his second."

"Well, if he shoots and kills Yancy Grant, fine. If not, then we have made an enemy," the shrewd Bumbee noted.

No one said anything, then Grace piped up. "Is there no way to stop this?"

"Doubtful," Serena said. "But there might be a bit of time because when DoRe delivered the letter asking for satisfaction, Yancy had already left for Richmond."

"Well, he won't refuse when he returns. Can't. He'd look like a coward," Bumbee said. "But if someone wishes, they might be able to bring them to terms and stop a duel."

"At least a duel solves the problem once and for all," Grace spoke.

"Oh, Grace." Bumbee smoothed out her skirt. "Sometimes it does and sometimes it doesn't."

"And what if Mr. Holloway is killed, which is more likely?" Liddy came over and plucked out an egg. "Then Maureen is a widow again and Sheba will be keeping her hand out to every suitor."

"No!" Grace was shocked.

"Honey, you need to learn how the world works. She's under-handed, greedy, and you'd better believe she will extract money and whatever else from the men lining up to marry that fortune. I can't believe anyone really wants to marry Maureen." Bumbee laughed.

"Maybe she's different with men than with women," Liddy posited.

"Aren't most women?" Serena raised her eyebrows. "And the men believe whatever the women tell them."

"Men hear what they want to hear. I can vouch from personal experience that Mr. Percy never heard a word I said."

They all laughed.

"I'd better get back up there. You know how Bettina can get. She's been flying all over the place this morning." Serena stood up.

"Serena," Grace asked, "do you think I'm going to be an old maid?"

"What brought that on?" the attractive young woman wondered.

"Liddy says I'm sixteen and I'm not married."

"Liddy, are you holding out your man as an example of the sweetness of marriage?" Serena gave Liddy a little dig.

"He's good to me." Her lower lip jutted out.

"Girl, he's good to some other women, too. Grace," she turned to the younger woman, "you aren't going to be an old maid and there are plenty worse things than not having a man. Men are work, I can tell you."

"Hear, hear." Bumbee grinned.

Liddy, still stinging from Serena's unwelcome information, kept quiet.

"Sometimes it works, doesn't it? I mean Momma and Poppa get along," Grace remarked.

Serena softened. "Does. You're too young to remember but

Bettina had a good man. Mr. Garth and the Missus were a match and really so are the girls and their husbands. Sometimes it works but don't go round looking for it. Let him find you." With that she swept out the door.

Liddy returned to her task without a word.

"Liddy," Bumbee took pity on her, "don't take it to heart. It will pass."

"Yes, Ma'am." She rolled yarn, head down.

Hours later, Catherine, John, Ralston, Tulli, and Barker O. had wished Jeddie a happy nineteenth birthday. Bettina sent down a small chocolate cake. Horses as always remained the major topic of conversation but that slid into Jeffrey Holloway's morning call, the news of which flickered through Cloverfields like fire.

"Mr. John, what will you do?" Tulli asked.

"What I can. The pistol Charles's father gave him before the war is such a fine instrument, balanced, just the right resistance on the trigger. I'll teach him with that if Yancy accepts the challenge."

"How could he not?" Barker O.'s deep voice filled the tidy tack room.

"He could show himself to be a forgiving gentleman and admit he was under the influence of spirits," Catherine answered.

"Oh, Miss Catherine, he might admit he was drunk as a skunk but I don't know as he would admit he was wrong." Ralston, an old mind in a young head, spoke.

John, next to his wife on a low bench, nodded. "I'm afraid he's right, my angel."

"Dear Lord, wasn't it bad enough we killed the British and the British killed us, now we're killing one another, our currencies are close to worthless, and," she threw up her hands, "is the world falling apart?" Then she caught herself. "Well, not on your birthday, Jeddie. This is a good day."

"Thank you, Miss Catherine." He beamed.

The distant rattle of a harness alerted them.

Tulli ran out, then ran back. "DoRe!"

"Seems to be a Big Rawly day." Catherine stood up, wrapped her shawl around herself, stepped outside with the men.

Daffodils survived the snow, peeking up everywhere. Forsythias threatened to bloom as DoRe drove the splendid coach-in-four toward the stable, the sides of the carriage gleaming.

The boys ran out as he stopped, dismounted. "Miss Catherine, Mr. John. Miss Selisse returns your carriage with thanks. She had us draw every single thing about this piece of fine work, including the bud vase inside the carriage." He grinned.

"That was fast," John remarked.

"The Missus is determined to be seen in the best carriage in the country. She can't steal yours so she's going to have one built."

"In Philadelphia?" John wondered.

"No." DoRe paused for dramatic effect. "Mr. Holloway and his father will build it."

The dramatic effect produced dropped jaws, wide eyes, and a moment of silence.

Catherine then said, "Well, DoRe, that is some news." Thinking of Bettina's hopes she smiled at the genial man. "Why don't you go on up to the house and tell Bettina? I'll be up shortly. Jeddie can drive you back to Big Rawly and I'll send Bettina with him so he doesn't have to drive back alone."

"Thank you." DoRe thought this an excellent idea.

As he walked up to the big house, his characteristic limp not slowing him down, Catherine put her hand on Jeddie's shoulder. "Take the carriage back so they can sit inside. Tie his horses to the back. Wait. Don't. This way DoRe has to come back for Maureen's carriage horses."

"Miss Catherine, how can I drive when DoRe's along? He's near as good as Barker O."

Barker O., pleased with the compliment, chuckled. "Son, I think DoRe will be just fine."

"Barker O., why don't you sit up with Jeddie and if he needs a lesson, well, there you are. Then the two of you can drive back."

"Thank you."

She reached in her pocket and pulled out some chits. "Here, Jeddie, Number Eleven. Barker O., Number Two. I don't think anyone's going to fuss but just in case."

They took their passes and Catherine took Jeddie's hand in hers. "Happy, happy birthday."

Then she and John started back up to the house, running into Charles, who walked out from the carriage barn, plans under his arm.

"Think I've got a way to store grain and reduce spoilage."

Piglet murmured, *"He never stops. He gets up in the middle of the night to make changes to St. Luke's and now this. I just wish he'd sleep through the night."*

"Piglet, you're talkative." Catherine adored the corgi.

John told Charles the news about the potential duel.

Charles shook his head, red-gold hair catching the light. "I'd hoped those words would be forgotten."

"When a man accuses you of consorting with, well, you know, and your wife is in the next room and her lady-in-waiting is literally waiting down below, I don't know." John sighed. "He has asked me to be his second."

"Good Lord, John." Charles stopped walking for a moment.

"I agreed. If Yancy accepts the duel, and we all think he will, then I will give Jeffrey some shooting lessons using your pistol."

A wry grin played over Charles's lips. "The spoils of war. One of these days you'll return my pistol to me."

"Maybe."

"You won the war, John, you don't need my pistol."

"You were my captive. Fair's fair." John enjoyed bedeviling his brother-in-law just a bit.

"You two." Catherine slipped her hand in John's. "Let's return to the problem at hand. Yancy left for Richmond. Surely he will be there tomorrow if he's on horseback. If he went down to Scottsville, boarded a boat, maybe tonight. We can hope his business there will take him two or three days, then two or three days to return. That gives us time."

"Time for what?" Charles appreciated Catherine's sharp mind.

"To see if there isn't a way out where each man saves face." Catherine watched chimney smoke rise straight up from the big house, a sign of good weather.

"My love, that would be a miracle." John squeezed her hand.

"Miracles do happen and, don't forget, Father's birthday is Sunday."

41

November 19, 2016 Saturday

"*H*ow can people let themselves get like that?" Harry blurted out, looking out the window of Liz's Barracks Road shop.

Susan chided her. "Harry, you can't say things like that."

"Why not? Fat is fat and if you're fat you're courting lots of sickness, plus you don't walk, you waddle," she shot back.

"Just don't say it," Susan replied.

Liz moved a bracelet on the counter. "Isn't that part of the problem? No one can say anything anymore? You hurt someone's feelings and you're a monster. Now, I don't think Harry should push open the door and tell that lady that she's one step closer to the grave for being fat, but she can say it to us. Which reminds me, I need to lose fifteen pounds."

"Liz, baloney," Harry said.

"Not baloney. Fat." Liz pinched her waist and a small roll of flesh did indeed stay between her fingers.

"If you want to lose that little bit of weight come on out to the farm and work with me for a week. Poof. That will be the end of that," Harry promised.

"She's got a point there," Susan agreed. "When I was young I don't remember so many overweight people, but then a lot of people worked outside jobs, physical labor. And housework qualified as physical labor. Our mothers had it easier than our grandmothers, but doing the wash, cleaning the floors, polishing furniture, keeping the fires going in the fireplace, women carried, toted, bent over, or got down on their hands and knees and scrubbed."

"We're spoiled." Liz nodded. "Now, Harry, what have you found out about the bullet in your Volvo?"

"The bullet in my Volvo. Same gun that killed Pierre Rice," Harry matter-of-factly reported.

Liz had not heard this so she froze for a moment. "Harry, that's—"

"Frightening." Susan spoke for her. "And you said you didn't see anything or anyone when you left the meeting."

"No, I didn't. The rain poured down." Liz looked behind her. "Someone stole that expensive dress. You are shot at. A man, successful, is killed. For what?"

"Don't forget the tombstones at St. Luke's," Harry added.

"What has that got to do with you, the Tahoe, all that stuff?" Susan leaned on the counter, taking the weight off her feet.

"I don't know. All I know is there's a string of weird stuff, murder, and that's weird, too. And you all can't point the finger at me and say I've stuck my nose in all this. I did not. But I'm in it somehow so I want to get to the bottom of it."

They both turned to her then, shut up as the door opened, and MaryJo Cranston pushed through it.

"Hey, what's up?" MaryJo smiled.

"The bullet in Harry's Volvo came from the same gun as the one that killed Pierre Rice," Liz stated.

"No!" MaryJo's hand came up to her heart. "No, it can't be."

Harry simply replied, "It is."

"I drove out that driveway before you did. I'm telling you there wasn't a car there or a lurking person. Nothing."

"Even if there were could you have seen it?" Susan exhaled.

"Maybe. A glint of light on a fender, movement behind a tree. I mean it was raining cats and dogs but I might have seen something. Nada. Nothing. Zero," MaryJo emphasized.

"Well, we aren't going to solve this here." Harry's voice carried an edge. "Anyway, we popped in here to see if you really are selling out, Liz."

MaryJo half laughed. "Me, too. Hard to shove away from the desk during the week, so here I am. Liz, are you?"

"I am. Thought I'd hang on through Christmas. I do good business around the holidays. Then I won't renew my lease. I'll close shop. Andy and I have done well, a good living for which I'm grateful. I'd like to travel. He swears if I go through with this then he'll turn the business over to our daughter once she graduates from the Darden School." Liz named the highly regarded graduate school of business at the University of Virginia. "Oh, he won't just quit, he'll work with her for a year but then we'll be free. I'm actually excited about it and I feel like I'll get to know my husband all over again."

"Sounds wonderful." MaryJo beamed. "I'm not sure I want to know Bruce all over again. I know him pretty well now." She smiled. "He's a good guy."

"We four married good men," Susan added. "Much as I love him there are times when I look at Ned and I want to just throw up my hands. I, of course, am perfect."

"I've been meaning to tell you that." Harry reached over to poke Susan in the arm.

"While I'm here, I want to buy that turquoise necklace I've been salivating over." MaryJo walked to the display case containing the necklace, which Liz removed.

"A knockout," the proprietor remarked as MaryJo turned around so Liz could come out from behind the case and fasten the necklace.

Harry and Susan *oohed* and *aahed*, and it was gorgeous and gorgeously expensive. MaryJo whipped out her checkbook and wrote a four-figure check on the spot.

"Would you like a box for it?" Liz inquired.

"No. I want to feel it on this sweater."

Then Liz reminded Harry, "You said you had an idea about all this stuff." She looked at MaryJo, filling her in. "Harry reminded me of how many truly odd things have happened. The murder, the theft of the dress from my shop, which was hacked, really, and the eagle feather—"

"I'm dying to hear. Being shot at after our meeting would scare me no end," MaryJo confided.

"I think this had to do with contraband." Harry folded her hands for a moment. "Exactly what, I don't know, but I suspect it has something to do with illegal smuggling of animals or animal parts. The eagle feather points to that."

MaryJo's mouth dropped open. Susan and Liz stayed quite still for a second.

"Harry, you mean like what MaryJo told us from her research at an earlier meeting?" Liz's memory was sharp, as always.

"Kind of. It might be otherwise, but for me the Tahoe was another clue. Whoever is behind this knew where to park that vehicle to hide it. And it may be that the storage building has been used for months or even a year or so to hide or store illegal goods. We don't thoroughly check it. When we do go to the schools we're concentrating on the actual schoolrooms. The other thing is whoever did this has a key or has cut the lock and had a duplicate lock made to match our keys. Isn't much but it's something."

"It can't be!" MaryJo was aghast.

"What else can it be? Even if this isn't about contraband, someone knows how to get into the storage building." Harry noticed the sky darkening.

Susan, speaking very slowly, putting this together, replied. "What you're saying could be true, but whoever is doing this took a risk."

"They did, but remember, whatever vehicles they parked in there were probably to be loaded or unloaded. And this was done quickly. In and out. If we'd stumbled upon a car or truck in there, whoever is behind this might have had a ready-made excuse. Surely they would have considered the possibility. But they are bold and sure of themselves."

"Harry, that creeps me out." MaryJo fingered her new, beloved necklace.

"Me, too," Susan and Liz said in unison.

"Harry, if you're right, you'd better be careful. You shouldn't be alone." MaryJo fretted.

"I'll be careful. Plus I have Tucker, Mrs. Murphy, and Pewter. Their senses are better than mine."

"Harry, don't be facetious." MaryJo's voice sounded like a schoolteacher's.

"I'm not. I'll be careful."

Once back in Susan's Audi station wagon, heading west for home, the first tiny snowflakes twirled down.

The weather, dramatic, changing, never failed to interest them or most people in central Virginia.

"First snow." Harry smiled. "Do you want to have a hot chocolate at my house or yours? Or mulled wine, I can make that."

The two of them always tried to celebrate the first snow with an impromptu party if possible.

"Yours."

"Good. I'll call your husband, my husband, Coop, that should do it. Oh, Miranda. Haven't seen her in an age." She mentioned the older woman she used to work with in the old post office now subsumed by a big new post office, burdened with so many federal rules. When Harry and Miranda ran the old, small P.O., they managed it with common sense. Those days and ways were gone. Everything had to be centralized, controlled, watched.

"Harry, have you told Coop what you think?"

"Yes."

They drove and the snow fell a bit heavier.

"A squall."

"The first snow, even if it's just a few flakes, is always such fun." Harry punched in numbers on her phone.

"Before your call, if you're right, the problem, the murderer, is close to home." Susan gave the wagon some gas as they climbed the steep hill on the other side of the creek, the eastern border-line of former Cloverfields and Old Rawly.

"I know." Harry turned to look at her dearest friend. "I know, but I don't know enough and I don't know why I'm the target. Did I blunder onto something? Could you do the same? I hope I find out before it's too late."

"Harry, don't say that."

42

April 1, 1786 Saturday

A blue sky filled with fleecy cumulus clouds promised true spring. The James River sparkled, batteaus, larger ships, filled the docks and slips. Traffic, thanks to the good weather and the ice having broken up, filled the wide river. Above the slip, walking away from the ceaseless activity, Yancy Grant and Sam Udall could still hear some of the shouting, a ship's bell ringing.

A young man hurried past them, tipping his hat to Sam.

"Mr. Udall."

Sam returned the gesture. "Mr. Parham." He commented as he swung his gold-tipped walking stick, elegant and expensive. "The young are ever in a hurry."

Yancy, his stick under his arm, wolf's head in silver at the top, nodded. "And it's spring."

Sam smiled. "I've always thought that high spring, when the dogwoods bloom, should be a respite from work. No one can think anyway." He laughed. "The sap is rising."

Yancy chortled. "Indeed."

They passed houses, the farther away from the docks, the more impressive. Had they stopped to look back and down, the tops of the tobacco warehouses would have reflected the light, row after row, of long, large buildings. The Old World could not get enough of Virginia tobacco. Hemp sold well and if apples were properly packed and the ship made good time, the English were awakening to some of the sweet varieties not found over there.

"Madam." Sam lifted his hat high, inclined his head slightly as did Yancy.

Yancy whispered, "Dazzling."

The redhead, accompanied by her lady-in-waiting, enjoyed the weather on her brief walk to a friend.

"Maria Skipwith."

"Ah, the Skipwiths."

"Mmm." Sam nodded. "Now of marriageable age, her mother has fantasies of the beauty marrying a noble in England or France." He paused, then related with relish, "And that divine creature said, 'I will marry an American or I will not marry at all.'"

They walked along, children playing, dogs playing with them, an open carriage rattling by, its deep green paint shining.

"Have you considered my proposition?" Yancy hoped his desperation didn't show.

"I have. I believe this will be a good year for corn, hemp, annual crops unless we suffer a July and August drought. One can never discount that, but it has been a wet winter and spring. I am prepared to lend you fifteen thousand dollars against your estate at five percent interest."

Yancy swallowed. Five percent was outrageous. "When would you wish repayment, Sir?"

"A year from April 15. You may pay quarterly or all at once. But I must have the total sum plus interest by April 15."

"We have never discussed what would befall me should I fail, not that I will," Yancy hastily added. "It's just that I had not considered such a dolorous event."

"The land becomes mine. I have the documents for you to sign, granting me the title should you fail or perish. All is in my office and we can review same on Monday. My clerk will be there and should corrections be needed he can do so."

"Would you keep the land or sell it?" Yancy sounded unconcerned, just curious.

"Sell. Mrs. Sel—I mean Holloway, whom I know through her first husband and, of course, I am adjusting to Mr. Holloway, has expressed interest."

Yancy's voice shot up. "Has she now? And how did she learn of my situation?"

"That, Sir, I don't know. Our dealings are in strictest confidence, but as I am one of the few financial men making speculative loans, someone could reach such a conclusion as we have been seen together. Naturally, I replied through a letter that I am not at liberty to discuss any such business and I had not made a loan to you, which at the time I wrote the missive was true."

Color flushing in his cheeks, Yancy, with his voice level, said, "I feel this uncertainty will pass. The land I purchased before all this confusion is valuable and I think I will be fortunate I did not let it slip through my fingers."

"Indeed. We must develop financial consistency. We need businessmen in Congress, men who understand something as simple as you cannot expect states to raise militias, train them, feed them, clothe them and yet only Congress can declare war. This is a burden that must be shared, a true national expense regarding our protection. As to our currency problems, again, businessmen must untangle this mess."

"Indeed. And what do you think will happen in Europe?"

"Ah." Sam's walking stick was raised up higher from the

ground for emphasis. "If the various kings live, we can consider a stable foreign policy. The men we send on missions to England, France, even Russia, seem highly intelligent, but, Sir, should a king die unexpectedly, who is to say? That's the terrible crisis of a monarchy, a sudden death or a king who is mentally unable to rule."

"They all seem healthy," Yancy murmured.

"Well, King George is fat." Sam laughed as they approached Georgina's.

Walking in the opposite direction, chattering away, were Eudes and Mignon, who opened the back gate to go to work. Eudes had given Mignon an early tour of houses close to Georgina's with lovely gardens.

Yancy stopped.

"Are you well, Sir?"

"Oh, quite." The horseman paused. "It's just that I recognize that tiny little woman."

"I don't believe I have ever seen her but the fellow is the cook, best cook in town."

"She's a runaway slave." Yancy spoke with emphasis on *runaway*.

"Ah, well, Sir, I would keep that to myself as I am certain she is not the only such woman at Georgina's."

"There is a one-hundred-dollar reward."

Sam's reply cut. "A pittance to a man of your standing. One should stay on the good side of Georgina. She has long talons. Do keep it to yourself."

43

April 2, 1786 Sunday

The gorgeous weather held, the temperature when all returned from church hovered in the midfifties. The doors to the big house stood open for fresh air but the windows remained closed. A bit of cooling in the house would be welcome, but once the sun set it would become cold quickly.

The late-afternoon sun drenched the meadows, the orchards with gold.

Pink and white hyacinths formed a low arrangement in the center of the table where cakes and cookies were piled on the table along with small wrapped gifts.

JohnJohn, Marcia, and Isabelle raced around the table screaming while Piglet chased them.

Ewing commanded the head of the table while his daughters and sons-in-law teased him about turning forty-eight.

Marcia grabbed a gift before Rachel could smack her hand and she leaned on Ewing's thigh to drop it in his lap.

"Birfday." She mangled the word.

"My, yes." He noted the name on the small card. "Piglet. Well, this will be good."

The three stopped to watch their grandfather open the box. He pulled out a handsome collar that one of the estate's leatherworkers had made.

"A collar for you, Grandpa!" Isabelle clapped.

They all laughed, then Ewing solemnly remarked to the children, "I believe Piglet has made this present for himself. Let's see if it fits."

Charles stood up, called his beloved friend to him, walking him to Ewing. Piglet sat down and, yes, the collar fit perfectly.

One by one the gifts, useful items such as gloves, cravats, an elegant silk bottle-green waistcoat, were opened with appreciative noises. The children did not find the clothing and books that thrilling but they did quiet down.

Finally, Catherine and Rachel disappeared into the kitchen, returning with Bettina, Serena, Weymouth, and Roger.

"Now, what are you all up to?" Ewing loved every minute of this.

The sisters approached their father, Catherine took the smallish beautiful wooden box that Bettina handed to her.

"Hiding things?" His eyebrows raised.

"Mr. Ewing, you can poke around." Bettina laughed. "But we all thought the pantry would be safe."

"Now, what is this?"

"Open it, Grandpa!" The three small children were flush with excitement.

The two sisters stood a bit nervously, as did their husbands.

He untied the ribbon, opened the box, and there nestled in royal blue silk gleamed a pocket watch, gold with his initials on the back in an elegant script.

Lifting it out, he admired the hands, the wonderful numbers, and was so very glad no one in his family had heard him at the dinner party crab about this newfangled piece of jewelry, a pocket watch.

"Father, it chimes the hours. May I show you?" Rachel held out her hand. He dropped the expensive watch into it.

She moved the hands to four o'clock and a low chime rang out four times, which made Piglet bark and the children scream again. Then Rachel reset the time, handing him the watch with its heavy gold chain, an oval at the end with *Cloverfields* engraved on it so he could wear the gift on his new waistcoat.

He stood and kissed his daughters, put his hand on his sons-in-law's shoulders, then picked up each child one by one for a big hug and a kiss.

"My dears, such a sumptuous gift."

"We couldn't stand the thought of everyone else pulling out their timepiece to look at it and our father having none. You are always the apogee of fashion," Catherine gushed.

As Catherine was not a gusher, her father realized how important the gift was.

Later, when the evening star arose, everyone was back in their house or cabin. Ewing threw on his coat to visit Isabelle's grave.

"My angel, how you would surprise me on my birthday. The kisses alone." He stopped. "Well, our girls have kept up your doings. I now have a timepiece so, like it or not, I am a modern man."

The watch chimed eight times, he flipped open the cover and the chime rang out deep and clear. The evening star, unnaturally bright in the rich Prussian-blue sky, flickered.

"Isabelle, the smartest thing I ever did was to marry you. My days are filled with our children and grandchildren. I am surrounded by love and always, always, and ever, I am guided by my love for you. You made me what I am." He paused, his eyes glistening. "Ah, my love, time is passing."

44

"*Colder up here.*" Pewter fluffed up her fur.

"*Always is,*" Tucker agreed.

"*Feels good in the summer. Maybe not so much now,*" Mrs. Murphy remarked. "*At least we have fur and an undercoat. She puts on layers. When it's really bitter, she looks like a doughboy.*"

At four in the afternoon, Harry wore an undershirt, an old cashmere turtleneck, many times mended, and her Woolrich red buffalo plaid jacket. A good pair of socks and boots, an unlined pair of work gloves kept her warm, as did heavier denim jeans. They'd driven up in the Ford F-150, parked in the turnabout more than halfway up the ridge. Becoming more and more certain that somehow this mess involved wildlife, Harry wanted to check for traps. Just to be safe, she'd slung her wonderful Weatherby rifle with the scope over her shoulder. As it was made for women it was lighter, the recoil didn't knock her shoulder out of joint. The rifle was well balanced and easy to carry over long distances, so easy that Fair ordered one for himself. Given his physical presence, Fair never needed to prove to himself or others that

291

he was manly. He considered all that bombast for weaklings. While he may have exhibited a touch of arrogance, his wife liked his attitude. She never needed to prop him up or massage his butch credentials. Harry figured one should take care of oneself. If he needed someone to whisper how big, strong, and handsome he was, that would be someone else. She had work to do. Then again, she never minded if someone told her she was intelligent, good-looking, and quick. But then Harry never said she was fair.

Right now, she wasn't feeling fair at all. She was worried and angry. The death of the truck driver didn't touch her. She didn't know him, nor did she know Pierre Rice, but meeting his sister, talking to Beverly Ely, she had a sense of him. Plus someone shot a hole in her Volvo, obviously intended for her.

Climbing near the top of the ridge, she stopped, walked parallel to the ridge, which was 2,500 feet, to check bear caves. She also knew where fox dens were tucked away. They had not been disturbed. The first bear den, lower down, maybe at 800 feet, showed no sign of occupation. For one thing, you could usually smell them. Bear scent was strong, they gave off an odor like wet wood. Couldn't miss it any more than you could miss deer in rut. That could bring tears to your eyes. Good the deer liked it. She didn't.

A prominent rock outcropping lured her. She moved slowly just in case. She'd learned if a bear does walk toward you, you make yourself bigger. Try to be aggressive up to a point. Fire your rifle in the air. If the bear has a cub, don't fool around. Back away if you can. Any mothering animal can be dangerous, even a house cat.

Nearing the entrance, she smelled bear. She tiptoed toward the overhang, and the two cats walked behind her while Tucker trotted ahead.

"If it's *Sweetpea*, *I'll warn her*," the corgi said.

It wasn't Sweetpea. A bear was using the den, but was out at the moment. A pile of leaves filled the back of the protective place. Berry bits scattered everywhere like tiny black punctuation points. Whoever lived in here ate well.

Harry nosed around, then backed out, heading upward again. She noticed high nests overhead. Raptors usually built high, big nests. The overwintering birds, smaller, filled up their homes in tree hollows with hay, clothing bits, downy feathers. Occasionally, a bit of straw or ribbon fluttered overhead. Each bird displayed architecture developed by the breed. Inside barns, the barn swallows, having left for the winter, also left their nests stuck alongside beams. Other birds used claylike materials to bind twigs together. Others wove slender grasses. The variety proved endless, each nest adapted for the needs of that particular bird. Some breeds lived in rookeries, kind of a bird high-rise. The gossip was endless.

Harry stopped to catch her breath. She unslung her rifle, leaned against a tree, perhaps two hundred yards down from the ridge. Had she not been wearing red buffalo plaid she would not have been visible.

A shot rang out. The bullet hit the tree with a *thunk*. Harry dropped to the ground, grabbed her rifle, slid behind the tree. The animals hid with her, then the cats climbed up the denuded oak.

"*He's moving down*," Mrs. Murphy called.

"*Who?*" Tucker asked.

"*Don't know, but he's got a rifle. Nudge Mom.*"

Pewter watched the shooter. He was either blind, dumb, or really arrogant, thinking he could shoot Harry without being shot himself. Then again he may not have seen her rifle. His face, the

bottom half, was covered by a bandana that he had pulled up for that purpose. He wore a leather coat. That was all she could see. He was within one hundred and fifty yards.

Tucker poked Harry with her nose.

A long association with her friends had taught Harry to trust their senses more than her own. She barely breathed. Then she heard the crackle of a snapped twig. She knew he was descending on her right.

She quickly spun to that side of the tree, raised her rifle, saw the human, pulled the trigger. Missed but the bullet whizzed close by. He stopped, turned, and ran.

Without a moment's hesitation, she stood up to chase him. Being closer to the ridge, he had the advantage. She had more uphill climb. When he reached the top, he knelt down, got her in his sights, and fired. That was too close for comfort.

Harry fired, fired again. She thought she might have hit him on the right shoulder because he grabbed it with his left hand and tore out of there. By the time she reached the ridge, he was already a football field's length away.

Tucker started to give chase.

"Leave it, Tucker."

Harry raised her rifle, took her time, and fired.

He zigged and zagged. Whoever he was, he wasn't entirely stupid. She watched him get away. She fired again for the hell of it to keep him moving.

Standing still for a moment, she heard a faraway throaty rumble. Being a motorhead she knew he had started his truck, a big one with a big diesel engine.

She took a deep breath, ran down to her old truck as fast as she could go. That took about seven minutes. Running downhill was tricky but she didn't fall. She picked up Tucker, put the corgi in the seat, and the cats jumped in and they coasted down the steep grade. Furious though she was, she wasn't going to go down that mountain at high speed.

Once at the bottom, she dialed Cooper on her cellphone.

"Coop."

"What's wrong?"

"I was on the mountain behind the farm and someone shot at me."

"Could you see who it was?"

"No, but it was a man. I had my rifle, thank God, and fired back. He would have killed me. I have no doubt." Her voice rose.

"Let me see if anyone from our department is near the top of the mountain."

"He had to have come down the old Chinquapin trail. Probably left his vehicle up near the top. He wore a camo shell and a bandana over his face. Made him hard to see, but I got off a good shot once he ran out on the ridge. I might have nicked his right shoulder, I don't know, but he was fit enough to run fast."

"Any idea why he was up there?"

"No, unless he was poaching traps or set them himself. Or followed me."

Coop gave clear orders. "Go home. Keep a gun with you. If anyone comes down your driveway and you don't know who it is, call me and don't open the door."

"Roger." She clicked off the phone, madder than before.

Once in the house, she hung up her rifle, took out the .38 Ruger from the side kitchen drawer. Mostly the revolver was there to scare off any marauder sniffing at the horses. Fortunately, that rarely happened, but one had to consider everything, especially if the food supply became scarce. Now it was plentiful.

She put her head in her hands as she sat at the kitchen table, trying to figure out what the hell was going on.

Mrs. Murphy jumped up on the table and rubbed Harry's hands with her sides.

Tucker, at her feet, promised, *"We'll take care of things. Don't worry."*

"My fangs and claws are deadly." Pewter sounded tough.

Twenty minutes later, Cooper drove down the driveway, parking near the back door.

"Cooper!" Tucker announced.

Harry stood up as her friend pushed through the now-closed-in back porch door. Harry opened the kitchen door.

"Not a damned thing." Coop nearly spat.

"I hope I did wing him." Harry grimaced. "You might as well sit down and have a cup of coffee or tea. I could use one."

"Yeah, but I can't stay long." She dropped in the ladder-back chair, noticed the flintlock pistol on the counter, stood back up and picked it up. "The revolver and this. A pistol-packing momma."

Harry, now at the stove, half laughed. "Well, the gunsmith showed me how to clean the flintlock when I went in to pick it up, said it was in perfect condition. He also said that at close range it was as deadly as any other pistol. He encouraged me to take up flintlocks. Said I would really like target practice. I had it out on the table to study it."

"We got a bit of a break today. The truck driver. Turns out, his wife found a key to a U-Stor-It. She drove to the unit, opened it, and there were cages in there, ropes, rawhide strings. Not a lot but the Louisville police called us."

"So this does have something to do with animal contraband? Who would have thought of this?"

"It isn't the first criminal activity that pops into your mind but it is becoming a big business. Also, if people are killing eagles, say in the west, people in other states tend not to notice. Has to be close to home." She paused. "You think someone is illegally trapping up there?"

"Yes, there is so much territory all you need to do is keep moving your traps. That way you lose your risk of being caught, being figured out because of routine. There's tons of game up in the Blue Ridge. Big bucks, songbirds, raptors. The kind of stuff MaryJo told us about a couple of meetings back."

"Right." Cooper sipped her coffee as Harry downed tea.

"I either interrupted him or, the worst-case scenario, he was coming for me. This is the second time I've been shot at. I don't much like it. If he was coming for me, he had a rough idea of my schedule."

"You'd think he would have the sense to lay low or clear out."

"Maybe he can't," Harry replied.

45

April 3, 1786 Monday

Rose sunlight filled the breakfast nook at Big Rawly. Maureen and the late Francisco had added Caribbean touches to the interior of the large house. For the breakfast room this took the form of interior shutters the length of the huge windows. When the sunlight became too strong, one closed the shutters but tipped the louvers for a bit of light. The color, a soft petal pink, added to the charm. A low fire gave off heat in the ornate fireplace.

Maureen, glad of the warmth as she swept into the room, flicked her right hand behind her, lifting up the silky morning robe as she sat down on a painted chair.

No sooner had her bottom brushed the chair than a young house girl brought in steaming chicory coffee, followed by another young woman bearing bread, jams, butter.

The lady of the house had taken the precaution of only allowing average-looking women to serve. No more raving beauties.

She reached over her plate, then noticed a light blue envelope, her name emblazoned on the front in Jeffrey's bold, attractive script. Picking it up, she ran her fingernail under the sealed back, carefully lifted it out, and read.

"Henry!" She bellowed.

The older, thin fellow appeared. "Yes, Missus."

"When was this put on my plate?" she demanded.

"I don't know, Ma'am."

Slamming the envelope down, she shouted at him, "Get me DoRe, get me DoRe right now."

Sheba sidled into the room.

Maureen pointed a finger at her before she could speak. "Pack my valise this instant. Do you understand?"

"What dresses—"

"The emerald-green and the shell-pink and gray cloak. Now! Now, are you deaf?"

Sheba shot out of the room.

As Maureen shoved the envelope between her bosoms, they could easily hold paper, she nearly ran for her closet, then stopped because she needed to see DoRe first.

"He may be crippled, but he can still move!" She rapped the table with her knuckles, then headed for the porch and side door since she figured he'd come up that way.

While she waited, John Schuyler heard hoofbeats drumming up the long Cloverfields driveway. Young, light, Milton Fahrney charged toward John and Catherine's house, skidding, dismounting before the horse—one of Maureen's good blooded ones— had stopped. John was hardly three steps out the door, going to work again on the back bridge. Charles, hearing the commotion, rose from his desk to look out the window.

"Mr. John, begging your pardon," Milton breathlessly apologized, handing him a light blue envelope.

John took the offered missive, opened it. "Good God."

Catherine reached for the letter, which he gave to her.

She, too, exclaimed, "He's lost his mind."

John asked, "Did Mr. Holloway send you?"

"Yes, Sir, he did."

"Does Mrs. Holloway know you are here?"

"No, Sir, I left before sunup."

Catherine, seeing the horse's heaving flanks, told the young fellow, "Take this horse to Jeddie and Ralston. Let them cool him out. Then you go to the kitchen in the big house and tell Bettina and Serena that I've sent you. Eat a good breakfast. Go on now, the horse needs attention."

"Yes, Miss Catherine." He bowed to her, took the reins, walking the horse down to the stables.

"What now?" She grasped her husband's forearm.

"He'll get killed." John's color drained a bit. "He'll get himself killed unless I can get there in time to delay or stop this."

"If he left at sunup, he's no doubt down by the river now. I expect he'll go by river. He isn't going to drive a cart or coach and he won't be riding. If he had, Milton would have mentioned it, I think."

"Yes, yes." John rubbed his chin. "If I leave now, I may be able to reach Richmond an hour or two behind him." He reread the letter.

"Two days?"

He nodded. "Perhaps a day and a half if the current is strong, but that brings up other problems. At least I know where he's headed, I think." He took a deep breath. "He's a fool but he asked me to be his second. I must do what I can."

"Darling, I'll pack a few things. You go on down and tell Barker O. to drive you on down to Scottsville. And I'll have Bettina put together a basket." She disappeared back into the house as John trotted over to the barn.

Rachel, having also heard the flying hoofbeats, saw Milton walking the gelding to the barn. She called over her shoulder, "Charles, something's amiss at Big Rawly."

"What?"

"Milton flew up our road to John and Catherine. I'm going over to the house."

"I'll go with you." He tossed on a jacket, Piglet at his heels, and they briskly walked to the duplicate white-framed two-story house.

"Catherine!" Rachel opened the back door. "It's Charles and myself."

"Come in. I'm upstairs packing for John."

Two sets of feet rang out as they climbed the wooden stairway with Piglet's nails clicking behind.

"What's happened?"

"Jeffrey Holloway has left for Richmond to personally challenge Yancy Grant. Grant made so much about the women for hire that night at our party. How does Yancy know so much? Jeffrey can't wait for Grant to return from Richmond. He wrote he can't sustain the attempt to dishonor him for any longer."

"Dear God." Charles shook his head.

"Throw in a shirt or two, socks," Rachel suggested.

"And my old pistol," Charles said.

"Why?" Catherine's eyes widened.

"Just in case."

"But if Grant does accept the challenge and he does choose pistols, Jeffrey won't be able to use yours . . . well, John's."

Rachel dryly added, "The family pistol. True, he will have to choose from the two shown him in the box by Grant's second."

"Jeffrey must have a second who can inspect the firearms." Charles exhaled. "This is madness. Noonday sun madness."

"Well, that it is." Catherine had calmed down. "But none of us has been accused of sleeping with nightingales."

Charles turned to go back out. "Rachel, I'll pack myself. Catherine, if you see John before I get to the stables, tell him to wait. I won't be long. This may take two of us."

"Then I'm going too." Piglet dashed after his master.

The sisters looked at each other.

Rachel said, "Men are fools. To die because of low gossip."

Catherine inhaled deeply. "What choice do they have? Who will do business with Jeffrey if he is dishonored? And even if they do because of his newfound riches, he will never have any respect. We wouldn't fight a duel but we don't need to. We have nothing to prove and little is expected of us. You and I can work in our husbands' shadows and who will know what we do or do not do?"

"Catherine, you can't hide your abilities." Rachel wasn't having any of it.

"Not completely, but I can certainly disarm men. They can only try to beat one another down."

"Our husbands aren't like that." Rachel's lower lip stuck out.

"Rachel, my husband is a war hero and yours proved himself at Saratoga. It wasn't his fault he was captured. Only a deranged man would challenge our husbands, because they are who they are, they could shrug it off. Or they could magnanimously refuse, citing their skills at firearms and fencing due to their military training."

"I never thought of that," Rachel admitted.

"Here, let's go to the stable. I've got what he needs."

As they walked out in the cool early spring air, Rachel wondered, "Do you think John and Charles can get there in time?"

"They just might. Even if Jeffrey finds Yancy and delivers his challenge via a letter or slapping Yancy in the face with his gloves, it would take at least a day to arrange the duel, find a quiet place to have it. There is some hope."

"What if Jeffrey kills Yancy?" Rachel inquired.

"Unlikely."

"I don't much care for Yancy. He's pompous."

"He can be," Catherine agreed. "But don't forget during the war he risked his fortune, he openly worked against the king. Had we lost he would have been hung along with our father. He is worth some consideration. But yes, Jeffrey is far more likeable and even this wild behavior is understandable."

"I suppose."

They reached the stable as Charles, small travel bag slung over his shoulder and Piglet racing in front of him, emerged from the house.

John looked up as Serena came down with a big basket of goods.

Catherine stepped inside. "Charles wants to go with you. He's packed."

"Good." John smiled. "Ralston, will you run up to the big house? Tell Mr. Ewing what happened."

Ralston tore out of the stable.

Catherine ordered Serena, "Go along. Tell Father we're down here."

She curtseyed, ran out of the stable.

Barker O. and Jeddie rapidly hooked up the simple wooden cart, painted a dark blue, harness all set. They drove around to the front and Jeddie hopped down. As he did so, Ewing puffed down from the big house.

On reaching the stable, the older man handed Charles a second lovely gun. "I have pieces of the story."

"Father, we will tell you all, but our husbands haven't a moment to spare."

The sisters kissed their husbands, who then swung up into the cart.

Ewing, deeply troubled, ordered Jeddie, "Go with Barker O., Jeddie." He then handed the two men brass passes, Number One and Number Four, having had the presence of mind to grab them.

As the cart rumbled down the packed dirt road, up at the main house cobblestones had been laid, Catherine and Rachel gave their father the details.

"To think this started at our house." He shook his head.

"Father, you aren't responsible for Yancy drinking too much and having a loose tongue."

"I know." He hung his head a moment, then looked up. "But what he said was designed to hurt Mrs. Holloway and inflame Jeffrey. Even drunk, he had to know a bit of what he was saying."

"You approve of dueling, Father?" Rachel took his hand.

"No, but I see no other way. Go to court for slander? A man would be a laughingstock. Gentlemen use lawyers for business, not for matters of honor."

"No honor in the courtroom?" Catherine's eyebrows lifted upward.

"Precisely." He half closed his eyes.

46

*M*ignon moved the long wooden rolling pin over dough on the back table while Eudes minced potatoes brought up from basement storage. Fortunately, the potatoes held out, a few more eyes than usual but good. The basement, dry, provided excellent storage. The two big ovens cooked chickens, the smell of hickory filling the kitchen as it slowly burned.

Herbs hung upside down from rafters, that odor pleasing as well.

"I'm sure we're past the last frost," Eudes hopefully predicted.

"I hope so. I'll be happy when the garden in the back gives us some early carrots. When all else fails, you can do all kinds of things with carrots, even make cake."

"True." He glanced up at the clock. "Where does the time go? We'll have this food ready just in time. The crowds are picking up, Georgina's happy, the girls are happy. The men are happy. The men are spending."

"Don't you ever wonder where they get all their money?"

He laughed. "Some I know. Others aren't worth squat. They live

306

off other people. The most worthless are the ones that haven't had to work."

"Why?"

"Oh," he smiled, "they inherited just enough money to make bums out of them." He paused. "Some good ones, of course."

The chatter intensified in the tavern. The murmur of voices floated into the kitchen. A good sign, always a good sign.

Then everything was quiet.

"Hmm." Eudes opened the kitchen door slightly to behold Jeffrey Holloway handing Yancy Grant a letter.

Yancy, who had stood as Jeffrey approached, opened it with his unused dinner knife, read it, threw it on the table. "I am happy to oblige. Let us give ourselves a week to put our affairs in order. Best we do this back home."

People figured out what was transpiring.

"I agree. I traveled here as I didn't want this to take more time than necessary. I thought I'd find you here. But I request that you tell no one but your second, as I don't want my wife troubled."

"No one will know other than our seconds." Yancy sat back down as Maureen, Sheba, and DoRe walked into the room to everyone's amazement.

"I told you he'd be here." Sheba gloated.

Maureen, eyes narrowed, rounded on her husband. "You beast!"

"I am here because I knew Mr. Grant would be here. Now you must leave."

Georgina rushed from her office, where Lolly had sped to warn her.

"What is the meaning of this?" Georgina demanded.

Binky picked up a thin log from the fire stack just in case. If the antagonists didn't explode, the boss might.

DoRe moved next to Binky. He didn't say anything but Binky was aware of a large presence by his right elbow.

"I've come to fetch my husband and put an end to this foolishness." Maureen threw her shoulders back.

"Mrs. Holloway, your husband has barged in here to offend Mr. Grant. I would be happy if you would remove him."

Binky looked up at DoRe. "That's Mrs. Holloway?"

"Yes," DoRe replied.

Binky dropped the log, walked toward Maureen. "Your runaway is in the kitchen. You promised a one-hundred-dollar reward."

"What?" Maureen was taken aback.

"The little tiny kitchen lady described on the bill. She's in the kitchen." Binky persisted.

Sheba whispered in her mistress's ear, "The thieving bitch."

"If you have my slave, I will demand compensation for the time lost!" Maureen shouted, furious.

"I do not have your slave." Georgina was wise enough not to block Maureen, Sheba, and DoRe heading for the kitchen.

Eudes, hearing it all, stood in front of Mignon, holding a meat cleaver.

As the door pushed open he warned, "You come near her and I will kill you."

"Mignon, you slut, working in a whorehouse," Sheba crowed.

Binky, also now in the kitchen, in his mind was already spending the money.

Jeffrey pushed past Sheba, nearly throwing her on the floor. "That is not our servant!"

Mignon had put on a bit of weight, looking healthier than she ever had in her life.

"I ought to know my own kitchen help," Maureen spit.

He grasped her elbow, drew his face close to hers. "My dear, she is close, very close, but you have suffered many shocks. Let us not add one more." He spoke to Eudes. "We are mistaken. I am very sorry."

Sheba screamed, "It's the thief. I know it!"

Jeffrey turned to DoRe. "DoRe, you knew the little woman. Is this she?"

"No, Sir, but she could be her sister. This woman is a little taller, lighter in color." DoRe stared at Mignon, who now stood beside Eudes, cleaver still in his hand.

Jeffrey then said to Georgina, "I apologize for all this. I had no idea my wife and her lady's maid were following me along with our coachman. As for my challenge to Yancy Grant, I do not apologize for that. He grievously insulted me and brought misery to my wife. She has suffered much in the last year." He drew Maureen closer to him. While stiff, she did not resist.

Georgina, business first, looked at Maureen. "Madam, I am sorry for your troubles. I want you to know your husband has only enjoyed food here with business interests. The men like to come, we serve the best food in Richmond. But he doesn't even look at the women."

Sheba's face fell.

"Thank you." Jeffrey then spoke to everyone, but mostly for Sheba's benefit. "My wife has witnessed her first husband's murder. She has been cruelly buffeted by fate. Anyone who adds to her worries, who preys on her as she recovers, will answer to me. And Sheba, if you are hoping that I die in that duel, I will not. I intend to live and to see my wife smile again."

Jeffrey may not have had the best education, but he had a pretty good sense of what had been going on.

Maureen relaxed a bit, leaning on him.

DoRe stepped forward to open the door. They walked through the hushed tavern, out into the front yard.

Binky had signed his own death warrant, but he was too stupid to know it.

Georgina clapped her hands together in the kitchen. "Back to work. We've got a full house and they're hungry. Binky, carry out the breads. Send Lolly in here. Let's get what we can on the tables." She looked at Eudes, shaking now, nodded her head, and left.

Once outside, Jeffrey said to DoRe, "Walk my wife away from here. This is highly irregular. I will be right back."

"You aren't going to fight with Yancy now, are you?" Maureen looked at him with doe eyes.

"Not here. But I do need to settle with the proprietress for the uproar we have caused."

DoRe, Sheba trailing behind, walked Maureen out to the sidewalk and a few steps away from the house. "Mrs. Holloway, shall I call a coach?"

A beauty was clattering toward them.

"Yes, yes, do. See if we can hire it. I will pay well, extremely well. I want to fly out of the city."

As DoRe negotiated with the driver of the coach, the owner inside, Jeffrey tiptoed into the tavern. He motioned for Lolly, putting butter on the tables.

"Will you please fetch Georgina?"

Within a minute, Georgina, a bit flushed, walked up.

"Mr. Holloway."

He reached into his inside coat pocket, pulling out five hundred dollars. "I do hope this will repair the problems I have caused."

She looked at this large sum. "You are most generous, Sir."

"If you will allow me, I would like to make good the terror caused to that poor woman in your kitchen. And I would also like you to know I am sorry about the reward postings. I did that to please my wife but I was wrong."

"Of course." She led him to the door, opened it, and stepped back.

Eudes and Mignon, tearstained face, looked up at him, dumbfounded.

"I deeply regret how you have been disturbed. Please accept this and if you have worries about anyone trying to declare you slave, I will see that manumission papers find you. You will be free even though you were not on Big Rawly." He looked her straight in the eye.

Mignon dropped her eyes, half curtseyed, then took the two hundred dollars.

Each knew the other knew. Each played their part. Jeffrey turned and left.

Tears rolled down her cheeks. She handed the money to Eudes. "I don't know anything about money. You take care of it."

"I . . ." He thought for a moment. "I will." Then he held her close, tears also running down his cheeks. "I will take care of the money. I will take care of you. No one will harm you. I will kill anyone who tries."

She held him tight. "I think you would." She released her grasp and smiled at him. "I don't know how to thank you."

"You don't need to thank me. You just need to accept that you will be spending the rest of your life with me."

The door opened, Lolly breezed in. "The animals are hungry!"

Outside, the owner of the coach, a fellow in his late fifties perhaps, beamed. He'd sold the coach, the harness, the horses, for two thousand dollars, a princely sum at an enormous profit.

DoRe climbed up, took the reins from the driver, then pointed down the street. "Mr. Holloway!"

Jeffrey, outside now, beheld John and Charles, Piglet leading the way, walking toward them.

"What are you doing here?" Jeffrey handed his wife up into the coach, then moved a bit away as she leaned out the window.

"We came to keep you out of trouble," John replied.

"Uh, climb up into the coach. I am partially out of trouble and please let's not discuss this in front of my wife. I will pay all your expenses. Thank you for trying to save me."

Charles lifted up his hands. "Someone had to."

Jeffrey walked back to the coach. "My dear, our neighbors will be riding with us."

"Of course." Maureen felt happier than she had in years.

She didn't know the duel was set but she'd seen her husband declare his love in his own way. She believed he did want to make her happy.

Sheba, by the coach, pouted. "We will be squeezed in."

"No, we won't. You sit up with DoRe," Maureen commanded.

Sheba's face fell as Charles helped her up. She sat next to DoRe, who refused to look at her.

The men climbed in, then Piglet was lifted up, and he jumped into Charles's lap.

The two-and-a-half-day trip allowed them to watch spring unfold from the falls of Richmond into the Piedmont. Spring, about ten days behind in the Piedmont, filled the air with fragrance. John and Charles kept offering to pay for lodging when they would stop for food, or to hire another coach that they might be less crowded.

Both Jeffrey and Maureen refused. And everyone had to admit it was a beautiful ride home, filled with talk of politics, of planting hay, corn, flax, even a bit of wheat.

The happiest creature was Piglet. He'd ridden in carts but never a coach-in-four. Surely there was no dog as stylish in Virginia.

47

November 22, 2016 Tuesday

Oak leaves shivered on trees. They turned gold or sometimes orange then brown. Many did not fall off the tree. Instead, they shook a little. If a breeze intensified, what seemed to be self-inflicted shaking grew more pronounced. The dried leaves would then loudly rustle. Harry often thought no other fall leaves sounded like oak. Virginia abounded in many types of oak. She couldn't remember if it was forty or fifty or what.

"Susan, how many kinds of oak are in Virginia?"

Next to her friend in the Volvo, Susan shrugged. "I don't know. Why do you think of these things?"

"I don't know." Harry smiled.

"No cat would waste time on that." Pewter tossed off this criticism.

"No human would waste time on catnip." Tucker, next to Pewter in the backseat, stared out the window.

"Oh, yes they do," the gray cat fired back. "They make catnip tea. Why you would want to waste a heavenly herb on tea, who knows?"

"All that catnip she harvested mid-September, hanging upside down in the high rafters of the tractor shed. How I wish we could get at it," Mrs. Murphy dreamed.

"*She'll bring it down for Thanksgiving and she'll also make you catnip socks for Christmas,*" Tucker predicted.

"*She is good about that,*" Mrs. Murphy affirmed.

Back in the front seat, Harry asked, "Did you like target practice with the flintlock?"

"I did, actually," Susan replied. "I'm glad you took me to the shooting range because I would have had a hard time without an instructor. What I found interesting was how good the pistol feels in your hand. Thanks for letting me use it."

"Does, doesn't it?" Harry nodded. "So many modern pistols are heavy. 'Course, most law enforcement people like Glocks. Coop uses a Glock. Actually, for a modern gun I still prefer a revolver." She took a curve on Garth Road. "So many people are dead set against firearms, but I find shooting targets at home or going to the range relaxing. Also, when you consider the history of guns and rifles, that's fascinating."

"Today is the day Kennedy was shot in 1963, speaking of firearms."

Harry thought a moment. "Right. Ever notice if you haven't lived through an event yourself, you might pay attention but it doesn't emotionally affect you too much? The people who remember it will be remembering where they were at the time. I'm glad we were born later."

"Richard Neville was born today in 1428." Susan held the hand rest as Harry turned right. "Speaking of dates, I've always been fascinated by the War of the Roses, and Neville was a brilliant man. I love Philippa Gregory's books."

"I think the world does." Harry slowed on the country road although it was paved. "Some people have the knack of making history come to life. Academics are snotty about historical fiction. I think it's a great way to learn."

"You went to Smith. You aren't an academic but you certainly received the best education." Susan said this admiringly.

"Did. I'm hoping over time I will get to know Marvella Larson better. She knows more than any of us and I really love the Virginia Museum of Fine Arts." She pointed to her right. "Don't you wish Cloverfields still stood? That was the site of the main house."

"I do. We're luckier than many other states. Virginia has preserved so much of her heritage," Susan agreed.

"Because we were too poor to tear buildings down at the end of the nineteenth century and for most of the twentieth when everyone put up big glass blocks. Most of that stuff is ugly as a mud fence."

They both laughed.

"Speaking of Cloverfields, do you have your chit underneath your sweater?"

"Do." Harry pulled up the brass piece on the box chain. "I wonder who wore this. I wonder about their life and who wore Number Five and Liz's Number Seven? It makes it real. I like to touch things from the past."

"That's what got MaryJo and Panto into all that tribal stuff. How long have people been wearing those skins, dancing, singing? Plus MaryJo sent away for the DNA testing, which she declares proves she has twenty-seven percent tribal blood. At least she's shut up about it finally. Remember when she'd constantly bring it up?"

"Yeah." Harry stopped at the crest of the hill at the back of Cloverfields. They looked toward the ravines where the bridges had been built, although you couldn't see down into the ravines. They were too far away.

"Sometimes, late afternoon, I like to sit with Grandmother

and Mother at Big Rawly, look over the fields. Think of footsteps down the hall over the centuries."

"That place is so beautiful and isn't it odd that Big Rawly survived but Cloverfields didn't? The Garths were supposed to be so highly intelligent but Fate doesn't always play favorites."

"Apparently not." Susan stared at the sky, long afternoon rays softening everything as Harry turned, drove over a cut hayfield stopping near the site of the old main house.

As they sat there, a brand-new truck barreled up from the slope to the ravine. Both women watched this $60,000 Ford F-250 diesel rumble by, hesitate as the driver beheld the Volvo near the house site, then move faster, speeding away.

"Isn't that Panto?" Susan inquired.

"Sure is. He must be making the bucks to buy that new big-ass truck."

They sat silently for a time.

"I'm going to follow him." Harry put down her window. "Hear that?"

"Loud."

"Sounds like he has a glass pack under there but Panto isn't exactly the hot rod type. That's the true sound of that beast of an engine."

"So what?"

"When I stood at the top of the ridge, shooting at whoever shot at me, I heard a truck start up. That's how loud the exhaust note was."

"Harry, this can't be the only truck in the county that sounds like that," Susan chided her.

"No and yes." She turned to Susan. "Something's wrong. Where did Panto get that kind of money? He's a lawyer who represents tribes. He's not representing Altria or Anthem. You get the idea.

Something is wrong. Plus he knows me. I think whoever shot at me knows me. I'm going to follow him."

"Harry, you're nuts, number one. Number two, this Volvo station wagon isn't exactly inconspicuous."

"Trust me."

"Dear God," Susan whispered.

The animals sat still, preparing for who knows what. When Harry took a notion, things happened, often bad things.

Out on Garth Road, Harry waited for another car to get between her and Panto. Then she pulled out. He drove down Garth Road to Owensville Road, turned left, then turned right down the drive of one of the expensive, lovely homes on the road.

"There. Are you satisfied?" Susan folded her arms over her chest. "He's going to MaryJo's. They work together all the time. Put your imagination to rest."

"I'm hungry," Pewter whined.

"We'll be home soon," Mrs. Murphy told her, as she, too, would be happy to eat.

They reached the intersection of Route 250, turned west, past Duner's, the popular restaurant at Ivy Commons, then the countryside opened up a bit.

Halfway to the right turn to Route 240 into Crozet, Panto's truck roared by them at such speed, Harry pulled over. Before she could pull back onto the road, a sleek Cadillac CTS also roared by her. They passed the 240 turn.

"Hey, that's MaryJo's car." Harry wondered what was going on.

Pulling out behind the wildly speeding cars, both Harry and Susan watched MaryJo tail Panto.

"People do this kind of thing if they're lovers and have had a fight," Susan observed. "I never thought of the two of them having an affair. Did you?"

"No. Jesus, they're going eighty miles an hour on a two-lane highway. I'm going sixty and that's fast enough."

MaryJo pulled next to the F-250, slammed into the truck, then dropped back as cars came toward her from the opposite lane.

"What the—?" Harry shouted.

"Don't go near them, Harry," Susan warned her. "They're crazy."

MaryJo again slammed into Panto's truck, pushing him partly off the road. Again, Harry had to pull back.

"He's going to head for 64," Susan predicted.

"I don't know." Harry looked in her rearview mirror to see three animals leaning against one another in the backseat, eyes wide open.

The stoplight on old Route 250 to turn to Crozet proper was red and a line of traffic headed east as well as a lot of people in the turnoff lane, including Panto with MaryJo right behind him.

"I'm going to call Coop." Susan pulled her cellphone out of her purse.

The unloaded flintlock pistol was sliding on the seat so Harry picked it up, dropping it on her lap.

Susan filled Cooper in on what was happening.

"You're the second report," the deputy told her. "I'll be on my way. I'm calling for backup."

Harry handed the gun to Susan. "Load this up, will you?"

"Why?"

"Just in case." Harry turned right. "I don't know, but do it anyway."

Once Panto drove under the railroad overpass, he turned left at the Amoco station and floored it. MaryJo, hot on his tail, did the same.

Cars, trucks driving in the opposite direction pulled off the road. Some honked. Most had the sense to pull off into a pasture if possible.

The two wild drivers thundered west, even the slightest curve at that speed courted danger.

Harry, no fool, stuck to sixty miles an hour, sometimes less.

"*Someone's going to die,*" Pewter prophesied. "*As long as it isn't me.*" She thought a moment. "*Us.*"

"*That's big of you.*" Tucker lurched to the right, bumping into Mrs. Murphy, who at least had claws to dig into the plush leather seats.

Panto slowed, allowing MaryJo to pull right beside him. He lowered the driver's window and fired. While neither Harry nor Susan could see the sidearm, they knew he fired because Mary-Jo's back window exploded as she had seen the gun and pulled slightly ahead of Panto, but still next to him. Furious, MaryJo hit his truck harder.

Her CTS, heavy, wasn't as heavy as the F-250 but she could still push. He fired again, hitting her in the shoulder, and in taking his eyes off the road, crunched off the highway with his right tires. He overcorrected and now slammed into MaryJo. Again, they sped, now on a straightaway.

Susan again called Cooper, who was approaching Crozet from Route 240 and drawing closer, five minutes away at most. Another curve loomed. Panto handling the large truck, tried to corner it but he slid, the heavy-duty truck leaning dangerously to the right and MaryJo used her moment, smashing into the truck with all her might. The new vehicle rolled over but landed upright. MaryJo pulled close, opened her own window, and fired. Harry and Susan saw blood spatter his windshield. MaryJo, half off the road herself, turned around, saw Harry behind her by perhaps fifteen yards. As Harry closed in, MaryJo leveled her .45 Smith & Wesson. She missed the humans but blew out the wide windows in the back. Harry, furious, grabbed the gun from Susan, pulled a U, not easy in the station wagon, and barreled down on MaryJo as the crazed woman was trying to get firmly on the road.

Using the flintlock, Harry fired and MaryJo's windshield shattered. The Cadillac stopped. Harry kept going.

Susan, adrenaline high, shouted, "Bull's-eye."

Covered in glass bits, thanks to the ball's perfect hit, MaryJo now focused on Harry and Susan, whom she could see just ahead. As she closed in after them, flooring it, Cooper prudently waited about half a mile down the road, as she could somewhat see what was going on. She let Harry pass, then fired her Glock at MaryJo's tires. One blew, but the woman determinedly tried to keep on. Cooper, a crack shot, blew out another one. MaryJo crashed.

Sirens blared from all four directions. MaryJo, though alive, was toast.

"Dammit," Harry swore, and she rarely swore. "Now I have to replace those windows."

"*Glass. Little bits of glass,*" Pewter bitterly complained. "*It will get into my paws.*"

Harry pulled into a church driveway near the town, stepped out of the car, lifted up Pewter, came round to Susan, and put the cat in her lap. Then she picked up Tucker and told the wonderful corgi to squeeze next to Susan. Lastly she picked up Mrs. Murphy, holding the tiger in her lap as she drove home.

"*She understood.*" Pewter was amazed.

"*Sometimes humans get it,*" Tucker replied. "*I've never seen anything like that. Ever.*"

"*Let's hope it was the first and last time,*" Mrs. Murphy added. "*A new Cadillac banging into a new truck. Usually if people spend money on something they take care of it.*"

"*He's dead. We'll only hear one side of the story once Cooper drags MaryJo out of the car,*" Pewter reasoned.

"Susan, let me go home after we give Coop our statements. Fair should be home soon and he can drive you back. I don't want to drive this car any farther than I must."

"Sure." Susan's heart slowed down a bit. "I think Panto or MaryJo would have killed us if they'd had the chance."

"Maybe they've tried before." Harry glanced at her friend.

"Dear God." Susan exhaled. "That was the craziest thing I have ever seen. If they'd hit people, other cars, deer, house, dogs, they wouldn't have stopped or cared. Lunatics. Madness."

"Sure was, but even mad men have a kind of logic," Harry replied.

48

April 14, 1786 Friday

*T*wo ghostly figures walked in the middle of a silver-gray ground fog covering a level pasture called The Downs. Invisible from the waist down they appeared to glide toward each other. On the opposite sides of this pasture waited carriages, an elegant small enclosed carriage driven by DoRe, a larger carriage driven by Everett Franks, enshrouded by the fog now beginning to rise with the sun. The carriages and horses also seemed otherworldly. Birds awakened. A chirp, a squawk enlivened the air. A herd of deer observed the horses and humans from the edge of a wood, only their elegant heads visible.

John Schuyler took off his hat, offered his hand. "Mr. Tapscott."

Henry Tapscott, a lean middle-aged man, did the same. "Major Schuyler, I regret the circumstances."

"As do I, Sir. I have encouraged Mr. Holloway to set this duel aside, to find another means of accommodation. He steadfastly refuses."

"I fear Mr. Grant is of like mind," Henry Tapscott, a childhood friend of Yancy Grant, dolorously replied.

"The surgeon we agreed upon is in Mr. Holloway's carriage."

"Thank you for bringing him. It was easier for you since he lives near to you. Young fellow but many of those he has treated have lived."

John craned his neck to look skyward. "The sun is low, but we should make certain they pace off in a north-south direction."

"Indeed." Henry nodded. "You would like to inspect the pistols, Sir?" He pulled the highly polished walnut box from under his left arm, turned it toward John, who opened it.

Two beautiful pistols lay side by side in satin, the metal, silver, the wood an even richer walnut than the box. John lifted up one, rubbed the nozzle lightly with his little finger. A thin coating of oil remained on his finger. Then he checked the trigger to make sure it hadn't been tampered with to fire faster. Putting it back, he picked up the other to repeat the procedure.

"Fine work."

Henry bowed slightly. "My own, Sir. Yancy has but one pistol, which he has modified."

John hesitated, couldn't think of anything else to say, then spoke, "We should get started. The mist is rising."

"Yes" came the subdued reply.

Both returned to their carriages.

John opened the door for Jeffrey and Thomas Downey, the doctor. Each man sat with his feet placed on a warmed brick.

Wordlessly, Jeffrey climbed down and removed his frock coat. He would be better able to move without it. Henry Tapscott performed the same service for Yancy Grant while Everett Franks, the driver, now on foot, held the horses quiet by their bridles.

The two antagonists walked to the middle of the flat pasture, where Henry repeated the rules of a duel.

"You will stand back to back. I will give the command and you will each walk ten paces, which I will clearly count out. Then you

turn and fire. One shot. Should one of you be killed or wounded, the other man shall immediately return to his carriage. Do you understand?"

"Yes," Jeffrey replied, holding the pistol he had picked out of the offered box.

"Yes," Yancy also replied.

"Back to back, gentlemen," Henry ordered.

John and Dr. Downey remained at the carriage. DoRe, sitting in the driver's seat, had an excellent view. The mist was rising fast. Shortly it would obscure their heads so Henry wanted to get the duel under way wherein each man could see the other.

Just in case, Henry did give them an opportunity. "Would you wish to wait until the ground fog is over your heads?"

"No, I don't give a damn about ground fog." Yancy wanted to get it over with, certain he'd drill Jeffrey.

"I agree. Let us begin," Jeffrey, his back now against Yancy's, said in an unwavering voice.

John gripped his hands together until his knuckles were white.

Henry, backed away from what would be the line of fire, called in a loud voice, "One, two, three."

The men, ramrod straight, took each step as called. However, the ground fog appeared to be swirling and rising faster on the south end, Jeffrey's end.

"Seven, eight, nine, ten. Fire."

Each man whirled around and for a split second Yancy squinted to see Jeffrey's upper body, the mist playing tricks. He leveled his pistol, firing.

Jeffrey grunted but stood his ground, firing a split second after Yancy.

"Great God." Yancy's left hand grabbed at his right knee while he dropped the pistol. He crumpled.

Jeffrey, standing, watched for a moment then walked, obviously in pain, back to his carriage. A line of blood trickled from his right biceps.

"You are hurt, Sir." Dr. Downey reached to roll up his sleeve.

"Please go to Mr. Grant first. I believe he suffers a more serious wound."

Rolling in the wet grass, tears flooded from Yancy's eyes. Henry knelt down with him, beheld the entry wound in his right knee-cap. Putting his hands under Yancy's shoulders he lifted him up, and Everett, knowing the horses were fine, ran over to help. With a man on each side, they supported him as he hopped in excru-ciating pain.

Dr. Downey, bag in hand, ran over as the two men leaned Yancy against the side of the carriage. One of the horses took a step so Henry quickly grabbed Yancy as he howled in pain. Everett ran to the horses, again holding them by the bridles, standing between them.

Tersely, Dr. Downey said to Henry, "Cut off the boot."

Henry reached into his inside pocket, pulled out a good knife, began slicing the boot along the back seam. "Forgive me, old friend, I know this is very painful."

Gasping, Yancy whispered, "Do what you have to do."

The boot off, Dr. Downey removed a sharpened pair of long-nosed scissors from his bag to cut away the breeches. Once they were cut above the knee, dropped into the grass, the young man knelt down, carefully examining the front of Yancy's knee and equally carefully lifting up his leg, then looked at the back.

"Your kneecap is smashed, Sir. The bullet has exited. I will not have to dig it out, which would only add to your distress, but I must lay you down flat, straighten your leg. Henry will hold you while I do so, as that will be painful. Then I must bandage your knee to immobilize it. You are bleeding but not profusely. Once you are home you must have the bone bits removed or you will always be in pain."

John hurried over to help lift Yancy flat on his back. Yancy, a big man, would be difficult for Henry to maneuver. First, Henry pulled a canvas cover from the carriage, spreading it on the ground.

John, enormously strong, picked up Yancy slowly and bent from his own knees to gently lay him down on the canvas, now with Henry's help.

"Do it now, Sir. Remove the bone bits."

Dr. Downey nodded, knelt down, too, began the work of cleaning away blood, bits of cartilage, and flesh. Henry held Yancy's hand as the man tried not to scream when Dr. Downey had to cut and fold back more flesh so he could see the damage. However, tears rolled down Yancy's face.

Looking up at John, he said, "Thank you and forgive me." He hoarsely continued, "I cannot stop these tears."

John took his other hand as he had remained on his knees. "I have seen generals weep, Yancy. No need for forgiveness."

"Then forgive me for being," he paused, "an ass. I caused such an uproar at Ewing's celebration."

John smiled at him. "No one was bored."

"I will never ride in a race again." The tears continued.

"No, but you will always be a horseman and you will breed animals that can run. I pray for your recovery." John stood up.

Yancy stifled a groan as Dr. Downey cut away another piece of torn cartilage.

"I must do this, Sir, else as you heal it will sometimes entangle what remains of your knee. This won't take much longer," he said consolingly.

"Do what you must." Yancy repeated the phrase, then said to John, "Is Mr. Holloway wounded?"

"Upper arm. He will be fine."

"I am glad." Yancy breathed deeply as more cartilage and bone bits were removed.

Dr. Downey, young eyes, worked quickly and carefully. He dabbed at the blood. Fortunately, there wasn't a great deal at the knee. Noticing this, John wished he had been the surgeon to his old regiment.

"Dr. Downey, we will wait until you have completed your work on Mr. Grant," John said.

"Ah, thank you. Better Mr. Grant not be in his carriage bounced around longer than necessary." He looked at Henry. "It won't be much longer." Then he looked directly into Yancy's eyes. "In time, some of your bone may grow a bit but this knee will never be able to support weight. You will need a brace and a crutch."

Yancy tried to smile. "At least I am alive."

"I will return to Mr. Holloway," John informed them all, then thought perhaps another kind of healing might take place. "Although wounded himself, Mr. Holloway insisted that Dr. Downey attend to you first, Yancy. I sincerely hope you two can find a way to reach an accord."

"I'll never like him, never." Yancy sighed, then took a ragged intake of breath as more cartilage was cleaned up as well as a bit of flapping flesh now sewed around the shattered knee. "But I will do my best to be," he paused "civilized."

John slightly bowed, then returned to the carriage where DoRe, down from his driving seat, had cut away Jeffrey's shirt. Jeffrey was bleeding more than Yancy.

"Do you think the bullet hit your bone?" John inquired.

"No." Jeffrey removed his hand from the hole in his arm.

"You are most fortunate. Dr. Downey can fix you up. He said he wouldn't be long with Yancy."

"What is his wound?"

"You blew apart his kneecap," John stated.

"Ah." The young man exhaled.

Three hours later, DoRe drove down the long Big Rawly drive as Maureen flew out of the house.

"You're alive! Oh, thank God, you are alive!" She went to hug and kiss him, she couldn't contain herself, and then noticed the torn shirt and the blood. "What happened? How bad is it? Oh, get out of this carriage and into the house."

John stepped out, smiled up at DoRe. "He will be fine, Mrs. Holloway, fine."

She never asked about Yancy, shepherded Jeffrey into the house, calling orders to all and sundry as she did so.

John climbed up next to DoRe as they drove to the stables. One of the young men brought out his horse, all groomed, relaxed and happy. John tipped the man, mounted up, and was at Clover-fields within forty minutes since he walked most of the way. The entire episode had exhausted him.

Catherine, down at the stables, hearing the slow hoofbeats, dashed out to see her handsome husband nearing the stable.

"How so?" She reached him.

"Both alive. Jeffrey's hit in the arm. He'll be fine. Yancy, on the other hand, has a shot-up kneecap. I suppose he will walk eventually with a cane or crutches but I doubt he will ride again."

"I do hope this is the end of it."

"I think it is. Neither one flinched. Let us hope this is a new day."

49

November 29, 2016 Tuesday

*I*n the hayloft, Harry, after opening the back high double doors, stood at the edge throwing out rich fragrant hay bales. The two cats watched this work, grateful they didn't have to throw hay.

"*Alfalfa bales can weigh up to sixty pounds,*" Mrs. Murphy noted.

"*Orchard grass and clover is heavy enough.*" Pewter saw Tucker, on the ground below, observing the pitched hay. "*She thinks she's helping.*"

"*Keeps her happy. The grass hasn't totally browned out yet, there's green. Our human is fanatical about nutrition for all of us.*" Mrs. Murphy admired Harry's sense of responsibility.

"*In that case, I'm in the mood for fried chicken.*"

"*What, no tuna?*" Mrs. Murphy wondered.

"*Fried chicken, and if she makes greens with fatback I can pick out all the fatback. Humans need to learn to cook for cats. Our palates are more developed than theirs. They eat tomatoes, remember?*" Pewter's silky eyebrows raised.

"*Odd. How about cauliflower?*" The tiger grimaced.

"*I'll eat it if she's melted cheese on those little white things,*" Pewter confessed.

Tucker, ears up, barked, "*Cooper.*"

"*Let's go.*" Mrs. Murphy dashed for the ladder, climbing down backward.

Harry, hearing the car, threw out two more bales, shut the doors, latched them from the inside, and slid down the ladder. She liked, when wearing gloves, to put her hands outside the ladder, hold on, and slide down with her feet also on the outside.

"*Show off.*" Pewter turned up her nose.

"*Looks like fun,*" Tucker, inside now, remarked. "*You're jealous because you can't do it.*"

"*At least I can climb up to the hayloft,*" the gray animal fired back.

"Coop, let me toss the hay into the pastures. Won't take a minute," Harry informed her friend.

"I'll help you."

The two women walked behind the barn, each picking up a hay bale by the string, chucking it over the fence. Harry then climbed over that pasture fence, fished a pocketknife out of her pocket, cut the string, rolled it up, stuffed it in her old Carhart jacket pocket.

This task consumed maybe ten minutes. Finished, Harry headed for the kitchen.

"Harry, I'm fine. You don't need to feed me."

"*I can eat!*" Pewter instantly refuted Cooper's comment.

"Well, I'm hungry and I have these poor starving animals. Got up at five-thirty and I just now finished the last of the chores."

Once in the kitchen, coats on the Shaker pegs, Harry warmed up the morning's coffee she'd made for Fair, put on the teapot for herself. Then she opened the refrigerator, cut up some leftover chicken, put it down for the animals, who raced for their bowls.

"Hey. I have liver pâté, fresh French bread, and farm butter. Also have jams."

"Liver pâté?"

"Coop, my husband now evidences an interest in more elegant

foods than my succotash." Harry smiled. "It really is good although I always feel bad for the goose."

"Omnivore."

"Sure, we'll eat anything."

The tall deputy waited for Harry to sit down before buttering bread.

"Not much of a Thanksgiving for you, was it?" Harry commiserated.

Cooper shook her head. "We got as much as we could. By the way, MaryJo died last night from her internal injuries from the crash, plus the wound from Darrel when he shot her. Damn fool, she's in the car, door crushed against her and she's still firing at us. Insane. Gone." Coop tapped her forehead.

"Conscious?"

"In and out but we did find out a few things. Bruce, her husband, swore he knew nothing. Thought all the money came from her investment business."

"Do you believe him?"

"I don't know. Rick and I talked about it, well, everyone on the force has talked about it. Rick says if wives don't know when husbands are crooks, is it not possible that husbands don't know about their wives? As long as the money rolls in, would you be suspicious?"

"I don't know. If people came in and out of the house at odd hours, I would be. She fooled us. She could have fooled him."

"She fooled us to the tune of six million dollars, give or take, over the last three years. She had a bursting account."

"My God!" Harry exclaimed.

"Selling illegal animal parts, feathers, fur, ground-up bones, is a huge worldwide business and she was the nerve center for the East Coast. She and Panto supplied everyone and anyone, and a big part of the business flowed from the tribal wannabes. The people who declare themselves to be of that blood but have inherited no regalia or implements from their ancestors."

"Do you think they are tribal members?"

"Not really," Cooper honestly answered. "Perhaps a few, but remember that white woman who declared herself African American to get a job? People do weird things especially if they believe it confers status. All I know is we now have records from her computer and there will be hundreds of arrests in the original thirteen colonies. People who don't get wind of this and run away anyway." Cooper slumped in her chair.

"So she and Panto were in business?" Harry asked.

"Yes, but she was in effect the major stockholder. We've got the financial records. Our computer whizzes really are unbelievable. They cracked her codes and we all read the financial statements with our mouths hanging open. The money!"

"So do you have a record of everyone she did business with?"

"Yes, but many of these accounts are under code names like Gray Wolf, Black Bear, that sort of thing. In many instances, the transfer was in cash. She was nothing if not slick."

"Did she say why she killed Panto?"

"No. She betrayed very little except to say her work involved religion."

"What?"

"No kidding. She could only say she was supplying goods for religious ceremonies." Cooper drank a bit more of the coffee, which wasn't bitter since it hadn't been sitting that long.

"How can that be?"

"Consider Quakers. Nonviolent people. They can choose not to fight in a war. Yes, they have to register as conscientious objectors but their wishes not to kill are respected. Or the Amish. There are things they can do or not do that the rest of us can't. This honoring of different faiths, if you will, is even more pronounced for tribes. They have treaties from the United States government allowing them their own government."

"A recipe for problems." Harry sighed. "Then again, look what we've gone through here just to get our Virginia tribes recognized by that same Federal government that herded people onto reservations."

"It is confusing. Do I think people are taking advantage of this? No. A few are and the really smart ones like MaryJo do more than take advantage. Once the media gets hold of this it will stir a political hornet's nest. A lot of MaryJo's customers are Asian, recently moved here, as well as people from parts of the world we regard as primitive. They believe in spirits and pacifying those spirits. Some of the things, shrunken whale penises, no kidding, are ground up and used as aphrodisiacs."

"For men, I assume." Harry started to laugh.

"Well, I'm not going to take it." Cooper laughed, too.

"It's a crazy world." Harry sighed.

"It is and our good old American way allows a certain amount of gaming the system. Remember the First Amendment. There can be no national religion. Mostly it's good and has served us well. When it doesn't you have to scratch your head, but remember, Harry, there are people here who believe the earth is flat."

"Good Lord," Harry whispered. "Back to all this, you think Panto wanted more money?"

"I do. And I think you were targeted because you shot your mouth off about contraband. Granted, you did not meddle, but somehow you were onto this in your own lopsided way."

Harry demurred. "I didn't really figure it out, it just seemed likely, given we found eagle feathers, a cage. Which reminds me, Pierre Rice."

"We think he was working for the Department of Wildlife and Fisheries. They were well aware of game being poached off our national parks and they were also well aware that this was a billion-dollar industry, much of the goods being sold in the U.S. Pierre, bit by bit, was closing in. He narrowed it down to the big rigs carrying contraband from the mid-South to all directions. First, he looked for big box trucks. But these folks are more subtle than that. They filled new cars being delivered with cages, boxes, et cetera, all cleaned up, of course, and hauled them to Afton pass on Route 64. There MaryJo, Panto, and the people who worked for them, we're still arresting drivers, met the rig, transferred the contraband."

"The dead driver's face?"

"Don't know. The medical examiner believes he was torn up by an animal. Possibly he realized Pierre was tailing him and he had something really valuable, stopped to free the animal or bird and the creature took his revenge."

"Good," Harry replied.

"MaryJo placed all the blame for the murders on Panto before she died. Said Panto killed Pierre, shot at you. Panto had killed Pierre at old Cloverfields, crossed the creek, and dumped him at Sugarday. Granted she was loaded on painkillers, but I wouldn't believe all that anyway. She proved herself an excellent liar and, if you will, a good businesswoman."

"Ever find Liz's Sioux Indian dress, the one that hung on the wall of the shop?"

"No. I have no doubt it is in some rich person's collection. Maybe in time. I'm amazed we've pieced together this much. And in some ways I think Bruce may be telling the truth because if he was in on his wife's criminal business he would probably have destroyed her computer."

"Didn't think of that."

"Pierre was very close," Cooper said. "But we don't know why he went to Cloverfields. Was he lured there?"

"The Rices are descended from the Cloverfields Rices." Harry folded her hands on the table. "Panto must have known about the chits. Lured him in some way."

"MaryJo swore Panto robbed Liz's store for his own personal profit. Anything she could pin on him she did."

"She wasn't stupid until the end."

Cooper nodded.

The phone rang. Harry jumped up to answer the old wall phone that she adored. "Harry here."

"Harry, can you come over to St. Luke's?" Reverend Jones's deep, deep voice asked.

"Sure. What's up?"

"The Taylors' grave has been opened. You need to see this."

"I'll be right there. Coop will be with me."

Within twenty minutes, Harry, Cooper, Mrs. Murphy, Pewter, and Tucker stood over the opened graves, spades resting on their sides at the piled earth.

"*I told you I smelled old bones,*" Tucker, self-satisfied, bragged.

"That pearl is as big as a pigeon's egg!" Harry gasped.

The skeleton, lying faceup on top of a lidded casket, shreds of mustard-colored silk still intact, wore her necklace, for it had to be a woman, a necklace of incredible value and the pearl, the centerpiece, was gigantic. Smaller, matching pearls were earrings. Given the size of the pearl in the necklace, smaller for the earrings was relative.

"Whoever she was, she was rich," Cooper declared.

"No doubt." The Reverend shook his head. "How did she wind up stashed on top of the Taylors? Whoever put her here knew the community well. Obviously knew that Michael and Margaret had died together. The earth would be easy to dig."

"Whoever killed her wasn't a thief," Harry posited. "Had to be hate."

The two fellows who had dug up the grave asked Reverend Jones, "What should we do, Reverend?"

"Coop?" The Lutheran minister looked to the deputy.

"Well, it is a body, so I have to call in the forensic team. Once we get all the photographs we need, you can fill this back in." She paused, smiled slightly. "I don't think anyone is in danger. Think we've had enough of that."

"Maybe." Harry considered the situation. "But someone had an idea about this, else why were the tombstones knocked over and knife marks in the soil?"

"True," Reverend Jones replied. "Let's do as Cooper said. This will be a big story for TV and the papers. Arouse a lot of curiosity. Someone may come forward. Really, no harm was done."

"You dug up the tomb?" Cooper inquired.

"Yes. I just got to thinking and my curiosity got the better of me." He smiled. "Usually it's Harry who gives in to her curiosity. I'm glad I did. I will pronounce the service for the dead before she's taken away."

"*Old bones. What can they tell?*" Pewter sniffed.

"*Sometimes if a bone is cut or smashed they know how a person was killed. And they most always can determine gender. 'Course, that's easy with these bones. Sometimes they can determine race and age, too. We'll see,*" Mrs. Murphy pronounced.

While the five humans, two cats, and one dog waited for the forensic team to show up, Reverend Jones did read the service for the dead and the humans acted as witnesses and mourners.

Not only did the sheriff's department get there, but so did

Channel 29, Channel 6 had a stringer, and The Daily Progress sent a reporter. This was going to be a big story.

As the skeleton was removed the Progress reporter asked Harry what she thought.

"There are so many stories about buried treasure at the old estates. Well, one turned out to be true."

"Reverend Jones," the reporter asked, "did you hear stories about buried treasure in the graveyard?"

"No, but I believe everyone in here is a buried treasure."

Finally on the way home, Mrs. Murphy said to her two friends and Harry, if she could understand, "I wonder who will get the pearl necklace?"

"It should go to the church," Tucker forcefully said.

"Nothing is that easy," Pewter grumped. "That necklace is worth a fortune."

"A bloody fortune," Mrs. Murphy added.

Harry commented as she turned down the dirt and gravel road to the farm. "It's been quite a day."

The blue jay swooped in front of the Volvo, screaming at Pewter inside.

"Fatty Fatty!"

"I understand why people will kill one another. I will kill that blue jay. I will. I will," the gray cat vowed.

Harry finished up the early-evening chores, her mind whirring. She never saw it coming with MaryJo. She never imagined a richly laden pile of bones would be tucked away in St. Luke's graveyard, either.

Petting Shortro, one of the horses, as she brought him in, she said to the handsome gray fellow as the cats and dog listened, "Shortro, I'm not as smart as I'd hoped I'd be."

"Humans worry too much." The gentle horse nuzzled her. "Some things you're not supposed to know."

Pewter piped up. *"And even when you find out, if you do, what difference does it make?"*

Harry walked Shortro, followed by his friends, into the barn. She looked at the evening star, large and luminous light in the sky, and wondered if it shone that brightly on the night the woman was killed.

Then wondered who desecrated the grave.

Shrugging, she stared again at the blazing star, said to her animal friends, "I wonder if we'll ever know who is behind this. If stars, trees, rocks could talk, we'd know most everything. Maybe it's better we don't."

Pewter blinked. *"I can't believe she said that, the world's most curious human."*

Mrs. Murphy's whiskers swept forward. *"It's true, though. What do we really need to know? The evening star saw as we changed from saber-toothed tigers to house cats."*

"Oh, Murph, the saber-toothed tiger turned into a tiger." Tucker laughed.

"Well, the evening star can watch you get swatted!" Pewter reached out to smack the dog, who dashed away.

So the evening star observed one puzzled, tired human as well as a merry chase.

50

October 15, 1786 Sunday

St. Luke's structure, washed in late-afternoon sun, testified to the progress Charles and the builders had achieved. The church itself, framed up, stood in the middle of the two wings, more or less roughed in as were the two smaller buildings, duplicates of each other at the ends of the arches. Charles decided to build with wood first, then cover that with stone. Usually the stone was done first but the press of oncoming winter encouraged him to try something different. The large log structure, now hidden behind the church, could serve indefinitely, but Charles learned if people could see progress they chipped in more readily.

The entire congregation of St. Luke's gathered in the new graveyard in the rear, the stone walls already constructed. The Taylors, respected and admired, drew friends from St. Mary's, as well as the Episcopal Church along with the various smaller Baptist churches. Father Donatello came, as did clergy from the other houses of worship.

Michael and Margaret Taylor, formerly strong and productive had wasted away. The cause was deemed the sweating sickness, malaria. At the end, both had lost so much weight as to be almost unrecognizable. In early middle age, they worked hard. He built snake fences, showing others how to do it, as well as stone fences. Michael oversaw the lovely stone fence for St. Luke's graveyard. It was he who told Charles that while buildings, important though they were, excited the parishioners, a proper graveyard needed to come first. The dead must always be respected and cherished. Who could have believed he and his wife would be placed there together on a brilliant mid-October day? Margaret expired first, Michael two hours later.

He had whispered to his eldest child, eighteen years of age, that he was sorry to leave her and her brothers, but he couldn't imagine life without his perfect Margaret.

To find the right mate provided progress, love, and respect. Catherine and John stood next to Rachel and Charles. Each of these young people knew of the fragility of life and each, like Michael, couldn't imagine a life without his or her partner.

The funeral was late in the afternoon so people from the other churches could attend. The Taylors had died that morning. As it was not unexpected, word traveled fast. The number of mourners testified to that.

Maureen and Jeffrey attended. Well, just about everybody did, but Maureen wanted everyone to see the carriage her husband had built with his father. Indeed, it was a beauty and people marveled that a local cabinetmaker mastered the skills so quickly. Just getting the angle of the big wheels correct on the axle took some doing. Jeffrey was not afraid to ask for help and to import same. The coach-in-four gleamed a deep maroon with gold pinstriping. On the doors, Maureen's crest had been painted. Yes, it was not the thing to do in a new republic, but Maureen's defense was that she was from the Caribbean. No one argued. Of course, there were those who thought she should return to the Caribbean.

The Shippenworths from Philadelphia were also there, having stayed in Virginia for the better part of the year. Their carriage, splendid but not flashy, would carry the Holloways and themselves to Hot Springs. If General Washington and Thomas Jefferson could take the waters there, so could the Shippenworths and the Holloways. The springs remained warm regardless of the season. Many swore by their medicinal powers.

The service, dignified, closed with "Ashes to ashes, dust to dust." Tears filled many eyes.

Rachel, wiping her own, said in a low voice, "They left us too soon, but they left us with a good example."

Charles, arm around her waist, nodded. "A short good life is better than a long, useless one."

As the assembled walked toward the log building, the main church was not yet ready for people, the delicious scent of food filled the air.

Inside, Bettina, Serena, even Bumbee, busied themselves. Ewing had asked them to honor the Taylors. He paid them, too, for intruding on their Sundays. The women and the other slaves working in the makeshift kitchen liked the Taylors. Bettina, having lost her own husband at a young age, thought death made all people equal, king as well as slave. It was not an equality she soon wished to experience.

St. Luke's parishioners, the white women, also worked in the kitchen. Cooking, serving food did seem to bind women.

"Miss Ix, this bacon is perfect," Bettina praised the German immigrant.

Given Bettina's reputation, Miss Ix smiled. "I do try, Bettina."

Sheba did not serve, but she did her mistress's bidding, as did Henry. DoRe popped into the kitchen, winked at Bettina, then popped out. How the ladies laughed even if it was a funeral.

"That man." Bettina pretended this was uncalled-for.

"Oh, Bettina, what would we do without their foolishness?" Lillian Bosum remarked.

"We'd get more done." Rebecca Smythers arranged sweetbreads on a tray.

Jutta Rogan nodded, then added, "Surely we would, Becky, but would we have as much fun?"

As they chattered, the front door opened, the people poured in. The hum of talk filled the room.

Given the distances, the constant labor, even a funeral provided warmth, gossip, the sense of belonging.

Ewing, legs tired from standing, sat on one of the graceful, simple backed benches.

"Father, what can I fetch you?" Rachel asked.

"Anything at all, my dear, but a pinch of punch would certainly restore my spirits."

"Right away." Charles, next to his wife, headed for the enormous silver punch bowl, loaned to the church for this occasion by Maureen.

Catherine, next to Maureen at the long food table, noted this. "Mrs. Holloway, what a kindness. If only the Taylors could see your contribution to their memory."

A solemn look flashed across Maureen's face. "Catherine, my dear, I believe they can. Nothing is ever truly lost except my husband's temper."

Catherine did laugh. "In a good cause."

"I am still shaking from that experience, but isn't it strange how men can try to kill one another, then make up?" She indicated with her head her husband talking to Yancy Grant.

Yancy, on his crutch now, also sat down, Jeffrey on one side of him with John on the other. John did not anticipate trouble but he felt either gentleman could be combustible.

"Mr. Grant." Jeffrey leaned toward the older man. "Your inter-

343

est in finance, well, let me put it this way, Mr. Shippenworth has a broad vision for our country's finances."

"Does he now?"

"I suspect he knows Sam Udall," Jeffrey replied.

Yancy considered this. "Mr. Udall has a sure grasp of value whether it be tobacco or land or hemp. He knows the day's prices. I wouldn't be surprised if the two have met."

John leaned toward Yancy slightly. "He and Ewing see each other frequently."

"If anyone knows money, it's Ewing." Yancy complimented the well-liked man.

The discussion between Ewing and Mr. Shippenworth was so lively other men gravitated toward them to listen.

"I tell you, Mr. Garth, we need a national bank to stabilize our monetary policy. It's not taxes that matter, Sir, it is monetary policy and we have none."

Men leaned closer.

Ewing, careful, replied, "You, Sir, are far better informed than I. I do not argue the point at all but I fear a national bank will offend our people. It's too close to the Exchequer in England."

A murmur of agreement attended this.

"We must go beyond the war years. There are things the English do that make great good sense," Shippenworth countered.

Big Billy Bosum, the parishioner passionate about building a navy, spoke. "The Europeans think of control. If they can control us through money, so be it. Controlling us by arms failed, but I do not think we can ever rest easy until we have a standing army, a large navy, and men committed to defending our shores and, I add, our businesses."

"Hear, hear," many said.

Catherine, plate filled for old Mrs. Ciampi, partially blind, circumvented the lively discussion.

"Mrs. Ciampi, what would you like to drink?"

"Oh, thank you, dear. Have they any sweet tea?"

"Always. I'll be right back." Catherine hurried to the drinks table, met Rachel there, and both sisters returned to the elderly lady.

"Thank you. It's a bit warm for mid-October. I find I am thirsty."

Rachel spoke. "Beautiful day, though."

"Oh, you two girls sit with me for a moment. I miss young people." Her little mobcap shook a bit as she spoke, for her head wobbled. "The loss of the Taylors distresses me. Such good people and in the prime of life. Oh, Margaret fussed about getting old and I would chide her, 'Old. Look at me! I was born in 1712. Don't talk to me about old.'"

They both laughed.

Rachel then said, "Mrs. Ciampi, you have more energy than women half your age."

This pleased the lady no end. "I will tell you my secret." She motioned for them to come a bit closer. "Never stop. Truly, never stop. Keep cleaning, cooking, chopping your own wood. Go on walks with the dog. Dig in your garden. We are meant to be busy. Idle hands do the Devil's work."

When the funeral gathering broke up all agreed that the number of people, the quality of the food, Mrs. Holloway's huge punch bowl, proved how valued were the departed.

Maureen and Jeffrey climbed into the Shippenworths' coach. Everyone went their separate ways. DoRe, now high in the driver's seat, waited for Sheba and Henry to get inside the coach.

Henry said not one word to Sheba nor she to him on the way to Big Rawly.

———

That evening, Sheba tiptoed into Maureen's bedroom. She knew where everything was. She put on Maureen's exquisite mustard-colored silk dress, the one with a low-cut bodice. Then she opened her jewelry box, for she knew where the key was. Picking up one glittering piece after another, she decided the colored stones would clash with the mustard color. Sheba possessed a good eye. Walking to the corner, she knelt down, then lifted up a loose floorboard. She took out the pearl necklace, the one with the huge pearl in the center, placed it around her own neck. Then she put the dangling large pearl earrings in her ears, the very pearls she had accused Mignon of stealing. Sheba longed for the day when she could wear what she had hidden.

"Looks better on me than that old bat," she murmured.

She couldn't help it. She wanted to walk outside in the cooling air. To glide, feeling herself a grand lady wearing a fortune in pearls.

As she swirled around, a figure approached her.

"DoRe," she acknowledged him. "Don't tell."

"Never." He came up behind her, put his hands on each cheek and twisted her neck so powerfully and quickly that he snapped it. She went down into the folds of the gorgeous voluminous skirt.

He walked slowly down to the barn, hitched up a simple hay wagon. He came back, picked her up like a rag doll, tossed her in the back, and threw hay over her.

As he drove out, Henry met him by the front of the house.

"Henry."

"DoRe."

"I trust you will say nothing."

"I will not. You've done us all a great favor."

"This is for my boy and for Ailee." He drove off.

———

Within forty-five minutes he was at St. Luke's graveyard. The earth was soft and easy to dig up on the Taylors' grave. Once he hit the casket, he quickly cleaned it off, placed Sheba on it, covered all with dirt, then tamped it down.

Driving back to Big Rawly, he realized the pearl necklace, the earrings would buy freedom. Then again, it could buy death.

Venus, the evening star, shone with brilliant light. He and his late wife would tell Moses stories about the stars when the boy was small. As Moses grew, father and son would identify stars, the Milky Way in the night sky. When his wife died, he told Moses, then a late teenager, that she was now a star. All would be well even though they missed her.

Looking up at the glittering planet, DoRe asked it, "Venus, shine your love-light on me."

Afterword

Once back at Big Rawly, Maureen did not mourn Sheba. No one seemed to mind that the lady's maid vanished.

Over at Cloverfields, the news of yet another missing slave from Big Rawly was met with resignation. Big Rawly leaked people like an old bucket.

The missing jewelry, though, caused talk. Did Mignon really take them or did Sheba? Did Sheba buy her way to freedom? Did she bury the treasure? Would she return for it?

As time went by, many folks believed Sheba was dead.

As for DoRe, neither he nor Henry ever spoke of things. DoRe had avenged a wicked abuser of a beautiful girl and his son ran for his life as she lied about Moses killing Francisco Selisse. Moses was making a good life in York, Pennsylvania, but his father missed him.

Bettina's response to all this was, "I didn't wish her dead, but I rejoice that she's gone."

About ninety miles east in Richmond, Binky, throat slit, was found propped up against a tobacco warehouse door. As no one claimed to know him, he was thrown in a pauper's grave.

Catherine, Rachel, John, Charles, and Ewing paid some attention to all this but fell into the routine of hard work.

The big news was that France was having difficulty paying its bills. That and the wonderful news that Catherine would have another child, due in June.

In the twenty-first century, things also died down. Harry felt sure that whoever had been troubling the Taylors' grave would eventually be found. She was right, but it would take time and cleverness. That would come next spring. The chits, too, would be found in good time.

Mrs. Murphy, Pewter, and Tucker lived in harmony with nature, although not always with one another. They evidenced no interest in divining the future. The day they were in proved sufficient for happiness. They had long ago given up teaching their humans this lesson.

Dear Reader,

You can see from reading this book that I am the one with the insights.

Also, I am not fat. My fur is dense.

Yours,

Pewter

Dear Reader,

Pewter is mental.

Dear Reader,

   As a corgi, I am calm, cool, and collected. Cats are irrational and emotional. Mrs. Murphy is somewhat doglike. Pewter is impossible.
   I hope you have a dog in your life to guide you.

Tucker

Dear Reader,

I am a saint.

About the Authors

RITA MAE BROWN has written many bestsellers and received two Emmy nominations. In addition to the Mrs. Murphy series, she has authored a dog series comprised of *A Nose for Justice* and *Murder Unleashed*, and the Sister Jane foxhunting series, among many other acclaimed books. She and Sneaky Pie live with several other rescued animals.

ritamaebrownbooks.com

SNEAKY PIE BROWN, a tiger cat rescue, has written many mysteries—witness the list at the front of this novel. Having to share credit with the above-named human is a small irritant, but she manages it. Anything is better than typing, which is what "Big Brown" does for the series. Sneaky calls her human that name behind her back after the wonderful Thoroughbred racehorse. As her human is rather small, it brings giggles among the other animals. Sneaky's main character—Mrs. Murphy, a tiger cat—is a bit sweeter than Miss Pie, who can be caustic.

About the Type

This book was set in Joanna, a typeface designed in 1930 by Eric Gill (1882–1940). Named for his daughter, this face is based on designs originally cut by the sixteenth-century typefounder Robert Granjon (1513–89). With small, straight serifs and its simple elegance, this face is notably distinguished and versatile.